by Karin Allaby

Jasmin

Copyright © 2016 by Karin Allaby

No part of this publication may be reproduced, distributed, or transmitted in any form or by any means, including photocopying, recording, or other electronic or mechanical methods, without the prior written permission of the author, except in the case of brief quotations embodied in critical reviews and certain other non-commercial uses permitted by copyright law.

Tellwell Talent

www.tellwell.ca

ISBN

978-1-77302-486-8 (Hardcover)

978-1-77302-485-1 (Paperback)

978-1-77302-487-5 (eBook)

CONTENTS

FAMILY LIFE 1
WWII 5
1943 17
1944 27
1945 33
JASMIN 41
TEENAGE CRUSHES 49
ENGLAND 67
HOTEL LIFE 75
FRIEND 85
ENGLISH FRIEND 99
PROMOTION 111
MR. TYLER 121
CALL ME MATTHEW 137
COURTSHIP 175
SURPRISES 211
THE MATCHMAKER 239
THE BALL 271
TRAUMA 337
HAPPY END 357
EPILOGUE 379

This is dedicated in honour of my father,
who refused to become a NAZI and to
my mother who taught me integrity.

FAMILY LIFE

1937 was a year of upheaval and turbulence in Germany, yet the shifting powers had no impact on the picturesque hamlet of Bergen, Mecklenburg. The tranquil setting was disturbed only by a cold wind that stirred up the snow from the previous evening. Heinz Claudius got on his motorcycle at his homestead to fetch Elsa, the midwife, who resided in Weeping Hollow, the next village over. His wife's birthing time had come.

The wind whipped around his head with icy fierceness as he sped along. He thought, "I must press through no matter what." He reached Elsa's house and she hurriedly packed her essential bag and braved the rear seat of his motorcycle for the seven kilometres to the Claudius farm. At almost three o'clock in the morning the baby arrived.

"Another girl!" Heinz exclaimed when the midwife put the small bundle into his arms.

"Now you have four girls and one son," Elsa commented.

"It is great to have many children," he remarked. "How is Cornelia?"

Elsa replied, "You can see her in a minute."

Heinz turned to his other daughters: Charmaine, ten; Camilla, nine; and Johanna, seven and said, "Come here, Charmaine; you can each hold her for a bit, and then to bed, you three." They each held and cuddled their new baby sister and then carefully gave her back to their father, who carried the infant to the bed where Cornelia was recovering from her ordeal.

"Cornelia, she is as beautiful as you are, my love," he spoke softly. "Take your deserved rest; Elsa here will take over for a while."

Several evenings later as they sat on the sofa near the white tiled floor-to-ceiling fireplace, Cornelia asked her husband a question: "I thought of calling our daughter Katherine. What do you think about that, Heinz?"

Heinz contemplated this idea for a while and said, "Perhaps something exotic and floral with a noble ring to it. Let's call her Jasmin."

Cornelia nodded her agreement and they had this name recorded at the township registry office. After a few days, Cornelia resumed her duties as a farmer's wife by managing the household and meat processing in the kitchen. The three older sisters took turns playing with the infant when they were not attending school, and the milk maids helped mind baby Jasmin after they had finished milking the cows.

Little Jasmin grew up well-nurtured. She went through the terrible twos and the energetic threes and got into everything. On one of those momentarily unwatched occasions when she seemed to have disappeared, her mama looked everywhere, and even waded through the miry pond trying to find her. Much to her relief, the maid Gertrud discovered Jasmin sound asleep in the cow barn, her light blonde head resting on a heap of hay.

Pigeons nested under the rafters of the barn and Heinz sometimes took the shotgun to shoot them down for a special lunch treat prepared by the cook. On occasion, Heinz would hunt deer in the woods and keep the antlers as trophies. These were mounted around the honorary plaque of his father, Heinrich, which depicted his three-hundred-year ancestral history. On one particular fox hunt, Heinz shot a red fox. He had the pelt cured and made into a stole by a furrier as a surprise gift for his wife. He came into the living room and said, "Happy Anniversary, Cornelia. Come open your present." The children gathered around to see what Dad had brought for Mom. Cornelia wiped her hands on her apron and gingerly pulled at the wrapping.

"Heinz," she exclaimed, using the clip to fasten the stole around her shoulders, "this is beautiful. How did you ever keep this a secret for so long?"

"I have another secret for you, dear: you can parade this around, because we are going out for dinner and to the theatre," Heinz stated.

WWII

Not many months later, the German Nazi party approached Heinz with an offer to join up, but he refused.

Cornelia asked Heinz, "Why don't you join them? You could make lots of money!"

Heinz shook his head, stating, "I don't agree with their philosophy."

A week after that he received service orders to register at the conscription office. He told them he would like to serve as a chaplain, but the officer in charge informed him that they had no need for chaplains! He would be shipped to Siberia after training. Heinz realized that his wife would not be able to manage the onerous responsibility of running the farm operation by herself, and so he arranged to lease the farm for the duration of the war. Cornelia and their five children - the three older girls, Hans, and Jasmin - would move to her empty parental home which she had inherited in the nearby small spa town of Black Creek.

The night before he was drafted, Heinz walked one more time around the periphery of his three-hundred-year-old heritage farm. He and his forefathers were God-fearing people. He watched the geese being herded in from the "Glistening Pond", the name the estate was known for. With an ache in his heart, he wondered, "Will I ever see my homestead again?"

The family settled in Black Creek and the children attended school in the city. In 1942, one more baby boy named Edgar was born. By now the war raged. Still, the family always made time for storytelling.

On March thirty-first, just before bedtime, Jasmin demanded, "I want my story!"

"We all have a story to tell you," her siblings said. The high school students enjoyed planning what pranks they were going to play on April first. They shared one favourite tale about their late grandfather, Cornelius Casper, who had owned the newspaper. He had loved to write humorous articles and funny but effective ads. On one particular April first edition he had printed a notice that Halley's Comet would be visible on the incline leading to the subdivision at ten p.m. that evening. As a result of this notice, at ten p.m. the whole town marched up the hill and stared up into the sky.

After about an hour, Cornelius shouted, "April fool's!"

Everyone walked home in a huff and the next morning the newspaper office was flooded with mostly outraged letters to the editor, although some of course laughed it off and called Cornelius a real ULK (joker). Cornelia thought, "I wonder which of my children inherited their grandfather's spunk," while she put Jasmin to bed.

On the evening of Heinz's homecoming from training, Cornelia prepared a feast of steaks, beer, and cigars for him. The siblings sat around the dinner table talking and listening as Dad told of his experiences. He was not in the infantry; he was an Adjutant to his

General. As always, Jasmin was put to bed at seven, but she missed the company in the dining room and whimpered. Little Jasmin was still small enough to fit into the iron crib. Heinz came into the bedroom, lifted her out of the crib, and held her. He spoke kindly, "Hush, hush sweet girl," and laid her gently down. He covered her with the eiderdown and patted her head in a traditional blessing he knew from seminary, saying, "The Lord bless you and keep you." This soothed her to sleep.

Marching bands filled the town square every other day with parades. Soldiers sang songs like "Auf der Heide blueht ein kleines Bluemelein und es heist: Erika" as they marched to the cheers of the townsfolk.

Jasmin called, "Mommy, let's look out the window and wave."

Cornelia picked up baby Edgar and opened the window while Jasmin waved vigorously. The square had been transformed into a fair ground with carousels, games, and ice cream booths. Jasmin enjoyed the swing carousel that made her fly high into the air. A huge electric punch card organ made music all day and well into the late evening, irritating nearby neighbours. Thankfully, the festivities only lasted a week.

The sound of war sirens woke them up many nights. The family would rush to the public air raid shelter, which was across the open area to the courthouse and into the earthquake-proof basement. They were fitted with gas masks and would wait until the "all clear" sirens made a different sound.

Life went on, complete with birthday parties and buying shoes. Jasmin received a pair of patent leather shoes which she loved very much. At bedtime, she didn't want them taken off.

She protested, "I want to keep them on in bed; I want to keep them on."

Cornelia waited to take the shoes off until Jasmin was asleep. For Christmas Jasmin received a wind up top and a celluloid doll. Brother Hans was given a book, her eldest sister was given a science book, and the two middle sisters were given spinning tops that could be spun on the sidewalk outside if they were hit by a whip.

On one occasion, when she and her siblings were asked what they wanted to be when they grew up, Jasmin said, "I want to be God."

Everyone laughed. Her second sister Camilla taught her a rhyme from a souvenir postcard about Greek gods. These statues of idols adorned a famous local bridge. The next day, her older brother Hans's duty was to take Jasmin for a walk. He was a "know-it-all."

He said to Jasmin, "If you want to be God, they are going to put you on top of a spear."

Jasmin didn't know what a spear was but it sounded gruesome.

When they reached home they were welcomed by company. Jasmin was handed around to sit on laps or between guests because she was so cute.

"What are you going to be when you grow up?" Aunt Mathilda asked her.

Without hesitation, Jasmin exclaimed, "I want to be a Mom with six children like Mommy."

At this everyone laughed, and the aunt said, "You may get your wish."

From time to time Jasmin was sent to the family farm where her grandmother still lived. She occupied the attached apartment on the left side of the main house. A picket fence surrounded her yard that was filled with apple trees and gooseberries. Perennials and annuals adorned the paved pathway. Her entry door led into the octagonal verandah with a granite floor and ornate furniture. The sliding pocket door that led to the flat had a taffeta curtain with a salamander pattern printed on it. The curtains were intended to keep out the draft on cold days.

Their grandmother "Oma" welcomed little Jasmin with open arms as she entered the sliding door, accompanied by her second oldest sister, Camilla.

"Here you are; I was concerned when your arrival took longer than expected," she said in a warm Low-German dialect.

Camilla mentioned that they had to get off the bicycle and walk the rest of the way, because her knees were tired and the carrier seat was beginning to hurt Jasmin. It was seven kilometres from the town of Garda where they had gotten off the train.

"Let's put your things right into the bedroom, and then you can wash up before dinner," Oma said.

They walked through the hall-like room with windows on each side and passed the dining area with the white tiled floor-to-ceiling fireplace into their grandmother's bedroom which also featured a white ceramic fireplace and twin beds. Jasmin hopped onto the bed and admired Oma's half-moon shaped alarm clock in coral Murano glass.

"Oma, your clock is pretty," she squealed with delight, as she let her fingers glide over the slick curved surface.

Camilla had gone back to the city by the time the sun rays coming through the window woke Jasmin up. She looked at the bird-covered branches touching the windows. She tried to crank the window outwards against the branches and the twigs pushed their way in.

"Oma, I can touch the leaves, and I see apples higher up in the tree."

Oma assured her that soon she could have apples. Jasmin was given home-made black raspberry jam on bread for breakfast; she liked the look and feel of the earthenware jar it was stored in.

The next day Oma said, "I'm running out of milk. I'll get some from the cow barn."

She came back with a jug of fresh warm milk and poured some into a cup for Jasmin. Jasmin put it to her lips and barely tasted it. She complained, "I don't like warm milk. It has to be cold. I cannot drink this."

Oma was patient enough to let it go, and the next morning she had cold milk from the cellar for her granddaughter. Jasmin loved her visits with Oma and was sad when she had to leave.

Hans liked climbing trees in the nearby woods of Black Creek. Once, as he and Jasmin walked through the forest, he let go of her hand.

"Jasmin, you stay down here while I climb up this one." He situated himself comfortably and called down to her, "You go home to Mommy the way I showed you. Go past the lilac tree, past the chain link fence, and through the back gate to the house. Ask Mommy to make lunch for us and bring it here in a bag."

Jasmin dutifully followed his directions and asked their mother for lunch as Hans had instructed. Thus armed with sandwiches and crisp raw turnip strips, Jasmin walked the path back to the forest and found the tree which Hans was sitting on.

"Here it is," she called.

Hans instructed her, "I'm a spy. I'm too important to come down. I'll let this string down and you tie the bag to it with my portion in and you can have yours down there. You can sit on the moss."

So she did. Once in a while he would tell her his discoveries from his lofty perch. He climbed down and taught her war games. Hans showed Jasmin to hold a stick in her outstretched arm and shout, "Hands up or I shoot."

The next time Jasmin went to see her grandmother, her brother Hans accompanied her. They had great fun together. He helped her climb high up into the straw piles, as high as the house. These square stacked bundles of straw measured about twenty feet high. He found a way to pull out straw bundles to make it possible to climb into the pockets, and then he helped Jasmin up. They felt as though they were on top of the world, and they jumped about.

The fun was short-lived, as the farmhands soon came running to the field. They hollered up, "You kids come down from there."

Defeated, they had to find other means of entertainment. Hans went to the backyard, dug a hole, filled it with water, and told her, "Here, Jasmin, go barefoot and play in the cool water."

He picked up some worms and threw them in the water, which frightened her. She jumped out and told their grandmother about it. Oma took her inside and gave her milk and sugar cookies.

Hans said firmly, "I did that to toughen you up so that you would not be so timid."

The next day, the kids helped Oma pick raspberries, strawberries, and gooseberries.

While Oma had her afternoon nap, Hans said to Jasmin, "Let's explore."

He coaxed her to follow him up the narrow back stairs of the grain barn past all the machinery to the third floor. This floor stored piles and piles of grain, with wheat in one corner and rye in a large bin. A window fitted with wire mesh became visible.

As they looked down from their vantage point, Hans prompted Jasmin, "See the chickens in the cobblestone front yard? They are trying to find something to eat. Throw some kernels of wheat down for them."

They grabbed some handfuls of grain and threw them through the wire mesh. As soon as the grains hit the ground, all the chickens appeared like magic and pecked and pecked and pecked the kernels off the ground. Jasmin clapped her hands with glee: "Look, Hans, more chickens came running; let's throw some more down." Soon the whole yard was filled with chickens running in all directions. It looked like a kaleidoscope with all three hundred chickens.

All of a sudden there was a commotion behind them and as they looked, the farmhand and a maid stood at the top of the stairs. "What are you doing? Stop that instantly!" they yelled. The children were escorted down the stairs and made to promise not to do that again. So the kids stayed inside with Oma and played a board game called 'Sorry'. Every once in a while they looked up at each other and grinned. They crowned the chicken feeding incident as the most fun prank they had pulled off in a long time!

In the city, Jasmin was pampered by her second oldest sister, Camilla. She told her, "Jasmin, your hair is blonde as the Loreley. It is as fine as silk." Camilla groomed, braided, and wove ribbons into this hair. She taught her sister the rhymes in the picture book and Jasmin memorized them. Camilla often took Jasmin on long walks through the woods and told her fairytales, some of which she made up as they went along. The woods came alive as Camilla, the artistic one, fed Jasmin's imagination with elves and gnomes. Gnarled tree trunks became faces and the mist of the meadows became fairies. A white majestic residence, barely visible through the leaves, became the object lesson for the enchanted castle of the Grimm's fairytale "Jorinda and Joringel".

In spite of frequent alarms and "all clear" sirens, life went on routinely. As the days grew shorter in early November, Charmaine, Camilla, and Johanna took Jasmin with them as they marched through the streets for the annual lantern parade. Suspended on a rod, their sun, moon, and star-shaped lantern supported a lit candle.

They sang, "Lantern, lantern, pretty lantern, sun, moon, and stars, don't blow my light out. Lantern, lantern, pretty lantern." On their way home, they took a shortcut through an alleyway near a long chain link fence with barbed wire on top. A group of women had congregated behind it. Jasmin stared at them screeching and putting their hands through the mesh, all excited and animated about the pretty Japanese lanterns. She was curious as to why they spoke a funny language.

Charmaine whispered, "Those are Russian prisoners; don't stop."

The following summer the family boarded the train to travel fifteen kilometres to the seaside resort. Aunt Martha operated a tourist home just off the beach. Her business supplied its own "Strandkorb", a beach chair with the company's name on it, and the family occupied this chair in the reserved spot. The two-seated recliner with a built-in canopy could be tilted backwards for sunbathing or forward for shade. Side shelves could be flipped down like a mini food tray similar to what they used inside of airplanes. The kids built sand castles and decorated the walls with seashells. In the evening their aunt gave them supper in the dining hall with the other summer guests before they went home by train. As the only reminder of war, one could hear mentions of "peace-time foods" because of the lack of certain fruits and coffee.

Jasmin's older sisters were very entrepreneurial and managed to organize a play to raise funds for the war effort. They used the hall of the inn and restaurant next door and sectioned off one-third of the area by arranging wardrobe stands in a row. They strung sheets and tablecloths on the upper edge, and fastened them all together like a curtain. Behind this camouflage they set up sceneries. Of course, the typical German example of culture was Grimm's fairytales. The German version of "Cinderella" was scheduled.

Jasmin was thought to be too small to participate, but she could run small errands. At noon, Mother sent her over to tell the girls that lunch was ready. Jasmin wandered over to the inn, did not see anybody right away, and walked through the table settings along the wall. As she walked, she looked up and spotted upon the high wainscot various flags displayed on small stands. She started to count them. She was proud to be able to count to twenty. She wanted to tell her sisters, who were the ones who had taught her to count. Jasmin came to a halt when the camouflaged clothes rack obscured the view. She pulled on the curtain to get a better look. As she pulled, the whole contraption fell down all at once into a big heap of steel and fabric. As she screamed from underneath it all, at the same time the "actors" who were changing out of their costumes also screamed. In the commotion nobody could see her, although they could hear her muffled cries. The eldest girl, Charmaine, ran home to fetch her mother.

Cornelia told Charmaine, "You stay here and watch the baby and I'll go over to the inn."

With the help of the volunteers, piece by piece they unraveled the strings, sheets, and drapes. They lifted the steel frames and found Jasmin huddled underneath the last tablecloth. Cornelia got her daughters Camilla and Johanna to carry Jasmin home. The sisters helped her up the stairs, laid her on the couch, and put a cold wet cloth on her head to comfort her.

The play was finally shown to a packed audience. Jasmin watched with rapt attention as Cinderella's dying mother admonished her to "be pious, so God will help you always and I will watch you from heaven." Cinderella heeded the advice and became acquainted with the prince who intended to marry her. However, her wicked stepsisters tricked him into believing she didn't exist. By providence from above their deceit was uncovered. The prince pursued his true bride-to-be, took her to his castle, married her, and they lived happily ever after. The wicked stepsisters received a severe punishment. Jasmin loved this fairytale.

Jasmin

The play was a rousing success and the children gave all the proceeds to the war effort. Everything seemed to be geared to the war effort. Charmaine, Camilla, and Johanna adhered to the instructions from high school to be environmentally conscious and nature friendly. They taught Jasmin to collect beech nuts in the woods. Hans collected dry bones from dog feeding areas for soap making. Wild mushrooms and chanterelles could be found in the underbrush for cooking and eating. Jasmin watched as Mom and her siblings followed instructions from guide books to differentiate between the edible and poisonous ones.

1943

The family moved into their custom-built house in a subdivision of Rese. Theirs was the only one-family dwelling beside two duplexes. It had a front door with frosted, beveled glass halfway up the curved top and a gilded door handle. The door on the left side of the hallway opened to the parlour, where one could see a dark brown ceramic tiled fireplace fitted in the corner. A French door led to the sunroom facing the backyard. On the right side of the granite-floored hallway a French door led to the dining room, which had a light brown glazed ceramic tile closed fireplace with side heating chambers that could be regulated by shutters for heating baked apples or just for warming. A French door led to the kitchen with mosaic granite floor tiles and two narrow pantry closets enclosing the hutch on the west wall. The hearth was located in the left corner adjacent to the wall of the fireplace with an extra warming chamber. The side door off the kitchen next to the sink led to the laundry room with granite flooring and a large round boiler for boiling laundry.

To get to the basement you had to go through the laundry room. All door handles were stainless steel. The basement had built in storage shelves on a nice clean polished cement floor. The French back door off the laundry room led to the yard and garden. The brick shed in the backyard had a latched door handle and a cement food trough for a small animal. It housed the Doberman Pinscher puppy. Jasmin and Hans had dog feeding chores and were expected to water the garden from the rain barrel. Cornelia and her three older girls managed their fruit and vegetable garden. Jasmin delighted in being allowed to go barefoot in the yellow sanded backyard in the summer.

Aunt Veronica returned from the Ukraine, where she had served as a secretary on the war front. She, Aunt Helen, and Aunt Martha escorted Cornelia to the secret baptismal service for Baby Edgar and Jasmin. During wartime, there was no church attendance other than for art displays, and so Jasmin's infant baptism had been missed when the war began. Aunt Helen dressed Edgar in a white christening gown and Jasmin in a white dress. As Cornelia's other children stood around the altar, watching, Aunt Veronica took baby Edgar from Cornelia's arms and held him as the pastor sprinkled Holy Water upon his head and gave the benediction. She promised to be his godmother. Aunt Martha held Jasmin's hand as they stepped in front of the baptismal basin. She promised to be Jasmin's godmother as the pastor sprinkled Holy Water upon her head, saying, "Jasmin, I baptize you in the name of the Father and of the Son and of the Holy Spirit." After a private family celebration, Aunt Veronica left for Italy.

Residents of the subdivision didn't have to travel unprotected to the air raid shelter in the city twenty minutes away. Instead, they could stay home, but they had to use blackout blinds in the evenings so that no light would shine through the windows. Everybody had

Jasmin

to be home by six p.m. because of the blackout. There could be no tear in the black blinds, or else there would be a knock on the window by those who imposed the curfew. Charmaine, Camilla, and Johanna used the glue from their school supplies to mend any tears.

Families were close-knit, clean, well-spoken, virtuous, disciplined, and patriotic. At night, bedtime prayers were said for the troops. Jasmin, very enthusiastic about being able to read and write, wrote a letter to her father, addressing it as "Heinz Claudius, Russia." She asked, "Mommy, could you put a stamp on it?"

Cornelia looked at the address and laughed, saying, "It needs a little more than that." She put his rank and location on the envelope.

On weekends, the older girls played social games with the little ones.

They blindfolded Hans and said, "Let's count books."

They guided his hand on top of the ironing board which was laden with books in a row and a bowl of water at the end. Sure enough his hand hit the water with a splash. He shrieked in surprise, and Jasmin did the same. For fun, the girls liked to dress Jasmin up in her mother's clothes and high heeled shoes. They took her to the local entertainment centre to make the audience laugh. They considered her to be so cute, especially when she said something funny. Cornelia discovered what they were doing and said, "What will people think about how I dress my child?"

Jasmin piped up, "Oh, people will think I dressed myself."

One evening, the family heard the distant sound of the siren. They were sitting around the living room talking quietly when an explosion rattled the dishes in the curio cabinet. It came from the big city Lubeck about ten kilometres away. They bent the flexible arm of the chrome office lamp way down into the cushions of the sofa, so as to see only the reflection. The older girls, knowing English, understood by short wave radio that there'd be more to come.

Charmaine, the eldest, who was of above average intelligence, brought projects home and taught the others. Through her enrichment program she became involved in the design of the first prototype Horton jet aircraft, though she could not reveal much classified information.

Father came home on leave from Russia. He had been at the military hospital for his wounds, which he had sustained while doing reconnaissance on his motorcycle. The leather of his glove had frozen to the skin of his hand in the Siberian winter. The glove had to be medically removed. He had also suffered thrombosis in his legs. Cornelia and her six children were delighted to have him home. He brought back funny dried Russian mushrooms and weird butter, but everything was appreciated since the hardships of the war had now begun. Heinz recovered enough to resume his duties and received promotion to special officer status in the Italian front. The family accompanied him to the military academy, where they played the popular war songs "Lily Marleen" (Lily at the lamppost) or "Erica".

Camilla, the artist, painted watercolours. She made figurines of fairytale characters out of very thin plywood with her jigsaw and placed them on the wall of her bedroom. Johanna, the acrobat, participated in gymnastics. Her extracurricular activity included acting in a theatre troupe.

Johanna or Hans took Jasmin to the movie theatre. Everyone had to see the first news reel about the victories the Germans had won against the enemies.

As a reminder of war, the phrase "Sugar is scarce" was familiar, especially when it came to baking. More than once, the neighbour sent one of her children over with a measuring cup, asking, "Could we borrow half a cup of sugar?"

Jasmin

The two middle sisters Camilla and Johanna helped Jasmin get ready for school. One sister would help dress her and the other would comb and braid her long blonde hair. They tied pretty ribbons at the ends to stop the braids from unraveling. But while she was playing "Ring around the Rosie, pocket full of posies" Jasmin lost one of her ribbons. This was a bad thing in the neat and tidy family, because now there was no match for the other braid. This meant that Mother would have to travel to the bombed out city. The department store was demolished. She found a makeshift shack and the lonely shopkeeper rummaged through the salvaged boxes to see if he had any ribbons. He did, but a ration card for canned goods had to be exchanged.

Aunt Veronica worked as a secretary in an engineering company in Milan. She came to visit the family and brought chocolate, coffee, and candies - rare treats in Germany. She also brought beautiful pale blue satin ribbons for Jasmin's hair. Camilla commented, "These will enhance your deep blue eyes. We will keep them for your visit to Oma."

During school break, Johanna took Jasmin to see their grandmother in Bergen. Oma took Jasmin on a long walk through a forest to see a friend who lived in a cottage-like home. To Jasmin's amazement the screen door didn't make any difference to the flies which were swirling around the dining table and hovering over the piece of bread with jam which had been offered to her. In the suburb where Jasmin lived, there weren't any flies or mosquitoes, neither were there any flies in Oma's house.

The next day, Oma and Jasmin visited a nearby family who lived in a nice brick house with a picket fence around the front yard. The elderly couple brought her up to the attic to play with antique dolls and even older high-wheeled prams. Jasmin put her imagination to work and acted out a fairytale. She selected garlands for make believe roses and pretended she was "Sleeping Beauty."

Back in Oma's house, she sat on Oma's lap. Oma read her a story in her Low-German dialect which put her fast asleep.

On one sunny afternoon, Jasmin pushed her doll stroller around the cobblestone front yard. When she flipped her braids to the front, she discovered that she had lost one of her pale blue ribbons. A jolt of dismay hit her as she glanced around and noticed the bow across the yard in front of the cow barn. She proceeded to walk over to the entrance to retrieve it. At that instant the farmhand opened the gate and the cows were let out to pasture.

Jasmin stared in shock and prayed, "Please dear God, don't let the cows step on my ribbon. Please don't let them step on my ribbon. Please God, don't let them step on my ribbon."

She continued non-stop until all forty-five cows had passed. Then she rushed over and picked up the ribbon. "Thank you God; no cows stepped on my ribbon!" she gasped in delight. She looked at her ribbon closely and found not one speck of dirt on it. She ran inside to Oma and showed her the evidence. "I lost my ribbon in the cow path and I prayed to God to save my ribbon and none of the cows trod on it!"

Oma undid the bow and tied it back in her hair. She said, "You'd better not go that way again." For the first time in her life Jasmin knew that God had heard her prayer and answered it. As soon as Johanna came to pick her up, she told her with awe about her rescued ribbon.

The subdivision where the family lived had an open area for more houses to be built. Jasmin saw many horse-drawn flatbeds arriving with building materials. Trucks unloaded sand into heaps for the workers to fill their wheelbarrows and start mixing the mortar. Jasmin's little brother Edgar had been given a toy wheelbarrow and

Jasmin

observed this activity with interest. Armed with his toy shovel, he wanted to copy the men. As the horses stood harnessed to the flatbed, Edgar set out with his wheelbarrow. Instead of walking around the front of the truck, he took a shortcut and marched right under the horses' bellies to where the pile of sand was stored.

When Jasmin saw where Edgar had gone, she screamed and called to her mother and sisters, "Edgar has gone under the horses' bellies!"

While they stood awestruck, Edgar appeared with his wheelbarrow full of sand, marching right back under the two horses and across the street to their front yard. Everybody rushed out to meet him. They hugged him, very glad he hadn't been hurt. Edgar looked up in consternation, not sure what all the fuss was about.

"Never go under the horses again," Johanna told him. He shrugged it off and continued to build his sand castle.

"Horses don't hurt small children," Cornelia said. "Children are protected by angels."

Camilla, the second oldest, had a summer job in Denmark and Johanna had a summer job on a nearby farm. Hans, the ten-year-old, was deemed mature enough to babysit Jasmin. He took her for walks to meet his friend and they would clamber through farm fences, climb trees, and wade and splash in a nearby brook. One day, Hans took seven-year-old Jasmin and Edgar, who was three by now, to the Au creek. The grassy bank was steep. After they had splashed in the water for a while, they stretched out on the grass. Hans went over to the fence to inspect an opening for a shortcut home, while Edgar, full of energy, collected small stones to throw into the brook. He threw one and tumbled down the bank all the way into the Au.

Alarmed, Jasmin cried out, "Hans! Hans, come here fast, Edgar fell into the water! Quick, he's drowning!" Hans turned and ran like a bullet. He jumped down the bank into the water, clothes and all. Wading into the midst of the Au, he pulled Edgar to safety. Even at only four feet deep, it was overwhelming for a three-year old. Jasmin and Hans wrapped towels around him. After he calmed down, they took Edgar by both hands and crawled through the wire fence. Cornelia saw them coming, and was surprised to have the children home so early.

"Hans rescued Edgar from drowning in the Au," Jasmin told her.

"What happened?" Cornelia asked. The whole story came out while she got everyone into dry clothes, hanging the wet ones on the laundry line with pegs.

Hans asked Jasmin to help make a smoking pit for the fish he had caught. They found an oversized old canning kettle without a bottom. He put sawdust inside the frame and lit it with matches so that it smoldered. Hans had some fence wire to string up the herrings across the inside frame. He used a sack to cover it and hold the smoke in. After an hour or so, he proudly presented his smoked fish for supper. While the fire was still smoldering, he said to Jasmin, "Would you like some roasted bread?" When she turned to see, he said, "The English call it toast."

Jasmin tried some and said, "It is very crisp."

Hans replied, "That's because it's our usual whole grain bread. The English use white bread."

Occasionally, Hans and Jasmin had to take the pull cart into the woods to gather sticks. Small branches lying in the woods were used for kindling. They marked a variety of different areas with a hatchet and cut down seedlings of spruce trees. After they had brought them home, they put them on the saw horse, used a bow saw, and sawed them into small logs. They stored them in the basement and everybody took a turn at chopping them on the chopping block. While gathering twigs for kindling near the railroad tracks, Hans once showed Jasmin where the "duds" (bombs) were. They stalked around them and Hans said, "You see that small dot at the end?

Jasmin

If you hit that with a hammer, it will explode. This is a bomb that didn't go off, it just fell to the ground." Jasmin took this knowledge all in her stride, matter of fact. Nothing to be frightened about.

For Advent, they suspended a wreath with four candles from the chandelier. On the first Sunday of Advent, Cornelia lit the first candle. The other candles would be lit on the next three consecutive Sundays before Christmas. The whole family gathered in the woods, hewed down a fragrant spruce tree, and hauled it home on the pull cart. Charmaine had learned how to make candles out of wax and used small medication glass tubes to shape them. She and Johanna put them up on the tree with metal clips. Cornelia had beautiful nostalgic glass ornaments to accent the tree and she finished it off with tinsel. Camilla crafted farm animals and pets for Hans and Jasmin out of plywood to play with.

1944

That winter of 1944 was unusually warm, so Cornelia decided to do her house cleaning then instead of in the spring. The girls were responsible for beating the carpet which was hung over the laundry line. They made a combined effort to move the furniture outside, and then they washed and waxed the floor. A very pleasant surprise came by way of a horse-drawn flatbed loaded with a wooden crate addressed to the family Claudius in Rese. After the delivery man had brought the crate inside the house, Mother rummaged around to find the box of cigars reserved for special occasions such as this and gave the man a big cigar as a tip. He thanked her several times.

Now, how to open it? They found a crow bar in the shed and pried the lid open. The box contained a sack of rice, chocolates, coffee, and oranges that could not be obtained anywhere in Germany. Two bottles of sweet red wine completed the gift. Heinz had shipped the gifts from Italy.

Jasmin used to look at the barometer over the sofa. Charmaine told her that when the arrow pointed left, snow was on the way. To everybody's laughter, Jasmin climbed up on the settee, reached her hand up, and knocked at it, hoping it would turn to the left. Over the next couple of days it gradually turned cold enough for snow. Pretty frost designs appeared on the windows. Jasmin rejoiced over them, saying, "See, I made it snow with the barometer."

She went tobogganing in the snow. Hans came to take her home for dinner, and the fragrance of baked goods wafted through the air. Mother and sisters had baked Christmas cakes and cookies and had prepared a torte that was cooling. The next day, Cornelia showed her daughters how to make icing. She used less sugar than she would have in peace time, but she still had spices like vanilla sticks and cardamom.

Hans explained to Jasmin, "Because it is Christmas Eve, we can stay up till midnight." They played and didn't seem to get tired. Cornelia and the girls gave the children small glasses of the sweet red wine from the gift crate to settle them down and put them to sleep.

Over the next few days Cornelia taught the girls how to prepare the rice. Everybody was delighted to taste the variety of ways this rice could be used. Cornelia, having been considered a "well-to-do daughter", had attended a women's college and knew the fine art of cooking. She also played the piano like a concert pianist. When Aunt Helen came for a visit, the girls showed her all the goods which Father had sent to them.

Charmaine said, "One thing I don't know about is this." Then she went to the broom closet and showed Aunt Helen the round green waxy ball.

Aunt Helen explained, "That is not wax, but Italian Parmesan cheese. You cut off the peel with a sharp knife and use a butcher's knife to cut off a chunk and grate it." She laughed as she demonstrated it. She had learned to cook in a fine dining establishment.

By spring it was Camilla's turn for confirmation at the Lutheran church. Cornelia had gone to the big city to an elite dress shop that wasn't in ruins and had purchased a suitable black dress for Camilla. This could be worn again the following year for Johanna's confirmation. The dress had a beaded accent pocket on it, but Camilla didn't like where the ornamental pocket sat, so they had the seamstress come to alter it. When the alteration was finished, everybody admired the dress on her. In adherence to tradition, on the afternoon of Confirmation Sunday Hans and Jasmin were sent to the families' houses where other confirmation graduates lived. They distributed congratulatory cards and in return the children were given cookies, pieces of cake, or home-made wrapped fondants.

The seamstress was often engaged to alter or mend outfits for the family, though not everyone wore hand-me-downs. For Jasmin, the seamstress was instructed to make a fashionable coat in a pastel grey wool fabric with a cape-like collar and a fitted waist. She also made a "Little Red Riding Hood" felt cap for it, and as an added bonus, she sewed an outfit for Jasmin's beautiful celluloid doll named Carmen. Jasmin insisted on dressing her doll without any help. But as she yanked its arm to fit into the sleeve, the arm came out of the shoulder socket. There lay the doll, broken.

Jasmin was distraught and cried, "Mommy, Carmen is sick, please help her to get better." Cornelia came and hugged her daughter, saying, "I'll have to take your doll to the 'doll doctor' in the big city" (referring to the customer service at the gift shop).

Although they lived on the outskirts of the city and didn't have to go to the air raid shelters, everybody had to practice fire drills. Air raids were now taking place during daylight hours. In rural communities, people had to throw themselves into a ditch if bombers were overhead. The school had concrete bunkers for emergencies. On the day when Cornelia took the tram to the "doll hospital" in the big city, an air raid happened at midday and the tram stopped to evacuate the passengers. They threw themselves into the ditch. Transportation was cancelled for the rest of the day, and so Cornelia had to walk home with the still broken doll.

School was let out early. The children came home and huddled around the backyard to see the fire in the distance. A factory had been hit. A few more planes passed overhead and the flak rose like shooting stars.

Camilla and Johanna brought supplies home from craft class. Dressed in make-believe nurses outfits, they repaired Jasmin's doll behind the closed doors of the sunroom. They came out and presented the repaired doll to Jasmin: "Here little sister, your 'Carmen' is healed." Jasmin of course was overjoyed and they all hugged each other.

A few days later, Jasmin was playing with Hans in the yard near the rain barrel. She noticed that the sky had become particularly grey and the sun was a barely visible disk.

She ran into the house to ask Mother, "How come everything is so still, and what are these fine fluffs and soft tissue things that come apart when you touch them? Hans is finding charred bits of ash."

Cornelia went outside and looked up at the sky. She looked around at the fine dust that was descending. She spoke with pathos: "Hamburg!"

Two of the sisters came out of the house and helped Mother back inside to sit down, while the eldest explained to Hans and Jasmin, "Hamburg was bombed last night and burned badly. These are the ashes carried by the wind from over 100 kilometres away."

To Jasmin this was just information, because war and bombs were part of life. But seeing her mother sad made her impulsively hug her and say, "Oh, Mommy please don't cry, I love you."

The new concrete row houses had been completed, and families from the bombed cities were re-settling there. All families were comprised of only women and children, because all the men had been drafted and sent to the front.

One fine summer day at noon, the family heard the flak again and suddenly the air was pierced by a loud roar. As the children looked up, the eldest grabbed Jasmin and Edgar.

Charmaine called, "Get down into the basement!" As Jasmin ran inside, she looked back for a second, and to her amazement she saw an airplane rapidly approaching the chimney of the house. For the first time in her life Jasmin experienced fear.

They rushed downstairs and Charmaine said, "Hold your ears to protect your eardrums and open your mouth!" They did this for a few minutes. As the sound that vibrated through the walls receded into the distance, they let go of their ears. Charmaine went outside to investigate. Cornelia called the children upstairs; everybody was talking at once.

Then Charmaine said, "The plane crashed about five hundred metres away into a field. The police have screened off the area. The pilot bailed out with a parachute."

Jasmin was ushered away into another room to prevent her from hearing more conversation. The older children were always instructed not to let any details of bad things come into her hearing.

The next day, Hans took Jasmin to the crash site. Some officials had removed the huge tires and left the inner tubes for a bunch of kids to play with. Hans took some metal bits and pieces and showed Jasmin the glass shards.

He declared, "That is not ordinary glass; it is Plexiglas. It does not crack or splinter; instead, it smolders and melts. The edges are smooth." They took home what they could carry and had something new to play with. Whenever planes flew overhead, Hans identified them. He named the Americans "Ami's" and the British "Tommy's." After more bombing raids parachutes were left behind in the brown and green camouflage colours. People took the ropes off and sold the nylon as clothing fabric. Charmaine, Camilla, and Johanna had blouses and dresses made from this "Fallschirmseide" parachute silk.

1945

The dramatic newspaper headline in the largest bold capital letters FUEHER DEAD devastated Cornelia, shattering everything she believed in. A national sorority had awarded the Blue Cross to Cornelia as the ideal German woman a year earlier. As a mother with multiple children, she received free health care, a one-week spa treatment and peat bath cure twice a year, as well as a free maid.

This event took place not long after his birthday had been elaborately celebrated. At that time Jasmin had brought flowers to school and a photographer had taken a class picture with the children standing beside a large portrait of Adolf Hitler. He had usually appeared in the media as standing on platforms arrayed with floral garlands. Mothers had lifted their babies and small children up to him to be blessed. The media had portrayed him as the guardian of families. After his death, many citizens walked around numb and bewildered. Jasmin didn't understand the significance of it, only that it made her mother sad, and so she clung to her all the more.

Social order as they knew it, had ceased. A rumour spread that for some reason, several city officials had committed suicide. School attendance was suspended indefinitely. They had to make room for the refugees.

Jasmin enquired, "What are refugees; where do they come from?"

"From East Prussia," her sisters said. "They are fleeing from the Russians."

The Red Cross erected camps, because the public buildings did not have enough space to house the onslaught of refugees. Johanna took Jasmin to visit one camp, where she learned the words typhoid fever and cholera.

"Don't go near there anymore," their mother admonished.

Plunderers came and broke into houses at night. Law and order didn't exist. Cornelia gathered her children around her to warn them: "Stay inside, and lock the doors. Charmaine, you as the eldest will have to be our 'Valkyrie' and protect us from the marauders."

Cornelia led Charmaine to the secret hiding place for the gun. She removed a thick round ceramic tile with a twist from the bottom shaft of the fireplace and gave it to Charmaine. "You know how Father taught you to use it; be at the ready." The family huddled together in the living room after supper. Only toddler Edgar slept in his crib. Just after dark, they observed the back door handle move.

Charmaine fearlessly shouted, "Hands up, or I shoot!" She clicked the gun. The family could hear shuffling outside. She stealthily walked to the window, opened it, fired one shot into the air, and shut the window fast. They heard the sound of footsteps running away. Charmaine put the safety clasp back on the gun and everyone rested for the night.

The next day Cornelia received terrible news from her brother. His son, drafted at sixteen, had been shot the first day he reported for duty at the front.

Charmaine, in true leadership form, took over. "Mom, come lay down on the couch and rest; we'll take care of you now." She instructed Johanna, "You make a cup of tea for Mom and mind Jasmin and Edgar. Stay in the house until we come back from shopping."

Charmaine and Hans searched for no longer existing stores. Somehow it was rumoured that the Russians were near. They followed the crowd to the famous jam factory which had opened their warehouses to the public because they didn't want their goods to fall into the hands of the enemies. The local dairy followed suit and opened their storage rooms for free cheeses. Some people rolled large Swiss cheeses the size of small tires home. The delivery vans for condiments and pickles with their logo "Pickles perk you up" stopped at street corners so that the townsfolk could help themselves to mustard and dills. The kids took what was handed to them, placed it into the pull-cart, covered it with a jacket to obscure it from view, and made their way home as fast as they could.

They found Cornelia sitting on the couch, her two youngest children beside her. Johanna was reading from a story book. Charmaine reported, "The shops are turning into trading posts. You exchange valuable items for food. Luckily, our cousin's bakery is still operating. They offered Hans a job as sweeper in exchange for one loaf of bread per day."

In the evening, Charmaine and Johanna listened again to the radio and declared to the family, "Germany has lost the war. There is going to be military police. The allied forces are dividing Germany into four sectors. They are making a border fifty kilometres east from here and giving the land to the Russians. Our farm is behind that border; we can never go back and visit Oma again."

That devastating news shook them all. What would the next morning bring?

Charmaine assured the family, "We will be in the British or American zone, and you don't have to be afraid of the Americans."

A messenger came to urge everyone to hang white sheets, handkerchiefs, towels, pillow cases, or anything white out over their window sills to indicate SURRENDER. People stayed in their houses, keeping the white cloths visible, and waited in fear. All at once, one could see tall and lanky foreign soldiers walking two by two up and down the streets. When they came to the suburb where Jasmin's family lived, the eldest sister whispered, "They are Americans!" Everybody jumped up and down, saying, "They are Americans!"

Camilla had to come back from Denmark. Her train stopped before her destination at Lubeck, still ten kilometres from home. She ran to the freight car to retrieve her bicycle, and she began pedaling towards home. As she came to a country crossroad, her tire went flat. An army truck stopped and a soldier stepped out.

He asked, "Do you need any help?"

She stared at him for a moment and asked, "Are you English?"

"No, I am an American," he said.

She pointed to her flat tire and he offered to give her a ride. They put her bicycle into the back of the truck and let her sit in the cab. She told them her home was about seven kilometres away. They brought her right to the front door.

Charmaine tried to teach Jasmin five English words: "Good morning, good afternoon, chocolates, cigarettes, thank you."

Jasmin practiced these words, and when her twin girlfriends came to play, they practiced these English words together. The next day they skipped behind the Americans and chanted, "Good afternoon, chocolates, cigarettes, thank you." The soldiers dropped packets of gum, chocolate bars, and half empty cigarette packages onto the ground behind them and kept on walking. The kids picked up these gifts with glee and took them home. Jasmin gave everything to her mother, who kept the cigarettes in a special drawer in the curio cabinet. Cornelia was able to obtain necessary food and meat items from local wholesalers and farms in return for these cigarettes.

The solders continued to patrol the streets, dropping goodies to the ground. When they saw Jasmin outside her home, they nicknamed her "Blondie" and gave her a handful of candy bars.

One afternoon, as Jasmin pushed her doll buggy in front of her house, the American soldiers walked by and one of them turned to the other saying, "There is Blondie."

The other one looked at Jasmin, walked toward her, and said, "Here, Blondie, I have something for you." He placed a gift box into her hands and put his other hand on top of her head. He said, "God bless you!"

They went on their way and as they turned left at the corner they said one more time, "Goodbye, Blondie."

Jasmin stood there looking till they were gone and thought, "The Americans are kind." She put the box into her doll carriage and wheeled it inside.

As she entered the front door, she called her mother, "Mommy! Look what the Americans gave me." Everybody rallied around her and sorted through the chocolate bars, gum packets, wafer cookies, and Californian candied fruit to be distributed around.

As her big sisters taught her how to chew the gum without swallowing it, she told them excitingly: "They called me Blondie!"

Cornelia, her mother said, "You are indeed the blondest of my girls."

Heinz reported to headquarters in Milan, but his assignment was in the agricultural area of Florence. When his post came under attack, he had to retreat into a bunker which then caved in. For three days they were cut off from the outside. Heinz said later,

"That's where my hair turned grey." They tried and tried to shovel themselves out of the rubble and eventually succeeded. As they came out into the daylight, Heinz and his group was picked up by an American army truck and taken prisoner. Although they were treated with respect, Heinz and his friend escaped from the prison. Heinz still had his bearskin coat and they hiked through the Alps on mountain trails of ice and snow for five days and nights. They came through Austria and hid in a friendly farmer's barn where they slept in the straw. The next day, after refreshments, they made it to Germany and boarded a train halfway home. Heinz walked the rest of the way, hoping against hope that his house would still be standing.

Jasmin was playing in front of their home with her dolls when she spotted her father from afar. She dropped her doll into the carriage and shouted, "Daddy, Daddy!" and ran towards him. Heinz, with his last ounce of energy, opened his arms wide, caught her up, and twirled her around. As they entered the house, the children flung themselves on him. Cornelia, coming out of the kitchen, wiping her hands in a towel, looked to see what all the commotion was about.

"Heinz," she gasped. Heinz put Jasmin down and held his arms open,

"Nellie," he embraced her. "I'll show you what I have brought for you," he said after he released her.

Cornelia turned to her children and said, "Gather around."

The family sat on the chaise and chairs, while Heinz opened his bag and rummaged around until he found what he was looking for. An empty toothpaste tube. He unrolled it and pulled out a silver ring. He held it in front of Cornelia and said, "I had it custom made for you. It is white gold. Look, one part is a smooth ring and the other is in a shape of a knotted rope. Six diamonds are crested in the knot. This symbolizes that our life is knotted together in love and the diamonds are for our six children."

"Oh, Heinz dear; it is beautiful, very impressive," Cornelia said as Heinz slid the ring on her finger. She held her hand up so that she and the children could admire her ring. "Now I can't do any work with my hands."

"Well, you can delegate the tasks," Heinz replied.

Cornelia asked the three older girls to set the table. She urged Heinz to take his place at the head end and told the three smaller ones to sit at their places. Then she proceeded to serve the dinner.

Within a few days the military police arrived in a jeep and requested that Heinz come with them. He smiled and waved to his wife and children as they took him away. They had to have documented evidence that he wasn't a Nazi. He had only served in the military. There was a distinction.

This section was now under British rule. The British officer who handled his case was very polite to Heinz. Addressing him as "Herr Claudius", he told him that according to his records, Heinz had conducted his affairs with discretion and integrity in the service to his country. He saluted Heinz and set him free.

JASMIN

Eight years later, Jasmin looked down the ramparts of the ancient fortress for the last time. This ruin dated back to the year 1130. The legend read that egg yolks, mortar, and straw held the walls of local slate together. Her brother had accompanied her up the spiral stairs into the tower, skipping over the odd missing steps.

"I sort of liked this summer job here at the clinic. The professor is a blueblood; he and his wife are both doctors. He is nobility linked with royalty. Even though I was only a servant to the patients and a cook's assistant, I breathed in the upper class atmosphere," Jasmin reminisced.

Hans walked over from the other lookout point and lectured, "When you have God in your heart you have nobility inside you."

"I have tried to be good all my life, just as Mom taught me," Jasmin retorted.

Hans explained, "It is more than that. God has a good plan for you, and I am going to pray for you every day."

Jasmin chuckled. "We are standing here like Jorinda and Joringel in the enchanted woods of the bewitched castle; the boy is watching out for the girl."

Hans laughed also. "You know, I'll be training for the mission field. As long as I am around in this area, I'll take the ferry across the river to see you in your new job. Remember, you are too young to have a boyfriend yet. When in time you might encounter someone, first make sure he fears God and do not go beyond holding hands until you get married."

"No chance for that with you around," Jasmin punched him in the elbow. "You scared off my first boyfriend when I was twelve. He simply wrote me a card after I moved. We went to private school together. There was no public schooling for over a year after the war because of the refugee crisis. We enjoyed studying together, and we competed in math and composition. He was the only person who was kind to me. Once he sent me half of his apple in a napkin via his sister. All I wanted was a friend."

"You are still too young for a boyfriend. Heed my advice and Dad's and live up to the honour of your name. Even if this new apprenticeship is not high society, do everything as unto the Lord, for he is king forever."

"O.K.," Jasmin consented. "Help me down the stairs. Do you know how thick these walls are? Six feet thick. At the base of the tower there is a chamber where the venison is stored. The cook instructed me to soak it in buttermilk for three days."

"What for?" Hans queried.

"To get the 'game' taste out of it," Jasmin explained. "After that, the cook marinated it in red wine and spiked it with bacon for roasting."

"Sounds gourmet," Hans commented.

Jasmin

They passed the now "off limits" well. Jasmin told Hans inconspicuously, "There is a secret tunnel leading from this well diagonally to the foot of the mountain."

"Something like an escape hatch?"

"Something like that, sure. We'll walk through the rose garden," Jasmin suggested. "This is where I used to daydream I was Sleeping Beauty as I waited for the prince to give me a wake-up kiss."

"You are still too young," Hans repeated.

"Well, a girl can dream, can't she?" Jasmin looked at him with a grin. "See there?" She pointed to the retaining wall of the building adjacent to the mountain. "Through that narrow crevice I climbed the night you brought me home from the movies and I faced the locked entrance door. I came up through there to the patio and entered in at the French door to the upstairs hallway."

"Why didn't you ring the bell at the front entrance?" Hans asked.

"I had done that once before. After I saw the stern expression of the housekeeper, I didn't want to face her again."

"Well, you always were a tomboy, Jasmin," Hans remarked.

"As far as tree climbing, fence climbing, and wall climbing go, maybe," Jasmin admitted. They entered the mansion through the large floor-to-ceiling French door, walked past the gallery of ancestral portraits, and down another hallway that led to the guest rooms of private patients. They came to the swinging door for the kitchen passage and Jasmin directed Hans to the front hallway exit.

"Thanks for the tour. Make sure you read the New Testament; bye," he said.

"Bye," she replied.

Jasmin's father had arranged an interview for her at a nearby tourist hotel and restaurant for an apprenticeship in hospitality in the Rhine river valley. This was to be a three-year contract. Jasmin had attended the interview with her dad and listened as they negotiated the details of the potential job. A few days later, her father received a phone call saying that they would be very pleased to have her work for them. Sadly, Jasmin had to give notice for leaving the castle atmosphere of nobility, but, as her father said, she needed formal training and schooling in something practical. The new job was a live-in position where Jasmin was to be trained in all aspects of the tourist trade.

At the hotel, the lady of the house showed Jasmin how to clean and polish the stainless steel counter in the front reception area and keep the glass-covered bar spotless.

Mrs. Manning said, "You are learning all the ins and outs of this operation behind the scenes. When you graduate, you will be able to supervise others. Mr. Manning will teach you all the finesses of customer service."

As a seasonal worker, the head waiter intended to leave for his home in Vienna, Austria. He gave a crash course in waitressing and hosting to Jasmin before he left. She had to practice holding the wine bottle in one hand and with a flick of her wrist pour just a small measure into the glass for the customer to taste. If he nodded approval, she poured the glass for the lady first followed by the rest of the guests and the host. At all times, she was to have a half-folded napkin over her left wrist. Jasmin displayed the menu, pointed out specials, and explained items on the list. She had to understand the French names for gourmet items like Chateaubriand and pommes frites. She set the dinner plates in front of the customers and served each meat and vegetable item from her platter by holding it between a spoon and fork and setting it onto their plates. Jasmin also escorted guests to the door as they prepared to leave and assisted them with their coats and hats. Her boss Mr. Manning supervised her actions. From January to March, when the management closed the hotel, the apprentices took vacations and then returned to help with furnishing and cleaning. The apprentices lived on the premises. Seasonal staff was hired by May.

Bus tour groups from the industrial areas came frequently. Many tourists came from Holland. The Dutch people loved travelling through Germany. These groups called ahead when they were ten minutes away from town to reserve meals. The boss took the calls and arranged that all had the same selection so that they were served rapidly. In the kitchen the chef put everything aside to have the forty or so meat items ready for frying, and the kitchen helpers made sure that enough potatoes were peeled and vegetables prepared. Jasmin helped with setting the tables. It happened sometimes that the meat delivery had not arrived that day, and when counting, the chef would find a shortage of chops. On these occasions Jasmin was sent to the local grocery store to pick up the extra meat pieces required. They knew her as Manning's apprentice and gave her what she needed right away. Of course, when she got back, she had to help serve. First, the group had their drinks of either sparkling water in bottles or beer in bottles. They drank draft beer with the main course. The driver and guide had their meals served in a separate area.

On Sundays, the busiest day for the restaurant, Jasmin assisted the head waiter in the two main areas. The upstairs terrace had one waiter and an assistant to manage the crowds. Outside during the summer season one waiter headed up the so-called sidewalk café with a dozen long tables and benches on a platform.

Tuesdays were designated as wash day in a rented laundry room in a nearby alley. The washing woman would spend the whole day washing, rinsing, and starching. At noon one of the dishwasher girls took lunch to her. In the afternoon Jasmin drew the pull cart loaded with a basket of wet bedding, tablecloths, napkins, and smocks down to the river bank to the public laundry lines. She had a bag of pegs and hung everything up to dry. After her afternoon break of an hour and a half, she went back and took all the wash down. She gave the large items to the housekeeper to be steamed, flattened, and put away.

When there were no customers to attend, she was reprimanded, "Don't ever stand around doing nothing. Keep busy!" Smocks had to be ironed by hand. This was Jasmin's duty in the alcove behind the front desk. This area was designated for the staff lunches. It had built-in benches along the back walls and two tables in front. She placed her iron on a metal stand on the wooden bench and plugged in the electric cord. Then she spread an ironing cloth on top of one table and ironed, all while keeping a watchful eye on customers. Sometimes when she was called away, she would forget to unplug the iron and the wood of the bench would blister from the heat. She learned to be mindful of this and so while attending the reception desk, she might tell the passing waiter to unplug it. Most of the time Jasmin had to multitask. She was always alert, striving to be perfect. Often she had to accompany an overnight guest to the only garage the hotel owned which was a block away. She would get out of the car and use an oversize key to open the huge sliding garage door. After the customer parked his car, she would lock the door and they would walk the block back to the hotel.

One particular evening when it wasn't especially busy at the desk, Jasmin filled her time with ironing. She didn't have to attend to the late guest because she had seen Mr. Manning give him the room key. She heard them say something, which she couldn't quite make out.

Then Mr. Manning called her, "Jasmin, please show the customer to the garage." She walked over to them, picked up the garage key, and did as requested. Upon entering the back entrance, she pointed the guest in the direction of his room and turned to go back through the interior restaurant door. It was locked! She reasoned that they had closed up early, and so she went upstairs to her quarters. As it

Jasmin

was her roommate's day off, she was alone. She went to bed. At three a.m. she woke up startled. What was it? Had she forgotten something? She couldn't think of anything. She prayed a childhood prayer, the equivalent of "Now I lay me down to sleep," when an image jolted her brain. She'd left the iron plugged in! She was frozen with fear. She didn't have a key to the interior room. The housekeeper who came in the early morning had it. She absolutely couldn't wake up her bosses. She prayed, "O God, please help me. Please help me. Please don't let the iron smolder the wood. I am so sorry, please don't let it smolder the wood. I promise, I'm going to be good, I'm going to be good if only you help me. You can do anything." She closed her eyes in exhaustion, then begged again, "Please dear God help me, don't let the iron burn the wood, I promise to be good, if only you help me."

Her prayers continued the rest of the night. She got up extra early and watched for the housekeeper through the window. When she saw her, she quickly ran down the three flights of stairs.

Mrs. Hoffman was carrying something in her hand. "You're up early, Jasmin."

"Yes," Jasmin said, "give me the key. I'll open up for you." She took the key out of her hand, dashed to the restaurant door, flew to the staff corner, and there, to her amazement, the iron sat unplugged and cool! Jasmin took a deep breath to calm her beating heart, pasted a smile on her face, and hung the key on the board.

The realization hit her: God had helped her! She remembered when God had stopped the cows from stepping on her ribbon. She remembered her mother saying that angels protected those who are good.

Just to be sure, she asked the waiter, "Did you unplug my iron last night?"

He said, "No."

She asked the head waiter, "Did you unplug my iron last night?"

"No, I went out the other door, why?"

"Oh, nothing," she mumbled. She thought, "I must tell my brother about this."

TEENAGE CRUSHES

The annual fairground festival attracted many tourists. Jasmin and the staff had the chance to go there at ten p.m. after working hours. She hung around with the other apprentices, and when it came close to midnight they paired off. One of the waiters, a university student on a summer job, escorted her home.

Jasmin was flattered that he, being well-educated and so much older than she, had taken an interest in her. She was only fifteen. Before they crossed the boulevard to the hotel, he turned to embrace her and asked, "Could I kiss you?" Since she was so awestruck, she didn't know what to say, so he kissed her and said, "Oh, you're so sweet." At the hotel door they parted: he to his quarters and she to the attic, where she shared a room with the senior lady cook. Jasmin thought about the kind words he had said about her. She was thrilled that he considered her to be "sweet", for this was a merit bestowed upon her that she didn't have to earn or work for. That he thought she was delightful filled her with confidence.

A knock at the door jolted her out of her reverie and Mrs. Manning burst in to say, "I'll talk to you in the morning."

"What was that all about?" asked the cook.

Jasmin said, "Mrs. Manning saw me and Gerald coming home, walking hand in hand. I have no idea why this made her angry."

The cook said, "She wanted to make sure you were in your room, not in his."

Jasmin laughed out loud, "That was the furthest thing from my mind."

Jasmin became more and more efficient in everything she did. As part of her apprenticeship training, Jasmin had to assist the chef with skinning venison or calf in the cool basement and understanding the different cuts. She made notes in her homework for trade school. This was the compulsory once-a-week class she attended alongside the apprenticeship training. She was enrolled in a three-year course followed by a diploma. The head chef also taught her to catch live eels with a burlap tied around her hand from the basin and to hold them tight to cut off their heads. That felt gruesome to her, and many times the eels slipped through her fingers and wiggled to the drain. But of course they couldn't get down through the perforated cover. She had to catch them again and grip them more fiercely as she decisively cut off their heads. They had to be cut open with a different knife and cleaned and rinsed off, even if their tail wrapped itself around her arm. Finally she brought them upstairs to hand them to the chef, who cut them into portions under running water and put them into the boiling water pot for the advertised delicacy, "Blue Eel".

In winter the banks of the Rhine stream froze although the water flowed underneath the ice. As it thawed, the narrow passage of the famous Lorelei Cliff became an ice jam. The engineers had to blast it so that the other towns upstream didn't flood. The ice flows

Jasmin

came rushing down river with lightning speed, taking everything with them that was loose including broken trees, broken docks, and debris. This made quite a show for the community. One particular spring season the flood warning caused everybody to be evacuated from the hotel to higher ground. Jasmin went home. When she came back to work, she could see the residue of the flooding on the walls and in the basement. Professional cleaners did the bulk of the work and renovating. Jasmin and the other cooking apprentice had to chip in by painting the storage areas. Jasmin had to whitewash the basement walls. But this assignment didn't last long, because in came unexpected customers.

She was called, "Jasmin, up front!"

She had to forget the dirty work, get cleaned up, put on her waitress uniform, and serve. Jasmin always wore black: either a dress or a skirt and top with a short white apron. Her money belt was tied underneath the apron. She took the order, registered it on the till, and gave the slip to the chef and the drink department. After serving the dinner guests, she collected the money from them, made change, and kept the money in the pouch until closing time. She tallied the register slips, made payment to the company, and kept the leftover money as a tip.

The boss had a new stereo radio installed in the restaurant with speakers in the two adjoining extensions. This radio also featured a record player for 45 and 78 records. You could load multiple records at one time so as to have continuing play when the usual radio program was finished. Jasmin was thrilled by this, especially since she could pick the latest pop songs. Soon they called her "Jasmin and the radio." She was synonymous with organizing the musical entertainment. Most of the songs were either American or Latin American translated into German.

One particular song hit a raw nerve in the displaced German public. The American title of the song was "Memories were made of this." The German singer's name was Freddy Quinn. People from the east behind the iron curtain whose properties had been stolen by the Russians found an outlet for their grief over their lost homeland through this song. They could never go back. It seemed so final, so hopeless. Jasmin could identify with her father's pain. His three-hundred-year-old heritage farm had been confiscated by the Russians and East German communists. It felt as if one's heart and soul had been ripped away. The song evoked a deep nostalgic memory that wouldn't go away, and it was played for years.

But life had to go on. In the so-called west, the occupying forces had returned properties back to the Germans. People started to rebuild and enter free trade, thanks to the Marshall Plan.

Another annual fair was in session and the staff were allowed to go to the amusement park after hours. Jasmin and her peers took to the bumper cars, and afterwards they stood around with some other youths. A fellow who had made eyes at Jasmin stuck with her the rest of the evening and escorted her through the park on the way home. They talked about who they were, where they worked, whether they liked what they were doing, and other subjects like that. He said he was eighteen and that his name was Hermann.

He explained, "I go by Harry though; it sounds more English." Jasmin understood, because most Germans nowadays wanted to Americanize or Anglicize their identity. They talked about the upcoming closing ceremonies of the festival up at the fortress. A dance band would be playing. As they sat for a while on the garden bench overlooking the Rhine River, Harry pointed to the cargo ships anchored for the night. He was employed on one of them. Jasmin pointed toward the hotel where she worked and had him check the

Jasmin

time. Then she decided to go back to the hotel across the boulevard to keep her curfew. Nothing particular was planned and they parted.

Jasmin gained confidence in answering the telephone located at the open end of the counter in a niche. Mr. Manning taught her how to handle bookings. One day, as she was fulfilling her routine duties behind the reception desk, the telephone rang. Jasmin answered, expecting a booking, but Harry's voice came on the line asking her to go with him to the dance up at the castle. She trembled for a moment, and then told him she got off at nine. She asked him to wait for her outside. She looked around to check if anybody had overheard the conversation. The busy staff paid no attention to her, except for the dishwasher girl who just smiled.

After work, she met Harry on the boulevard. He escorted her all the way up to the castle where they joined the crowd at one of the long tables surrounding the dance floor. After dancing the evening away, by midnight everybody was given a torch so that they could follow through the catacombs and out along the ramparts into an ancient armories assembly hall. One of the leaders gave a closing speech, and then the band began to play. They encouraged everybody to join in the anthem, "Germany above all". For a moment, it struck Jasmin that she had heard somewhere through the grapevine that this song had been banned or at least censored, the same as the marching song "Erika". But she didn't dwell on it, thinking that maybe Germany didn't have a new anthem. Jasmin and Harry made the long trek home.

They talked and held hands. After a short embrace, Jasmin tried to open the back door, only to find it locked. She called, "Harry, come here please!"

He turned and said, "Yes, what is it?"

Jasmin whispered, "I can't get into the door; help me climb into the window of the first floor." She could use the ridges and vines along the down-spout for balance.

She urged, "Give me a lift to the door frame so I can reach the outer sill of the upstairs window." First Harry lifted her up high by the waist, and then he cupped his hands for her to step into and raised them so that she could get a footing on the concrete ridge of the door frame. From there she climbed into the open first floor window above. She waved a silent goodbye and made her way up the stairs to the staff floor into her bedroom. She exhaled a sigh of relief and made up her mind to ask for a key the next time.

Harry wrote letters to Jasmin from where he boarded his ship to alert her of when he would be in the vicinity of their town. His ship sailed from Holland to Switzerland via the Rhine, ending in Basel. As Jasmin wheeled the laundry to the public park, she looked intensely toward the cargo ships going upstream. When she spotted him, they waved to each other. When the ship anchored in her town, sometimes he showed up at the window across her desk in the evening. She would hurry to finish her work and rush out the back door, and then they would take a stroll along the river bank.

Harry had a few days' vacation and met Jasmin on her day off. They rode the ferry to the other side of the river and took a leisurely walk along the mountain road to Jasmin's home. She introduced him to her mother and father. Jasmin's mother liked Harry, but her father was not too impressed. However, they parted cordially and the two walked back on another nature trail through vineyards and sat on the bench looking at the beautiful scenery on both sides of the Rhine river valley.

When they met a few evenings later, Harry said, "My sister watched us with her binoculars while we were sitting on the bench."

Jasmin found that amusing. She considered it flattering to parade a boyfriend around at sixteen, but she saw no future in it.

Her father had mentioned, "As a sailor, he is no better that a 'Knecht' or a farmhand; you can do better that that." Jasmin liked Harry's friendship, but when he told her what other girls did to turn him on, an alarm went on in her head and she lost interest.

She still received correspondence from him and also from other admirers, even one from the neighbour boy in her hometown. One card came from a cooking apprentice she had met in class. He came to visit her after hours and brought an expensive gift, a silver dresser set. Jasmin graciously received this gift. It piqued her vanity of course, but she remembered her mother's admonition. On first dates one does not usually receive gifts, other than flowers or maybe a box of chocolates. Jasmin appreciated the gesture, knowing he wanted to impress her, but she didn't particularly wish to keep up the friendship with him.

After a few dates, she said, "I really don't want to keep that gift. You might want to give it to somebody who likes you more."

But he assured her, "No, it was a pleasure giving it to you; please keep it." They parted, with no strings attached.

In her last year of school, she occasionally rode on the train with a local boy, Dietrich, who attended high school. Their paths didn't cross often, except when he took the later train, which was the one Jasmin usually took. Jasmin liked his disciplined persona and educated language. He wanted to become a lawyer. This fascinated her, since her sister Camilla had married a doctor. Her third sister, Johanna the actress, had become engaged to an opera singer. People of higher education and professions impressed her. She enjoyed intelligent conversations.

Dietrich lived in the village above the tourist town. Some of the hotel staff had planned to attend the Plum Festival in that village.

Camilla, the dress designer, had made a dress for Jasmin for this occasion. After the dance was over, the young people congregated at somebody's house with several parents present. The adults served cake and coffee into the wee hours of the morning. Dietrich played American pop songs on the piano and added some jazz. Everybody had a good time.

When it came time to break up the party, Dietrich spoke to Jasmin, "I'll have to take my father's car back home. I'll drop the others off first, and then I'll walk with you down the mountain trail. I'll have to catch the early morning train anyway."

Jasmin got into the back seat of the crowded vehicle and one of the boys tried to get fresh with her. She slapped him, putting an end to that! Finally the others left.

Dietrich said to Jasmin, "Wait in the car while I go in the house and change into my school outfit and pick up my books. I'll walk with you to the hotel." Jasmin rested and closed her eyes. Dietrich returned with his backpack and offered his hand to help her out of the car. He guided her down the mountain. Time was of no importance at the moment; it could have been four in the morning. Slowly, they wandered the winding paths towards town. Dietrich kept hold of her hand to make sure she wouldn't stumble. Jasmin felt comfortable in his company, similar to how she felt when she was with her brother. They rested for a moment on an old log and talked about what they thought about life. He intended to take psychology as well as law. He wanted to learn about what motivated people. Jasmin asked him which university he planned to enroll in.

He said, "Mainz."

Jasmin inserted, "My brother-in-law studied there and he took my sister to the campus dances where they played American pop songs."

Dietrich smiled, "In the Mood? String of Pearls? Boogie Woogie Bugle Boy?"

Jasmin agreed, "Same songs that you play. Where did you learn to play piano?"

"Here. I began lessons as a five-year-old. Listen, I'll have to get you back to the hotel and I don't want to miss my early train. I'll see you next time when you go to your school."

Before they entered the clearing to the road, he asked, "May I kiss you goodbye?" Jasmin looked up at him and barely nodded. He brushed a gentle kiss on her lips. Jasmin was thrilled and felt a sweet sensation.

"Let me walk with you to the end of your corner. I'll watch till you are safely inside your door," he offered. They parted and waved as long as they could see each other. Jasmin went upstairs to her room for a couple of hours sleep before starting her morning shift.

A few days later a letter arrived for her. She put it into her pocket and anxiously awaited her afternoon break to open and read it. It said:

Dear Jasmin, or dare I call you dearest?

Your floral name invokes the most intoxicating feeling. You are the most adorable girl I have ever met. Your beauty surpasses the famed Venus De Milo. You are a living doll, poetry in motion, gracious and enthralling. I want to spend my days just watching you, admiring you. I want to spend time with you, dream with you. You have enraptured my heart. I can't wait to see you again next week.

Your truly devoted friend,

Dietrich

Jasmin held her breath. She had never in all her seventeen years heard anybody say anything even remotely something like that to her. She had hardly ever received praise, only reprimands. She read her letter over and over, relishing each word. She had considered Dietrich a dear friend but had never expected him to develop into an ardent admirer.

She kept the letter in her purse, took it to school, and flaunted it like a conquest to her peers. At the hotel she showed the letter to her colleagues, the kitchen staff, and to her roommate. She didn't realize that sharing secrets with girlfriends could have disastrous consequences. Whenever Jasmin thought about Dietrich she imagined those adoring words he wrote. However, she didn't meet him on her weekly school day. She had hoped to hear more from him, but there was no news. She couldn't understand why someone who had written such an endearing letter wouldn't try to pursue her any further, or even try to communicate. She didn't see him the next school day either.

She heard through the grapevine that Dietrich's sister worked at the local beauty salon. With that information in mind, Jasmin made a hair appointment. During the curling session, she casually asked Dietrich's sister, "How is Dietrich?"

"Oh," his sister said, "our father got wind of Dietrich's infatuation with a girl and strictly forbade him to have any contact with her, since he was only eighteen. He has to attend to his studies, get his diploma, and spend long years at law school. He is not to be closely involved with anybody. Father watches over him like a hawk. He changed Dietrich's train schedule so that he wouldn't see her by chance."

When her style was finished, Jasmin looked into the mirror. Dietrich's sister gave her an admiring look, and said, "You are beautiful."

Jasmin

Jasmin thought, "I don't feel beautiful, if you only knew the truth."

Dietrich's father was the station master. When she purchased her weekly train ticket for school, Jasmin wore a stoic expression. She straightened her shoulders and held her head up high. The pain of rejection was etched in her countenance. Jasmin wondered who had betrayed her, "Cherchez la femme?" She cried quietly when no one was in her room. She missed being talked to kindly and approvingly, especially from someone she could have admired.

Her life consisted of work, work, study, and more work. She did it methodically and tensely, trying to do everything according to the book. Jasmin had to study theory and demonstrate what she learned for the Examiner from the Hotel Association. He inspected the class category of the establishment. He checked everything and everybody.

He said to Jasmin, "Remember you are a servant to the public. You have to smile, smile, and smile some more, if you want to pass the test in the fall."

Jasmin thought, "Grin and bear it, no room for emotions in my life."

As this was an extraordinary busy season, Jasmin had to work non-stop through many lunch hours. Suddenly, she felt a sharp pain in her heart. Mrs. Manning had noticed Jasmin's face turn pale. She took her by the arm and led her to the seat in the staff corner.

She pointed to the maître d' and ordered, "Call an ambulance!" Within a few minutes, they had rushed her to the hospital, where she stayed three days for testing and observation.

Hans came to visit. He asked her quietly, "What is really on your heart, Jasmin?"

She began to cry, "Why can't I be friends with somebody without it being perceived as something bad?"

"Tell me about it," he encouraged her.

"I made friends with a law student who walked me home from the Plum Festival." She continued, "A week later, I received the most adoring letter from him. He said beautiful things about me and he wanted to see me again. But I have not have any communication from him since. I heard in a round-about way that he was grounded because somebody had told him something negative about me, but even so, I feel that a true friend would have found a way to contact me."

Hans put his arms around her shoulders. "Jasmin, it's quite alright to cry and grieve over loss. It'll be alright; you don't have to internalize it and think you are bad. Indeed, a true friend would have continued to express his care for you. Now dry your tears and listen to two pieces of advice. One, the time was not right, as you are still too young to have a boyfriend. Two, there are more fish in the sea." Jasmin thanked him for his love and wisdom. The doctor prescribed a tonic for Jasmin and advised her to take it easy for a month after she was discharged from the hospital. She was to check back with him monthly for evaluation. The Manning' gave her a lighter work shift.

The drinking age at that time was sixteen in the company of adults. At seventeen, Jasmin still preferred soft drinks. However, because of her job, she had to serve wine. As part of her curriculum, she went to wine tasting sessions to differentiate between vintages. She sipped a small sample, rolled it around in her tongue, and spit it out. She took a piece of bread to clear the taste away and try another sample. Wine Queen Parades were a big tourist attraction in the area. Local vineyards elected a yearly Wine Queen, who would wear her braided hair on top of her head like a crown. All the teenage girls, including Jasmin, imitated that hairstyle for a season, as it had become a fad. The boss's family owned vineyards across the river and the grape harvest came along in October. The apprentices, daily kitchen workers, and dishwashers went to help for the day. So, first thing early in the morning, off they went by ferry to the other town where they met the vineyard warden and climbed up the winding paths called "serpentines" to pick grapes. Everyone received a basket, filled it with clusters of Riesling grapes, and dumped the contents into a bin at the end of the row. By ten in the morning the group had their late breakfast with a tall glass of wine. This time Jasmin couldn't avoid it, and she laughed as she drank it. By noon they had lunch with more wine. Everybody cheered and filled their baskets with glee. They worked as a team the rest of the day and lined up to catch the last ferry at eight p.m., singing and swinging. The chef prepared supper for them and nobody had to do any more work that day. They just fell into bed, very tired.

The owners kept skeleton staff in the off-season: one cooking apprentice, one kitchen helper, and Jasmin in the reception. Mrs. Manning had prepared the Christmas room in the German tradition. She decorated the tree and set up individual tables laden with gifts for each staff member, including her own mother and aunt who helped in the business. She locked the room. At six on Christmas Eve, a night which is called Holy Evening in Germany, she rang a bell and invited everybody in. You could hear a collective "Ah" when they entered, seeing the lit Christmas tree for the first time. Mrs. Manning led each guest to their gift and enjoyed watching their reactions. Jasmin received a very modern leather purse to match the coat she had previously purchased. She was also given a wallet with cash, a pretty scarf, a photo album, and of course a full Christmas goodie hamper to take home.

On Christmas Day, which in Germany is called the First Christmas Day, Jasmin went home to her parents' house. They attended the church, which was halfway up the hill to the castle.

On Boxing Day, known in Germany as the Second Christmas Day, Jasmin's sisters commented about how quickly she had grown up. She had almost reached marriageable age. Camilla promised to sew her wedding dress, but Jasmin retorted that marriage was not on her agenda!

In February the Carnival season began. The Mannings had closed the business for renovations, but it opened one night for the local townspeople to have a costume party. They came disguised as clowns, gnomes, knights, princesses, you name it. Jasmin was in charge of decorating the two main restaurants of the hotel with tinsel, garlands, and colored lights. In the evening Jasmin passed around trays of finger food to the guests and served lots of alcoholic beverages. A couple of musicians played for the group until midnight. Then they closed the hotel again.

Jasmin got permission to go out one evening to a fancy dress-up ball at the competition. She had no qualms going alone across the square up the block. She donned a long black veil to obscure her appearance; besides, her brother had taught her self-defense. Jasmin normally wore her hair in a ponytail, but tonight she had let her long blonde hair down so that no one would recognize her easily. Jasmin wore a mermaid costume, designed for her by Camilla. It consisted of a tight fitting sequined green top, green net stockings, and a white satin-lined tail that was also covered with green satin. A sequined mask over her eyes completed her costume. Jasmin carried a fan in her hand.

She entered the hall, and a few heads turned her way. As the rule of carnival, girls took the initiative. They didn't have to stay seated and wait for the guys to bow before them and ask them to dance. On this night, girls could just tap boys on the shoulder and then they would dance with them. Jasmin mingled for a few moments and when the music began to play the next song, she turned to the first guy she saw who was reasonably good looking. Then she tapped him on the shoulder with her fan to invite him to dance with her. Guys were eager to be picked. She danced with several acquaintances and even with her doctor who had treated her when she had the heart attack. He murmured, "I sure would like to know who is behind that mask."

"Well," she quipped, "as the saying goes, 'At midnight all the cats turn grey.' You'll have to be on the alert or the magic disappears." She accepted a drink from somebody and the evening went by with lots of picture taking and polonaises.

When the clock struck twelve, in true tradition, the announcement came to take the masks off. Everybody turned to see this mysterious mermaid reveal herself.

The doctor looked incredulously at her. "It is you, Jasmin, and I thought you were a celebrity from out of town! You sure look healthy now."

Jasmin quipped, "That was not I; it was a Nixe, now I am a prim and proper girl who goes home, and my curfew is up." She turned to the young man she was dancing with, and said, "I am leaving now."

The fellow said, "I'll walk you home."

She replied, "Don't bother, as I have only a few steps to go. I'm O.K."

But he insisted. As they came to her door, he wanted to come in and kiss her, but she wouldn't let him embrace her.

"I hardly know you. Thanks for walking me home," she said, as she slipped inside the door and shut it. Jasmin had enjoyed flirting in the masquerade. Playing the role of an enchantress had transported her into a make-believe mood while in the mask. As soon as it came off, the game was over, and she had no amorous emotions or intentions. This way Jasmin guarded her heart.

After graduating from her apprenticeship she held a position as a fully paid associate, and then she stayed on for one more year. During the off-season, she served dinners to the sporadic guests. Jasmin knew how to present and sell the best items on the menu and suggest the appropriate wines for the best cuts. She was favoured by management, customers, and staff. She hosted everything from "Champagne Breakfasts" to children's parties and family get-togethers.

One more carnival party for the local townspeople was arranged by Jasmin and her employers. Again, the rival hotel also hosted a costume party. Jasmin was allowed to go, but this time her employer and his wife accompanied her. Jasmin felt secure in the company of her "surrogate parents". She came dressed up as a harem dancer, and the guys actually lined up waiting to be picked. She didn't even have to go and tap them with her fan. She merely beckoned with her index finger to give them a turn. Jasmin thoroughly enjoyed that. She pretended she was on a stage playing a role, and then she won the prize for the best costume. At midnight, when the masquerade was over, Mr. and Mrs. Manning escorted their prize girl home.

The Mannings were members of the Hotel and Restaurant Association. Their seasonal periodical had advertisements where companies looked to hire staff. When the Mannings came across an article that said England was opening their borders for German individuals who could work on a yearly contract in domestic services, they approached Jasmin and some waiters and asked them to consider it.

They suggested to Jasmin, "You could gain experience in the field and learn English at the same time. We'll give you a reference and in your application you could stipulate that you would like to be in a better category than domestic services. The tourist business is expanding all over Europe, and being fluent in English will be a great asset for you. If you come back here after your contract, we will hire you as manageress for the new affiliate we intend to lease." Jasmin talked it over with her parents and they considered it wise to explore the world on a working permit, especially since the hotel business afforded room and board. She would be well-chaperoned.

Her father admonished her, "Always live up to the honourable standard we taught you."

She applied for the position, and about a month later a job offer came from a six-hundred-room hotel in central England. Her contract read that once she could speak English she could manage the coffee shop, although initially she would have to be hired as a domestic. Jasmin became very excited about this new adventure in her career, and the summer flew by with preparations for the big change in her life. She got a clean bill of health, her first passport, and new outfits. Her co-workers and friends wished her well as she prepared to leave.

Jasmin recalled the time in grade four when her school teacher had announced her upcoming trip to England. Miss Krause boarded the first ferry boat that allowed Germans to visit England. Upon her return she talked about the Belisha beacons. Orange poles with lights on top were used as warnings at street crossings and zebra stripes were painted on the roads. Jasmin thought, "I'll get to see that now."

She had another recollection from her earlier childhood when she had lived with her aunt. The scarcity they experienced had caused her aunt to send Jasmin to a particular house in the "Black Market" with a twenty mark bill (equivalent to twenty dollars at that time) to buy two eggs. Another scene came to mind from her time at the seaside resort where a section of the beach had been segregated for British personnel from the German public. One aunt had been swimming while the other aunt had sat with Jasmin on a blanket on the beach. They had noticed a British family sitting on the other side of the fence on a beach mat having a picnic. Suddenly the English gentleman had come over around the edge of the fence with something in his hand.

He had walked closer to Jasmin, given a sizable package to her aunt, and said, "For the child." The other aunt came out of the water, wrapped a towel around herself, and was stunned. "For you as well," he added. Both aunts thanked him profusely. He left, lifting his hand like a salute. Aunt Helen and Aunt Martha had unfolded the wrappings and shared with Jasmin the very white English sandwiches. This gift of sandwiches had left a lasting impression on Jasmin about the kindness of the British.

Hans made a point to speak to Jasmin alone before she set out on her new journey. "Remember, we will be worlds apart, but there is no distance in prayer. I will always be praying for you to be guided, protected, and channeled in the right direction. The Lord will help you and surround you with favour, if necessary, by angels."

They shared a hug. "I believe that," Jasmin concurred, and said goodbye to her family.

ENGLAND

The day arrived for her departure by a train that would take her to Brussels. She wore her new mohair two-piece suit and carried the cute grey leather purse and one suitcase. She had booked a room at a small hotel close to the station where the friendly innkeepers welcomed her. They provided an evening snack and promised to wake her at six the next morning. She asked for directions to the city centre and found it within walking distance. Jasmin took snapshots of the ornate buildings which had the same architectural Patricia features as in south Germany. Amazed that the stores stayed open until eleven p.m., she bought souvenirs.

    The next morning, she embarked upon a new endeavour: first by train to Hook of Holland, and then by ferry to cross the English Channel. The ferry docked at the harbour in Folkston, England. Jasmin boarded the train to London. Facing a porter, she pointed to her ticket. The porter escorted her to the train for Middleton. That started the last leg of her journey.

When Jasmin arrived, she hailed a taxi for the Excelsior Hotel in Middleton and entered the reception area.

The doorman asked her, "May I help you?"

She said, "I've come to work here," and showed him her work permit form.

"Oh," he said, "wait here a moment. I'll get one of the housekeeping staff for you."

A pleasant young woman came to meet Jasmin and told her in German that they were expecting her. She directed the bellhop to carry Jasmin's luggage to the elevator and up to the sixth floor. Jasmin entered a large room with four beds. When the bellhop left, the housekeeper introduced Jasmin to the other occupants of the room and directed her to the vacant bed designated to her.

The housekeeper instructed another German girl, Renate, to escort her to the staff kitchen in the morning for breakfast and then to the office for further instructions.

Before leaving, she asked Jasmin, "Are you hungry?"

Jasmin replied, "A little."

The housekeeper turned to Nancy, the English girl, and said, "Go to the room service pantry on the fifth floor and arrange for a sandwich to be brought up and a cup of tea." Nancy did as she was asked. She went to the pantry, had the waitress order a snack and tea, and then she waited until the dumb waiter bell rang, pulled it, and brought the tray to Jasmin.

The next morning, Renate showed Jasmin which elevator to take, and how to operate the time clock. She introduced Jasmin to the timekeeper, who immediately addressed her: "Hello, Smiler!"

Renate took Jasmin to the staff kitchen. Jasmin observed everything laid out for breakfast including cereal, eggs, bacon, toast, sponge cake, jam and butter, juice, coffee, and tea. Renate translated everything so that Jasmin could get her bearings. Jasmin already knew the word toast. She remembered from her childhood how her brother had tried to improvise toast in the smoking pit. "Now, I am getting the real thing," she thought.

At the office they properly registered her and gave instructions and papers to take to the Employment Office in the city. The hotel encompassed several city blocks, making everything within walking distance. Renate showed her inside and helped her to understand the attending officer. They were very kind and she signed up for domestic services. Unemployment insurance and pension had the same system here as it had in Germany. Back at the hotel, Renate took her to the third floor and left her in the care of an elderly maid, Mildred. She had just made some tea and invited Jasmin into the maid station, which was a closet-like room with a window, a table, two chairs, and some cabinets. Mildred poured tea into two cups and offered Jasmin cream and sugar. She said, "You never start work without a cup of tea first." Jasmin could hardly understand anything she said, but she nodded. Renate came by occasionally to translate when needed.

"But," Renate said, "the reason you are not assigned to me is that you wouldn't learn English."

Mildred put on her chain belt with the pass key and took Jasmin along to the fifteen rooms in her charge. She motioned to her what she needed assistance with. First she checked for a tip, either on the dressing table or the bedside table. Then they began stripping beds, cleaning sinks, getting fresh linens from the linen closet, and vacuuming the carpets.

The third floor consisted of a total of sixty bedrooms, with fifteen rooms per section. Mildred pointed to the intercom located on each of the four corners of the square with the chart to be filed. Since Jasmin had to work as a housemaid until she could communicate in English, she had to scrub the corridors after the regular maid service hours had ended. After the lunch break, she worked from two p.m. until five p.m.

After two weeks they promoted her to chambermaid. Now she didn't have to scrub floors anymore (the daily staff did that), and she had her own housemaid who cleaned the bathrooms. Jasmin received her own chain belt with the pass key and reported on the floor every morning at seven a.m. First, she had to check the chart on the intercom shelf for wake up calls. Next, she had to tap on the door of the guest's room and enter, leaving the door wide open.

She would then say, "It's seven-thirty," (or eight, or whatever the time of the wake-up call) and "May I draw the curtains?"

When the sleepy person replied, "Yes," she would march to the windows and pull the heavily-lined drapes to let the daylight in the room. Then she would make her exit.

Sometimes the guest would ask, "What type of day is it?"

Jasmin would then reply, "It is sunny." Even on cloudy or foggy days, she would say, "It will clear up." She always said something positive.

In her new shift, she finished at two in the afternoon, but had to be back to work at seven p.m. till ten p.m. In her free time off work she went to afternoon classes at the "Further Education School" for her English upgrading. That meant no more relying on girlfriends to translate; she would be learning English at the source. She did her homework and memorized new vocabulary. She also interacted with the other foreign workers including French chefs, Italian waiters, and Spanish maids. Even though they couldn't communicate much in English, they communicated with each other in their own way. They all carried dictionaries with them, but when it came to getting a point across they found a way with gesticulations, like playing charades.

An Italian young man approached Jasmin, and said, "Oh, your name means 'love.'"

A French boy asked, "Rendezvous?" and everyone knew it meant a date. Everybody understood café or coffee bar as these were international words. Jasmin liked the fun of afternoon dates, going to coffee bars, or window-shopping, all the while practicing new words. However, the International Club proved to be a short-lived novelty for her. The majority of the members came from Pakistan, although these students emphatically told her they weren't Indian. It didn't make any difference to her, but she was more inclined to meet local Englishmen. Once more she attended the club, participated in a board game, and a young English boy (she guessed he was about her age) asked her to go to a movie some time. She thought it wouldn't hurt and told him that the next day she had off, she would go out with him.

She attended some meetings at the YWCA, where at least there were English people. The Salvation Army had group meetings with travelling missionaries. Jasmin was fascinated by a speaker who had just arrived from Nairobi. She hardly understood a word but the gentle tone of his voice gave her great comfort. In a way it reminded her of a dialect in Low-German, the softer nuances of her own language.

At her work station, the laundry man always greeted her by saying, "You're a cracker," while blinking his eyes.

Jasmin asked another maid, "What does he mean?"

The maid replied, "He says you are pretty."

Jasmin blushed and went about her business. She noticed that when she was walking down the streets, guys would often give a short sideways nod of their heads and sometimes wink one eye in approval, or click their lips. Some even tipped their hats and let her pass. She would just smile.

Within two months her English had somewhat improved and her supervisor offered her an opportunity to babysit for a celebrity one evening. Jasmin hesitated, thinking that her English wasn't good enough yet, but the housekeeper assured her that she wouldn't have to talk much; she just had to be there. They gave her the number of the room and told her the time to be there. When she arrived at the room, a beautiful blonde American actress and her escort were awaiting her with instructions to entertain her two sons. Jasmin nodded, although she hardly understood a word. The actress gave her a packet of American cigarettes and left. Jasmin sat on the big bed with the boys, who played a board game. (She understood the numbers in this game, but not many words.) This went on for a little while and when their eyelids began to droop, she tucked them in and turned the light down low.

Jasmin tried one of those cigarettes, and after she put it out, she nestled into the easy chair and dozed off. She startled awake when the gentleman tapped her on the elbow. He and the lady just smiled and gave her a generous tip of two pounds and two theatre tickets for the matinee of the play in which the actress performed as the leading lady. Jasmin went to the live theatre the next day and enjoyed it immensely. She didn't understand too much, but the actors used the word "collaborator" a lot.

Jasmin liked weekend shifts when guests stayed over in the hotel for special events, conferences, or parties. Not many rooms were booked, so she supervised two sections. Instead of fifteen rooms, she was responsible for thirty rooms. Although the guests wouldn't require wake up calls, they often had breakfast served in bed by the room service. Others just rose late. On such occasions, someone would call, "Maid!" and as soon as Jasmin rushed to attend, they would give her a generous tip. For VIPs, the housekeeper arranged flowers in the suites. Upon departure, Jasmin could keep them, if they were still good, plus the tip.

One time a gracious lady pointed to the cigarette holder on the dresser and said, "I'm not using that anymore; you can have it, if you would like."

Jasmin bowed her head and said, "Thank you very much."

Jasmin and her roommates liked to go to the department store and shop at the ground level for poppy seed buns, pumpernickel bread, and camembert cheese. They even found the odd corner delicatessen for European treats. This might have been nostalgia rearing up, although Jasmin didn't suffer from homesickness as much as the others did. One Sunday evening, Jasmin and Renate came home late. Jasmin asked the food manager what to do for supper, since the staff kitchen was closed.

He replied, "Go to the larder; there should be someone there. Tell them I sent you."

HOTEL LIFE

Well, this opened an entire new world for them. They shyly walked the long sawdust-covered passage that divided the hot kitchen from the cold kitchen and went down the steps to the larder.

The "Cold Chef" looked up and said, "What are you two beauties doing in a place like this?"

Jasmin replied, "Brian the food manager sent us down here because we're late and we missed the staff dinner."

The chef interrupted, "What can I offer you? Cold chicken, ham, cheese, lettuce, tomatoes - anything you want. Grab a platter and I'll pile it up for you. How many of you are there?"

Renate replied, "Four." He gave them several slices of Virginia ham, four half chickens, and a variety of cheeses on a bed of lettuce and tomatoes. The chef also had his assistant fetch some soft drink bottles and napkins, which Jasmin took while Renate carried the tray. The girls giggled and the tray wobbled precariously in Renate's hands until one of the chicken pieces rolled off the platter and down into the sawdust. Jasmin retrieved it with her free hand and wiped it with a napkin. They reached the guest elevator and when the door opened, the floor manager Robert came out.

He looked at them and raised his eyebrows, saying, "Having a party?"

All the girls could say, was, "Yes." They got in the elevator, still giggling. This particular elevator only went to the fifth floor, so they had to walk up the staircase to the sixth floor.

Finally they arrived at their room. Jasmin made a bee line to the sink where she washed off the lost chicken and dried it with more paper towels. Then they presented their feast to the other girls: Claire the Austrian and Nancy the English one.

"Where did you get all that?" they queried.

"Just eat and enjoy," they said. "Don't look a gift horse in its mouth."

At the end of their meal, Nancy said laughingly, "You German girls get all the favours." Nancy was otherwise a wealth of information who had told them about the house detective, the house doctor, the nurse's station, the beauty salon, and the valet service. They lived in a city within the city.

All staff had the privilege of obtaining complimentary railway tickets. Jasmin took this opportunity to go on a trip to Sheffield on her day off. She visited Siegfried, a waiter from her previous German employment who had got his working permit for England at the same time as she. They had intended to touch base at some point to see how they were each getting along in England and to talk about how to cope with culture shock. They went sight-seeing. He told her all about Sheffield being a steel city and how his hotel was also well-run. They had coffee and cake and wished each other well. Then Jasmin boarded the train back to Middleton.

Jasmin

On the way home another passenger in the train started talking to her. He asked the usual questions about where she had come from, where she was going, what was her name. He said he was an American from Mexico. Jasmin wasn't familiar with the American geography and couldn't speak enough English to ask him to explain if he meant American or Mexican. But she understood he was an engineer, and this sounded educated to Jasmin. They agreed on a luncheon date for the next day in Middleton, since her shift wouldn't begin until that evening.

At the restaurant he asked for Tabasco sauce, which they didn't have. She had him spell this word out for her, but she didn't find it in the dictionary. She didn't eat anything except for a few pretzels from the basket. Rather than focusing on the food, Jasmin merely liked meeting with people in appropriate places so that she would have someone to converse with in English. They decided to go to the popular ballroom dancing hall for an hour during their afternoon session. It had two orchestras: one full thirty-piece band and a six-piece Latin band. This was a nice place to go to when you had nothing else to do. Jasmin had taken dancing lessons at thirteen while living with her sister and could differentiate between the Latin beats. She was puzzled when he got into a Mexican hat dance instead of the Samba that played, but she laughed it off and took it in good sport. After a while she got bored and they left. They walked through the city window shopping until they reached the staff entrance of the hotel.

She said, "Nice to have met you." He said something in response, but she didn't understand, so she just nodded and went inside.

A few days later, he was waiting for her at the timekeeper who called her on the intercom. Jasmin came down, saw the Mexican, and thought, "Oh my, that must have been what he asked me." She told him that she had misunderstood and hadn't firmed up a date. Then she thanked him for his interest and said goodbye.

The housekeepers of the hotel acted as chaperones for the live-in girls, and the midnight curfew applied to all. Jasmin never stayed out later than ten when the movies were finished. One day a local boy from the International Club left a note at the timekeeper, inviting her to a movie. She went with him to see a film called *Love Me Tender*, even though she couldn't fathom the rave about Elvis Presley. Jasmin went to the movies to improve her English the easy way.

In the cinema, as it is called in England, before each showing they played the national anthem while everyone stood and sang. The cigarette girls came up the aisles with their trays of chocolates, candies, ice cream bars, juice, popcorn, and cigarettes. After everyone made their selection and paid, the movie began. The cinemas usually featured three showings: one matinee, one early evening, and one late evening show. Some people liked the movie so much that they stayed for more than one showing - one ticket paid for it all. Jasmin preferred to go to the one-hour cartoon cinema for fun and to of course learn English.

On another evening the English boy, Tim took her to a pub and treated her to Baby Cham, a favourite drink for the young people at that time. It was a very small bottle containing a mixture of sparkling wine and champagne. He complimented her on her green corduroy dress with a tiered skirt and said that it would twirl nicely, should they go dancing some time. However, this time they had planned to see the movie *Oklahoma*, which she enjoyed enormously. He wanted to hold her hand during the show. Jasmin wasn't into holding hands, since her philosophy was look but don't touch. At that precise moment, the spotlights shone on the cigarette girls walking up the aisles with their trays.

Jasmin

She smiled sweetly and asked, "Which do you want: popcorn, an ice cream bar, or a Coke? It's my treat." He settled for popcorn and Coke. After the movie he walked her home and she told him thanks, goodbye. She found it easy to have dates but also boring.

Sometimes two or three girls went together to see a movie. They pretty much saw a movie every week. Because of their shift work, they attended matinees and didn't have to stand in line. However, nobody called it a line; here it was called a long queue. The busses all had long queues of people waiting to ride them.

The maids sometimes met during break or when passing by the intercom or linen room. On occasion they sat on the wide window sills in the hallway where they would observe the new building being constructed across the street. Like clockwork, they would see a make-shift stove with a whistling teakettle. Someone would brew tea and then the men would stand around having their cups of tea. The German girls were amazed at the strict labour laws in England for provision of tea breaks. People worked better when they had tea pauses, and they didn't get as fatigued from long hours. The German girls adopted the English relaxed attitude of unhurriedness; "take it easy" was the first phrase they enjoyed.

On one of the rare occasions when all four girls came together in their room during the day, Renate told of one guest, a Jew, who had shown her his bare back with scars on it. He stated that he'd received them while in a concentration camp in Germany. Jasmin listened, totally aghast. She thought, "That's not the kind of Germany I know." She didn't even know what a Jew was, although she vaguely remembered in third grade religion class how it had something to do with God helping them. Within the circles where she had grown up, Jews had never entered the topic of conversations. Claire, the Austrian girl who had been in England for almost a year, had observed that many Jews now lived in England where they owned and operated many delicatessen stores. Kosher chefs catered to Jewish functions in the hotel.

Jasmin had started using makeup and putting mascara on her eyelashes, but it irritated her eyes. The hotel doctor gave her the name and address of an eye specialist.

Nancy told Jasmin, "He is excellent; he's Jewish."

Jasmin went to Dr. Dawson's house and met his wife who would be assisting him. During the examination he talked kindly to Jasmin and gave her eye drops. He advised her to use only hypoallergenic mascara. He enquired about where she came from in Germany. Jasmin told him that she had originally come from the north, but their ancestral property was behind the iron curtain and therefore inaccessible. She had grown up in the Rhine river valley, the wine country.

He recognized the area and said with much emotion in his voice, "We loved Germany."

Groups who booked banqueting rooms for their functions needed cloakroom attendants. The housekeeper asked Jasmin, "Are you interested in manning the cloakroom for a function of the Anglo-Swiss Club? You get paid overtime and you can keep your tips."

Jasmin asked, "Do I have to say anything?"

"No more than good evening and thank you," the housekeeper replied.

Jasmin laughed, "I learned that when I was a little girl."

This was another new experience for her. She took the coats, which were mostly fur, pinned numbers on them, and gave the copies to the guests. Then she hung the coats on the coat racks and laid the excess items on the single bed in a neat row. Jasmin took her schoolwork into the room and worked on it during quiet moments. Just as she was starting her English assignment, the waiter came carrying a tray for her evening meal.

Jasmin

He asked her, looking at her notepaper, "You're new here, aren't you? Oh, reading, writing, and arithmetic."

Jasmin nodded, "Yes, I know reading and writing, but what is arithmetic?" She got out her dictionary. "Oh," she read, "Mathematics."

He asked again, "You're a German girl? How long are you here for?"

Jasmin held up her index finger and said, "One-year contract."

He carried on the conversation she didn't understand, and so she just smiled till he left. The ladies came back after their meeting. Jasmin smiled and nodded, not knowing at what. They were very gracious and mostly found their own coats, giving her a generous tip.

On Christmas Eve, one of the older English maids called Jasmin around three p.m. "Come to Nancy's station."

Once there, Nancy handed her a glass with gin in it and added some Orange Crush. "Have you ever had gin and orange?"

"No," Jasmin admitted.

"Well, enjoy. Merry Christmas. How do you like it?"

"Very tasty," Jasmin said. They invited the other German girls and the English room service waitresses from the pantry. They had also left messages in the dumb waiter to the other staff one floor up and one floor down to meet at Nancy's station. The group crowded together, sitting on window sills, tables, stepping stools, and boxes, talking about what they were planning for Christmas. Some asked the German girls how they liked to spend Christmas, and found they had similar traditions. Some mentioned that the German soccer teams came regularly to play here. Others told about how a lot of German prisoners of war had decided to stay in England and live here. Some German girls whose contracts were up had decided to stay on in private homes as nannies.

Mildred, who had been employed in the hotel all of her working life, was nearing retirement. She said, "You Germans are such likeable people; I don't know why there was ever a war between us."

Everyone cheered about that and clanked their glasses together. Gradually, one by one, they wished each other "Merry Christmas" and dispersed back to their stations until closing time when they would finally go off-duty.

Jasmin and Nancy were in their own bedroom when Paula, another German girl, came in. She approached Jasmin. "There's a get-together of German waiters and cooks, but they are short one girl to pair up. We are going to have a party at one guy's apartment. It's going to be an all-nighter; come and join us."

Jasmin was not comfortable with this arrangement and said, "This is not my idea of a party."

Paula shrugged and said, "O.K., suit yourself, if you want to be unsociable and prudish," and she left. Nancy had overheard the conversation, but she didn't understand German.

She asked Jasmin, "What was all that about?"

Jasmin told her, and then Nancy encouraged her by saying, "Don't take it to heart; there are lots more fish in the sea."

"Yeah," yawned Jasmin. "Better no company than bad company."

The hotel closed for Christmas Day, and Jasmin joined the other staff for Christmas dinner at one of the banquet halls. As per English tradition, they listened to the Queen's speech. This impressed Jasmin as she listened intensely. The housekeeper asked if any of the maids were interested in waiting on tables on New Year's Eve, and urged them to let her know right away.

"You get overtime pay plus tips." This new opportunity added interest to her life, so Jasmin signed up.

On New Year's Eve, she showed up at her place of service in the large banquet hall. At the long tables guests sat squeezed together

Jasmin

so tightly that you could hardly move between the chairs. When the midnight clock struck and the New Year was ushered in, everybody kissed each other. Jasmin was carrying some empty plates when a guest, a waiter, and a chef started kissing her.

She put the plate between her and the next guy and said, "I'm out of here."

The supervisor called her and the other helpers and led them to a secluded pantry for a delicious meal and a glass of champagne.

FRIEND

In January, the room service waiter, Bernhard - a German boy whom she had passed several times - asked, "How do you like the job here so far?"

Jasmin answered, "Not bad."

Bernhard said, "My contract is up in May and I have to decide soon if I want to renew."

"Where do you want to go after here?" Jasmin enquired.

"I have a few options," Bernhard said. "Listen, we can't talk long here on duty; do you want to go for coffee in your free time?"

"Sure," Jasmin said. "What are your hours?"

He answered, "I'm off on Monday."

"So am I," Jasmin replied.

Bernhard suggested they meet at the timekeeper. On Monday they met and walked together to "Prego", the new Italian coffee bar, where they talked over cappuccino about their life in general.

They decided it was better to converse in English, to help Jasmin advance her English.

He said, "I heard about you not going to the party on Christmas Eve."

"What? Were you there?" Jasmin asked.

"No," he said, "I also do not do all-nighters and I don't invite girls to my apartment. I have a sister who had the misfortune of having an illegitimate child. I wouldn't do that to a girl. My parents are very supportive of her, but it could have been avoided."

They made another coffee date at a different location, down the block but still within walking distance. This time they met in the evening. Jasmin brought the cigarette holder she had received as a tip and inserted the American cigarette she had saved. She flaunted it like an actress.

Bernhard chuckled, "Now, whom are you impersonating?"

Jasmin cocked her head and said, "A famous movie star."

They talked about imaginations, movies and the world of make believe, and the latest pop songs. Jasmin couldn't do or say anything wrong in his eyes; he approved of everything. They went to movies together, and would often go the cartoon cinema for a laugh. Bernhard suggested they go to Aintree for the Grand National horse race. That would be something classy to do. With their complimentary train tickets, they had spare money for bets. Although they didn't win anything, they enjoyed a fancy dinner afterwards.

All of a sudden, Gertie, one of the other German girls who assisted in the hotel's Danish Snack Bar, called on Jasmin to tell her she'd be leaving her post and would Jasmin be interested in managing the food counter? She'd have to arrange the popular Danish sandwiches in view of the customers.

Jasmin hesitated, "I'm not sure I speak English well enough."

Jasmin

Gertie replied, "No need to say much; the waitresses will take the orders from the customers. They'll tell you what to do. You'll prepare the salads or the open sandwiches and they'll take them to the customers, including the ones who sit at your counter."

"O.K.," Jasmin concurred. "I'll do it. When do I start?"

"Come with me to the office." Gertie led the way.

The clerk arranged the change. Jasmin visited her new living quarters which she would share with just one roommate. Gertie took her to the larder to get cold cut trays and helped carry them to the back entrance of the Snack Bar. After that, they went to the upstairs pastry and selected the pies, fruit, desserts, and specialty cheesecake made exclusively for the Danish Snack Bar. After displaying the trays at the back buffet, Gertie introduced Jasmin to Carla, another German girl who would be her new colleague. Then Gertie left Jasmin in Carla's hands for instructions. Luncheon guests arrived from eleven till two, when the doors closed and the staff had their meal in the narrow hot kitchen. The break lasted until five-thirty p.m., and then the restaurant opened again till ten-thirty p.m.

Jasmin went to the third floor. She entered the pantry for the room service and told Nellie and Beatrice of her promotion to the contemporary Danish Snack Bar. She asked them to tell Bernhard to meet her at the timekeeper at three p.m. Bernhard was eagerly awaiting her at the timekeeper's booth when Jasmin got off the elevator.

"What do I hear; you're the snack bar assistant in the Danish Room?"

"Yes," said Jasmin exuberantly, "I have my own niche. Carla and I share the post. It's very modern and first class."

"Let's go and celebrate at Prego's. How long is your break time?"

"Till five. At that time I'll have to get stuff from the larder because the doors open at five-thirty for the dinner guests. Wait here while I go upstairs to change out of my smock and I'll be back down in ten minutes."

"O K," Bernhard said. "Hurry; we'll have a lot to talk about."

Jasmin came back, still excited. They walked the two blocks to their favourite coffee bar, found a booth, and ordered cappuccino.

Jasmin said, "I prefer the idea of meeting the public this way, because I will have my own counter as a guard rail so to speak. People will come up to me rather than me having to go to them. I never liked waiting on tables, although I was trained in that and did my best. I always felt more secure behind the reception desk. The waitresses are supposed to take the orders, even for guests sitting at my counter."

"How many waitresses are there?" Bernhard asked.

"First," Jasmin said, "there's the head waiter, who is like an overseer; the head waitress, who serves; and two regular waitresses, Maureen and Rose - she is Irish. Across the floor from us is the bar, managed by two bartenders."

"Do they also serve hot dishes?" Bernhard enquired.

"Yes," Jasmin said, "they have their own small hot kitchen behind the swinging door."

"That makes sense," Bernhard said. "It would be a long way from the main kitchen. What do they have on the menu?"

"Oh, traditional English food: roast beef with Yorkshire pudding, liver and onions, fish and chips. They also make flaming waffle desserts; I mean, when it is brought out the head waiter does the 'flaming'."

"I know how to do that," Bernhard exclaimed.

"Do you?" Jasmin asked. "I know in theory, but when I had to serve it, my boss usually lit the flames right at the table in front of the guests. As I said, here in this place I like my vantage point and I won't ever have to eat in the staff kitchen again. We eat in our own

Jasmin

tiny kitchen, where the chef prepares the hot dishes I mentioned. Whatever is on the menu for the day, we can have too. Carlo the chef is Italian, and his assistant is Georgios."

Bernhard said, "I like the hotel business."

"I do too," Jasmin added.

Bernhard tapped his forehead, "Oh, I almost forgot, this weekend I am going to Glen Eagles, the famous golf course, to attend a big golf tournament. With my complimentary train ticket it's so affordable. I'll see you when I get back. I'll put a note on your time card slot."

After a few minutes, Bernhard asked, "What are your career plans?"

Jasmin replied, "Receptionist, management, functions coordinator, possibly ownership. I have a job in management waiting for me if I decide to return to Germany."

Bernhard said, "I find that for me it's a very desirable situation being able to travel the world on a working visa. My next goal is perhaps Switzerland. The hotel association has a thorough screening process for staff. Well, Jasmin, I really enjoy talking to you. I will see you when I get back."

They strolled back to the hotel. Bernhard said goodbye to her at the staff entrance, and he went to board the bus to his flat. Jasmin took a short nap in her new room and changed into her uniform to start her shift. First she went to the larder for the prepared cold trays of smoked salmon, smoked tongue, cooked Virginia ham, and the cheese tray. Her assistant helped with carrying the items. They made several trips and remembered to go to the pastry kitchen for the cream caramels, apple pies, fruit salad, and fresh cream. The waitresses took care of the coffee corner by switching on the coffee machine and pouring milk in the steamer for white coffee.

The head waiter nodded at each person in their post and unlocked the doors for the public.

Jasmin and Carla planned to take a trip on the British Railways to Edinburgh, Scotland. They had selected the long Easter weekend and were booked to stay at a hotel in Edinburgh. Their train would be leaving at midnight from a different station across town, and so they asked the porter at the front lobby to arrange for a taxi. A guest overheard them and offered, "Girls, I'll give you a ride; it's on my way." He escorted his lady friend to the car, had the porter put their suitcases into the trunk, and ushered the girls to the back seat. When they arrived at the train station, Carla and Jasmin politely thanked the couple and boarded the train. It was an eight-hour ride to Glasgow and another hour or so to their destination of Edinburgh. They checked into the hotel and were about to crash, but breakfast was underway. They had a quick nap after breakfast and arranged for a picnic lunch to be given to them to take on their booked tour of one famous bridge and other tourist attractions. Their heads were spinning from all the new impressions. After dinner they finally crashed. On the following day the girls took a tour of Edinburgh castle. The tour guide took great care to explain extra intricate details. When he heard that the girls had come from Germany, he told them that he liked German people.

They had one more day for sightseeing and decided they'd go window shopping. To their delight, they saw that the stores were open, even on Easter Monday. Jasmin tried on several dresses and to her surprise she found a matching lightweight coat for a dress she already owned. This would make a perfect ensemble. One particular store featured a specialty section of kilts. Jasmin chose a brightly coloured one in red, green, yellow, and orange - a Royal Stewart Tartan. Carla got a green, blue, and black - a Modern Douglas. They didn't have enough money on them to purchase them outright, so the store keeper offered to ship them as soon as they sent a money order. Filled with excitement they travelled home. They decided to get their money from their post office savings accounts and send the money orders.

In Germany, when you buy a money order at the post office and give the address of the recipient, that seals the deal, and the post office forwards it. So with this in mind they waited a couple of weeks, but nothing happened. No parcel arrived. They had a distraught look on their faces.

Rose the waitress asked, "Why are you girls so glum?"

Carla said, "We are waiting for the kilts we purchased in Edinburgh. We wrote to the store to ask why they are not here, and they wrote back to say that they haven't received our money orders. But we sent them right away; we have the receipts."

Rose said, "Let me see the receipts after your break."

So Jasmin produced her receipt and the original, "Here, look at the date."

Rose laughed, "You still have the original. You have to put it into an envelope and mail it to the store."

"Oh," gasped Jasmin, "I didn't know that; they do it differently in Germany. I'll get it mailed right away."

One week later the parcel arrived and the timekeeper called them up on the intercom. Jasmin and Carla rushed there as soon as the afternoon break started.

They called to Rose and Maureen, "Come to our room and look while we unpack."

They signed off at the timekeeper, took the elevator, met the other girls at the top, and rushed to their room. Simultaneously they cut the cords off of the parcels and opened them. The kilts would be wrapped around the waist, held by two leather straps, and fastened with the large pin. Rose felt the wool fabric between her fingers.

Maureen suggested, "That deserves to be shown off. Let's go to the Ceylon Tea Centre and have a tea party."

Not that they needed any food, but they wanted to be in a smart environment. As Jasmin and Carla walked back and forth to the buffet and selected a morsel or two to have with their tea, they incurred admiring looks. It was fun, but most of all the skirts fitted well. In the mild weather they sauntered across the street back to the hotel.

Once inside, Bernhard was waiting for Jasmin. "I had hoped to catch you before you go on duty," he said. "When can we get together? I have a lot to tell you."

"Probably tomorrow afternoon," she said.

"O.K. I'll pick you up here," Bernhard smiled and was gone.

The next day they met and walked to their favourite coffee bar. Bernhard said, "Let's sit on the barstools at the counter so I can admire your fancy kilt. Is that new?"

"Yes," Jasmin said. "Carla and I got kilts in Edinburgh on our Easter excursion and guess what? I found an evening coat to match a new dress that I had bought here earlier, and also white kid gloves."

"Oh, that brings me to the topic I want to talk to you about. I have just the place in mind to take you to where you can wear it; it's a dinner dance at the Renaissance Inn, and I have two tickets. Would you like to go?" Bernhard asked.

"That sounds interesting; when is it?"

"Next Friday night; it starts at seven," he replied.

"Oh," Jasmin said, "I have to check if I can change my day off with Carla; I'll let you know."

They tapped their cappuccino cups together, and said, "To a new experience."

Jasmin

The week went by in a blink. On her day off she put on the new outfit and kid gloves for the occasion. Bernhard was once again waiting for her at the timekeeper's booth.

"We'll get a taxi," he said.

He escorted her through the interior of the hotel to the front lobby. He talked to the doorman and shortly the vehicle took them to the outskirts of town. Bernhard offered his hand as she exited the taxi.

"Let me touch your delicate gloved hands, my lady," he commented, looking at her fondly.

At their reserved table for two, the head waiter held the chair for Jasmin and she was seated.

"You belong in a beautiful atmosphere," Bernhard remarked as he sat across from her.

"Thank you," she said. "I feel comfortable in a classy environment."

"Will you go back to Germany when your contract in England is up?" asked Bernhard.

"I haven't thought much about it," said Jasmin. "I might take further education courses here. What about you?"

"I intend to gain more experience in my field and work in different countries like Switzerland, for instance in one of the elite hotels, and ultimately I would like have my own place somewhere."

"Something like this?" she asked.

"Possibly," he said.

Bernhard helped her out of her coat and draped it over the back of her chair, but she kept the long gloves on because her dress was sleeveless. The wine waiter brought a light white wine which Bernhard expertly found suitable and after it was served they ate some bread sticks. The music began to play and some couples danced.

"We have some time before the dinner is served. Would you like to dance?"

He got up and bowed before her, she accepted, and they ambled to the dancing area. They began swaying with the music to a popular tune.

During the dinner conversation, Bernhard said, "If I were your future beau, I'd put you on a pedestal."

Jasmin blushed. "Bernhard." (She understood his words to be a typical German expression of idolizing a woman).

He held her hand and breathed a kiss on it.

A few days later, he came to the timekeeper booth and left a message for her to wait for him.

When she showed up, he said, "There are new films at the cartoon cinema. Would you like to go during the afternoon break?"

"Sure," she said, "I'll just go up and change. See you shortly."

They watched the "Bugs Bunny" show for laughs, and then they ended up going to the Italian coffee bar to chat.

Bernhard said, "I like your company."

Jasmin said, "Me too."

At the Danish Snack Bar, Mr. Tyler, a longtime guest, said to Jasmin, "You look all aglow."

Jasmin looked away and overheard his lunch companion say, "She must be in love."

Jasmin busied herself at the other end of the counter and said to Rose, "Please attend to Mr. Tyler."

"What's up?" Rose asked.

"He is teasing me."

"Leave him to me." Rose strolled over, and asked, "What's it going to be today, Gentlemen?"

While bending near Mr. Tyler, she warned, "She is too young for you."

Jasmin

He looked up in mock astonishment.
On their next date, Bernhard said, "I won't renew my contract here. I have an offer of a job in a big hotel in Switzerland."
"Oh, how exciting for you," Jasmin said. "When are you leaving?"
"End of May. I'll be here for the staff party; will you be my date?" he asked.
"Sure, sounds like fun," Jasmin said. "So, tell me, is it a ski resort?"
"Actually, it is an all year round establishment where jet setters vacation," Bernhard said. "I will write to you of course, and when your year is up here, maybe you might want to change places too."
"Well, we'll see about that," Jasmin said. "I shall miss you; you admire everything I do or wear or even when I smoke the occasional cigarette."
"Don't forget the cigarette holder," Bernhard added. "I'm working steadily and for the next weeks I shall very be busy with a double shift at room service. The two waitresses are taking vacations while I am still here. Why don't you come up to the pantry tomorrow and we can chat there."
"Sounds terrific," Jasmin said. "I'll pretend we are in a little tea house and you can wait on me."
"Delighted," Bernhard bowed.
When Jasmin met Bernhard the next day, he had set up a small round table with a fancy cloth, teapot, creamer and sugar bowl, cups and saucers, silverware, and a high tea tray with petit fours. He held out the chair for her to be seated.
"Shall I pour?" he asked, lifting the teapot over her cup.
"Yes, thank you," Jasmin consented.
After he poured the tea, he reached for the sugar tongs and asked, "One lump or two?"
She said, "One."

He offered, "Cream?"

"Yes please."

They ate the goodies and sipped tea. Bernhard was called on the intercom for service. He attended to the request and told Jasmin it wouldn't be long. When he came back, he passed the order to the kitchen on the other intercom and stood by the dumb waiter until the bell rang and the guest's food came up to the pantry. Then he placed the covered dishes on a trolley and wheeled it out the corridor down to the room.

When he came back, he smiled and said, "Thanks for staying. Let's pick up where we left off. I'll give you my new address now. This is the hotel in Switzerland where I will be working and staying. It is a resort high in the Alps. I'll write when I'm settled in and give you more details."

"I shall miss talking to you," Jasmin said.

"Well, think about this way: you will have more opportunities to speak English with me not around because we always drift back into our own mother tongue," Bernhard replied. "And if you are conversant in English, you can go anywhere in the world and we'll stay in touch as friends."

They had several more afternoon tea parties and then came the staff party. Everybody sat at long tables for dinner and enjoyed the entertainment. They danced half the night away. At midnight Bernhard said, "Come, I will escort you to the staff elevator and then I'll go home to pack for my early morning trip. Will you meet me at the train station?"

"Gladly," Jasmin said.

They shared a goodbye hug and then her elevator opened. She entered and waved goodbye.

Jasmin

Jasmin was at the station the next morning at nine. It was a convenient time for her to be there because she didn't have to start work until ten thirty.

She heard a voice behind her saying, "Hello beautiful."

Jasmin turned abruptly and saw Bernhard.

He held a bouquet of yellow roses in his outstretched hand, and he said, "Let this be a sign that we will see each other again. Please take them from my heart and enjoy them."

Jasmin gasped, took the roses, and brought them to her face to smell the fragrance. She thanked Bernhard while he picked up his bags and waved one more time. She waved back, turned slowly, and walked back to the hotel with a heavy heart. She made a detour to the third floor pantry where she showed the flowers to Nellie and Beatrice and asked if they had a vase for her.

They hugged her and said, "Bernhard is such a nice guy."

They gave her a glass jar which Jasmin took up to her room. She filled the jar with her roses and placed them in front of the window. She reminisced about the fun times she had shared with Bernhard. Could he have been her future beau? She found the long cigarette holder, cleaned it up, and doused it in cologne. Then she dried it, wrapped it in tissue paper, and placed it inside her locked memory box. She knew she wouldn't use it again, nor would she smoke anymore.

Rose told Jasmin about a new movie that was even better than *Around the World in Eighty Days* called *South Pacific*.

"You must see it."

Jasmin went alone on a Sunday afternoon. At first she found it exhilarating and then she felt sad about the death of the lieutenant in the story. He reminded her of the American soldier who had called her "Blondie" when she was a child.

At the Danish Snack Bar, Mr. Tyler, a lawyer, liked to challenge Jasmin with a difficult English word on occasion.

Jasmin would retort, "How do you spell that?"

When he told her, she would look it up in the dictionary she kept under the counter. One day he asked her if she would always stay in this type of job. She replied that for the time being she would, and she would continue attending afternoon school to improve her English. He suggested that perhaps she might consider taking secretarial or administrative courses as well.

"An interesting thought. My aunt from Canada wrote the same thing to me," Jasmin replied. "I'll look into it."

On her day off she inquired at the school for further education and found they only had full time courses. Since there were no part time studies available, she dismissed the notion.

ENGLISH FRIEND

One Sunday afternoon Jasmin and Carla decided to take a train trip to a seaside resort. Carla had the Monday off as well, and she intended to extend her trip to the next town to meet up with another girl who lived there. This particular day she would spend with Jasmin. After they got off the train they went to the beach for a swim. They sunbathed, swam some more, and had their picnic on the mat they had brought. When Carla left to catch her train for her next destination, Jasmin decided to walk along the beach for a while since she had another hour to spare before her return trip. Eventually she sat on a bench in the beach front park, facing the North Sea. She took her time drying off her feet and putting on her sandals. She rolled up her towel, stuffed it into the beach bag, put on her sunglasses, and leaned against the back rest. She was just about to close her eyes, when she heard the crunching of footsteps.

A tall, young, rugged looking man sat beside her and began a conversation. She had no qualms with being spoken to in a public place such as this, in front of the resort hotel. She couldn't quite follow what he was saying, so she explained that she was German and her English was limited. He then introduced himself as Roger. He asked for her name, and that much she understood. She told him Jasmin. He admired the beauty of her name and then he enquired as to her occupation and several other things that she didn't quite catch.

She stood up saying, "I'm going to catch the train, goodbye."

Roger followed her. When he had caught up with her, he said, "If you are going to Middleton that is my destination too."

They boarded and sat down in the train cabin, facing each other as he talked non-stop. Jasmin had a difficult time understanding him. Judging from the briefcase he carried, it occurred to her that he probably attended university. Eventually, she surmised that he liked jazz music. He asked if she would like to go with him to a jazz concert at the Free Trade Hall. She told him she would think about it and he could contact her at her work. As they got off the train, he hailed a taxi and offered to take her home too. She accepted and told the taxi driver to let her off at the staff entrance. Roger came out with her, and she thanked him and waved. Inside she laughed to herself.

The timekeeper looked up. "Hey Smiler, what's got you so amused today?"

Jasmin said, "Funny thing, I show up somewhere and somebody wants to make a date with me."

"That's because you're drop dead gorgeous," he said with a wink.

"No, it can't be true; I am just an ordinary student who wants to be able to carry on an intelligent conversation in English," Jasmin commented.

"You could have fooled me," Ernest interjected.

Upstairs, on the sixth floor, she put the wet towel into the laundry chute. She collected her bathrobe from her room and went to the

Jasmin

common bath room to soak in the tub and wash off the beach sand. Then she rushed to her room and fell into bed.

Back at work, she really enjoyed her daily tasks. A customer called Mrs. Benson struck up a conversation with Jasmin.

"I have a daughter about your age, Alicia, who is going to take studies in German. She would like to meet you. Would you like to come visit at our home some day?"

Jasmin noted the address of Mrs. Benson and promised to visit on her next day off. Alicia and Jasmin formed a casual friendship which also helped Jasmin with her English. As it turned out, the daughter took up an internship with the United Nations that resulted in her travelling overseas and they kept up their relationship by correspondence.

Mr. Tyler enquired how Jasmin was doing with her plans for secretarial school. She told him there weren't any part time studies available. He suggested she could take private lessons.

He went on, "Are you interested? I'll gladly find out for you."

Jasmin thanked him and shrugged her shoulders.

Roger, her beach acquaintance, came to the Snack Bar entrance and handed a letter addressed to Jasmin to the cashier, asking would she pass it to Jasmin. The cashier, Gloria, came out of her booth because it wasn't busy.

She gave it to Jasmin, smiling, "You are coming up in society, girl."

Jasmin put the letter inside the pocket of her smock while she attended to the customers' orders. After her shift, she went up to her room and opened the envelope. Out fell one ticket to the jazz festival at the Free Trade Hall with a note from Roger asking if she would meet him at the entrance of the hall on the following Wednesday at six o'clock. She took it to understand that he expected her to do so, because they had discussed it and she had told him her schedule, so it was not necessary for her to reply. She just had to show up. This flattered her nonetheless and she anticipated the event for the whole week. At the appointed day, she walked the one block to the auditorium and saw Roger waiting for her.

He smiled at her, and said, "Glad you could make it, shall we go in?"

She just nodded. People were milling around in the foyer. He directed her to some armchairs and asked if he could get her anything like champagne, wine, or gin. She opted for the champagne. They chatted as he told her about his studies which often took him on field trips to various airports. She asked him what he was studying. He told her aeronautical engineering. She couldn't quite comprehend this and had not brought her dictionary with her, so he explained that it had to do with designing airplanes.

When the doors opened to the auditorium, he helped her up from the chair and they went in to find their seats. During the concert, he glanced over towards her, hoping to see that she enjoyed it. She smiled back and nodded.

At the end, Roger asked, "Did you have fun?"

"Oh, yes," Jasmin replied, "I like modern music."

As they walked slowly toward the hotel around the corner to the staff entrance, he held the door open for her and said, "There is a new play at the theatre. I'll get tickets and leave a note again at the cashier for you, alright?"

"Fine. Thank you for a pleasant evening, good night." He waved his hand.

Jasmin took the elevator up to her room and pondered the evening's events. She realized that she lacked enough vocabulary to carry on a lengthy conversation, and thought about how she should brush up on that. She was glad that Roger wrote notes, because at this point she could read and understand better than she could speak. She wasn't particularly attracted to Roger; she thought of him more like a puppy dog. But he was English, courteous, and well-educated, and that counted for something.

A few days after that, as the lunch crowd came in, Mr. Tyler occupied a barstool at Jasmin's counter and gave his order to the waitress.

He bent slightly towards Jasmin, saying, "I have something for you. Here is a card with an address and telephone number of a tutor; he is a client of mine. He has his own studio for teaching various specialty subjects. He could teach you secretarial skills, accounting, and business administration. You could do this in less than a year, while at other schools it would take about three years. When you are ready, I'll tell him to expect your call."

"Why would I want to do that?" Jasmin asked.

"You could expect a higher salary as a bank teller, a customer service clerk, a manager, or a legal secretary just to name a few and you would also have your evenings free," he explained.

"All right," she said, "on my next day off, I'll contact him."

"When would that be?" Mr. Tyler asked.

Carla overheard what Mr. Tyler said and whispered, "Do you want to switch with me? You can have tomorrow off and I will take your next day off."

"Tomorrow then," Jasmin turned to Mr. Tyler.

"Fine," he said. "I'll make an appointment for you at one o'clock. Are you acquainted with that part of the city?"

"I'll take a taxi until I am familiar with the bus routes," Jasmin said.

"Sounds fine," he said, getting up.

He left a generous tip, which Jasmin put into the tip jar on the shelf above the small fridge. The head waitress collected it at the end of each day and divided the tips each week with the other girls.

The next afternoon Jasmin arrived at the studio, a Tudor style house. A middle aged man who introduced himself as Mr. Arthur Worthington met her at the grand staircase facing the foyer. She could see several closed doors to the right. Mr. Worthington led Jasmin to the first room which was furnished with a table, a desk with a typewriter, several chairs, and a bookcase. He wished to know if she had any typing experience. Jasmin replied that she had some typing experience from her earlier teenage years. He suggested in that case she wouldn't have to be in the Beginners category but could go right into the Intermediate group. As far as bookkeeping was concerned, she'd have to start from scratch as well as learn shorthand and business English. They arranged for her to attend classes three times per week to leave time for homework. She would also need time to study for her monthly exams. She decided to drop the English school since she would be so busy with her new studies.

Jasmin knew she was able to pay the fee without using her tip money. As the meeting closed, Mr. Worthington said that Mr. Tyler had left a message to tell Jasmin that his secretary had her old typewriter for sale. If Jasmin wanted it to practice on, she'd meet Jasmin on her lunch hour and then take her home afterwards. This extra consideration surprised Jasmin. Before she could say anything, Mr. Worthington suggested she take the offer, because she definitely needed to have a typewriter for her homework assignments.

Jasmin agreed and let him call Mr. Tyler's office to give directions to the secretary. Jasmin asked about the bus route and Mr. Worthington gave her the information. She waited outside the door and saw a pleasant woman emerging from the parked car and walking toward her.

"I am Myrna. Are you Jasmin?"

"Yes," Jasmin replied. She asked her how much she wanted for the typewriter.

Jasmin

Myrna said, "Five shillings, if you please."

"Sure," Jasmin said and paid her.

The secretary then invited Jasmin into the car and then she drove her home. At the staff entrance to the hotel, she helped her carry the heavy box to the door and waved goodbye. Jasmin took the box to the elevator without saying anything to the timekeeper, who just glanced up from his newspaper. The elevator bell rang and the door opened, and she went in and pressed up. Inside her room she made space on the top of her table and set a chair in position for typing practice. She took the chart from her purse and started on the first page of her assignment. She became so engrossed in her work that she didn't hear Carla come into the room to get her smock. She looked up when Carla rushed out again to start her shift.

The next afternoon Jasmin again worked on her assignment right until she had to report for duty. She hurried to the elevator. It was stuck, so she made her way down a flight of stairs to the guest elevator which stopped at the first floor. Then she walked through the "staff only" door down a half stairway to another hallway, passed the passageway that divided the hot kitchen from the larder, and went down the steps to pick up her display trays of cold meat. The cold chef stood waiting for her, wondering if he should send word for a pick up.

She asked, "Do you have someone to bring up the rest of the stuff for me, so I don't have to make the second trip?" He called Pete, who had just come out from the deep freeze carrying a half side of beef. He put it on the chopping block. Wiping his hands, he asked what he could do to help. The chef told him to get the small trolley, load it up with the rest of the platters, and follow Jasmin to the Danish Snack Bar.

Pete took this opportunity to say hello to Rose, whom he was sweet on. Jasmin put the goods on the display shelf. She still had to make one more trip up to the pastry kitchen for the dessert trays and pies.

The pastry chef turned to his assistants and said, "Look, here comes the pretty Jasmine flower; help her with the pies and sweets and hold the door for her."

Jasmin blushed, but she appreciated the help. She rushed out the door, down the stairs, through several alcoves and corridors, and finally to her post in time to see the head waiter signal the doors opening for the evening dinner guests. It was busy the whole evening until closing, and Jasmin gave a sigh of relief when the last thing was put away. She punched out at the time clock and got into the empty waiting elevator. She reached her room. Exhausted, she fell into a deep sleep.

In the morning, as she reached for her card at the time clock, the postman handed the mail to the timekeeper.

He called, "Smiler, here is a letter for you."

She thanked him, glanced at it, and slid it into the pocket of her smock. The lunch crowd was sparse and nobody occupied a place at her counter, so she nestled near the coffee machine in the pantry and ventured to open her letter. It was from Bernhard in Switzerland. He wrote that he very much enjoyed his work there and liked the whole environment and would probably stay in St. Moritz. He asked about the happenings in her life. Jasmin knew she wouldn't have time to think this through for a while. In her afternoon break she practiced her typing assignment over and over again until she was confident she had it mastered. She had barely time for a quick nap before returning to her work routine. Her next private lesson at the tutorial studio was shorthand, business English, and accounting followed by more typing homework. She comprehended everything very well and felt this was the right time in her life to widen her educational horizon. She wrote a quick letter to Bernhard about

Jasmin

what had transpired in her private tutoring and told him that she had renewed her contract for another year in England.

A note arrived at the cashier for Jasmin from Roger. He offered to take her to a play at a country playhouse on the outskirts of town. She rearranged her schedule so that she could attend the matinee. Though she managed to skip classes for that day, she realized something would have to give if she wanted to keep her goal of improving her status for the future. Jasmin fondly remembered her father saying that it was important that she could stand on her own two feet, meaning she should be able to support herself so that she didn't have to depend on a husband or family for a living. She should be self-sufficient. On the other hand, life shouldn't be all work and no play. She reasoned within herself that meeting with Roger was to improve her conversational skills in English.

At the studio she befriended a middle aged lady, Mrs. Harman, who had decided to take a refresher course in typing and shorthand.

Mrs. Harman said to her, "I am amazed by how easily you pick up stenography and typing in a foreign language, and accounting also."

"Thank you. It's not too difficult actually, because shorthand is phonetic and numbers are the same in all languages," Jasmin said. "I am on my way out; do you want to walk to the bus stop with me?"

"Sure, I take the same one as you but I have to transfer later as I live in another suburb. This crash course enables me to get a job at my age of forty-eight. Mr. Harman's watch repair business isn't doing so well. We bought a house in Stent and are renting out rooms to tenants to help with the mortgage."

"Where did you work before?" Jasmin asked.

"At an insurance company for twenty years, but the company folded and I haven't held a secretarial position since."

With that, Mrs. Harman got up at the transfer stop and waved goodbye. Jasmin wondered about the words mortgage and insurance.

She missed having the dictionary with her. 'Just as well,' she thought, "I'll ask around and have it described to me in English. That way I learn even more."

Mr. Tyler sat on his favourite barstool in front of the Snack Bar counter facing Jasmin. He opened his newspaper and started reading. When Rose the waitress came to his side, he ordered his food and folded his newspaper.

He looked at Jasmin and commented, "A little bird told me you are doing very well at the tutorial school."

"How did you find out?" she asked.

"I have my ways," he said smugly.

"I need to ask you two words. I didn't have time to look them up in my dictionary," she said. "One is mortgage."

He interrupted, "Easy enough." He went on to explain that when you buy a house and don't have enough money to pay cash, the bank advances you the money and you sign a contract to pay it back over time. In the meantime, you can move into the house and possess it. She nodded in understanding, saying she followed his explanation. They were interrupted by his dinner being served and she got busy filling orders too. Before he left, he asked her for the second word and explained it to her. Then he changed the subject by mentioning he had heard about the interim graduation party at the school. Would she invite him? His question caught her off guard. She said she hadn't been aware that there would be guests, and besides, it was only an intermediate graduation - the real one was at the end of the term. He smiled and left.

On Fridays, the theatre crowd came early for supper and during the lull from seven-thirty till nine-thirty, one of the girls could go for a break. They had enough time to visit the cartoon cinema at the corner of the block and be back for the next rush to serve the returning theatre goers. Just as Jasmin was about to ask permission

Jasmin

for her break time, she glanced over to the cashier's booth and saw Roger handing the note to the cashier. She couldn't go across the floor of the restaurant.

She asked Rose, "Go catch Roger before he leaves and tell him to wait for me outside the staff entrance."

She hurried upstairs to get her coat and came back down and out the door to see Roger standing there. She told him she had some free time, and they could walk and talk. He was delighted with that and they sauntered toward Prego coffee bar. They ordered cappuccino and Jasmin told him of her busy schedule. She explained that she had to spend her day off on homework. Three afternoons a week were taken up with classes, the other afternoon with homework, and that only left her with Sundays for socializing. Roger told her he had intended to invite her Sunday evening to the theatre, to see Spanish dancers.

"Shall I get the tickets and we could go early so we have time to chat in the foyer during the cocktail hour?" he asked.

Jasmin replied, "You know, you shouldn't always have to treat me; I should contribute something too." "Oh, don't mention it. I like your company and wish to get better acquainted with you. This seems to be a pleasant environment to do so. At the university campus there is only the cafeteria, the library, or the gym, and I don't think you would be interested in any of those places."

"O.K., you win. Maybe the library, but I already have my head full of studies. Besides, at the library one couldn't talk anyway, only whisper. On Sunday you can pick me up at the timekeeper and I'll be there."

"Around six then?" he asked.

"Sure," she said. "By the way, if I am not downstairs waiting, you can always ask him to call me on the intercom."

Jasmin looked at her watch, saying she had to get back on duty. They walked the two blocks back to the staff entrance, then they shook hands and parted. There was mail waiting from Bernhard. He wrote about missing her and asked her to consider taking a vacation and coming to Switzerland. "You could stay at your sister's in Biel and I'd travel from St. Moritz and meet you there."

Jasmin remembered the silver dresser set, which had been given to her by a jilted beau. She had stored it in her home before she had left for England. When she heard that her third sister intended to marry her beloved opera singer, she wrote to her mother asking if she would please give this set to Johanna. Her mother had complied with her wish, and had shipped the dresser set to Biel in Switzerland for the wedding. Jasmin thought dreamily, "I wonder what it feels like to be sung to by a suitor." She felt nostalgia and homesickness for her siblings, and yet now she realized she was beginning to grow new roots in England. This was becoming her world. She was learning things of her own choice. She was enjoying herself and she was fulfilled in her present vocation. Though she missed the way Bernhard had made her laugh and how comfortable she had felt in his company, she explained to him that she wouldn't be able to come at this time. Jasmin needed to put everything emotional aside and focus on work, classes, and homework.

PROMOTION

One of the German liaison workers approached Jasmin with an offer of a possible job change. She said, "There is a new lounge opening within the hotel called the Concordia Bar that requires a female food counter attendant. It features marinated trout in a tureen, French onion soup, fresh oysters, and French bread, with Gruyere cheese, lettuce, and mango chutney. All you have to learn is to open the oysters with an oyster knife and oh, you must also serve escargot. This place is actually referred to as an oyster bar. Hotel patrons have direct access from within the hotel. The wet bar is manned by two bartenders. You can do it; we'll show you how. You have a pleasant personality and you like meeting the public. You would be perfect for the job, and the hours are almost the same as the Danish Snack Bar."

This new promotion surprised Jasmin and she followed the leader through a maze of corridors to the swinging door of the Concordia Bar. She scanned over everything the lady had told her.

Jasmin looked out over the counter and admired the comfortable cane armchairs and glass-covered wicker coffee tables adjacent to a grand piano.

She commented to her guide, "Quite sophisticated, isn't it?"

"Well, do you want the position?"

"Yes, certainly, thank you," Jasmin answered.

"You start tomorrow morning at ten. Let me show you the way back."

Jasmin didn't know whom to tell first at the Danish Snack Bar. Meanwhile, all the seats in front of the food counter were taken. She filled several orders without pause until the dessert orders came in.

Rose asked her for help: "Jasmin, could you take a white coffee to Mr. Tyler? I have to serve another customer at the table." As they stood in front of the coffee machine heating the milk for the white coffee, Jasmin whispered to Rose, "The management moved me to the Concordia Bar; I start tomorrow morning."

"That's fantastic," Rose said. "I can't wait to tell Pete."

Carla was appalled when she heard the news. "Who's going to fill in your post and help me here?" she whined.

"An English girl from room service," Jasmin said. "Don't worry; we still share the same room and my hours are similar as here, except my day off is no longer a weekday, but Saturdays instead."

Jasmin hurried to gather her things and get ready to catch the bus. Today she had classes. When she returned she barely had time to change into her smock and be downstairs to pick up hors d'oeuvre trays for the last time at the Danish room. The staff wished her well.

Mr. Tyler was all perturbed when he came on Friday for lunch at the Danish Snack Bar and saw a new face behind the counter. He demanded, "Where is Jasmin?"

Jasmin

Rose hushed him, and explained, "Jasmin has been transferred to the new Concordia Bar, the oyster bar that you can only reach from the interior of the hotel."

"So she hasn't left town?" he asked.

"Of course not. It all happened so fast, and she didn't have time to say goodbye to everybody. If you want to see her, you'll have to visit her there," Rose replied. She winked at him and he understood.

Jasmin had suggested to Rose, "Come up to my room on Saturday. You know where I live from the last time when we fitted your outfit."

"Yes I do," Rose said.

Rose had bought a two-piece suit on sale a month back and had heard that Jasmin was a handy seamstress, so she had asked her to shorten the hem. As she entered Jasmin's room she described Mr. Tyler's reaction to her absence. She stated, "I think Mr. Tyler has a crush on you; mark my words."

Jasmin laughed out loud.

"Looks like you have a couple of guys interested in you," Rose mused.

"Three actually, counting my pen pal in Switzerland," Jasmin corrected. "I'm in no hurry to get serious, though it's nice to have acquaintances."

Rose began again, "Now to my news: Pete and I are getting engaged and we are buying a small chocolate store on "All Saints Squar" right on the corner. It sells newspapers, cigarettes, and candies as well. The owner is retiring, so we got a deal. It has a tiny apartment upstairs with a living room and kitchenette on the second floor and a bedroom on the third floor."

"That is so great, I am so glad for you, when is the wedding?"

"Last day in November, and you are invited," Rose said.

"Thank you, I will be glad to attend," Jasmin affirmed.

"How are your studies coming?" Rose enquired.

"I keep current with all my assignments. Midterm graduation is coming up at the end of the month. I spend most of the weekend on homework, except tomorrow evening I have a date with Roger. I must tell him about my job change. If he wants to communicate with me, he will have to leave a note at the timekeeper," Jasmin explained.

"Well, if anything serious develops, I want to be the first to know," Rose said. "Promise?"

"Promise!" Jasmin vowed.

Rose prepared to leave for her home in the city. Jasmin offered to come down in the elevator with her. They parted at the timekeeper. Jasmin went to the main kitchen and had one of the chefs prepare something for her. As long as she went there before or after the usual meal times for the guests, she was technically kitchen staff and could eat in a special alcove right there. She could have anything from the hot kitchen, the grill, the soup kitchen, the vegetable kitchen, and of course the larder at the lower level. For pastries she had to make a special trip upstairs to the pastry kitchen that also prepared fruits and fruit salads.

As it was the weekend, her roommate Carla had gone on a trip, so Jasmin had the room to herself. She spent her time typing, transcribing her shorthand notes, and working on her accounting assignment. For a break she listened to the radio tunes, "Love and Marriage" and "Quai Sera, Sera". On Sunday evening Roger picked her up for the theatre. She told him all about the changes in her life including the job promotion, different work schedule, classes, and her upcoming monthly exams. As they sat in the foyer with glasses of champagne in their hands, Roger told her about his research experiences and his upcoming transfer to Scotland. He would be gone for a month and hoped she would be able to see him when he returned. She looked at him intently as he spoke.

Jasmin

He asked, "Am I talking too much?"

She told him that her mind formulated the symbols for the stenography of his words because they were phonetic, and she wanted to practice on ordinary conversation, not just dictation. He laughed at her explanation, commenting that she always had school on her mind. Anyway, he hoped to be able to write a letter to her.

Jasmin said, "The address should be easy enough to find." They took in the Spanish dancer show and at the end he asked her how she liked it.

"I found it a bit loud with those blocks on their shoes," she said.

"Yes, I felt that too, although it was colourful and exhilarating," he added. "There might be another jazz concert coming up when I am back."

"Sounds interesting," she said, nonchalantly.

As they came to her entrance, he held her hand and hesitated and for a moment she tensed and thought he might want to kiss her. She saw the longing in his eyes, but he lifted her hand to his lips and kissed it instead. "I'll get in touch with you," he said softly.

"Goodnight," she whispered. He held the door open for her, she waved, went inside, and breathed a sigh of relief. Back in her room, Carla had returned from her trip and was waiting up for her.

"How was your date?" she asked.

"Fine," Jasmin yawned.

"Just fine? Tell me the whole story, every bitty detail," Carla insisted.

"He kissed my hand."

"He what?" Carla shrieked. "That's what Lords and Ladies do!"

"Yes, it felt kind of like high society, but I have no amorous feelings for him; besides, he is leaving for Scotland and wants to write to me."

"So that makes two absentee boyfriends," Carla laughed.

"Story of my life," Jasmin sighed. "Let's turn the lights out and go to sleep; tomorrow is a busy day."

In the morning, the girls went down the elevator together to the larder and salad corner, and then Jasmin went to the bakery for fresh French baguettes, pastry, sweets, and fruit. She had to come back for the oyster barrel, the tureen with trout, and the cheese tray. She asked the junior salad chef to wheel her supplies on the trolley through the hallways for her. He did, and he also put the French onion soup pot on the burner outside her swinging door entrance. She made sure everything was displayed appropriately. The condiments must be freshly filled and everything must be polished clean. She made entries in the ledger for all the items supplied and again at the end of each mealtime to record how much was sold. In the evening after closing, everything left over was taken back to the larder.

Jasmin took the time to answer her brother's letter in which he wrote he was going to missionary training in Switzerland.

Dear Hans,

Remember the prayer you said for me before you left, that I would be channeled in the right direction? I've been promoted twice. The first time according to my contract, that in itself was expected. Now, this second time, I have been promoted to an even more favourable position in this first class establishment. I have my own realm of influence in the gourmet food department. I meet the public and engage in interesting conversations. At present I am enrolled in an elite private institution for further business education. I have met some people outside of work as well, to have meaningful conversations in appropriate settings.

If and when anything further develops, I will ask your advice. Your devoted sister,

Jasmin

Jasmin continued going to afternoon classes every other day and manning her post at the oyster bar. Some people liked to order half a dozen oysters and have them with cocktails before going for dinner in one of the formal dining halls. Certain groups engaged a pianist as part of their booking. The pianist played soft contemporary tunes to create ambience.

The management decided to have a street entrance built to attract local customers who appreciated this classy atmosphere. While the renovations progressed, they invited a newspaper to write an article about it. The reporter sat in front of the bar and made his notes as he sipped his free drink. He turned and saw Jasmin preparing an appetizer for a client. He asked the barmen if she might be on staff. They said, yes, he should go over there and interview her. The reporter said, "That will make my article appear on the front page."

He walked slowly across the lounge floor towards her food counter and took a barstool at the end. He waited until she had served the customer. "Good afternoon, I am Marvin from the *Evening Chronicle*, the weekly paper, have you read it?"

"I have seen it," Jasmin replied.

"Do you like working in this place?" he asked.

"It is very pleasant," said Jasmin.

"Would it be alright if I brought a cameraman to take a picture of you here?" he asked. "Then you might tell me a little more about it."

"I suppose so," she said.

In the evening, some customers hung around the bar and talked to the barmen, while one person came and sat at Jasmin's bar. He had the bartender bring his glass of lager and lime over and ordered a ham sandwich on rye bread. He asked a few questions and since it wasn't busy, Jasmin sat on her barstool on her side of the counter and talked a little bit too. She felt at ease saying that she was taking courses in steno, typing, and bookkeeping.

He asked, "Would you like to practice your shorthand with me now?"

"Sure," she said, reaching for her steno pad.

He said a few sentences and then said, "Let me order another beer and we can carry on." He waved to the bartender, placed his order, and then spoke about his daily rounds of visiting businesses, displaying his brochures, taking orders, and securing contracts.

She looked up and offered, "Let me repeat this back to you."

He listened and said, "You have a distinct accent but your English is impeccable."

She blushed and said, "Thank you."

He got up to leave and mentioned he would be back next week. She said, "I'll transcribe this and we'll see if my spelling is correct." He laughed and waved his hand on his way out. She closed up shop, filed her report, and called it a night.

The next day a letter from her parents was waiting for her at the timekeeper. Her father suggested she find a church to attend where there would be suitable people for her to socialize with. Jasmin took this advice to heart and decided to do something about it. She looked around for a Lutheran church and found a group that had formed in a suburb. The young pastor engaged her in a conversation about her standing faith-wise. She told him that she had gone to confirmation instructions at thirteen, but hadn't actually been confirmed when she was fourteen because she had moved to another city to stay with her sister and train as an office assistant. When she had returned to live with her parents, she began working in her summer job at the clinic in the castle and had dismissed the importance of it.

Jasmin

He suggested she could take catechism classes in her spare time. Jasmin laughed. "With no boyfriends around, I probably have some spare time."

She explained her full time working schedule. On her time off she took afternoon classes and on weekends she did homework, but she could come on Saturday mornings. They settled on the following Saturday and Jasmin hurried home to study for her exam.

The midterm graduation came up for all the students from their various programs. There were painters, sculptures, singers, accountants, woodworkers, interpreters, one welder, and two gentlemen who were training to be butlers. They all wanted to upgrade their skills on a fast track. Jasmin and Mrs. Harman were the only two in secretarial class. Jasmin had left a note in Rose's slot at the time clock with the date of her graduation. She took the bus to the Worthington mansion. There she met Mrs. Harman who showed her in which order they had to appear to receive their diploma. All of the students lined up behind the back door of the salon from which they would enter and walk across the platform at the back of the room. The guests entered through the formal double doors from the foyer. The tutor had invited potential employers, mentors, or sponsors according to the vocations his students had chosen.

The housekeeper counted the number of the people present and told them to wait for the signal. She whispered, "I'm going to prepare the punch as soon as the first one of you parades on the stage."

At this time Mr. Worthington ushered the guests to their seats in two semicircles in the salon with the higher backed chairs at the back and the club chairs in front. The rocking chairs were positioned at each side.

Mr. Worthington took the stage, positioned himself behind the lectern, and said a few words to the small assembly of about twenty-five guests. Then, turning his head to the right, he called the name of the first graduate. The young man walked toward him, received his diploma, shook hands with Mr. Worthington, stepped off the stage, walked along the hall, and waited for the others.

MR. TYLER

One by one their names were called out. Jasmin followed Mrs. Harman, and after receiving her certificate, she too lined up against the wall. She looked through the room and didn't see Rose. When her eyes fell on Mr. Tyler, he winked at her. She blushed and lowered her eyes.

After everyone had received their paper, Mr. Worthington said, "I see punch is served; please make your way to the sideboard over there and mingle."

A theatre agent approached the singer and had a conversation with her. The welder stood in a corner where a rugged looking man walked toward him, introduced himself as the foreman of a company, and offered him a job. Mrs. Harman was greeted by an architect who asked if she would be interested in working part-time. Jasmin turned her head and suddenly saw Mr. Tyler standing by her side with two punch glasses in his hand. "Congratulations," he said, handing one glass to her.

She took it and said, "What are you doing here?"

"Seeing you, of course. Rose told me this was your day, and at the same time I came to see how my client Mr. Worthington is getting along."

"My course has not ended actually; I'm going to continue the next term."

"Oh, does that mean you're going to stay in England longer?" he asked expectantly.

"Yes; I have renewed my contract at the hotel for another year."

"Terrific," he said. "By then you should be well acclimatized."

"Probably," she smiled. "Now I have to leave to catch the bus back to work."

"May I take you home?" he offered.

"Oh, no, I don't want to trouble you," she said.

"No trouble; it will be a pleasure. Let me show you to my car."

Jasmin looked for Mrs. Harman who stood at the other end of the table, writing in her pocketbook. "Goodbye, keep in touch," Jasmin said.

"I will," Mrs. Harman said.

The others still milled around. Mr. Worthington broke away from his small group and approached Mr. Tyler, addressing him, "So glad you could come by and see the progress of your protégé."

"Much pleased," was the answer.

Jasmin mulled over that word in her mind: "Protégé, did he mean me?"

On the way out Mr. Tyler asked Jasmin, "Are there any other words you have trouble comprehending?" While reaching over to open the car door, he touched her just below the shoulder blades.

"Security," she turned as she said it, facing him. For a moment time seemed to stand still, as she had felt a jolt of electricity, so to speak, because of his close proximity.

Jasmin

"Oh, I would very much like to be your security," he murmured.

"What do you mean?" she questioned.

Mr. Tyler took a deep breath and said affectionately, "I mean that you're an exceptionally beautiful young woman. You don't realize the power you have over a man, yet you have a refreshing innocence about you that makes one want to protect you. I would like to be the one to befriend you honourably, someone you can count on."

"I see," she said thoughtfully.

He got into the car and started it. While he drove, he asked, "What will you do tomorrow?"

"I am starting a six-week catechism course at a Lutheran church here," Jasmin explained.

He laughed, "For confirmation?"

Appalled, she asked, "What's so funny about that?"

"Oh no," he apologized, "I didn't mean it's funny. I did that when I was fourteen years old."

"Well, you didn't have any interruption in your upbringing like I have had due to adverse circumstances," she quietly said.

"You formulate your sentences very well. You could be a diplomat. Yes, by all means I find it commendable that you're taking this step now. You have gone up another notch in my admiration for you," he said with pathos. "Can I enquire about you how you are getting along with all your plans within a month or so?"

"I have to think about that," she said, as the car came close her entrance.

He stopped and said, "Wait till I open the door for you; this Jaguar is a very low-seated car." When Mr. Tyler stretched out his hand for her, she took it and let him assist her. "I hope to see you soon," he said. Jasmin smiled, took a few steps to her door, and was gone from his sight.

The evening business was moderate. She sold some trout, some oysters, and escargot. The bartender came over and said, "The gentleman over there wants to treat you to a drink. What will you have?"

"I don't drink on duty, but say thanks and take the money for a lager and lime. Tell him I will have it at closing." She smiled and mouthed "thank you" to him and he waved. This occurred often, and it meant nothing except that the customers wanted to express their appreciation for services rendered. In this case, he liked the food, and since he combined payment for it with the drinks it was an extra tip for her.

Jasmin kept busy with confirmation class, homework, as well as typing, business math, and bookkeeping assignments. The salesman who now came regularly once a week took his steady seat at her counter and when the opportunity presented itself, he gave some dictation to Jasmin, who took it in shorthand. This way she kept her skills current.

Jasmin pondered the catechism class. The fifth commandment to honour thy father and mother meant more than that. It extended to employers and people in authority. One must also speak well of them.

Eventually the renovations were completed and the newspaper reporter came back, this time with his cameraman. He took pictures from many angles of the Concordia Bar and several of Jasmin. Marvin came over to her counter and asked, "Now can we finish the interview we began a while ago?"

"Certainly," she said.

"You mentioned that this is a pleasant place to work. Would you expand on that?"

"The hotel itself is well known for its first class service and accommodations. It has internationally-known culinary features.

Jasmin

It's a city within a city, with excellent management and carefully selected staff. The Concordia Bar is another example of how eager they are to please guests with individual tastes. Clients are invited into a non-threatening atmosphere of ambience. The different alcoves offer unique feelings of nostalgia. Someone might like to sit at a round table with a Roman glass of wine and some pretzels. Someone else might use the Bistro setting for his French bread. Cocktails of distinction transport you in your imagination to distant ports of call. The philosophy here is to make customers feel at ease and comfortable."

"Well done," Marvin said, "I couldn't have said it better myself. Thank you very much." He put the article into the paper in time for the official opening to the public and the Open House went very well.

Just before closing one evening, Mr. Tyler came through the new entrance door, making a beeline towards Jasmin's station. He nodded to the barman and said, "Bring me a Perrier water over there." Taking a seat at the barstool in front of her counter, he grinned. He unfolded the newspaper from under his arm and held it in front of Jasmin so that she could see the front page. "Perfect shot," he said.

"I didn't know it was on the front page," Jasmin said, somewhat flustered.

"A fine article for a rookie reporter. He quoted your comments verbatim. You could be in advertising. I'll see if Mr. Worthington can give you a few sessions in Public Relations. You may not need it, as you have a natural talent for expressing graceful words. I thought I'd better come and snatch you up before too many suitors line up for you, Jasmin." He looked deep into her eyes while lifting the glass with the sparkling water.

His words gave her momentary pause, but then she calmly said, "I just did my duty of speaking well of my employer."

"Your modesty is winning even more hearts than your looks. It is beginning to win mine," he whispered.

"Oh, Mr. Tyler, you are only flattering me," she didn't know how else to respond.

"Well, I will let you rest on your laurels and scoot out of here. I have several court cases pending which will keep me quite busy for some time, but I hope to eventually have a formal outing with you, O.K.?" He rose from his chair.

"O.K.," she said.

The next afternoon before her break, the catering manager came by and asked Jasmin to come to the office. She followed him and met the Resident Manager, Mr. Arlington, who stood beside the accounting clerk. He stretched his hand toward her for a handshake. She took it, and after he released it, he said, "Jasmin, your good words have brought much business to the Concordia Bar and an excellent reputation to the hotel as a whole. We are going to give you a one-time bonus. Mrs. Goddard here will give you a check." Then he left.

"Thank you very much," Jasmin said. Mrs. Goddard handed an envelope to her, saying she could deposit it into her bank account. "I don't have a bank account, only a post office savings account," Jasmin said. She deposited the check as soon as her afternoon break started.

By now, Roger was back in town. In the note he left at the timekeeper, he wrote they could go to a newly opened basement coffee shop and talk on Sunday evening; he would pick her up. Reluctantly, Jasmin got ready. She donned a scarf over her head, put on her raincoat, and fetched her Mackintosh umbrella. She saw Roger through the window of the entrance door. He walked down the steps, half-opened the door, and said, "I'll get a taxi. You wait inside until it has arrived, and then I'll come for you." Roger went

Jasmin

to the front lobby and asked the doorman to order the taxi for him. It came right away and Jasmin appreciated his concern. As promised, Roger came toward her door and held the umbrella over her.

He laughed, "That's England for you; have you gotten used to it by now?"

She smiled and said, "You mean the rain? It comes with the territory; one just has to be prepared for it at all times. I actually lost my brand new fashionable raincoat and red Mackintosh on my trip to Scotland. I left it in the back of the taxi and didn't realize it until we boarded the train. So I had to scramble to find another set to buy."

"Speaking of Scotland, I have a lot to tell you. We are here at the café; let's get inside." Roger paid the driver and got out. He held the umbrella over the opened door for Jasmin, took her arm, and entered the establishment under the canopy. They found a table in a corner and ordered their refreshments. Then Roger said, "First tell me what's happening with you these days."

Jasmin told him about her mid-term graduation but left out the part with Mr. Tyler. She went on about her constant studies, homework, her daily routine at the Concordia Bar, and her catechism sessions. Roger had the same reaction as Mr. Tyler, wondering about the relevancy to adult life. Jasmin said, "I honour my father's request to catch up with what I missed when I was a teenager."

"I realize I don't know enough about you to fully understand, but I would like to get to know you better," he quietly said.

"Let's hear about your Scotland experiences," Jasmin quipped, while she took a sip from her hot chocolate. He explained about the intricate mechanisms in all of the aircraft's functions, and noted how mechanics and pilots alike have to understand them all. The tower personnel have to know everything as well as the administrative executives. He in particular intended to specialize in building simulators for training facilities that would take him all over the world.

"Fascinating," Jasmin said. She listened to many more details about future designs of jets and supersonic jets. She made up her mind to look up some words in the dictionary to understand them.

Roger said, "You listen so patiently. I enjoy talking to you and I like your company."

As the evening went on in friendly chatter and more hot chocolate and cookies, they decided to see each other again in two weeks when he came back from an assignment in London. She mentioned it was time to leave, and then Roger helped her up from the chair and followed close behind up the stairs to the door. The rain had let up and he suggested, "Should we walk the few blocks?"

"Yes, it's nice to get out in the fresh air," she agreed. He carried her umbrella until they came to her door, and then handed it back to her. He took her other hand, kissed the tips of her fingers, and left.

Jasmin kept thinking about this relationship. She realized that she enjoyed carrying on an intellectually stimulating conversation with Roger, predominantly to improve her English. She was interested on a friendship level and in being treated with respect. She wished for their relationship to stay that way, as she felt at ease in the company of professionals.

When Bernhard wrote to her again, she compared his station in life with that of Roger or Mr. Tyler. True, Bernhard was only a waiter, but he had ambitions and he did the best he could. He was humble, sincere, and would sacrifice a lot to please her. Plus he made her laugh. He would probably own a hotel or a specialty restaurant in a few years. She kept up the correspondence and encouraged him in all his endeavours. He told her that he had taken up French lessons in his spare time from being in such an isolated place. She commended him on spending his idle time constructively.

Jasmin

In analyzing her emotions, it was brotherly affection she had for Bernhard. Now, as Mr. Tyler came to mind, she recalled the sensation she felt when she heard the timbre in his voice, the thrill when he barely touched her shoulder, and recently when he looked into her eyes. She wondered if romance as she imagined was somehow attainable to her.

"I am going to sleep on it," she said to herself. "It will sort itself out."

Not many days later, one middle aged gentleman came through the street entrance and looked around. Upon noticing Jasmin, he walked towards her counter. He took a barstool and sat down. Then he smiled at Jasmin. "I'm expecting someone here, but in the meantime I shall have one of your French bread deals."

"Certainly Sir, would you like something from the bar as well?" she asked. She nodded to the bartender, Martin, who was waiting for her signal to come over and take the drink order.

"My name is Achilles James," he started to say, and stopped while his drink was being served. "I have wanted to meet you ever since I read the article in the newspaper. I thought there is more to that young lady than just a pretty face."

Jasmin looked up from her work, handed the plate with the sandwich to him, and said, "Thank you." She knew how to accept a compliment.

He took a bite from his sandwich, wiped his mouth with the cloth napkin, and said, "I own the Birkdale Lodge, are you familiar with it?"

"I can't say that I am," she said. "Is it in the city?"

"Actually, it's out in the country close to Stockport, an old provincial town with cobblestone streets and a market square," he explained.

"Sounds charming," she said.

"I have run this place for a year now. It has ten bedrooms, a fully staffed kitchen and bar, a nice dining room, and a small dance floor. During the week we cater to travelling salesmen or tourists on a tight budget, and on weekends we have a band. Once a month we invite a special singer or performer. I used to operate the Sunnydale tourist home, which I sold before I purchased this one. I have a great following in this city. I hired someone through the Worthington studio."

"I am enrolled there also," Jasmin cut in.

"Commendable," he said. "I see the person I am to meet has arrived. It was my pleasure talking with you. I'll come again some other time." With that he stood up, said hello to his companion, and led him to an empty table near the piano.

The bartender came over to clear the glass away. "What was that all about?" he queried.

"He told me about the hotel he is running," Jasmin said.

"I hope he doesn't want to hire you away from here; we need you," he said.

"Just small talk," Jasmin assured him.

"By the way," Martin the bartender said, "Mr. James wants to treat you to a drink. What shall I charge him for?"

"A gin and tonic, but put the money into the tip jar," said Jasmin.

She had a fair share of repeat customers, as did the bartenders, and the tips were shared weekly. Jasmin enjoyed the camaraderie among them. She didn't miss having a social life because she continually met interesting people and her tutoring classes occupied much of her time. Jasmin continued with her homework and still kept her steno pad at hand in case she found an opportunity to practice at work.

Jasmin

On one particular evening, shortly before closing, Mr. Tyler came bursting in. "I'm glad you are still open," he said, and he told Martin to bring a dry martini over to Jasmin's counter.

"Good evening Mr. Tyler, how are you?" she said warmly.

He answered, "I'm not my usual cool, calm, and collected self. I need a place to unwind, and you are just the person I would like to unwind with."

"What do you mean?" she said.

"Your presence has a calming influence on me, and I like talking to you. I've had a harrowing day at court. The case is adjourned and the jury is sequestered, but of course I can't talk about that."

Jasmin still had her steno pad in her hand from the previous customer. She flipped the page and asked, "Could you repeat the two long words you just said?"

He moistened his lips with the aperitif and said, "Adjourned and sequestered."

She showed him the pad, "See, I got it."

He looked and said smilingly, "That looks Greek to me."

It's shorthand," she corrected.

"I know it is," he chuckled. "I'm just joking; I like teasing you."

"Would you like something to eat while you are here?"

"Sure, give me some of your delectable French bread treats."

She filled a glass with ice water and set it down in front of him. Then she prepared his dish, adding a spritz of lemon to the lettuce. "Bon appetite," she said as she placed his plate on the counter.

He nodded, "Thanks." She covered the other platters and put the fresh produce into her tiny fridge. Then she sat on her barstool at her side of the counter to provide pleasant company.

When he was halfway through, he drank some water and murmured, "So how is your love life?"

She cocked her head and said, "Secret."

He raised his eyebrows and frowned. "Does that mean I have competition?"

Now she raised her eyebrows and said, "I didn't know you were in the running."

"If I were at a formal affair, I would ask for your dance card, My Lady," he offered. She giggled and cut a rectangular piece of paper, crimped it, and did some scrolled writing. She wrote:

Miss Claudius

He ate the rest of his meal wondering what she was up to and curiously craned his neck to see what she had done. Then she folded the paper and handed it to him. "If you want to play formal, I can be formal."

He opened it, read it, bowed his head slightly, and declared, "Miss Claudius, I'd be honoured to call on you in the very near future."

"There might be a possibility," she allowed.

He put the notepaper into the pocket of his waistcoat and said as he got up, "Have a pleasant evening." He walked towards the door, nodded to the bartenders, and left. Martin came by to clear the glass. Having overheard the last word, he asked, "Why did he not say 'goodnight'?"

Jasmin said, "He adopted some French culture when he studied there. The French never say 'bon nuit', or good night; they always say 'bon soir', or good evening, because they say the night life of a person is nobody's business. He indicated that I was not a 'lady of the night'."

Martin nudged her with his elbow, "You are alright, kid."

The days that followed were busy and intense as Jasmin continued to develop all her faculties and focus on her goal to be the best trained in her future career. She met with Roger again for a jazz concert. He related his new understanding of different concepts in the airline industry and she listened. He commented on her intelligence and told her that she was a pleasant person to be around. Roger said he would really like to keep seeing her again, and enquired about her plans for Christmas. Jasmin indicated that she might go for a visit to Germany over the holidays. He hoped he could firm up a date before that, and she left it open for discussion closer to the time. There was more correspondence from Bernhard, who still pined for her, hoping for a get together maybe in Germany or Switzerland. He would need a reply soon so that arrangements could be made. She didn't want to be pressured into making a decision at this time about personal things. To be honest, she wondered why Mr. Tyler hadn't contacted her as he had hinted he would. She thought, "Is this the same situation as with Dietrich - someone declaring his interest in me and not following through with it?"

Meanwhile, Mr. Tyler was busier than ever in the various aspects of his legal practice. Court cases were won: some public, and some dealing out of court. He acted as corporate lawyer as well as a mortgage broker. At present he was a Barrister and Solicitor. His ultimate goal was to be a Q.C. (Queen's Council) as his father had been, but that of course would be a few years from now. He looked again and again at the slip of paper in his pocket. Sometimes he imagined Jasmin's face and contemplated what to do. He felt an urgency to come up with a decision.

He lived at his parental home, since there was no reason to move out until he started his own family. His mother and he shared the cost of the upkeep and the servants. He took some files home to work on after supper one evening.

Mrs. Tyler found him in his private office. "Matthew," she said, "I planned to have your suit and waistcoat picked up for the dry cleaners and I came across this slip of paper with a name on it. Is it important? I didn't want to throw it out without consulting you."

Matthew Tyler looked at his mother and said, "That, dear mother, is what has been churning in my mind for some time now and I'm glad you have given me an opportunity to talk about it. Miss Claudius is a fine young lady I've spoken to for a few months now, and I believe I have grown very fond of her."

"Does she know that?" asked his mother.

"I am hoping to tell her soon," he said.

"Will I be able to see her?" Mrs. Tyler enquired.

"As a matter of fact, she goes three times a week for afternoon classes to Arthur Worthington's studio. You are acquainted with Emma Worthington, aren't you?" Matthew said.

"Actually, yes, I've been meaning to invite her for tea. You can introduce me to Miss Claudius and I will invite her too."

"Sounds like a plan," Matthew said excitedly. He jumped up, hugged his mother, and told her to get ready for Friday afternoon.

On Friday after classes, Jasmin asked Mr. Worthington if she would be allowed to make a call, since she didn't have a telephone. She had kept the number for Mrs. Harman's office. Mr. Worthington said, "Certainly. Go right to the office; my wife is in there."

"Mrs. Worthington, will it be alright for me to use your phone to call Mrs. Harman?" Jasmin asked. "Yes, of course. Please say hello to Mrs. Harman for me. Do you need privacy? I can leave," she said. "That won't be necessary," said Jasmin. "Mrs. Harman told me to let her know when my confirmation was so she could come to the church with me. I have been taking instructions and my confirmation is this Sunday."

Jasmin made the call and thanked Mrs. Worthington, saying she had to catch her bus home. As she turned to leave, there stood Mr. Tyler with an elderly lady. He introduced her, saying, "Jasmin, meet my mother, Mrs. Tyler. Mother, this is Jasmin."

"Charmed," said Mrs. Tyler, stretching out her hand toward her.

Jasmin

Jasmin took it and said, "I'm pleased to meet you, Madame."

Mrs. Tyler smiled and said, "I've come to invite Mrs. Worthington to tea. Emma, how are you, my dear? When is it convenient to have you for tea? Perhaps you might bring your present company too." They turned to the very surprised Jasmin and asked if she was available on Saturday or Sunday.

Jasmin gathered her wits about her and said, "I have my last instruction session tomorrow with my pastor, and on Sunday I have my confirmation."

Mrs. Tyler said, "Let's make it Sunday for lunch." Turning to Mr. Tyler she said, "Matthew, why don't you bring Jasmin to our house after her church?"

Jasmin jumped in, saying, "I have to think about it, but now I am leaving to get my bus. Thank you for your invitation."

Mr. Tyler spoke up. "I can take you back, if you like, while my mother visits with Mrs. Worthington."

CALL ME MATTHEW

"Thank you that will be fine." She walked briskly in front of him toward the main entrance. As he rushed to hold the door open, he pointed to where his Jaguar was parked. He unlocked the door and stepped back to let her inside.

After getting in and before starting the motor, he turned to her and said, "Jasmin, I mean Miss Claudius-"

Jasmin interrupted, "Are you suddenly tongue-tied, Mr. Tyler? What happened to your eloquence?"

He laughed. "I recall last time we spoke, we had fun with words, and the best thing that came to my mind was a ladies' tea, so I wanted to formally extend an invitation to you and my mother wanted to take part in it too."

"So, you got your mother involved in the plot?" Jasmin laughed out loud, as they drove.

"Well, the opportunity presented itself; you were there." Now Mr. Tyler laughed too. "First of all," he said, "will you call me Matthew, please?"

"Oh, we are getting familiar now," she laughed.

"I'm serious," he said. "Jasmin, my name is Matthew."

"Pleased to meet you, Matthew," she demurred.

"Another thing," he said as they were nearing the hotel, "what time on Sunday morning is your church service? I will be glad to pick you up and take you there. Then you won't have to take the bus."

"It's at eleven, but we will have to leave here by ten thirty," she said. "And thank you; your offer is very much appreciated."

"I wouldn't miss it," he replied. When he turned the car off, he reached over for her hand, held it in both of his for a moment, and then slowly let it go. He got out of the car, walked around the back, and opened the passenger door for Jasmin. He helped her get out. While she briskly walked to her hotel door, they both waved goodbye. Once inside, she brushed by the timekeeper and punched in her clock. Then she turned her head toward him, smiled, and headed toward the elevator.

He called, "Hello Smiler, how are you?"

"Great," she said. "Actually, I am on cloud nine."

He came out of his booth as if to hear more gossip. "Must be an exciting date."

"Could be," she shouted as went down the hallway straight to her place of work, since she had no time to change.

She took her smock off of the hook behind the door and put it on over her outfit. Then she uncovered all the dishes on display and waved over to the bartender, who was just about to open up their bar. They were ready for business. The evening guests drifted in sporadically to enjoy some hors d'oeuvres and drinks as the pianist played to create a relaxed atmosphere. At closing time, Jasmin said to her colleagues, "See you Monday." They said the same to her. She gathered up the rest of her dishes, took them to the kitchen, made out her report, and went up to her room.

With a sigh of relief, she plunked down on her bed and said, "Oh, what a day!"

Carla, who had been half asleep, turned and asked, "That bad, eh?"

"Oh, no," Jasmin said. "Quite the opposite: it was full of surprises. First, I met Mrs. Worthington at the studio when I went to the office to make a call, then Mr. Tyler and his mother walked in, and as I was about to leave to catch my bus, they invited me for tea. When I declined the first suggested time, they doubled their offer to make it lunch on Sunday. In addition, Mr. Tyler offered to take me to church and lunch at his house, plus he wants me to call him by his first name, Matthew."

Carla gasped, "Well that is quite a string of events, what else?" She looked at Jasmin, noticing her dreamy eyes, and queried, "I'm waiting."

"Well," Jasmin mused, "He ever so gently helped me out of the car. I felt like a porcelain doll."

"A different sensation than with Roger, right?" Carla asked.

Jasmin thought for a moment, then said, "They are both perfect gentlemen, but with Matthew, when he touches my hand it feels like electricity."

"So," Carla asked, "are you going to let Roger go?"

"Probably," Jasmin said, "if Matthew wants to keep seeing me. I'm tired; let's go to sleep."

Before she drifted off to sleep, Jasmin thought, "Did I reveal too much of my inner emotions to Carla?"

In the office of the Worthington studio, Mrs. Worthington closed the door, rang a bell for the maid, and offered a chair to Mrs. Tyler. The maid came from the kitchen entry door and asked what she could bring. "Tea for two and some biscuits," Mrs. Worthington ordered. Smiling, she faced Mrs. Tyler. "Now, Martha, tell me all about it. Matthew is really smitten with that girl, isn't he?"

"Wouldn't you know, Emma, but this is the first thing I heard about it. Matthew told me last night that he was interested in seeing a young lady he had noticed and had some brief conversations with. What do you know about her?"

"Jasmin is an exceptionally intelligent student. She is diligent and well-mannered. She comes three times a week for afternoon classes, and the other days she completes her assignments. She is in England on a working permit at Excelsior Hotel, where she manages the food counter at an exclusive lounge within the premises. Her main reason for studying here was to learn the English language, and then she branched out into secretarial and accounting classes. She might advance into administrative courses."

"She is very beautiful," Martha cut in. "How old is she?"

"I can look that up," Emma said, going over to the filing cabinet. "Jasmin is beautiful, yet she does not flaunt her charms. In fact, there is a maturity about her. Here, let me see what I find. Yes, she comes from Germany, recommended from the Hotel and Catering Association, having served an apprenticeship at a four-star hotel there. She is twenty going on twenty-one."

"Not quite of age yet," Martha said thoughtfully. "Matthew is heading towards thirty. I've been secretly hoping he would find a nice young woman and bless me with grandchildren soon."

They sipped their tea. Emma said, "Matthew hasn't shown much interest in the usual society ladies, has he?"

"No," Martha said, "his passion is race cars."

Jasmin

"Let's see if this particular young woman will wrap him around her finger," Emma said. They tapped their teacups together and laughed. Emma offered to take Martha home. Martha accepted, as she knew Matthew would have to return to his office. They said their goodbyes and agreed to the time of one p.m. for the luncheon on Sunday.

Jasmin hurried to her last confirmation class on Saturday morning at the new congregational church that had formed after the war. Pastor Gruber walked her through the order of service for Sunday and the questions he would ask her and the answers she should give, according to what she had studied and memorized. Then Jasmin came back to the hotel. She did some more practicing on the typewriter using her memory-verses and the answers she had to give the next day on paper. This would keep the material fresh and seeing it typed helped her form a clearer picture in her mind.

Jasmin walked to the soup kitchen and let the soup chef give her a sample of his latest concoction, creamed squash soup with nutmeg and almond slivers, which she consumed in her usual alcove. She praised him for its excellent taste. After that she went up to the pastry kitchen and asked, "Is there any leftover cheesecake from the Danish room?"

Ken, the red-headed assistant, gushed, "We saved a piece just for you, Angel." He placed the cheesecake in the take-out box and added a mince tart to it.

She blushed, said, "Thank you," and took the food up to her room to have later with her cup of tea.

On Sunday morning, Jasmin drank a glass of water before she got ready for church. Matthew was waiting beside his car as she came up the steps through the staff entrance. "Good morning," he said, as he opened the passenger door and offered his hand to help her inside. He went around to the driver's side, looked up and down the street for traffic, and slipped into his seat.

"Nervous?" he asked while starting the engine.

She was taken aback by that statement, but then controlling her emotions she said, "Somewhat, but I am focused on the task at hand."

"Your discipline is another quality I admire in you," he said as he drove.

"Thank you," she said. Her face grew warm as she lowered her eyes, hoping she wouldn't blush.

They drove in silence for a while. "You have picked a nice day today," he started the conversation again.

"It's very pleasant," she agreed. She looked towards the small church and spotted Mr. and Mrs. Harman waiting outside the door. The pastor was also standing beside them. Jasmin pointed them out to Matthew, saying, "You see the tall gentleman on the right? He is the pastor. The woman is Mrs. Harman and I presume she is with her husband."

Matthew parked the car, helped Jasmin out, and walked with her towards the group. The pastor faced him and Matthew stretched out his hand. He introduced himself as Matthew Tyler. "Conrad Gruber," replied the pastor, as they shook hands. "Excuse me while I whisk Jasmin away to direct her to her special place today," the pastor said.

Matthew smiled and gave her an encouraging nod with his head. So did Mrs. Harman, who made the introduction, "Mr. Tyler, meet my husband, Paul Harman."

Mr. Harman stretched out his hand in greeting, saying, "Pleasure to meet you."

Matthew took his hand, saying, "Likewise."

Mrs. Harman continued, "I've gotten to know and like Jasmin very much. She is like a daughter to me and I am truly fond of her."

Jasmin

Matthew said very agreeably, "Jasmin is certainly a very likeable person; shall we go in?" They were seated together in a middle row. While Matthew craned his neck to see where Jasmin sat, Mrs. Harman nudged him, leaned her head slightly at an angle, and looked at the end of the front row. Matthew looked in that direction and spotted Jasmin sitting there.

The service began with several hymns, followed by announcements and a warmhearted sermon on the love of God. Then the pastor announced the special occasion of the day: the confirmation of one person who by her own free will desired to do it. He introduced Jasmin and asked her to step forward. He stated that although this celebration was usually encouraged to take place in earlier teenage years, there is no age limit by which a person may study to grow into the full stature of Christ.

He turned to Jasmin and asked, "Are you willing to declare before this congregation your statement of faith?"

She said "Yes, I am."

He then said, "Please recite the Apostles' Creed."

Jasmin faced the congregation and said with a lilt in her voice, "I believe in God, the Father Almighty, Maker of heaven and earth. And in Jesus Christ, His only Son, our Lord, who was conceived by the Holy Spirit, born of the Virgin Mary, suffered under Pontius Pilate, was crucified, died, and was buried. He descended into hell. On the third day He rose again from the dead. He ascended into heaven and sits at the right hand of God the Father Almighty, from thence He will come to judge the living and the dead. I believe in the Holy Spirit, the holy Christian Church, the communion of saints, the forgiveness of sins, the resurrection of the body, and the life everlasting. Amen."

Pastor Gruber asked the congregation to stand, and then he moved a step closer to Jasmin. He placed his hand on her head and said, "I bless you in the name of the Father, the Son, and the Holy Spirit."

Jasmin felt a strange sensation. She suddenly had a flashback to being a nine-year old, visiting at the seaside resort with her aunt, and going to church. She had looked around, craning her neck backwards and upwards. Just then a sunbeam had illuminated large wooden capital letters forming the verse, "Lo, I am with you all the days even unto the end of the world." Now Jasmin felt the same sensation. She thought, "It must be God."

Pastor Gruber turned to the congregation and said, "Let us sing the closing hymn."

He quietly spoke to Jasmin, "You may now join your friends." As the hymn was being sung, Jasmin strode slowly among smiling faces to the row where Matthew stood next to Mrs. Harman. He stepped out into the aisle and let Jasmin slip in beside him. He held the open hymn book for her and pointed to the line they were singing. Matthew revered the ceremony. He was mesmerized by the glow on Jasmin's face and couldn't take his eyes off her. As she had approached him from down the aisle, his heart had skipped a beat.

After the singing stopped, Pastor Gruber pronounced the Benediction: "The Lord bless you and keep you, the Lord let his face shine upon you and give you peace."

The congregation made their way into the foyer and crowded around Jasmin. They shook her hand in congratulations before they dispersed. Matthew said, "You did very well, Jasmin."

Mrs. Harman said, "When you stood there up front, I could have sworn I saw a halo around you."

Jasmin replied, "You are too kind."

Pastor Gruber had now finished saying goodbye to the rest of the people. He came over to them and said to Jasmin, "God bless you in your walk of faith." To the others he said, "Thanks for coming; hope to see you again."

Mr. Harman said, "I didn't want to miss the opportunity to shake your hand, Jasmin. Congratulations."

Jasmin hugged Mrs. Harman and said, "We'll get together real soon."

Back in the Jaguar, Jasmin said to Matthew, "One day I would like to take them somewhere for a treat. Mrs. Harman is such a motherly friend to me."

Matthew agreed, and said, "The thought occurred to me also to invite them to my mother's luncheon, yet it seemed too short of notice."

"True," Jasmin said. "Sometimes our emotions get ahead of practicalities."

"I hope you have some spare emotion left for me," Matthew said jokingly.

She said, "You are very kind."

He asked, "What else?"

She cocked her head and said, "Considerate."

"Any more?" he asked.

"I don't know yet," she answered.

He asked her slowly, "Would you like to find out?"

"Matthew," Jasmin said, "I am not sure."

"Well," he said lightly, "two attributes are better than none. What do you say?"

They neared the driveway of his mother's house and he stopped in front of the main door. He turned off the engine, took the key out, and looked at her closely when she didn't respond. He neared his face close to hers, held the look for a moment, and said, "If I were to kiss you, would you slap my face?"

She retorted, "Indeed I would," and reached for the door handle. He laughed out loud. When he came to her door and assisted her out, she laughed too.

As they neared the steps of the front door, it was opened and Mrs. Tyler stood there with open arms. "Here you are," she exclaimed. "What were you two laughing about?"

Matthew said, "Just some friendly banter." He let the blushing Jasmin go ahead of him, where she was embraced by his mother.

Mrs. Tyler beckoned Matthew. "Come on in," she said. "Our friends are here." She walked ahead of the two toward the dining room, where Mr. and Mrs. Worthington stood in front of the curio cabinet holding small glasses of orange juice. Matthew tipped his head in acknowledgement.

Mrs. Tyler said, "I'll let the cook know we are ready to dine now. Please be seated." She pointed to the right for one couple and to the left for the other couple, while she reserved the end chair at the head of the table for herself. The maid brought in a bottle of white wine and set it on the service cart beside the table. "Matthew," Mrs. Tyler asked, "would you do the honour of pouring the wine?"

"Certainly," he said as he rose from his chair, took the bottle, and poured first for his mother, then Mrs. Worthington, Jasmin, and Mr. Worthington. Lastly, he filled his own glass, set the bottle back onto the trolley, and sat down.

"Now, Matthew, tell us all about this morning's events," Mrs. Tyler encouraged.

"Well," he began, "Mr. and Mrs. Harman were already at the church when we arrived."

Matthew was interrupted by Emma Worthington, who said, "Mrs. Harman is such a dear person."

He continued, "The pastor, Conrad Gruber is his name, introduced himself and ushered Jasmin to her reserved spot for the ceremony,

Jasmin

so I chatted with the couple and we took our seats together. The service was very comforting, and towards the end, Pastor Gruber conducted the question and answer period with Jasmin. He explained the solemnity and at the same time the joyfulness of the occasion. Jasmin did her part and came through with flying colours."

Mrs. Tyler lifted her glass and said, "Let's propose a toast to Jasmin!" Everybody lifted their glasses and said in unison, "Jasmin."

Jasmin smiled, took a sip, and said, "Thank you."

The cook stood in the doorway and announced, "Dinner is served." Emily the maid brought side dishes of steamed vegetables to the table, and then served individual meat portions to each guest. Mrs. Tyler offered to say grace and everyone enjoyed the traditional roast beef with Yorkshire pudding and all the trimmings. Jasmin took small bites while participating in the conversations. She didn't wish to be the centre of attention all the time, but she answered questions about her peers and the kind of entertainment she liked.

She said, "One of my friends, her name is Rose, is from Ireland, and she's engaged to be married. She has no family here other than her future husband and his father. I'm invited to her wedding."

"I love weddings," Martha Tyler blurted out, looking at Matthew, who glared at her.

"Mother."

Emma Worthington came to the rescue. "So are you looking for an appropriate gift for your friend, Jasmin?"

"Yes, I am," said Jasmin, "I would like it to be a surprise, yet it should be something she really wants and needs."

Martha Tyler took over again, "What you need is a bridal consultant who arranges a registry at the stores. Then you get a few girls together who find out what Rose's wishes are. The consultant makes a list with the stores and the participants buy the desired gifts. Where is she going to live?"

Jasmin replied, "They've bought a chocolate store at a street corner and will be moving into the apartment above the shop."

Matthew said, "My firm handled the legal transaction for them."

Emma Worthington now cut in, "All you need now is a place for the bridal shower."

"Shower?" asked Jasmin. "What do you mean by that?"

Matthew now got his word in, "It is a party for ladies to shower the bride-to-be with gifts." As he was speaking, he looked at Jasmin while he slowly said 'bride-to-be' and held her eyes for a moment.

Jasmin simply lowered her eyes and said, "I see." The two ladies at the table exchanged an understanding look.

The maid came in and asked, "Would you like to have your coffee in the parlour or in the library, Madam?"

"We'll have it in the library, and then we will have a view of the garden and the conservatory," Mrs. Tyler directed. This time she arranged the seating so that Matthew faced Jasmin around the coffee table. That way they could look at each other and also see outside when turning their heads.

Emma Worthington suggested that their studio would be the ideal place to have the party. Turning to her husband, she asked, "Couldn't we pretend it is a semi-graduation party for Jasmin so that Rose could be invited without it being too conspicuous?"

Mr. Worthington advised his wife, "Emma, that's your domain; you'll think of something."

Martha took over again, "Now we have to make sure Rose is going to come. We'll have to involve her fiancé; does he have a car?"

Jasmin replied, "No, they spent all their savings on the purchase of the store."

Matthew piped up, "Since our firm is involved, I could have our associate offer them a ride to the place saying that Pete and Rose

Jasmin

both have to sign some documents at a neutral place to finalize their deal on the business."

Emma spoke up, "Jasmin, you will need to give me the names of Rose's friends and associates so I can contact them. You will also need to give a list of gift items to Martha so that she can reserve them at the stores."

"Let's enjoy the coffee and pastries," Martha suggested.

"The pastries are delicious," Jasmin commented.

"We've had a lovely afternoon," Mr. Worthington said. "We'll be on our way, and congratulations again on your confirmation, Miss Claudius."

"Thank you," Jasmin bowed her head slightly.

"I will see our guests out; please stay, Jasmin," Martha Tyler said.

Matthew got up and closed the double doors of the library. He sat down again, looking at Jasmin, and asked, "How do you like this turn of events?"

"My head is spinning actually with so much to do, but the good thing is, I have the weekends free."

"Would you like to step out into the conservatory?" Matthew asked.

"Gladly," Jasmin answered. He took her hand and opened the sliding glass door. They walked the narrow aisle through the flower beds and tropical plants.

"I love gardens and flowers," Jasmin voiced her opinion.

"I should like to have a garden planted with a profusion of Jasmine just for you to match your name and beauty," Matthew said with pathos.

"Don't get all romantic on me now, Mr. Tyler," Jasmin said jokingly.

"Jasmin, tell me, is there anybody I should consult with in regards to courting you?" Matthew asked.

"Courting?" she asked.

"Yes," he said. "Should I ask your father if I may take you out to places and get to know you better? I do have good intentions about you."

"Why don't you ask me?" she said.

"Miss Claudius, may I have the pleasure of taking you to the Christmas Ball? They are booking two months in advance. It's a formal affair in a large ballroom."

"You mean the old fashioned kind, with dance cards and all?" she asked.

"Yes," he said, "as long as I have the majority of the cards."

"O.K.," she said. "It might be fun, only I don't have anything formal to wear and I don't have much money left after I pay for my lessons."

"You could rent an outfit for one evening. My mother knows a place for that, and she would be delighted to help you with the selection," he offered. "While we are on the topic, Mr. Worthington has a dancing instructor every year to help couples brush up on their steps. I have a mind to take in some lessons; would you like to join me?"

Jasmin said, "I really can't accept too many favours from you."

"Oh, you would be doing me a favour. It will be my lesson and I will need a partner to practice with. You only have to be there; please say yes."

"All right," she said.

"I shall take you home now; you've had a full day. I have enjoyed spending it with you."

Matthew led her through the doors to the hallway, looking for his mother to announce Jasmin's departure. She spotted them and came closer, saying, "There you are, Jasmin. Again, congratulations on your step of faith. It has been a pleasure having you here. Emma and I will be in touch with you about the bridal affair. We usually go to the Steiner Beauty Salon at your hotel. We'll send you a note with the busboy and you can respond with your information and give it to him."

They exchanged a light hug and then Matthew escorted her out the door to his car. He opened her door first and helped her in, and then he got in on his side and they drove away. He said, "Your father and mother told you to associate with people who go to church? We also go to church. It is different from yours, but it is based upon same foundation of faith."

Now Jasmin giggled. "Is that supposed to mean you feel eligible to date me?"

"Yes," he sighed, "in a way. I also want to see you live up to the best of your potential and I wish to have a part in it. Most of all I desire to see that glow on your face you came with one morning while you still worked at the Danish Snack Bar. Somebody did something to put that there, and I want to see that glow directed at me."

Jasmin listened and remembered exactly what that was: when Bernhard gave her the bouquet of yellow roses. She said with a flirty look, "That is for me to know and you to find out."

"I am determined," he said. He stopped the car when they arrived at her entrance, helped her outside, and walked her to the door. Then he added, "I'll take you to the party for Rose's shower when it happens. Have a good evening." He held the door open for her, turned, and left.

When Jasmin passed the timekeeper's booth, a voice sounded, "Are you Smiler?"

"Oh, yes, where's Ernest?" Jasmin asked.

The young fellow said, "He is on vacation and I am filling in temporarily till he gets back. He told me to watch for Smiler because she is always in before curfew. He said you're a good girl."

"Ha, ha, Jasmin Claudius is my name. Here, look at the punch clock: there's my card. Now you can put a name to my face."

"Oh, I won't forget your face," he said. He looked at the chart board with the employees' names and pulled out her name and number. "Jasmin sounds like Jasmine the flower. By the way, I am Bill Bromley."

"You know flowers, Bill?"

"I learned about them when I went on a school trip to the Royal Conservatory; they have a beautiful fragrance," he replied.

Her elevator dinged. Jasmin stepped into it and waved goodbye.

"Bye, Jasmin Smiler," he shouted as the door closed.

Jasmin came to her room and saw that it was empty. She took a short nap. Afterwards she went down to the larder and let the junior assistant who was on duty fetch some cold cuts and salad which he put into a take-out box. She thanked him. Then she found something sweet in the pastry kitchen and made her way back up to her room. This time Carla was there, eagerly waiting for her.

"Look, I already made tea for us, knowing you would be here any minute," she said. "Did he kiss you yet?"

"No," said Jasmin, "I wouldn't let him. I felt it was too soon. I needed to sort out my feelings for him. I know he's a perfect gentleman. In the meantime, he wants to court me."

"Court?" squealed Carla. "Let me look that up in the dictionary." Jasmin took a few bites of her supper while Carla fished out her dictionary from underneath her bed. "Courting is very formal, a prerequisite to engagement leading to marriage," she read out loud. "So, what's the next step?"

Jasmin

"The first thing I have to do," mumbled Jasmin between bites, "is to let Roger go. I have to figure out how to break it to him gently. He is a fine man, but I have no feelings other than respect for him. I shall have to write him a letter."

Carla checked if the tea had steeped long enough and poured two cups. She passed one cup over to Jasmin and uttered, "Poor guy."

"Yes," agreed Jasmin, "but I hope he finds somebody else." She changed the subject. "Now, to the business at hand: tomorrow when you go to work, make a list of Rose's friends who might want to come to her bridal shower party. If you meet Pete in the larder, take him aside and tell him to keep it a secret but be in on the conspiracy. He has to make sure Rose is coming to the party at my tutoring studio under the guise of having to sign the final papers on the purchase of the store they are buying. If I see him first, when I get my supplies from the larder I will tell him and let him know that you are in on it."

"O.K.," Carla said. "What's next?"

Jasmin took a deep breath and continued: "Make sure Rose keeps Saturday two weeks from now free. Then find out what exactly she needs for her apartment and what her wishes are, what her colours are, and what she already has. I need the list of items by Wednesday morning and the names of friends by Friday. I'll take the list to class and type the invitations. Mrs. Worthington will provide the cake and Mrs. Harman will help with the decorations. Mrs. Tyler will go to the store and arrange a bridal registry, so that everybody only needs to go to one store to select the gifts that they want to buy. It's going to be a ladies' affair, so after Mr. Tyler drops me off, he will take Pete and his associate out for an hour and a half to a pub and come back to the party when it's time to eat the cake and have tea or hot chocolate."

"Great," Carla said. "I'll get right on it first thing in the morning."

"O.K.," Jasmin said, yawning, "let's call it a night. I am going down the hall to the common bath to soak in the tub."

On Monday at lunch time, Mr. Tyler took his usual place in the Snack Bar. He left some space between him and the other customers so that he could talk to Rose without being overheard. He gave his order and when she came back with his drink, he said, "I want to ask you something, Rose. You remember when Jasmin first worked here, she came in one morning and looked all aglow and my friend said, "she must be in love." Who was the guy Jasmin dated?"

"That was a German waiter who made her laugh and he gave her a big bouquet of flowers, roses, I think, but he's since left, although, as far as I know, she still corresponds with him," Rose informed him.

"Bouquet of flowers," Mr. Tyler said with a faraway look. He thought, 'I wonder if I'll win Jasmin's heart that way.'

Rose nudged him on the elbow, "Get yourself together."

"Yes, yes," he said slowly, and didn't say anything else. He ate his meal when it arrived, got up, paid the cashier, and left.

Jasmin went to work early to get her supplies on Monday, hoping she would see Pete in the larder. He had just come out of the deep freeze, and she motioned for him to meet her near the bread cutter. He sauntered over to where she stood. "What's up?" he asked.

"It's got to be a secret," Jasmin whispered. "We are having a bridal shower for Rose and you have to be sure to get her there under the guise of having to sign important papers for your store purchase deal. Your lawyer's assistant will drive you there because it has to be a neutral place to get the signature witnessed. We will all be there. The shower is a surprise for her. Mr. Tyler will take you and the other man out for an hour and a half while the ladies have their party, and then you can come back and enjoy the refreshments and take the gifts home. You know my tutoring studio?"

"Yeah, I know," he said.

Jasmin

"Oh, one more thing," Jasmin said. "Give me a list of items you guys need for the apartment. Give this list either to me or Carla, she is in on it, but don't breathe a word to Rose, got it?"

Pete's face finally lit up as the understanding slowly dawned on him. "O.K.," he said. "Do you need help with your stuff?"

"Sure," Jasmin said. "Bring the French onion soup pot and put it on the stove outside my swinging door. Then light the flame under it, thanks."

She prepared her station, arranged the oyster barrel, and called over to the bar to fill her ice buckets. She sat on her barstool with pen and clipboard to check off the items listed. The noon crowd kept her moderately busy. Only once did she have to leave her post to take an order to a couple who occupied one of the alcoves. Then she put the bill on the spike at her counter so that the bartenders could pick it up and add it to their tab.

As she glanced up, Mr. James come through the street door. He walked toward her counter. Just as before, he greeted her. "Good afternoon, Miss Claudius, how are you today?"

"Very well, thank you, Mr. James, what may I serve you?" Jasmin asked.

"Do I smell something delicious?" he pointed his head toward the swinging door.

"That's French onion soup," Jasmin informed him.

"I shall have that, thank you," he said. While she went out the door to fill the bowl, he ordered his drink from the bartender, who had come over.

"Mr. James, a dry Martini?"

"Yes please," was the reply. As he waited for his soup to cool down, he added some crackers to it. Then Mr. James asked Jasmin, "Have you always worked in the hotel business?"

"Yes," she said, "I'm here on a working permit from Germany. I also attend several classes at Worthington tutorial studio in business, English, secretarial skills, and accounting principles. Currently I am completing the latter."

"So, you are busy day in and day out. Not much time for a social life, is there?" he wondered.

"Actually there is," she replied. "At the present time I'm arranging a bridal shower for my Irish girlfriend Rose, and I am going to take a list of names to my typing class to type invitations."

"She's lucky to have a friend like you," he said.

Jasmin countered, "She has no family here, and I have empathy for her. I want this to be a surprise."

Mr. James asked, "Did she book her reception yet?"

Jasmin said, "As far as I know, it's only a civil ceremony. Her fiancé knows somebody who has an empty room above a warehouse for rent, and they have a record player and free drinks and snacks. They spent all their savings on purchasing a chocolate shop with an apartment above the store where they are going to live."

"I have a suggestion," Mr. James said. "Why don't you tell her she can have her wedding party at my lodge? She won't have to pay for renting the room, we provide our band for free, and the guests will only need to pay half price for their own meals. The wine for the toast will be on the house, and if the guests want more drinks they can buy them at the bar. We have a small dance floor. It will be a little more festive than a bare room; besides, we are putting up Christmas decorations early this year. It will be an appropriate setting for a memorable occasion such as this."

"You are very kind," Jasmin said.

"Don't mention it," Mr. James answered as he rose from his barstool, waved to the bartender for his bill, smiled, and left.

Jasmin

Jasmin hurriedly covered the food trays, put things into the cooler, closed up everything else, and made her way to the larder with the empties to be refilled for the evening session. She craned her neck to find Pete, but didn't see him, so she went to the Danish Snack Bar to see if Rose might still be there. She found her in the coffee pantry emptying coffee grounds and replacing the filter.

Rose said, "What brings you here?"

Jasmin took a deep breath and said, "Have you booked that room yet for your wedding reception?"

"No," Rose said. "The fellow wanted too much money for it, so Pete is looking for something else."

"Tell Pete not to bother," Jasmin said. "Hear me out; I just talked to Mr. James from the Birkdale Lodge, and he will let you and your party have the room, the dance floor, and the band for free. Your guests will only have to pay for their meal at half price, which is better than potluck and they will be served. Mr. James will provide the wine for the toast, and if anyone wants more drinks, they can pay for them at the bar. Also the place is going to be decorated for Christmas with extra white lights around the head table. You can take pictures that will be memorable. What do you say?"

Rose gasped, "I am speechless; how on earth did you manage to do that?"

"Let's just say this is your lucky day," Jasmin smiled. "Do you have the list of guests you are planning to invite?"

"I gave it to Carla," Rose said.

"O.K. She is probably upstairs; I will get it from her," Jasmin said on her way out.

As soon as Jasmin walked into her room, Carla got up from her chair, waving two lists in front of her. "Here," she said, "I have ten people as wedding guests and twenty items of gift suggestions."

Jasmin said, "I know Mrs. Harman will come too. That makes eleven besides Mrs. Tyler and Mrs. Worthington. I'll take the gift list to work and give it to Mrs. Tyler when she comes for it tomorrow. If I had cards, I could write the shower invitations out on my typewriter. Do you think they might have something in the office that they could spare?"

"I don't see why not," Carla responded.

"Now, the next change of events is the reception. You know that Rose and Pete intended to rent that room above the warehouse and have the guests bring potluck. Well, Mr. James of the Birkdale Lodge offered his restaurant for free." She gave Carla the details. "As far as the wedding guest list goes, to Rose it is just that, but we will use these names for the surprise shower. Did you see Pete today?"

"Yes," Carla said. "He said he will get her there, even if he has to kidnap her. He is so thrilled and humble with gratitude at the same time."

"So, O.K.," Jasmin sighed as she neared the door, "I'll see what kind of stationery I can round up, and make sure the items on the gift list are readable. Are you going out, or are you going to stay here? I'll need to type them too."

"I'll stay," Carla said.

The office door was open but Jasmin politely knocked pro forma and smiled at Mrs. Goddard, who looked up from the paper she was perusing. "Oh, hello Jasmin," she said. "What can I do for you today?" She put down her papers and looked at her.

"It might be an unusual request, but I will ask you anyway," said Jasmin hesitantly.

"Yes?" Mrs. Goddard waited.

"Would you by any chance have some spare stationery, or some small cards or place cards, something like that?" Jasmin asked.

"What do you need it for?" Mrs. Goddard queried.

Jasmin

"It's for a bridal shower. I have a gift list and an itinerary for Rose and Pete's wedding. The shower is a secret and I need to get the invitations into the hands of the participants as soon as possible. I have my own typewriter in my room, so if I had some supplies, I could do it now. I only need about fifteen."

"So Rose is getting married," Mrs. Goddard said. "Come with me to the storage area and I'll see what we can come up with. You can put me down for the shower too. When is the R.S.V.P. deadline?"

"This weekend," Jasmin followed closely.

"So, come down on Thursday during your afternoon break and I will let you know if I will attend. Now, here we are: let's look on these shelves and see what may be suitable." They found some pre-printed wedding invitations, shower invitations, program sheets, place cards, and envelopes. Mrs. Goddard gave Jasmin a stack of each plus some extra embossed notepapers and sent her on her way.

Loaded with an armful of papers, Jasmin entered her door. She let Carla take them off her and put them on the sideboard. "O.K.," she said, "let's see that gift list again. Give me a few minutes and I will type out three copies while you count out the invitations for me."

Jasmin typed the items on the lists, inserted the lists in envelopes, and started on the invitations for the shower. She put the address of the tutorial studio on them but left the name of the store for the gift registry blank. Then she typed the address and details for the reception on the fine notepaper and inserted these in the appropriate envelopes along with the R.S.V.P. cards. She instructed Carla to give these to Rose. Carla would ask Rose to write the names of her friends on the envelopes by hand, and to be sure to keep track of the number of guests who would be attending. She would then get back to Jasmin with the total.

"O.K.," they both said simultaneously, "we still have jobs to hold down." They changed into their smocks and went to their supply places for the evening dinner crowd.

Jasmin thought, "I hope we are not busy tonight." She organized her display shelf and went out of the swinging door to have a snack near the hot stove. When she returned she put some ice in her water glass, looked around, and went back out again to sit on that old kitchen chair beside the stove. She stretched out her legs for a few moments before attending her post.

Some customers occupied the tables in the room. A few ordered hors d'oeuvres, while others sat at the regular bar and talked with the bartenders. Later, Mr. Larson, a salesman who came periodically, visited her food bar, ate his snack, and asked how her studies were coming along. "Now that you mention it," Jasmin said, "I haven't practiced my steno for a while since I am mostly into accounting. The only typing I've done lately was today when I typed invitations for a bridal shower and a wedding."

"So you are a social convener too?" he asked.

"Let me write that down," Jasmin said, picking up her steno pad from the drawer under the counter. "What was that word again? Actually dictate the whole sentence to me; I want to see if I'm still fluent in shorthand," she said.

He dictated the sentence again. Then he added more words by telling her about his day, the weather, the road conditions, the places he visited, the new contacts he'd made, the plans he had for the next day, and the delightful conversation he was enjoying with her. "Enough," she laughed, putting her pencil down. "Flattery will get you nowhere."

The rest of the evening passed with lighthearted chat. The bartenders closed up shop and Jasmin took the food stuffs back to the larder. Then she went to the time clock to punch out. Bill,

Jasmin

the assistant timekeeper, spotted her and handed her a letter. "This came for you, Smiler," he said.

"Thank you," Jasmin said, and she took the letter, smiled, and took the elevator upstairs.

At noon the next day, the bellhop came through the hotel entrance, asking the barmen, "Where is Jasmin?" He couldn't see her right away because her food counter was separated by the interior swinging door. They pointed to her, and he turned his head. From this angle he noticed her and handed her the note waiting a reply. She knew it was from Mrs. Tyler. She read the note and wrote back that she needed to know by Wednesday which store had the registry. Then she handed her own envelope with the list and the reply note to the bellhop.

Matthew Tyler confided to his mother that he intended to take Jasmin to the annual ball at the Regency Hall. He asked his mother to help Jasmin with selecting a rental gown for the occasion. He also mentioned that he had decided to enroll in a brush up course on ballroom dancing because he didn't remember very much since his college days. He planned to go to Mr. Worthington's studio.

"Excellent idea!" Mrs. Tyler exclaimed.

Matthew said he needed to know Jasmin's birthday, because he wanted to give her a surprise party. His mother remembered that Emma Worthington had Jasmin's records on file. She offered to check that out and promised to call him at his office about it.

In the meantime Jasmin learned that the store which had the bridal registry was on the fourth floor at the Carlton, manager's desk. She took it up to her room during afternoon break and left a note for Carla to fill in the blanks on the invitation since she had to go to class. She hurried to get her books and worksheets together and walked briskly to catch the bus. Jasmin handed in her homework and picked up her previous assignments with the marks on them.

She had received straight A's. Then she listened to the instructions for today's assignment.

As she was getting ready to leave, Mr. Worthington came into the classroom and said, "Miss Claudius, do you have a moment?" He stepped aside to let her pass him out the door and she noted Matthew Tyler standing there. Mr. Worthington explained, "Matthew here has signed up for private dance instructions. He will need a female partner to volunteer for the lessons. This means that the teacher is teaching Matthew the steps. Of course, he'd also show them to you. There is no charge to you because you are taking the part of the female teacher and we don't have one who gives private lessons. Will that be all right with you?"

"When will these lessons take place?" Jasmin asked.

"They will be on Saturday afternoons," Mr. Worthington said.

"That should be fine. I am a day time person," Jasmin said, "but now I have to leave to catch the bus."

"I'll take you back to work," Matthew offered.

"Thank you, Matthew," she said. Turning to look at Mr. Worthington, she said, "Goodbye, Mr. Worthington."

"Goodbye," he replied.

As they walked to the parked car, Matthew explained, "Court finished early today, so I took the opportunity to drive here and arrange for the dance lessons in person and talk to you since you don't have a telephone."

Jasmin smiled and said, "You could write me a letter."

Now he smiled. As he opened the car door for her, he stood close to her and asked, "Will that put the glow on your face?"

She straightened her shoulders, held her head up high, looked at him sideways, and said, "It might; depends on the content."

He tipped his head in understanding. When he was seated in the driver's seat he started the engine and put the car in reverse. Then

Jasmin

he looked at her and began a new conversation. "I understand your arrangements for your friend's shower are nicely underway," he said while changing gears and looking over his shoulder, left and right. Then he drove onto the road, keeping his eyes in front of him, but giving her a quick glance as he awaited her reply.

"Yes," she said, and she told him the latest developments of how she was able to secure a fine establishment for their reception offered practically for free by a gracious philanthropist.

Matthew commented, "You're a remarkable young lady, giving of yourself in service for others."

"I enjoy doing it," she said. "I remember my sister telling me that in the hallway of our ancient homestead there hung a plaque which said, 'There is no greater joy than to give pleasure to others.'"

"A beautiful sentiment," Matthew said thoughtfully. He stopped the car at their destination and went around the back to hold the door open for her. "I'll pick you up here on Saturday at two thirty." He came down the steps with her to the entrance, held the door open, and then he drove away.

When Jasmin got to her room, she saw Carla hunched over the papers and writing on the cards. She looked up and said, "I'm almost finished. Let me do the last two and I'll show you."

"O.K.," Jasmin said. "I'll just go to the powder room and change. I'll be back in a couple of minutes." She found the unopened letter still in the pocket of her smock and read it. It was from Roger, saying he was back in the dorm of the university and she could reply to that address. That gave her an idea as she walked back to her room. She entered, sat down on the empty chair beside Carla, and planned her strategy.

"You know," Jasmin said to Carla, "this letter is from Roger wanting to meet me again. I don't have animosity toward him. He's a nice guy, and he would be a good friend to associate with in a group setting. How would you like to accompany me next week to the coffee bar? We could sit around chatting for a while and include him in the conversation so he doesn't feel rejected by others just because I don't take to him."

Carla said, "This would give me a chance to meet an English guy socially."

Jasmin checked if the shower invitations had the admonition of secrecy on them and gave the stack back to Carla. "You know what to do; give them to the friends within the hotel or put them into the slot at the time clock downstairs. Are there any that need to be mailed?"

"Yes, two," Carla answered.

"Fine, hand them to me so I can type the names and addresses on these envelopes. Are there any stamps around?"

"I have some," Carla offered.

"Thanks," Jasmin said. She put the envelopes into the typewriter, typed the names, inserted the cards, sealed them, and reached for the stamps. "I'll give them to the timekeeper for the outgoing mail when I go down to punch in," she said, getting ready to go downstairs. "I'll also give these itineraries to Rose so she can distribute them to the guests herself."

Jasmin went downstairs to the timekeeper's booth and gave him the two envelopes. "This is for the morning's mail going out. Keep these from Rose's eyes; it's for a surprise bridal shower,"

"O.K. Smiler," he said, taking some other mail and piling it on top, "consider it done."

Jasmin punched her clock card and made a beeline to the kitchen to pick up the garnished trays waiting for her. She loaded the trolley and wheeled it to her station. She fastened the swinging door with a doorstop and placed the dishes on the display shelf behind her counter. After she had made sure that everything looked fresh and

Jasmin

appealing, she snapped the doorstop off, waved over to Martin, and called, "Do I have five minutes till opening time?"

He checked the time and said, "Eight."

"Right; I have another errand to run. If I am not back by then, you know I will be here shortly, so cover for me, will you?"

"All right," he said.

Jasmin hurried through the maze of corridors to the Danish Snack Bar where she cornered Rose in the coffee pantry, half out of breath, "Here," she said. "Rose, all you have to do is put these invitations into the envelopes, address them, and mail them first thing in the morning."

"Sure thing, thanks again," Rose said.

Later that evening, back in her quarters, Jasmin picked out a sheet of the fine notepaper she'd received from the office clerk and began to write the letter to Roger. She told him what she had mentioned to Carla. She appreciated his friendship and wished to continue this in a casual group setting. She asked if she could bring her girlfriend when they met at the Prego coffee bar to have leisure conversations and keep abreast of the happenings in each other's lives. They could be available next Tuesday afternoon and would plan to see him there. She addressed the envelope, placed one of Carla's stamps on it, and sealed it. The next morning she made her way down to the timekeeper's booth and asked, "Has the mail gone out yet?"

"Almost," Bill said, holding open the mailbag for her. She quickly dropped her letter into it. "Now, it will, Smiler," he said as he bundled up the mailbag. Jasmin walked to the time clock and punched in her card. Looking back she saw the postman enter the door, come down the steps with new incoming mail, and then take the full bag off Bill.

Mr. Tyler brought his associate Jeff Kerr to the Danish Snack Bar and took his usual seat at the food counter. They ordered their cold cuts and salad from Rose and engaged in a conversation about current affairs. When they were having their dessert and coffee, Mr. Tyler glanced up and asked Rose, "What are those papers sticking out of your apron's pocket?"

"Those are wedding invitations," she said.

"Am I invited?" he asked jokingly.

"Now that you mention it," she said, and she pulled out two invitations. "Sure, and you may bring a companion too."

He smiled, took the invitations, and gave one to Jeff who said, "Looks interesting."

On the Thursday, as promised, Jasmin went to the office during her afternoon break. Mrs. Goddard saw her coming around the corner through the open door. She smiled and said, "Ah, Jasmin, how are all those plans of yours coming along?"

"Very well," Jasmin replied. "Here is your shower invitation with the address, date, and time, as well as the gift list. It's registered at the Carlton, fourth floor." She handed the invitation and the guest list to her.

"By the way," asked Mrs. Goddard, "has Rose ordered a bouquet yet?"

"I honestly don't know," Jasmin said, "Why?"

"With winter approaching," Mrs. Goddard said, "it should be ordered in advance at the International Floral Boutique. They specialize in tropical flowers like orchids from Italy and roses from Greece."

"Oh, I don't think Rose wants anything fancy. Seems to me I heard her mention some time ago that she is happy with some daisies, maybe carnations," Jasmin said.

Jasmin

"Pink carnations would be perfect," Mrs. Goddard insisted, "as her colours are pink and navy blue. Find out from Pete. If she hasn't got the flowers arranged, I'd be glad to order them for her and put a note into the shower card with the promise of it. Two days before the wedding we could have them delivered to this office. She has to come down here to get her pay anyway."

"What a great idea," Jasmin conceded. "I'll check with Pete and let you know at the shower. I am going up for my break, see you later."

During the evening hours most of the customers had their hors d'oeuvres and snacks served at the tables by the bartenders. Occasionally Jasmin brought some orders to the tables too, but she didn't have to clear the dishes. The barmen did that by placing the dishes on the trolley next to the hotel entrance behind a partition. Jasmin sat on her own barstool behind her counter and hummed along with the tunes the pianist played.

On Saturday she didn't allow herself to sleep in. Carla had already gone out on a shopping spree, so she decided to skip breakfast and do some homework on her accounting assignment and practice her typing of numbers for a few hours. Afterwards she went down to the main kitchen. She located the grill chef who offered her steak. While he put it on the grill, she looked for the junior vegetable chef. He served her a variety of legumes onto her plate. Then she strolled over to her usual alcove and enjoyed her lunch. Later, she made her way up to the pastry kitchen and had the baker give her some freshly baked cherry pie. He asked, "Do you want ice cream on it?"

She asked in consternation, "Ice cream in winter?"

"Sure," he affirmed, "the pie is still warm and the ice cream will melt right over it."

167

"Sounds yummy," Jasmin laughed. They put the pie into a covered dish for her to take upstairs. In her room she enjoyed it with a cup of tea.

In the afternoon, Jasmin contemplated what to wear for the dancing lesson. Normally on a cool day she wore a suit with a tight skirt, but for the dancing lesson, she decided on the pleated Scottish kilt. She chose a V-neck sweater, placed the St. Christopher's pendant (the latest craze) around her neck, and wore just a light shawl instead of a coat. Then she went downstairs to wait inside the door, glancing periodically through the window for Matthew's car. He drove up within minutes, stopped, and came out to see her to the passenger door. "Good afternoon, Beautiful," he greeted her with a smile.

"Good afternoon, Matthew," she said as she got in.

While they were driving he said, "I'm looking forward to this new venture."

"Venture?" she asked.

"Yes, venture, spending time with you and learning something new at the same time," he replied with a grin.

"Let's see what happens," she said in a non-committal way.

At the tutorial studio, the adjudicator Mr. Townsend greeted them on the way to the salon. They walked across the polished dance floor and past the elevated stage with the record player, and then he motioned to a chair on the side for Jasmin to take a seat. Then he said to Matthew, "Before I start the music, I will show you the steps. Follow exactly as I do." They did that three or four times, and then Mr. Townsend instructed him further: "Now you have to memorize the steps. Don't look at your feet, and follow an imaginary line with your head. It's called the line of dance, and it goes straight down the centre of the room. The steps I have shown you go diagonally across the line of dance to the right, and when you turn you go diagonally to the left, then again straight up the line of dance and to the right, turn, to the left, turn and continue this way all around the ballroom floor. We will try it together once. I will step backward and you will follow forward so we do it in unison." He counted, "One two three four, one two three four, turn, two three four, you are getting it." They made it to the end of the round, and then Mr. Townsend started the music. Matthew and Jasmin had to listen for the beat that accented the melody.

Mr. Townsend encouraged Matthew to rest his hands on his shoulders and he guided him through the music, all the while counting the beat. When they came to a halt near the stage, he stopped the music and walked over to Jasmin and asked, "Have you followed everything I've shown Matthew?"

She said, "Most of it."

He offered his hand to her, then held her in dance position to show Matthew how to hold and guide a lady in dance. "I will walk with you through the steps once so you get the feel for it, and then Matthew will proceed."

Looking over his shoulder, he asked Matthew, "See how I follow the line of dance?" To Jasmin he said, "As you will be walking backwards, flex your knees to get into the swaying motion." As he guided Jasmin through the step sequence, he said at each turn, "this is a quarter turn; don't overturn."

They came to the stage and he said, "I'll do this once with the music for you before I turn you over to Matthew." He told Jasmin to hold her head up high, firm up her shoulders and move from her hips. Then he counted the beat and moved her with his wrist as he guided her through the dance.

He stopped the music and showed Matthew how to hold the lady. "First," he said, "you raise your elbows halfway up to form an arch. The right hand is positioned just above the lady's waist, and the left is raised up to hold the lady's hand. Jasmin, your left elbow rests upon Matthew's elbow and your left hand rests upon his upper arm. Matthew, your right arm is the centre of gravity and direction and the left arm is for balance. Now, with the music, wait for my count after four, then one, etc." The music started and he counted, "One two three four, now two three four."

Matthew and Jasmin moved in unison hesitantly, then more confidently, and after the first turn they moved more fluently. They continued in tune with the music for two rounds until Mr. Townsend stopped the music. "That was a good start. Before I show you any other dances, you will have to practice this one until you are able to recognize the tunes that fit these steps. On Sunday evening from seven to nine we have an open session for students of this club. You are free to attend. There is of course the big dance hall in the city, but they don't open on Sundays. Do another round and we will call it quits. O.K., mind your posture, ready when the music starts, wait four beats, then go." He started the record and they began to dance, a little stiff at first, then flowing more easily.

Mr. Townsend booked another lesson that would take place in two weeks, because the shower would occupy the salon next week.

As they drove home Jasmin started the conversation. "So, do you label this venture rewarding?"

Matthew answered with a question, "You mean the dancing or your presence?"

Jasmin saw the smile in his face and said, "Take your pick."

He said very analytically, "It surprised me how much knowledge the dancing required. There is much to think about and to concentrate on. While this is indeed rewarding, your presence superseded it all." As they had stopped at a stoplight, he took the time to look full into her face and he held the look for a moment.

Jasmin

She looked at him, then lowered her eyes and asked, "Do you use this flowery language in the courtroom?"

He admitted, "It's your lovely persona that causes these graceful words to pour from my lips."

Jasmin leaned her head back, closed her eyes, and whispered, "Thank you." She'd learned to accept compliments gracefully.

After a few minutes he asked, "Would you like to know how fast this car can go?" He was looking at her with a glint in his eyes to find out if she wanted to have some fun.

She picked up on the light mood and laughed, "You mean now we go from venture to adventure."

He assured her, "It won't be dangerous. I know a straight country road just out of town. Put your seatbelt on." They left the perimeter of the city, turned down a treed street, and came to a wide open space with fields on either side of the paved road. As Matthew sped up with a whoosh, Jasmin's hair whisked back and she held onto her seat. He slowed down at a cross road, stopped at the side, and asked, "How was that?"

"Exhilarating," she said. "It took my breath away; now what?"

"It's still early. We could go for a cup of tea in the pleasant atmosphere of the Ceylon Tea Centre. They are open till seven."

"That would be nice," she answered.

Matthew said calmly, "I'll go at a moderate speed." Jasmin nodded her approval. They drove in silence, comfortable in each other's company. Once inside, Matthew and Jasmin let the waitress show them to a booth. As they settled into the Far East décor of the surroundings and placed their order, he asked, "How are the bridal shower arrangements coming along?"

Jasmin perked up and said, "Very well indeed. Everybody who is coming has been notified. They are aware of the gift list and know that secrecy is the code. Actually, that brings to mind a comment

Mrs. Goddard, the lady in our office, made about flowers. She said there's a new florist in the city called the International Floral Boutique. Apparently they import roses from Greece and orchids from Italy just to name a few."

They ate some of the Petit Fours and other treats, while Matthew looked at her dreamily. Jasmin paused to ask, "You aren't saying anything; is too much girls' talk boring you?"

"Oh, no," he insisted. "On the contrary; I am interested. Orchids from Italy and roses, no doubt white roses from Athens. I'm familiar with that particular florist, as my office arranged for the mortgage on the property. As yet I haven't had the occasion of being a customer, though my mother has."

They engaged in some more small talk and set the meeting time for the following Saturday. "I look forward to this 'conspiracy'," Matthew said.

"It will be, unless the secret gets out," Jasmin concurred.

They stood up. Matthew placed the shawl around her shoulders and said, "I will leave my car in the parking lot and walk you across the street to the door of your hotel."

"Fine," Jasmin consented. She absolutely adored walking arm in arm with Matthew. She pondered whether it was time to write to her brother about Matthew. At her entrance door, he tipped his hat and said, "Thank you for the pleasant afternoon. I shall be here next Saturday at six thirty sharp."

Jasmin waved to the timekeeper on her way to the elevator. When she came to her room, she saw Carla cutting wrapping paper and measuring it to fit one of the boxes spread on top of her bed. "Oh," she said, "You are just in time to look at the gifts before I wrap them. This is a six-piece dinner set in two boxes and that over there is the dessert and tea set I bought for you with the money you gave me. Here is your change. You can wrap your gift with the other paper over there."

"How pretty," Jasmin exclaimed, "what a lovely pattern." They talked over the events of the day while they wrapped and taped the gift boxes and put ribbons and bows on them.

"By the way," Carla said, "The head waitress Mrs. Shaw is giving Maureen and me a ride to the shower. We are going to her house on our afternoon break on Monday, so she can store the gifts there inconspicuously until Saturday."

"Great idea," Jasmin said. "While I think of it, when you see Pete on Monday ask him if he or Rose have arranged her bouquet. If not, tell him not to, because I have a plan. I will let you know soon."

"O.K.," Carla answered. "I am going downstairs for something to eat. Do you want me to bring you something?"

"Sure," Jasmin said. "Check for teabags, etc. and bring a chicken salad on a croissant.

COURTSHIP

Matthew drove home deep in thought. He was trying to recall what Rose had said to him a few weeks earlier when he had asked her what made Jasmin all aglow. "The young man made her laugh and gave her flowers. I make her laugh sometimes. Did she give me a clue? Maybe flowers, or yes, she said 'write a letter'."

He arrived at his house and sought his mother in the parlour. She was sitting at her opened roll top desk. Nonchalantly, he walked over and said, "Good evening, Mother," while eying where her stationery was stored.

She turned to him and said, "Ah, you are home. I'll have Emily bring tea." And with that she left for the kitchen. Matthew took some of her embossed blank notepapers and envelopes and went to his own office. He sat at his desk, held his pen, and looked out the window for a moment. Then he stared at the paper, imagining Jasmin's face. He began:

My Dearest Jasmin,

I call you dearest because my mind dictates me to think of you that way. You have captured my heart from the moment I saw you by the way you turn your head, the way you look at me, and the way you form the words with your mouth.

I am fascinated by the lilt in your voice when you laugh and I am challenged to tease you when you cock your head with a pretend frown. Your graceful demeanor when you walk is like a mirage come real. All my reserve is melted in the emotion to adore you and cherish you. Your gentleness is like the morning dew and your smile lights up the atmosphere around you. I am ecstatic in the anticipation of seeing you in person again soon.

Your most devoted admirer,

Matthew Tyler

He folded the letter, breathed a kiss on it, inserted it into the envelope, wrote her address, and placed a stamp in the corner. The next morning he took it personally to the main post office.

On Monday, when Jasmin arrived at the studio for classes, she found a note on her desk saying to call Mrs. Harman from the office. She finished her studies early so that she could call Mrs. Harman before catching the bus. She knocked at the door, and upon entering she saw the welcoming smile of Mrs. Worthington.

"Jasmin, dear, go ahead use the phone," she said.

Jasmin dialed Mrs. Harman's direct line at the architectural office, and when Mrs. Harman answered, she said, "Hello, this is Jasmin."

Jasmin

Mrs. Harman said, "Yes Jasmin dear, I wanted to tell you I have purchased the shower gift and I will be there on Saturday. But the main reason I called is to ask if you would like to come to church with me on Sunday. We would be glad to pick you up in the morning at ten thirty from your hotel, and have you for lunch at our home afterwards."

"That will be fine," Jasmin said. "You know the side entrance of the hotel where to stop the car? It's on Central Street around the corner from Main Street."

"Yes, thank you, I'll see you there," Mrs. Harman said. They both hung up.

Jasmin turned to Mrs. Worthington and said, "I am on my way out, see you on Saturday."

"Perfect," Mrs. Worthington said. "Everything is arranged for the party."

"Fantastic," Jasmin shouted as she hurriedly left the building.

Jasmin made it back to the hotel with fifteen minutes to spare. She weaved her way through the other staff who crowded the timekeeper's hallway and took the elevator up to her room. She changed her outfit, tidied up her school books, and went back down to punch in her time card. She heard "Smiler" and turned her head for a quick glance.

The timekeeper scurried towards her, waving a letter in his hand. "This came in the evening mail for you."

She took the letter and said "Thank you." Then she looked at the sender's name and her face went red.

The timekeeper stared at her and whistled. "Must be something special," he grinned as she walked away.

Jasmin quickly slipped the envelope into the pocket of her smock, took a deep breath, and went about her business as usual. She attended to her evening guests and filled some orders for the bartenders until there was a lull. Then she put things in order, refreshed the platters, and decided she had a spare minute to look at the letter that was burning a hole in her pocket.

She stepped out through the swinging door to sit quietly beside the stove and opened the envelope. There seemed to be a faint perfume fragrance. Jasmin read those wonderful words about her and they sank deep into her soul. She looked up and stared into space, wondering when she had ever received accolades for something she didn't earn, something she didn't work for, and something she didn't try to achieve.

She heard the barman come through her food bar, and before he opened the swinging door, she folded the letter and shoved it back into her pocket. She got up.

"Jasmin, you have a customer. Everything alright?" he asked.

"Sure, fine." She walked behind him through the door and smiled at the customer. She was in perfect control and ready for service. The customer ordered what she recommended and had his drink while he was waiting for her to prepare it.

"This is the first time I'm visiting Middleton," he stated. "My predecessor has been transferred to another region and I shall have to get my bearings first thing in the morning."

Jasmin finished preparing his dish and set it before him. She asked, "Could you use a city map?"

"That would be helpful, yes," he replied.

"The bartender can get you one so that you can look at it tonight. When he has a minute I'll ask him for you." With that, she opened the other swinging door a slit and motioned to Martin to come over to her. She asked, "Could you find the bellhop to bring a city map for this gentleman?"

"Sure," he said, and sauntered out to the interior hotel door. In the hotel business, any extra service meant more tip money. In a short while Martin came back. He walked to the guest side of the food counter and handed the map to the guest. "Here you are, Sir," he said.

"Oh, much obliged, thank you," he said, tipping his head. He finished his food and drink and paid the barman with a large bill. "Keep the change," he said, and left.

Martin winked his eye at Jasmin and she bowed her head slightly in acknowledgement. They closed up shop. The barmen took the used dishes and cutlery away in the trolley and Jasmin took her empty trays back to the larder for replenishing in the morning. After she had punched out her card at the time clock, she considered for a moment where she could find privacy. She took the elevator to the first floor, then slowly walked up the guest staircase to the Mezzanine where she sat in an obscure corner on one of the armchairs.

She slowly read the letter several times more, folded it, and carefully put it back into the envelope. Jasmin contemplated where to store it. It occurred to her that Matthew wanted to trust her with his heart. She didn't want to share something so precious with Carla. She remembered the time a few years ago when she had received a similar adoring letter. She had shared it with her girlfriends and bragged about it. They had tattled on her and she had lost her boyfriend.

Luckily, when she came to her room, Carla was just on her way out with a bathrobe in her hand, saying, "I am going to have a bath." Jasmin waved her off and closed the door. She found the lockable box in her suitcase, put the letter inside, locked the box, and stored the key in her wallet. She prepared her own clothing for the laundry service and laid out her outfit for the next day. Then she read a few pages of her English assignment and went to bed.

Her restless thoughts went to the letter from Matthew. She thought about what she meant to him, and how much he cared for her. Did he mean anything to her? Did she have any ounce of care for him? What did she feel about him? What did she like about him?

She made this statement in her mind: she liked the sound of his voice.

She found it scintillating the way he teased her and how he let her tease him.

She admired his eloquence: his words were not shallow but carefully thought out and sincere.

She relished walking arm in arm with him.

As she drifted off to sleep, she put her mind at rest that she had the whole week to analyze this.

The next morning Carla said, "I talked to Pete and promised that you would explain further about the flowers before he made any decision."

"Yes," Jasmin said, "I'll find the time to see him when I pick up the bread at the bread cutter."

When she came to the larder, she spotted Pete while he was placing the tureen onto the trolley with her other supplies. "Oh, Pete," she called, "could you wheel it over to my station while I carry the bread?"

"Sure thing," he said, and he went ahead of her through the two corridors to the back of the Concordia Bar, stopping behind the swinging door next to the stove.

Jasmin caught up with him and said, "Pete, this is the plan: Mrs. Goddard will have Rose's bouquet ready for her the Friday before your wedding when she comes to the office to get her pay, O.K.?"

"Thank you very much," Pete said.

"How are you holding out with the secret for Saturday?" Jasmin enquired just to be sure.

"Oh," he said, "Rose has no qualms about going there for the so-called signing of papers. I want to take a picture of her surprised eyes."

"Good idea," Jasmin said. "Now let's get back to work."

Pete left. Jasmin clipped the swinging door into the stopper and placed all her food items on the display shelf. This day she was especially busy with oysters. She had one of the bartenders help her open them with the spare oyster knife and asked him to send for more to replenish the wooden barrel with fresh ones from the cold kitchen.

The next afternoon was the casual date with Roger. Jasmin hoped that he would take the transformation from seeing her exclusively to a group get together in stride. The girls found a small corner table and kept the extra chair available by putting their purses on it. Before they even ordered anything, Roger showed up. He walked towards them in his slightly awkward way, smiled shyly, bowed his head, stretched out his hand to her, and said, "Jasmin."

Jasmin took his hand, shook it, and said, "Hi Roger, this is Carla."

Roger tipped his head. "Carla. Have you ordered anything yet?" he asked them.

"We were just about to," Carla said.

"Let me get it," he offered. "What will you ladies have?"

"Cappuccino," they said in unison and laughed. He turned to the coffee bar attendant and made the letter 'C' and three fingers, that was enough. There was only espresso or cappuccino available anyway. For espresso it would have been thumbs up.

"I wonder who had the busiest week so far," Jasmin opened the conversation.

Roger responded, "My week as yet has been absolutely unreal. My professor had the whole class redo our assignments because he said we hadn't paid enough attention and hadn't studied thoroughly.

He gave us an ultimatum to have the new corrected ones on his desk by this weekend."

Carla asked, "What exactly was the topic about?" Now Roger launched into several technical details; he was thrilled to have such a captive audience. Jasmin regretted not having her steno pad with her or she would have jotted down technical terms, but she was glad she had diverted his attention from herself to Carla.

Carla was diplomatic enough when there was a breather to cut in and say, "At least you're not the only one to have had a horrendous half week, and it is not over yet."

"Tell me about it," said Roger, really animated. "But first let's have some more coffee, O.K.?" Everybody nodded. Roger asked Jasmin what her week had been like. She told him how busy they were with the oysters. The barman had to help her, and since nobody could leave their post, they had paged the bellhop to fetch more from the kitchen. Sipping her coffee, Jasmin encouraged Carla to tell her tale.

Carla told how they had gotten so busy that they had to call the room service waitress to help out and man the coffee pantry. When it was all over, Maureen had whispered to the head waitress about the shower gift she had bought, and with Rose overhearing "shower", Carla had to put on a poker face and say she was due for a shower. Then Carla explained to Roger about the secret bridal shower and the wedding plans for Rose.

Roger said, "This was a real fun get together; why don't we do this again next week, same time, same place?"

"Good enough for me," Carla said.

"Fine with me too," Jasmin agreed.

"Thank you, Jasmin," Roger said, rising from his chair. The girls stood up too.

Everybody said, "Goodbye."

Jasmin

On their way home, Jasmin said to Carla, "I will come with you to see Roger next week, but after that you are on your own. Why don't you invite him to the wedding? You will need an escort anyway."

"Sure," Carla said, "he is a likeable enough fellow."

Matthew had had a hectic week with open cases, and on Friday evening he brought some files home to peruse them in peace and quiet. He worked on them early Saturday morning as well. By noon he decided to go to his club for a work out in the gym. He also wanted to touch base with his associate, Jeff Kerr, and go over the evening's activities to make sure everything went well. They had lunch together, and in parting they laughed, "Let's not make these social activities as tense as court cases."

When Matthew came home he saw a note on the hallway table from the maid who'd been off duty since two p.m. The note read: "Mrs. Tyler, your chauffeur will be here at six p.m. His supper is in the kitchen in the covered dish. I shall serve tea for you and Mr. Tyler at five p.m. in the library before leaving for the evening."

He took a shower, and instead of going to the library afterwards, he went into the conservatory. As he looked around, he contemplated if it were appropriate to have a flower in his button-hole or even bring one for Jasmin, but then he thought otherwise. Back inside, he took a seat at the game table and opened the newspaper that lay on it. His mind couldn't concentrate on what he was reading, so he folded it again, put it away, and leaned back in his chair. He closed his eyes and imagined Jasmin's face. He wondered how she might react to the words in his letter. Would his letter warm her heart? Would she understand it wasn't flattery? Would she read between the lines and recognize his utter devotion to her? He realized there had to be a continuation of gentleness on his part of wooing her.

After tea, his mother got ready saying, "This should be a fun evening for us ladies. What are you guys going to do?"

"I'll take them for a spin in my Jaguar to test the speed for a while, then we will go to a pub nearby and meet you at the party for treats afterwards," he informed her.

She half-turned back toward him as she reached for the door handle and said, "Just remember, the guardian angels only travel as fast as the speed limit." With that she left. She found the chauffeur in the kitchen and instructed him to put the gift boxes into the trunk. Matthew drove to the hotel to pick up Jasmin. He was a little early, and so waited in his car. He hoped to note something in her demeanor that would indicate she was pleased with his letter. He looked at his watch and slowly got out of his car. Then he stood waiting, leaning against the passenger side. Suddenly the door opened. There was Jasmin. Someone was holding the door for her while she balanced the boxes in her hands.

Matthew's heart skipped a beat. He walked down the steps toward her with outstretched hands and looked into her eyes. "Allow me to take these for you," he said gently.

"Yes," she breathed.

In that instant he saw the glow he had been looking for in her, and he knew that it was directed toward him. He caught his breath and said, "Let me put these into the trunk." He unlocked it, placed the boxes into it, then snapped the lid shut and opened the passenger door for Jasmin. He very gingerly closed it when she was seated. He rushed around the back of the car, entered, and looked at her again to find that rosy blush still on her face. For a while they drove along in silence.

She finally broke the silence. "I thoroughly appreciate your letter; it means a lot to me. I'm keeping it in a special place. I don't know how else to respond."

He turned his head and looked at her for a moment. Then he looked straight ahead at the road and reiterated, "Your consent to keep seeing me is response enough. You are always on my mind, and if you will let me, I will share more of my heart with you."

Jasmin smiled shyly. She didn't want to break the spell, but she took a deep breath to calm her beating heart. Matthew turned into the parking lot, stopped, and said in a light tone, "We are here. Let's make some people happy, shall we?"

Now Jasmin laughed too, and said, "Yes, for sure."

As they neared the Worthington mansion, the maid was waiting and ushered them into the wide open French doors of the salon. She pointed them to the empty chairs in the circle. Everybody else was there. Mrs. Worthington arranged that the lights be turned low until Rose appeared, and then they would all shout in unison: "Surprise!" and simultaneously the lights would come on. That was Mrs. Harman's job.

The maid, who was stationed at the door, said, "I hear a car coming."

Everyone held their breath, and the doorbell rang. The door was pulled back, and blaring lights and "Surprise!" echoed through the hall. Rose stood there, stunned, as several cameras flashed to capture her shock.

Jasmin walked toward her, took her by the hand, and said, "Welcome to your bridal shower, Rose."

At that time, Matthew took Jeff Kerr and Pete aside for their "guys' time" out.

Rose finally got her voice back and asked, "For me?"

Jasmin nodded and led her in front of the stage to the special high backed chair decorated with garlands of silk roses and ivy leaves. The gifts were placed along the edge of the stage. Her two attendants stood in front of their chairs on either side of her, and the rest of the ladies sat in a semicircle facing her. Two room dividers formed a backdrop behind the chairs so that the room didn't appear too large for the group of under twenty. At a cue from Jasmin, Mrs. Worthington played a tune and everybody sang "You are my sunshine" and "Bicycle built for two". Then a quiz game was introduced that produced a lot of laughter. The other six girls sat on one side of the circle and the head waitress, Mrs. Tyler, Mrs. Harman, Mrs. Worthington, and Jasmin completed the group. The two attendants, Maureen and Carla, pretended to be reporters and they interviewed Rose alternately about how and when she met Pete. When the interview was over, the gifts were distributed. Maureen handed the gifts one at a time to Rose. Carla was the scribe, recording each gift on the accompanying card.

Then Maureen brought each opened gift box to the group for viewing. They passed them around to the next person until the end, when the last one was brought back to the stage.

Finally, it was time for punch. Rose walked among her peers, amazed at how they had kept this secret. Carla told of how each of the elderly ladies had a part in it. Rose was still so overwhelmed by it all, but she had enough grace to step up to each of the senior ladies to thank them. When she came to Mrs. Tyler, the lady said, "You can thank Jasmin; it was her idea."

Rose took Jasmin in her arms and held her with tears of joy. She said, "Thank you so much."

The maid announced that the cupcakes were served at the table by the wall. There were several varieties of squares, tarts, and petit fours. Everyone helped themselves. Jasmin took a couple of trays to the ladies who preferred to stay seated.

Suddenly the door burst open and the guys showed up. "I hear there is something to nibble on," said Matthew upon entering with his friends. Rose pointed to the sweets table and Pete and Jeff went to help themselves.

Matthew saw Jasmin holding a tray in front of his mother and the thought flashed through his mind, "She always puts others first." She turned, brought the trays back to the service table, and held one up to him. He took one piece and asked, "May I take this tray off your hands?" Then he held it in front of her, asking, "Would you like to try a morsel?"

She took a piece, "I don't mind if I do, thank you." She flashed a grin at him, took a bite, swallowed, and said, "There is punch over there."

He looked in the direction she pointed and offered, "Shall we?" He lightly touched her elbow. Jasmin felt as if the world stood still at that sensation; she felt wobbly on her feet as they made their way to the other side. She took a deep breath to pull herself together.

He lifted a glass and asked, "Shall I fill this one for you?"

"Yes, thank you," she said smiling. He filled the punch glass half full and handed it to her, observing that glow again. In that instant he knew that she appreciated his serving gesture. Still smiling, he poured some into his own glass. "You made this evening a great success. What are your plans for tomorrow?"

"In the morning," Jasmin started to say, when Mrs. Harman came over to have some punch, "I'm going with Mrs. Harman to church and to stay at her house for lunch."

"How pleasant for you," Matthew said. "I had thought we would go to the open session here for dance practice in the evening. Will that be possible for you?"

Mrs. Harman cut in, "Jasmin, you could stay the afternoon and watch some television with us and have tea. Then Mr. Tyler could pick you up from our house." Turning to Matthew, she said, "Why don't you join us for tea at five thirty, and then you can go together from there?"

"Thank you very much, Mrs. Harman," Matthew said. Looking at Jasmin, he asked, "Is that agreeable with you?"

"Fine," she said. Matthew wrote down Mrs. Harman's address.

Jasmin looked around to see if anybody needed help with their gift boxes. She set her glass down and walked over to the diminishing pile of cartons. Some of the girls were helping the maid with clearing the wrapping paper and bows away, while others were saying their cars were full now and they were leaving.

Mrs. Tyler said, "In my car there's room for more boxes; in fact, I can have all these brought to Rose's address. I'll have Charles, my chauffeur, load them and take them to your door. If you go ahead, we will follow you."

Pete gave Charles the address of the store where he and Rose were going to live. Then he left with Rose in Jeff Kerr's car.

At the store, Rose and Pete opened the storage vault and with Jeff's help they stored the boxes as they came in. Mrs. Tyler waited patiently while Charles brought all their boxes right to the doorstep. Eventually, the others came and unloaded their cargo. Then Pete locked up and he and Rose got a ride to their separate flats.

After everyone had left, Jasmin said to Mrs. Worthington, "Thank you so much for providing this beautiful environment for the bridal shower."

"Oh, I was glad to be of help, my dear," Mrs. Worthington replied. "Ah, my husband came out of hiding," she smiled, seeing him standing next to Matthew making small talk about business.

They walked closer to them and heard Mr. Worthington say that he would make sure the pictures would be developed by a photography student who liked to practice his skill. "In fact," he added, "if the couple don't have a photographer yet, our man would be glad to do the pictures of the wedding as well; all they have to provide is the film."

Jasmin

Matthew turned to Jasmin and said, "Looks like you have another chore to co-ordinate." He smiled encouragingly. To that, she just tipped her head and smiled back.

"We shall be leaving now," Matthew announced, opening the door for Jasmin.

Mr. Worthington said, "Goodnight then; we will see you here tomorrow evening."

In front of his car, as Matthew opened it, he held Jasmin's hand in both of his. He squeezed her hand, saying, "You're doing a fine job, Jasmin," and then he assisted her into her seat and gently closed the door.

When he got in and the dome light was still on, he looked into her face and softly said, "I like looking into your blue velvet eyes." She blushed, and at that moment he again noticed that he had found one more thing to put that glow in her demeanor.

They drove in silence and when he walked with her to her door, he said, "I shall look forward to seeing you at Mrs. Harman's tomorrow. Good night, pleasant dreams."

"To you too," she said. Then she smiled and went inside.

Her Sunday outing was very relaxing and Jasmin enjoyed the conversation and interaction with the Harmans. They watched the news on television and anticipated the "London Palladium" that would be aired later. Then they decided to play Monopoly for a while.. At tea time Jasmin offered, "What can I help you with, Mrs. Harman?"

"Thank you, dear," Mrs. Harman said, "you may set the table. The cutlery is in that drawer."

Jasmin found a linen cloth, laid out the silverware, and added napkins as well as a nice centrepiece of chrysanthemums to the table. Her mind wandered to Matthew, as she was joyfully anticipating his arrival, when Mrs. Harman came out of the kitchen with trays of sandwiches and scones. Then Mrs. Harman went back to the kitchen to bring raisin bread, jam, and butter.

Mrs. Harman said, "As soon as Mr. Tyler arrives, I shall bring the tea pot. Would you fetch the cream and sugar for me, Jasmin?"

"Certainly," Jasmin responded.

Promptly at five thirty, the doorbell rang. Mr. Harman got up from his armchair, walked to the vestibule, and welcomed Matthew. "Good evening, Mr. Tyler, it's good to see you, come in please."

"Good evening," Matthew greeted back. "Good evening ladies," he acknowledged them with a smile. He took off his hat and coat, and then followed Mr. Harman to the dining table.

Mr. Harman directed each person to their chair and then he sat down himself. Matthew said, "Thank you for having me." Mrs. Harman came with the teapot and announced she would pour the tea. Matthew held Jasmin's cup up to be filled and then his own. He also passed the cream and sugar to her first before helping himself and then passing it around to the hosts.

"Please help yourselves," Mrs. Harman encouraged them, pointing to the sandwich trays and scones. Matthew lifted a tray in front of Jasmin to let her take something, and then he passed it around to the others.

"Have you had a lovely day so far?" Matthew turned to Jasmin first, then the others.

"Yes, thank you," Jasmin said, and the others agreed. "We watched some television too, which is a new experience for me. In Germany the television is still in the beginning stages and not as common in most homes as it is here."

Mrs. Harman directed her question to Matthew, "How have you spent your afternoon so far?"

He swallowed his bread and said, "My friend and I selected two deserted country roads that ran parallel to each other and tested the speed limits of our cars, checking our stop watches as to who arrived first at a designated spot."

Mr. Harman chirped in, "Yours was the first, no doubt?"

"Well, yes," Matthew admitted.

"Is yours a race car?" Mr. Harman probed.

"It's a Jaguar sports car," Matthew corrected. They talked about current events and winter sports.

Jasmin interjected, "In England, ballroom dancing is considered a social sport which includes square dancing and formation dancing. The large dance halls are built to accommodate competitions and practices, but they are open to the public as well. They only serve soft drinks."

"You are very knowledgeable about that, aren't you?" Matthew asked.

"Yes," Jasmin answered. "Mr. Worthington taught that in our English class."

"Dancing is one sport I'm really getting to enjoy with Jasmin!" Matthew reported while rising from his chair. Matthew pulled Jasmin's chair back and took her hand as she rose to leave with him. Mr. and Mrs. Harman said a few more words by thanking them for their company. Then they helped their guests into their coats and wished them a good evening.

When Jasmin was seated inside the car, he reached over to help her with the seatbelt. As he closed her door and went around to get in himself, Jasmin thought, "I don't know how long I can stand this tension; first the touch of his hand, and now the closeness of his face as he fastened the seatbelt." She took a deep breath and made up her mind to be placid.

At the studio, several couples had already arrived and introduced themselves to Jasmin and Matthew. They stood around in small groups while Mr. Townsend selected the records. He announced the beat of the tune and encouraged them to start dancing. To Matthew and Jasmin it sounded somewhat unfamiliar, and so they sat that one out. Matthew said, "Your dress is very becoming, Jasmin; it suits your personality. And I like the way your name rolls off my tongue; I could say it all day long."

Jasmin lowered her eyes and shyly said, "Thank you."

When the music stopped, Mr. Townsend gave a short lecture. "Although the ladies should have learned their steps, it's up to the gentleman to lead. The lady is to follow his lead, and not get ahead of him. The object of ballroom dancing is for two people to move in unison. Also," he continued, "the sequences you have learned here fit this room; however, in a large ballroom with many people it's wise to go with the flow. Here you may do a few straight steps and turn and go along the other side of the room, then turn etc., but in a large rectangular room you will have to adjust your steps along the line of dance, doing more straight sequences until you get to the corner. Then turn; you'll have to watch out for other dancers. I will give you an example."

He beckoned one lady from the group to join him. He held her in dance position and did a routine that Matthew recognized. Then he stopped and explained how to adjust this for a larger room. He demonstrated this clearly. "And remember ladies, your posture must be head erect, shoulders back, firm but not rigid." He finished his talk and escorted the lady back to her partner.

Matthew bowed before Jasmin and led her to the dance floor. They listened for the beat and moved in unison down and around the room. Mr. Townsend promised to teach something new after the break. By now everybody who was coming to the open session had arrived.

Jasmin

As they drank some Orange Crush, one couple spoke to Matthew and Jasmin: "Hi, we are Verna and Lloyd. You two are new here, aren't you?"

"Yes," Matthew laughed. "This is our first lesson. You can tell, can't you?"

"Oh, no," Lloyd said, "you dance very well together. I meant that we haven't seen you here before."

"I'm Matthew Tyler and this is Jasmin Claudius."

"What a beautiful melodious name," Lloyd exclaimed. Matthew felt a possessive streak, but before he could figure out what to do about it, Verna asked, "Are you the barrister Matthew Tyler?"

"The one and the same," he replied.

They watched as Mr. Townsend introduced a couple who were to demonstrate a new step. The couple showed four steps that could be incorporated into a routine at any time. When the music started they did it again a few times and then Mr. Worthington had everybody line up and copy it: first without music, and then with music. He encouraged them to do these steps once per round. After that, the last dance was announced and Lloyd came over and asked Matthew if he could dance with his partner.

"Ask the lady," said Matthew with a gesture to Jasmin.

Lloyd bowed and Jasmin said, "As long as you don't make me stumble; I don't know too much yet." Then she rose up and followed him to the floor. Lloyd led Jasmin into a twirl that looked attractive.

Matthew planned his strategy by analyzing his opponent's tactics, just as he would have done in the courtroom. He stood up and countered Lloyd, smiling, "That was an interesting maneuver you did there, is it difficult?"

"Not at all," Lloyd offered.

Matthew said, "Dance with Verna and show me how you do it."

Lloyd motioned for Verna to come over. He held her and said, "Just a flick of your wrist with your right hand on her hip, while you hold your left arm high above her head and guide her through the turn."

Matthew followed the motions on his own and then asked Jasmin to do it with him and it worked.

"Thanks Lloyd, you're a good sport," he said.

On the way home, Matthew said, "You've had two full days, haven't you? How do you feel?"

"It has been exhilarating and exhausting at the same time," Jasmin sighed. "I find that my social life can take more energy than daily work routines."

"Would you change anything if you could?" he asked.

"No, not really," she said. "You can't have all work and no play; you need both. I like the work that I do and I like people."

He asked, "Do you like my company?"

She cocked her head and said with a flirtatious smile, "It's tolerable."

"Tolerable enough to accompany me to Rose's wedding? She gave me an invitation, you know," he asked expectantly.

"Rose invited you?" Jasmin asked.

"Yes, she did. Is that so hard to fathom? I am a nice guy, or haven't you noticed?" he said.

"Well, we might bump into each other there," Jasmin conceded.

"I could give you a ride to the wedding," he offered.

"We'll see," she said. "Actually, my pastor asked me if I could help decorate the church for Christmas next Sunday afternoon."

"Oh, I'd be glad to take you to church," Matthew cut in. "Are you staying for lunch at their house too?"

"No," Jasmin said, "he is not married."

"Why don't I take you to church and lunch afterward somewhere and then drop you off back to the church for the afternoon? Then I could come back in the evening for the dance routine at Worthington's. Don't forget we still have Saturday afternoon booked for new lessons."

"Matthew Tyler, you have my head spinning with your premeditated planning," Jasmin laughed.

"Is it a deal then? We can firm it up on Saturday when I pick you up at two thirty. I won't see my tropical flower for a whole week."

With that, he stopped at her hotel, helped her out in his usual gentle way, and took her to the door. "Goodnight, Jasmin."

"Goodnight, Matthew," she whispered, and went inside.

"Smiler," came a shout from the booth.

"Ernest, are you back?" Jasmin asked.

"Yes, for good," he said.

"Were you away on vacation?" she enquired.

"Well, sort of. It was a sad occasion though. My sister passed away and I went to the funeral. Now I have nobody left on the whole earth," he said sadly.

"Oh, I am so sorry for your loss," Jasmin said kindly. "But you know you're not alone; all the staff here love you. We're like a large family." She held his hand, patted it, and went to the elevator. She made up her mind to get him some flowers.

Her thoughts went back to the evening's activities, and she thought about how comfortable she was with Matthew. She enjoyed the dancing routines and tried to analyze her emotions. There was no sensation in the closeness or movements because she was highly concentrated on her deportment and steps. She also felt good and as light as a feather when she danced with Lloyd, especially when he'd led her to turn around in a spin. She chuckled to herself when she recalled the competitive spirit in Matthew when he challenged

Lloyd to show him the new movement. He had wisely told Lloyd to dance with his own partner to display it.

Now, she recalled the sensation she felt when Matthew expertly flicked his wrist and made her spin. With that thought she drifted off to sleep.

The next day at the Danish Snack Bar, Matthew ordered his lunch. At an opportune moment, he asked Carla, "Tell me, is Jasmin seeing anybody seriously?"

"Well," Carla said slowly, "there is this aeronautical engineering student who took her out a few times."

"Anyone else?" Matthew asked.

Carla leaned over and whispered like a conspirator, "She let him kiss her hand."

Matthew raised an eyebrow, but put on a poker face nonetheless. "One more thing," he started again, "I want to give Jasmin a surprise birthday party. I need to get her to my mother's house under false pretenses. Do you want to be in on it? You can bring a friend. I'm going to ask Rose and Pete. Could you ask Maureen and her boyfriend? Here's a card with my home address. It's on Saturday evening at seven. I'll be by on Friday at lunch to firm things up."

"O.K.," Carla said, and she went about her business with other customers. Rose at last came over to hand Matthew his bill and he asked her also to come to the surprise party with Pete, to which Rose said they would be thrilled to come.

On Tuesday, as they were getting ready to go out to the coffee shop, Jasmin said to Carla, "I'll stay long enough until Roger is there at Prego, then I will have to excuse myself to go on an errand."

"Good enough for me," Carla said with sparkling eyes. "I'll keep him entertained."

They ordered their cappuccino and waited until Roger arrived out of breath, apologizing for his delay, which was only two minutes.

Jasmin

He didn't have a car and had missed an earlier bus. "So what's going on with you guys?" he asked after he had ordered his own drink.

"We pulled off a surprise bridal shower," Carla said. She told him how they had Rose completely in the dark about it to the last second, and how she was almost blinded by all the flash cameras, and how it was a great success.

"The pictures should be ready soon," Jasmin added. After hearing what Roger had to say for a while, Jasmin got up and said she had to get some flowers for a person who was mourning and so that is why she was leaving early. "Carla still has time on her hands though. Bye Roger," she waved.

When Roger got over his disappointment, Carla said, "I want to tell you a secret: we're planning a surprise birthday party for Jasmin. She is going to be twenty-one, and the same people who helped her with the arrangements for Rose's shower are going to host this party for Jasmin. Would you like to come? I have the address here. I'm glad I have this opportunity to talk to you about it, because I wouldn't have known how to contact you otherwise."

"Oh, that is splendid. Sure I would like to be in on it. When is it?" he asked.

"This Saturday evening at seven," Carla informed him.

"How will you be getting there?" Roger now asked.

Carla answered, "I'll have to get a ride with somebody."

"I can pick you up," Roger offered. "I usually get a taxi for anything special anyway. I can be at the staff entrance by six thirty, if you can be ready by then."

"That's great. I'll be right at the door looking through the window for you," said Carla.

"O.K., we are all set then. Let's call it a day. That gives me time to get something I have in mind for Jasmin," Roger said.

"Me too," added Carla. "See you, ta, ta."

Jasmin went to the International Floral Boutique to select a suitable arrangement for Ernest. The florist asked about the occasion and the age of the person. Jasmin explained that he was in his early sixties and bereaved because his only relative had passed on. The florist suggested a small arrangement with chrysanthemums in brown and yellow with a yellow rose in the centre. When she asked her name to write on the card, Jasmin said, "Jasmin Claudius."

The florist asked, "Like Jasmine without the 'e'?"

"Yes," Jasmin replied.

The florist wrapped up the arrangement and placed it into a box. She gave it to Jasmin with the admonition to tell the person to water it. "That way," she said, "it will last a month."

Jasmin smiled, picked up the box, thanked her, and left. The florist let her eyes follow Jasmin through the window until she was out of sight. Jasmin took quick steps across the square, crossed the street to the hotel, and walked around the side to the staff door and down the steps to see if the timekeeper was still on duty.

There he was, shuffling some papers. When he looked up he said, "Smiler, what have you got there?"

"Ernest this is for you," she said, handing him the box.

"For me?" he asked, "What's in it?"

"Open it up," she encouraged him.

He still hesitated, so she lifted the tissue paper that loosely covered the top. "These will help dry your tears and have good memories about your sister every time you look at them. There are instructions of how to care for them."

"Thank you my dear," he said with tears in his eyes. "You are so thoughtful. I will never forget this."

"God bless you," she said. "I must get to work now." She punched in her card, went straight to her private closet, donned her smock, and went to the kitchen for supplies.

Jasmin

When Jasmin got to the Concordia Bar, she checked to make sure everything was in order and refreshed. She glanced over to the bar to see if they were ready to open, and only saw the junior bartender. Leaning over her counter she asked Richie, "Where is Martin?"

"He is delayed for a few minutes. I am going to open up tonight," Richie called back.

As soon as the doors opened, customers streamed in, and Jasmin got busy with oysters. Richie mixed the cocktails and served drinks. Since Richie couldn't leave the bar, Jasmin had to go over to fetch the drinks for her own guests and also take food to the tables in the alcoves. Finally there was a lull and Martin came rushing in. Jasmin was still busy writing up the bills as best as she could remember, and she piled them up on the spike so he could take them. She saw him talking to Richie while looking at her. Jasmin went out the swinging door and took a sip of ice water, then came back in and sat at her bar stool in the corner behind her counter making notes.

Martin came over to take the bills off the spike and said, "That was a pretty decent thing you did for Ernest. The word is getting around that you are a real angel of goodness."

"Oh, that," Jasmin said quietly. "He was so sad about his sister dying. I remember mourning my grandmother, whom I loved dearly. I know what it is like when a close loved one has departed and I wanted him to be consoled."

"He is consoled alright," Martin said.

At that moment a customer came by, sat on the barstool, and said, "I'll have some of that French onion soup you serve here."

"Certainly, Sir," Jasmin said. "Would you like French bread or bread sticks?"

"I'll have French bread with just butter, thanks," he said. To Martin he ordered, "You can bring me a lager and lime."

"Sure, Sir," Martin walked over to the bar and brought it back to him.

"What a pleasant place this is," the guest said after a while. "I am from Leeds, actually, and I have several contacts here in the city and the surrounding areas."

"Do you need a city map?" Jasmin enquired.

"Yes," he said. "I thought about that. I shall have to get one somewhere in the morning."

"Oh, we can get one for you," Jasmin waved to Martin and met him at the interior swinging door, whispering, "Fetch a city map."

Martin signaled to Richie that he would be right back. Within a few minutes he came with map in hand which he gave it to Jasmin, who placed it in front of the guest.

"Thank you very much," he said.

She pointed to a spot on the map, saying, "This is where we are." She took a pencil and marked it for him.

"You'd make a good secretary," he said.

"Customer service," she said smiling, tipping her head slightly.

He motioned for the barman to come over to write up his bill. "Well, I'll be going up to my room to study this map and compare it with the addresses I have in my file. Put a drink for the lady on my tab will you?"

"Sure," Martin said, looking at Jasmin. "Usual?" he asked, meaning the amount of money the drink would cost.

She nodded, then said to the guest, "Thank you kindly; I'll have it later."

After he left, Richie and Martin exclaimed, "With the money you make on tips, you could buy this joint."

Jasmin laughed then said, "At this point I am replenishing my education fund."

Jasmin

Alma Loren, the florist at the International Floral Boutique, was looking at the clock and considering closing up when she heard a car coming to a screeching halt in front of her store. A gentleman emerged from the vehicle and walked straight to her door. As he entered, she recognized him. "Mr. Tyler," she smiled, "you gave me a start with those squealing tires."

"I wanted to get here before you locked up. I apologize," he said.

"Apology accepted," she replied. "What can I do for you?"

He took a deep breath and asked, "How much notice to you need to order a genuine Jasmine flower made into a wrist corsage?"

"Jasmines from Spain will take from five to seven business days," she said. "The wrist corsage can be prepared when it arrives. Are you in a hurry for it?"

"As a matter of fact, I am," he said. "It will have to be here for next Saturday the thirtieth at the latest."

"I can check with my supplier now, if you would like to wait," she offered.

"Fine," he said. While she was on the telephone, she looked at Mr. Tyler and pointed to a chair in a corner beside a display table for wedding flowers. He walked over towards it, chiding himself for having waited so long. Then his eyes fell on some pictures and he imagined Jasmin in a wedding gown with a bouquet in her hand.

He was jolted out of his daydream when the florist called him over. "Mr. Tyler, we can have the Jasmine by next Thursday. That gives us Friday to prepare it and it can be delivered the same day or Saturday morning."

"That's splendid," he exhaled a sigh of relief.

She took a pen in her hand and asked, "To whom is this to be delivered?"

"Miss Jasmin Claudius," he said.

"How appropriate," she paused. "Address?"

"On second thought," he said, "I'll pick it up myself. I shall pay for it now."

"As you wish," she responded.

On Thursday, Mrs. Goddard cut her lunch hour short to go to the International Floral Boutique to select the bouquet for Rose's wedding. "Hello Catherine," the florist greeted her, "what a pleasure to see you. Do you have time for a cup of tea? I'm just brewing one."

"Yes, Alma, thank you," answered Mrs. Goddard.

Alma carried the tea tray over to the wedding display table, brushed the magazines aside, and motioned for Catherine Goddard to take a seat. As she poured, she asked, "Any special reason for your visit today?"

"Just a bouquet of pink carnations for next Saturday's wedding. This is a small affair for Rose, one of our waitresses at the Danish Snack Bar. They are having a civil ceremony, but will have a party in the evening. I'll pick up the bouquet, because it is a secret gift."

"Talk about secrets, I tell you," started Alma, while sipping her tea, "I'm dying to know who a certain young lady is."

"Oh?" Catherine questioned.

Alma began, "On Tuesday this beautiful girl came in and bought a small arrangement for a gentleman who was bereaved. She signed her name as Jasmin Claudius. Then yesterday, Mr. Tyler, you know of Tyler Associates, came by and ordered a real Jasmine flower from Spain, he paid five pounds for it, and guess who this was for?"

"Jasmin Claudius!" they said in unison. Mrs. Goddard laughed out loud.

"What's so funny?" asked a very perturbed Alma Loren.

"That girl," Catherine Goddard said, after she took a quick sip of tea, "that girl, Jasmin, is considered by all the kitchen and restaurant staff to be an angel. Ernest the timekeeper was so distraught and depressed about the loss of his family member that it affected his

Jasmin

concentration on the job and nobody knew what to do for him. Then Jasmin got him those flowers and spoke comforting words to him. It made all the difference in the world to his demeanor. And two weeks ago she singlehandedly organized a bridal shower for Rose and Pete who are getting married, but had no money to spare because they spent all of their savings on that chocolate shop with an apartment above the store, so somehow Jasmin got Mr. Tyler's mother and Mrs. Worthington together to arrange a bridal registry at the Carlton. All the invited staff purchased the gifts and met at the Worthington studio for the secret bridal shower. On top of that, she talked Mr. James of the Birkdale Lodge into allowing his facility free of charge and the food half price to the guests. Mr. James even offered to provide free wine for the toast, so Rose and Pete don't have to pay anything. Even before that, when the Concordia Bar was renovated, the management was hoping to make a go of it and hadn't had much luck with advertising. Out of the blue Jasmin was interviewed by the newspaper and spoke so graciously that the bar and the hotel as a whole is doing a tremendous business."

"Wow, quite a report. How does Mr. Tyler fit into this?" queried Alma. "He ordered a wrist corsage for next Saturday. I presume we are talking about the same wedding?"

"Yes," said Catherine, "I suppose that since there isn't a formal wedding party, or bridesmaids who need bouquets or corsages, he didn't want to show them up by making Jasmin wear one. So the wrist corsage is somewhat more discreet. He is her escort. I think he has been looking for a reason to get her flowers."

"Is that all?" asked Alma.

"From what I overheard," Catherine said, "at the party there was another middle aged lady, a motherly friend of Jasmin's called Mrs. Harman. She said to Mrs. Worthington that Mrs. Tyler was hoping they'd be engaged. I think he is waiting for her to be twenty-one. Let's see what happens."

"Pretty formal courtship!" Alma considered.

"I'd say," Catherine agreed.

Matthew Tyler finished his lunch on Friday and leaned over the counter to task Carla, "All set for tomorrow?"

She nodded, "O.K."

"Where is Rose?" He looked around till he saw her come out of the coffee pantry. "Rose, I've got to leave; do you have my bill?"

She wrote it up and handed to him, "Here you are."

He whispered to her, "Are you all set for Jasmin's birthday tomorrow? Everyone else also?"

"We wouldn't miss it for the world," she assured him.

Matthew zipped down the road in his Jaguar and parked in front of the jewelry store. He went straight to the desk and told the attendant, "Quick, there are only ten minutes allowed for parking. Do you have the bracelet I ordered?"

She looked in the drawer and took out an envelope with Matthew's name on it. Then she opened it and showed him the slim box with the bracelet inside. "Would you like me to gift-wrap it?" she asked.

"Yes, please, if you don't mind," he said, checking his watch.

"No trouble at all." She swiftly wrapped it, expertly put a bow on the box, placed it into a shopping bag, and handed it to him.

"Thank you, goodbye," he rushed out and drove down the road a few more blocks.

Luckily there weren't any parking restrictions. He stopped at the theatrical agency and was greeted by the owner. "Ah, Mr. Tyler, here is your receipt and the information. The magician and his assistant have their own transportation, and they know your address and phone number. They will be at your place at six forty-five sharp."

"Good, thank you," Matthew said, and they shook hands goodbye.

Now, Matthew had to get to the Justice Building since court had been recessed until three p.m. He had fifteen minutes to get there. He took a shortcut through a one way street, which took him to the parking lot at the back of the building. He locked the gift in the trunk, took his briefcase, and entered the building with five minutes to spare. After a short deliberation, the case was dismissed. Matthew shook hands with his colleagues and went to his office to organize his files. He was about to go home, but first he pondered for a while if he should go to see Jasmin at her workplace. He imagined other fellows being interested in her, and felt a tad jealous. He dismissed that, and told himself that she doesn't date customers. He was proud of her. "What about me," he thought, "would she have dated me when she was still at the Danish Snack Bar? Probably not. But now I am officially courting her and I am sure she'll welcome another letter."

At his house he began with that task. First, he took the gift box and locked it in his safe, and then he found his mother in her sitting room and gave her the information about the entertainment.

She said, "We will have the party and the entertainment in the drawing room. When will the guests arrive?"

Matthew said, "They should all be here between six forty-five and six fifty-five. I'll try to be a little later, something like five after seven."

Mrs. Tyler commented, "Emily will see to the door, and when you arrive, she'll give us all a cue for the lights out."

"All right," Matthew said. "Then I will bring Jasmin into the vestibule and say, 'Come with me; I shall get the lights,' and then you can flick the lights on and surprise!"

His mother clapped her hands with glee, and said, "Great."

After supper, Matthew retired to his office. He sat at his desk and put his head in his hands. Then he closed his eyes and let his mind wander for a while before reaching for the envelope and putting Jasmin's address on it. He laid it aside. Then he took the perfumed paper and began to write:

My very dearest Jasmin,

The more I see you and have conversations with you, the fonder I grow of you. The aura of your presence illuminates the atmosphere around you. Your smile can heal a wounded soul.

Your compassionate care brings out the best in everyone. Your true desire to please people is so admirable, you personify angelic virtues.

I am very much drawn to you in my wish to explore what makes you happy, to seek out and fulfill your heart's desires.

What will give you fulfillment over and above knowing you have done a good job or helped someone in a special way?

You are of such incomparable beauty, inimitably delightful, so wonderfully poised. Jasmin, in my imagination I inhale the fragrance of your name.

I wish to be the one who showers you with good things from a caring heart, giving you comfort and encouragement when you need it, and offering you all the intangibles of unconditional love

Jasmin

just because you are you. The time transpiring until our next meeting feels like pure agony, yet sweet anticipation.

I am your humble servant,
Your true admirer,
Your truly devoted,
Your adoring,

Matthew Tyler

He blew a kiss on the paper before he folded and inserted it into the envelope. Then he put a stamp on it and slipped it into his coat, as he intended to mail it in the morning.

The next afternoon, he waited in anticipation for Jasmin to emerge from the staff door. She was prompt as usual. As he assisted her into the car, he heard the rustling of her skirt fabric. When she was settled inside, she loosened her outer coat because it was quite warm in the car. Before he started the engine, he looked over at her and noticed the dress she wore. He said, "That is a pretty dress you have on; is it new?"

"In a way," she answered. "My sister, the fashion designer, made it for me especially for the Plum Festival. I haven't worn it since."

"No occasion to wear it?" he probed.

"Not exactly," she replied.

He noticed a shadow of sadness pass over her countenance and asked, "Any other reason?"

She had now collected herself and said, "It did have an unpleasant memory attached to it."

Matthew had slowed the car down and pulled over to the side. When he stopped, he looked full into her face. "A broken heart?" he asked gently.

"Yes," she whispered.

"Jasmin," he said seriously, "I would never break your heart." They held the look for a moment, then Jasmin lowered her eyes, took a deep breath, and smiled. He started the car again and they rode in silence till they reached the dance studio. "Remember, we have two dancing sessions today. We can't come next Saturday because of the wedding," Matthew reminded her with a smile.

Mr. Townsend welcomed them and started right into the lessons. He reviewed what they had learned previously and the new steps which they had picked up at the open session. He showed them a new dance called the Foxtrot, a slower version of the Quickstep with longer strides. He then gave them the names of certain step sequences. "The standard steps, you should know by heart, but if you lead the lady into an intricate step pattern, you should prepare her for it," he said to Matthew. "I'll demonstrate for you." Mr. Townsend explained, "Furthermore, typically you will do a twirl only at the end of the dance in the Quickstep. In the Foxtrot, you will do the lunge, or the fanning out, same as the Waltz."

He put the record on the record player and played the song "Fascination", to which Matthew and Jasmin thoroughly enjoyed dancing.

"In the next lesson I will show you the Tango. It has what is called a staccato movement. These four dances are designed to flow around the perimeter of the ballroom."

He introduced them to the sound and beat and demonstrated the movements. He told them the upper body has to be rigid, whereas the knees should be bent. They should grip the floor firmly with their heels during the fast twists and turns so as to keep their balance. He showed them one basic routine, then he let Jasmin and Matthew practice their steps individually. Next, Mr. Townsend did the steps with Jasmin. At last he put Matthew and Jasmin together. He counted

Jasmin

and made them count and dance, first without music and then with music. As he watched, he admonished them, "Head erratic to the side, sharp turn, bend knees, twist, toe kick, carry on."

Matthew said, "This one is right up my alley; I like it the best."

Jasmin laughed and asked, "Are you sure there isn't some Spanish in your ancestry?"

Now he laughed too. "There may well be, perhaps Italian or French, who knows. How about you, Jasmin?"

"I have French ancestry," she said.

"You don't say," he said in awe.

They did one more routine until they had it down pat. Then Mr. Townsend showed them one variation called the Contra Check. He admonished Matthew to warn the lady beforehand, since he had to support her firmly and it was fast. They did that over and over again, until they were out of breath. As they walked to their chairs for a break, Matthew said, "That movement feels - French, for lack of a better expression."

"Argentinian!" Jasmin corrected.

Matthew laughed and asked, "Jasmin are you teaching me new words?"

Jasmin put her nose up. "Just imparting my knowledge unto you, Mr. Tyler."

He rose from his chair. With a flair he made a mock salute, took her hand, and said, "Much obliged, Miss Claudius." At that moment time stopped. He slowly lifted her hand to his lips and kissed it, looking deep into her eyes. She let her hand linger and looked into his eyes, awestruck.

A door opened, breaking the spell, and then Matthew released her hand with a smile and she smiled back. Mr. Townsend, who had left the room earlier, came back and said, "One more round before we call it a day? Let's do the new routine in the Quickstep so you won't forget it. Tomorrow evening you can practice all you have learned."

When they had finished their routine they headed for the door. Matthew helped Jasmin into her coat and they entered the car.

Jasmin thought, "The dancing is like an exercise in gymnastics, but the sensation I felt when he held my hand and kissed it is one I have never experienced before."

Matthew thought, "I saw a connection in her eyes when I kissed her hand." Out loud he said, "I know a quaint teahouse not too far from here; shall we go there for tea?"

"Thank you, that will be fine," she said.

They came to a cottage with a thatched roof nestled among trees and shrubs. "Oh," Jasmin's eyes filled with tears.

"What is it?" Matthew asked in distress, "is it something I said?"

"Oh, no," Jasmin swallowed, smiled, and said, "Just a flashback to my childhood."

"Let's go in and you can tell me all about it," Matthew said, turning towards her. "I want to drink in every nuance of your life."

SURPRISES

The tea room had several tables dressed with embroidered tablecloths which were situated near windows overlooking the garden. Floral room dividers between each table gave privacy to the conversations. The hostess directed them toward a table for two with a lit candle in the centre. Matthew held out a chair for Jasmin and then he sat down also. Jasmin looked outside and back at him and said, "How delightful."

"I am glad it pleases you," Matthew said.

The waitress came with tea and a sandwich platter. Matthew offered the tray to Jasmin, and after she had taken a couple of sandwiches he served himself. He began, "Jasmin, I do wish to hear what brought on the change in your emotions."

Jasmin sighed. "I was reminded of my childhood when I visited my grandmother on the farm. She had a ground floor apartment adjacent to the main house that was occupied by the caretaker. He had leased it from my father while he served in the military. One of the barns had a thatched roof that housed a large stork's nest. The storks fed on frogs in the ponds, had their young in the nest, and many congregated on the peak of the gable. I used to sing to them, 'stork, stork, bring me a baby brother or a baby sister.' That homestead was to me the epitome of comfort. After the war our property was confiscated by the communists and the Iron Curtain prevented us from ever visiting there again. We couldn't even go to my grandmother's funeral."

Matthew put his hand on hers, and said, "Jasmin, I'm so sorry you had to experience such loss in your young life, but believe me: for every loss there's a new beginning. You have your whole life in front of you and I want to be there for you till you find happiness." He released her hand and looked at her encouragingly.

She smiled and said, "Thank you."

Between bites of sandwiches, Jasmin asked him about his youth and upbringing. He talked about his college days. He had spent one term at the Sorbonne in Paris, France.

Jasmin looked in awe at Matthew and said dreamily, "Fascinating!"

He smiled and accepted her admiration. Matthew went on to say that he had joined his father in his legal practice, until his father had passed away seven years ago. He said he enjoyed his profession but his hobby was fast cars.

He then brought the subject back to the present by saying, "My mother has a seamstress over at her house with several samples of dresses for the Regency Ball. She would like you to try some on. I'll take you there and drive you home afterwards."

"That's wonderful!" she said.

He took her arm as they walked out onto the gravel driveway so that she wouldn't trip with her high heeled shoes. It was dark by now. He looked at his watch and saw that he still had fifteen minutes before Jasmin's surprise birthday party. He didn't want to arrive at his destination too soon in case any of the guests were late, so he said, "Let's take a quick spin up the country road; you game?"

"O.K.," she laughed.

"Put your seatbelt on," he admonished.

Once he was out of the parking lot, the car gave a roar as he pressed the gas pedal hard and sped down the road. After a few miles, they finally came to a halt. "How was that?" he asked.

"Hilarious and scary," she said.

"O.K.," Matthew consented, "we will go at a normal speed now."

When they arrived at his front door, he cautioned, "Take my arm, there are two steps." She did, fully trusting that they would be expected by Matthew's mother, but when they came inside, it was dark! Matthew held her hand and guided her through the hallway. Suddenly a bright light blinded her, followed by a loud "Surprise!" shout.

She fell back into his arms, and asked, "What's this?"

"Don't you know what day this is?" he whispered.

Before she could answer, "Happy Birthday to you," sounded from the crowd. Now she recognized Rose, Pete, Carla, Maureen, Martin, Roger, Jeff Kerr, the Harmans, the Worthingtons, and Mrs. Tyler. "Happy Birthday, dear Jasmin," the song ended.

She put her hands on her cheeks. "I'm totally shocked," she said. "I don't know what to say, thank, you, thank you!"

Everyone crowded around her, wishing her well.

Matthew said, "Let's have champagne."

Jeff Kerr assisted in popping the bottles and filling the glasses while Rose and Carla led Jasmin to her honour seat. They sat beside her, with the mature ladies next, and the men sat behind them in a semi-circle.

Mrs. Tyler announced, "Before we give the gifts, we have some entertainment for you." She clapped her hands and motioned for everyone to join her.

In came the magician with his assistant. He bowed in three directions and pulled out several silk scarves from Jeff Kerr's lapel pocket. He neared Roger and pulled out of his jacket pocket some coins, and out of Matthew's waistcoat a deck of playing cards. Everyone cheered and hollered. The assistant held his top hat and produced a rabbit, and then he somehow disposed of it behind his cape. The team presented several other tricks with batons, doves, mind games, and a juggling act.

After being heartily applauded, they left, and then Mrs. Tyler announced, "It's gift time. Gentlemen, you may replenish the drinks, and Carla and Rose will assist Jasmin." Two of the guys placed the chairs to face the half circle and they moved the oval coffee table with the gifts in front of Jasmin.

She received tiny figurines suitable for a mantel or bookshelf as well as small charms, wall plaques, and picture frames. From Roger she received a figurine of an airplane. The card read, "A memento of the long conversations we shared about aeronautics. Sincerely, Roger."

The gift of a diamond bracelet from Matthew was accompanied by these words, "A little bird told me you play tennis. Let this tennis bracelet enhance your wrist. In fondness, Matthew."

Jasmin said, "I'm absolutely stunned and overwhelmed by your kindness for the party, the gifts, and your friendships. Thank you again." The hosts and guests cheered.

The maid announced, "Supper is served."

A buffet at the side wall displayed finger foods with salad plates at one end. Mrs. Tyler led the way and she encouraged the group to follow Jasmin and help themselves. Jasmin took a plate and placed a perfunctory Petit Four on it, and then she moved along to let the others partake of the goodies. She was still too excited to eat.

Out of the corner of her eye she saw Matthew talking with Roger. Jasmin went up to Maureen and Martin. They raved, "What a fine party; you deserved that."

"Oh, I don't know about that. I feel so humble and pleased at the same time. I had no clue. How did you keep it so secret, Martin?"

Nudging Maureen, he mumbled, "That was easy; I didn't even know about it until yesterday." They had gone in on a wall plaque gift together.

"So next thing on the agenda is Rose's wedding isn't it?" Martin affirmed.

Jasmin replied, "Yes," as she moved over to Carla, who had just come back from thanking Mrs. Tyler for having invited her to such an extravagant party. "Have you invited Roger to Rose's wedding?" Jasmin asked Carla.

"I was about to, when Matthew steered him away," she replied, looking in their direction.

"I wonder what they're talking about," Jasmin voiced.

"Probably about you," Carla commented.

"It looks jovial enough, not like they are about to have a duel." Jasmin laughed.

Rose came over. "Having fun?" she asked.

"Let's go have some punch." Jasmin took the two by their arms and moved to the punch table.

A few moments earlier, Matthew had scanned the crowd for unfamiliar faces, walked over to Roger, and introduced himself with an outstretched hand, "Matthew Tyler."

"Roger Halliday," said Roger, shaking the hand Matthew held out. "Good party," Roger began.

"Glad you could join us," Matthew replied. "Have some food."

"I don't mind if I do," was Roger's response. "The university cafeteria doesn't have delicacies like these." He filled his plate, took a bite, swallowed, and said, "Great that Carla invited me. I've been meaning to find an occasion to give that plane model to Jasmin, and this presented itself as an excellent opportunity."

"Have some punch," said Matthew, while devising a strategy to avert Roger's interest in Jasmin. He sauntered over to the younger group, put on his most charming smile, and said to Carla, "Carla, your guest is thirsty," pointing to Roger. "Offer him some punch." Carla followed his cue. She filled a glass and motioned for Roger to sit at a side table. She sat down with him and talked him into coming to the wedding with her next Saturday.

A couple of hours later, as the guests were preparing to leave, Matthew asked, "So, did you guys have a good time?"

"Best party I've ever been too," Martin said.

"Me too," echoed the others. "Thanks for having us."

"Thanks for coming," he replied.

"Thanks for making my birthday so memorable," Jasmin said. She looked over at the older couples who were about to leave and moved towards them. Matthew followed.

"It was a lovely party, very entertaining," they said to Matthew and his mother. "Happy Birthday again to you, Jasmin."

Eventually, everyone left. Mrs. Tyler busied herself with the maid and cook, and Matthew said to Jasmin, "I shall take you home too, but first let me put on your new bracelet for you."

"Oh, Matthew, I couldn't accept something so expensive from you," she hesitated.

He had already taken the bracelet out of the box and lifted her hand. "Hold it steady," he said. "No strings attached. A twenty-one year old young lady deserves to have an appropriate birthday gift, there," he said, fastening the clasp. He stroked her wrist, let her hand rest in his for a moment, and then let go.

He suggested that they let the maid box the rest of the gifts and he would bring them to her place another day. She thanked him for being aware of her curfew. On the way home, he looked at her to see her reaction to the happenings of the day - the glow.

Matthew asked, "Did you have a good time?"

"It was amazing," she said. "Nothing could have topped it."

"Nothing?" he asked.

Jasmin inhaled, then said dreamily, "Nothing; you know there's a German saying, 'wunschlos glucklich'; this means totally happy without a wish."

"My ambition is to make you totally happy, Jasmin," Matthew said with emotion in his voice.

"Matthew, you are so good to me, thank you," Jasmin answered.

"I'll be here in the morning," he said as he took her to the door. "See you," he waved. She waved back with her new bracelet glittering in the moonlight.

Matthew made a beeline home. He wanted to check the box that the maid had brought up for storing the presents. Emily was half finished re-wrapping them when he arrived, and he said, "I'll be glad to finish that task for you, thank you so much." He searched till he spotted that airplane model. He held it in his hand, felt the patina, and mumbled to himself, "That must have cost him a bundle." He looked up, staring into space. "I wonder how close their relationship was or is. Maybe it would be wise for me to check out the competition. Whom do I know at the faculty of the university who might be working on Sundays? Chaplain? Librarian?" Before he went to sleep, it came to him: "Professor Mayberry, he lives on campus." Bingo!

On Sunday morning, Jasmin got ready for church. She wore a slim black dress with a short "A" line jacket, and she carried a small suitcase and her purse. Matthew greeted her, "Good morning, Jasmin. Would you like me to put your suitcase on the back seat?"

"Yes please," she said.

"You look 'très chic' in that attire," he said admiringly.

"Thank you," she smiled back at him.

When she put on her seatbelt, the bracelet slipped forward to the back of her hand. Matthew noticed it immediately. After he had started to drive, he said, "I see you're wearing your new bracelet; it's very becoming on the black sleeve."

With a sigh she said, "I couldn't take it off last night, so I just kept it on."

"You mean you slept with it; did it give you sweet dreams?" he laughed lightly.

"I slept soundly, thank you, Mr. Tyler," Jasmin pretended to put on a formal face.

"I know I would have sweet dreams if I had something of yours on my pillow," he teased.

"Not going to happen," she said, "but I appreciate your sense of humour."

At the church, they were welcomed by the pastor and Mr. and Mrs. Harman stood close by. After exchanging greetings with some other people, they sat in the same row as the Harmans. The Pastor spoke about the virtuous woman of Proverbs, 31, 10-31. KJV. When the service was over, Matthew whispered in Jasmin's ear, "I couldn't have described you any better than that."

Jasmin said to Pastor Gruber, "I shall be back around two to help with the decorations. Which door will be open?"

Jasmin

"I'll show you the side door," he said. When Matthew and Jasmin followed his lead, he continued, "There will be a couple more people to help as well. Thank you for helping, see you later."

Matthew took Jasmin to the same tea house as before, and he said, "I have made reservations for brunch, you will like it." During their meal, Matthew asked, "Are there any more nostalgic places you remember?"

"Believe it or not, I travelled more in my earlier childhood, because of the refugee crisis. Every time I formed a friendship it was interrupted by another move, and it became more difficult to make lasting friendships. I have bittersweet memories," Jasmin sighed.

Matthew laid his hand on hers and said admonishingly, "I hope our friendship is going to be a lasting one."

Jasmin closed her eyes for a moment and answered, "So do I."

"One more thing," he added, "I'm sorry about that trick I pulled on you, saying it was going to be a dress fitting. I could not think of a better reason at the time. Will you forgive me?"

She laughed lightly, "Well it was a pleasant deception, hopefully the only one, yes."

"I promise," he said. "Notwithstanding there's going to be an actual dress fitting at the rental shop. It's in the block next to the International Floral Boutique, and within walking distance of your hotel."

"I've seen the sign," Jasmin said.

"It will be the following week after Rose's wedding," Matthew said. "I'll tell you the exact time next Sunday."

"Yes, thank you, and thank you also for brunch," Jasmin said.

"You are more than welcome," Matthew replied as he held out her jacket.

When they arrived back at the church, Jasmin asked Matthew, "Would you hand me the suitcase please? I'm going to change my outfit in the church."

In the church auditorium, some young people were opening boxes of decorations when Jasmin and Matthew entered. Pastor Gruber came towards them, saying to Matthew, "Why don't you come back at five thirty for tea? The ladies group is setting it up for the helpers, and there will be plenty to eat."

"I might just do that, thank you," Matthew said. Turning to Jasmin he said, "See you later."

Matthew estimated the time it would take him to go to the university and back and was satisfied he could make it easily with traffic being light on weekends.

Something was brooding in his mind. "How could a bookworm like Roger Halliday manage to have two girls interested in him? What does he have that I don't have?" He could only come up with, "It must be his intellect."

The campus was located in the centre of the city, so Matthew parked on the street. He walked directly to the library, not needing any directions, as he still had alumni membership to the law library. Out of the corner of his eye, he saw somebody coming in the same direction with books in his arms. When he got closer, he recognized Roger. "Good," he thought, 'I won't have to inconvenience the professor.'

"Hello there, Roger, good afternoon, study work completed?" he stretched out his hand in greeting, Roger took it with his free hand.

"Good afternoon to you too, yes, partially, I have to pick up one more textbook though."

"Looks like you need a break; want to check out some aerodynamics on the ground?" Matthew offered.

"What do you have in mind?" Roger asked.

Jasmin

"I'll take you for a spin in my Jaguar," Matthew said.

"Now?" asked Roger excitedly, totally forgetting that he had been about to ask Matthew what had brought him here.

"Sure," Matthew assured him, "as soon as you drop off your books. I'll wait here at the copy centre."

Roger's opinion of Matthew was that of an elder brother. He had no animosity toward him, although he perceived that Matthew had won Jasmin over. He took his books back and found the new one he was looking for, checked it out, and rejoined Matthew.

Matthew was still in thought about how to formulate his question about Jasmin, when Roger opened the conversation with, "Carla asked me to go with her to Rose's wedding you know, we're each paying our own way, but do you think I should get a flower or something else for her?"

Matthew thought, "That's music in my ear." Out loud he said, "Definitely, something small like a corsage or a wrist corsage, pink carnations. They can do that at the florist for you and you would just give it to Carla when you pick her up. Do you need a ride?"

"Oh, no thanks, I've already booked the taxi for Saturday; thanks anyway."

When they reached Matthew's car, Roger's fingers felt the smoothness and the curvature of the lines of the exterior. As he got in and fastened his seatbelt, he glanced over at the dashboard and let Matthew explain the meaning of the symbols to him; his analytical mind comprehended everything immediately.

While Matthew slowly drove his car out of the city limits, he ventured to ask Roger innocently, "So, how long have you known Carla and Jasmin?"

Roger replied, "Carla recently, but Jasmin I've known since she didn't even speak enough English to complete a sentence."

"Is that so?" Matthew raised an eyebrow.

"Yes," Roger said, "but she's a good listener and a good friend."

They had reached the isolated road that Matthew used for fast driving. "Hold on, here we go," he announced, and within sixty seconds he was up to full speed, racing down the lane. He slowed down as they came to a crossroad and went at a steadier pace. "What do you think about that?" he asked Roger.

"Excellent acceleration," Roger said. "Engineers who make good quality cars also make good airplanes."

"I've never flown before," Matthew said. "Have you?"

"Yes," Roger said. "It's similar to your car, as there is a 'rush' when you're going up in a plane and when you're flying in the plane. But there is a different 'rush' when you're at the controls and taking off. The sensation is indescribable; out of this world, no pun intended."

"Fascinating," Matthew said. "We'll get together again sometime after next Saturday."

They had arrived back at the university and Matthew let Roger out of the car. "I'm glad to have made your acquaintance, see you again."

"Same here, goodbye," Roger waved his hand.

Matthew pondered the situation. He could tell that Roger highly respected Jasmin and valued her friendship. He felt somehow accountable to Roger as if he wanted his approval. He would like to make it known to him that his intentions for Jasmin were honourable.

When he arrived back at the church he went through the side door and observed the change in the décor. He walked to the back where he saw an opening and discovered as he came closer that it was the kitchen. Some ladies had prepared a long linen-covered table ladened with goodies. They were putting on the finishing touches, when one turned and said, "Good evening."

Jasmin

Jasmin, now wearing a different outfit, said to the lady, "Mrs. Kramer, this is Mr. Tyler."

Mrs. Kramer said, "I'm pleased to meet you, Mr. Tyler. I'm Pastor Gruber's housekeeper."

"Pleasure to meet you too," Matthew bowed slightly.

Pastor Gruber emerged from a group he was talking with and encouraged everyone to take a seat at the table. He looked around, bowed his head, and said, "Let's give thanks." Everybody closed their eyes, and then he prayed, "Lord God, we give you thanks for this house to worship in and bless all the willing helpers who decorated it for this Advent season. Now bless this food we are about to partake. Amen."

When tea was over, Matthew and Jasmin excused themselves and said goodbye. Pastor Gruber saw them to the door and said, "Hope to see you next Sunday?"

"Possibly," Matthew said.

In the car, Matthew offered, "I would certainly like to take you to church next Sunday; will that be fine with you?"

"I think so, thanks," replied Jasmin.

At the dance studio, a teaching couple introduced the Rumba. The gentleman explained it was an ideal dance for a small dance floor. Unlike formal ballroom dances where partners move close together in the same direction, in this Latin dance, partners are positioned apart and do separate steps from each other. The couple directed the men to one side of the room and the ladies to the opposite side. The teacher showed the steps to the men and his partner showed the steps to the ladies. They counted the beat and explained one-quarter turns, three-eighth turns, and full turns.

When they thought that everyone understood, the teacher took each lady and danced with them so that they would get the right feel for it. His partner did the same with the men. After that, Mr.

Worthington put the record onto the record player and the teacher counted the beats and called out the figures. He then encouraged the students to take their partners and do the steps without music, just by counting and memorizing moves. Finally, they allowed the music to be played, but over it they counted for them the beats, steps, and moves. After the break, everyone was encouraged to form two circles with ladies on the inside and gentlemen on the outside. Then they moved one step over to the next person, did a routine, then the next one, until each had danced with a different partner once.

After two or three other dances, the evening came to a close. Matthew said to Jasmin, "You look like poetry in motion when you do those moves."

Jasmin laughed, "I don't know about that; all I can think of is 1 2 3 4, turn one-quarter, etc."

Matthew said again, "It looks good to me, though I've only got eyes for you, and I like what I see."

Jasmin lowered her eyes, took a deep breath, and let him put her coat over her shoulders. They left for the parking lot. Inside the car, Jasmin turned to him and asked, "Matthew, would you be so kind as to unclasp the bracelet for me? I can't do it on my own and I shouldn't wear it at work. I have the case for it right here." She pulled the case out of her purse and held it open with her other hand.

He said, "I will gladly do it." She held up her wrist. He released the clip and let the bracelet slip into his fingers, then he held her hand for a moment and placed a kiss into her palm while looking deep into her eyes wordlessly for a few seconds before putting her hand down. He placed the bracelet into the jewelry case, still looking at her, smiling all the while. He didn't want to disturb the magic. Finally he placed the case into her lap and started the car. She opened her purse and slid the case into it, still in a daze.

Jasmin

When they arrived at her hotel entrance, Matthew said, "I have the box with your gifts with me. I'll carry them to the elevator door for you."

"That is so considerate of you, thank you." Jasmin took her small suitcase out of his hand. He took the box, opened the staff door, held it open for her to get through, and walked with her to the elevator. He waited till it opened and handed the box of gifts to her.

"Can you manage from here?" he asked.

"Yes, thank you dear. Goodnight, see you next week," Jasmin replied. She realized what she had said as the elevator closed.

To Jasmin, all the routines of work became celebrations of love. She felt a team spirit with the staff. She kept up with her lessons and homework. When she went downstairs to punch the time clock, the timekeeper called her over to his booth.

"How are you today, Ernest, are you taking good care of your flowers?" she asked.

"Yes," he said, "they're doing fine. Their fragrance fills my whole house."

"Wonderful," she said.

"Here's a letter for you, Smiler. It looks special. I didn't want to put it into your card slot, out in the open." He gave her a delicate envelope.

She knew exactly what it was. She thanked Ernest and quickly put it into the pocket of her smock. Up in her room, she stretched out on top of her bed and opened the letter. She imagined Matthew's voice when she read the lines. She read them over and over again to let them sink deep into her soul. Jasmin folded the letter, took out her treasure box, unlocked it, and placed this letter with the other one.

She took out her stationery and began to write to her brother:

Karin Allaby

Dear Hans,

I hope this finds you well. There's something I need to discuss with you. Remember when we were at our house and two village boys came over one evening? We all played a board game and one wanted to take me out on his new snowmobile. You stated, "If any of you dare to get fresh with my sister, you have to deal with me." You scared them off for sure. I'm laughing now. Other times you said I was too young to have a boyfriend. The last time we talked, my heart was emotionally broken because although it seemed I had been honourably pursued, it had all burst like a bubble. Now I have met a fine man; I've known him for almost a year. He introduced me to his mother, he takes me to church, he speaks to me kindly, and he likes everything about me. He is courting me and intends to ask Father for my hand. He is disciplined and we never go beyond holding hands, although I would welcome his embrace. He wrote me two letters similar to the one I received from Dietrich, when I was a teenager. He describes me in superlatives. I know that beauty is in the eyes of the beholder, but I believe he really wants to please me and win my heart. He is an accomplished lawyer. He is serious but not somber or stuffy. He is understanding, like you. He witnessed my confirmation and believes like I do. Somehow I feel he is the right man for me and the time is right, but I have a fear that won't let me go, that something will happen to stop the dream from becoming reality. Even from

Jasmin

a distance you surround me with your prayers, please continue.

Your special sister,

Jasmin

The next day, before her morning shift, Jasmin gave the letter to the timekeeper for mailing.

On Friday afternoon, during their break, some of the kitchen and restaurant staff lined up at the office to receive their paychecks from the office assistant. Mrs. Goddard sat behind her desk and watched out for Pete and Rose. When she saw them, she called them over and handed the wrapped bouquet and an envelope to Pete. "Here's an anonymous gift for you two." Rose was aghast, but Pete took it and thanked Mrs. Goddard. Some of the guys in the line clapped their hands and let the couple pass by them out the door.

Matthew, after a long day in court, folded his papers, said goodbye to his client, and made a beeline for his office. Myrna his secretary was still in the office and she handed him a slip of paper with a message to call the florist. He took the message, gave the files to her with several instructions, and said, "I'll call the florist from my office."

When he sat down at his desk, he dialed the number.

"International Floral Boutique, Alma Loren speaking," a voice said.

"Hello, Mrs. Loren, Matthew Tyler here."

"Mr. Tyler, I have your Jasmine flower prepared," Alma Loren replied. "It will have to stay in its airtight container in a cool place or refrigerator until the last minute."

Matthew asked, "Will the conservatory do?"

"As long as the temperature isn't over ten degrees," Mrs. Loren cautioned.

"I'll come right over and look at it," Matthew said.

He closed his office, told Myrna to have a nice weekend, and drove to the florist.

When Matthew entered the flower shop, Mrs. Loren was waiting for him and she led him directly to the cooler where the finished Jasmine corsage was mounted inside a clear plastic case. Around the wristband were tiny petals crested with seed pearls on silk.

"Ah," he said, "it's magnificent."

She said, "I'll demonstrate to you how to place it on the wrist." She directed him to the mannequin and wrapped a sample on the forearm of the doll, showing him where the small Velcro fastener was. She added, "If at any time you wish to change it into a regular corsage to be worn on a dress, you will find two pins in the side of the mount. Ideally," she continued, "you wait until the lady has deposited her coat in the cloakroom before placing the corsage on her wrist. When it's taken off later, it can be put back into the box and you have to blow air into it like so," she showed him on an empty box. "Close the box decisively; that way it will keep for up to two weeks in a cool place."

"So," he queried, "I should transport it in the trunk of the car because it is cooler, rather than inside with the heater on?"

"Yes, definitely," she assured him. "There isn't any frost yet."

"I'd best leave it here then until the last minute tomorrow. You close up at six thirty, don't you?"

"Yes," she said.

"I shall be here at six fifteen then."

He turned to leave, then asked, "One more thing: did Roger Halliday order a corsage?"

Jasmin

"Yes, he did. He picked his up already; it doesn't need to be refrigerated," she said.

"Goodbye till tomorrow," Matthew said when he left the shop.

"Goodnight," she waved as she locked the door.

Jasmin looked into her closet and pulled out the new dress she had bought earlier in the month. It was still in the garment bag. She pushed the bag up and felt with delight the velvet, and then she laid it out onto the bed. The black velvet dress had a bow neckline and small shoulders without sleeves. It was fitted in the waist and hips and clung to mid-thigh. The attached flared black satin skirt reached to the knees. This was held by a wide satin sash and tied into a large bow at the side below the right hip. Jasmin decided that to complete the outfit she needed long black satin gloves. She went to the same specialty store where she'd obtained her dress, and sure enough, they had what she was looking for.

Now she still had to keep her hair appointment at the beauty salon she frequented once per week that was down the street from the hotel. The Swiss hairdresser often tried out new styles on her. This time he asked if she wanted the flip that was so popular. Jasmin looked at the picture of it first, and then said, "Go ahead."

Kurt then added, "Your hair is so easy to work with; it has the right length for this new creation I will design." When his work was completed, he gave her the hand mirror to see the back of her head. He exclaimed, "It looks like a halo around you."

Jasmin chuckled as she stood up, and joked, "Let's just stay with the flip."

Kurt said, "Close your eyes," and then he added more hairspray. As they walked to the cashier every head turned to look at her and everyone clapped their hands.

Jasmin crossed the street, turned to the right at a fast pace, rounded the corner of the block to the staff entrance, and went down the steps. She rushed to the elevator, pressed the button to the third floor, and took a deep breath.

Ernest the timekeeper came out of his booth, followed her with his eyes, and shouted, "Smiler, what's the hurry?"

The bell dinged, the door opened, and Jasmin went in. She shouted back, "I'll tell you later."

Nellie and Beatrice stood leaning against the cupboard, smoking cigarettes, when Jasmin entered the door. It had been about six months since she had been promoted and she had not kept in contact with them. Surprised, they put out their cigarettes in the nearby ashtray and stretched their arms out to her. "Jasmin," they cried together. "We haven't seen you in such a long time."

"You look fantastic," Nellie said.

Beatrice added, "We heard about that bridal shower you pulled off for Rose and the posh wedding reception; you must have friends in high places."

"Just kindhearted people," Jasmin replied modestly.

"You want a cup of tea and something to eat?" asked Beatrice. "We were just going to send this fresh leftover tray back down with the dumb waiter. Look, it's chicken and ham salad with croissants."

"You know what?" Jasmin said, "That would just hit the spot; thank you. I haven't had any breakfast or lunch yet. Let me just go down the hall and wash my hands, then I'll show you what I bought."

Nellie put the kettle on while Beatrice prepared a luncheon plate for Jasmin. Nellie poured a cup of tea for Jasmin and when she came back she pulled over an extra chair to the tiny round table so that Jasmin could eat there. Jasmin said between bites, "Look in my shopping bag."

The ladies carefully undid the tissue paper and held the black satin gloves. Nellie slipped her fingers into one and asked, "Are these for tonight?" She carefully put them back into the wrapping.

Jasmin answered, "Yes, they will complete my outfit."

Beatrice exclaimed, "We have to see that. What time are you leaving?"

"I'm being picked up at six thirty at the staff entrance," Jasmin informed them.

"We will be here till seven, so why don't you stop over on your way out; we absolutely must see it." They both eagerly awaited her answer.

"O.K." Jasmin said. "Six twenty."

Jasmin went up to her room; now she had two hours to get ready. She so wished she could have a nap, but that would spoil her coiffeur and she didn't want to risk that. So she sat on her chair in front of the dresser and began carefully applying foundation cream and powder. She was about to put on mascara, when Carla came into the room.

"I like your hair," Carla said, and then she proceeded to get her own wardrobe ready. "Roger is picking me up a half hour early so that I can be at the Lodge to bring those place cards you gave me and match them up with the seating plan."

Jasmin waited until Carla was gone to do her eyelashes without interruptions. Then she held her eyes steady for a few minutes so that the mascara wouldn't smear. At last, she stepped into the black velvet dress. It had a long zipper she couldn't quite close and Jasmin wished that Carla had stayed to help her. She decided to go a little earlier to the third floor pantry and ask the ladies there for help. She put on the gloves and jacket and picked up her clutch purse. She checked if anything was amiss, but everything seemed fine, and so she took the elevator down to see Nellie and Beatrice. Nellie was tidying up while Beatrice was putting stuff into the dumb waiter. They smiled when Jasmin entered the swinging door.

"Here you are, girl; let us look at you," said Beatrice.

"First," Jasmin said, "I need help with my zipper." Nellie held the jacket while Beatrice zipped her up.

"Turn around," said Nellie.

"Oh, you look gorgeous," both of them exclaimed.

Beatrice slid her fingers up Jasmin's forearm, pulling the gloves tighter at the top, and then helped her into the cape-like jacket. She fluffed up the collar fashionably and said, "I will escort you down and hold the door so that you don't have to touch any door handles. What time is it?"

"Six twenty-five," said Nellie. "Have a fantastic evening, ta, ta."

Beatrice pressed the elevator buttons and walked with Jasmin to the exit door. "What kind of car does your beau drive?"

"A Jaguar." Jasmin was nervous by now...

"I see one stopping," said Beatrice. "He is coming to the door."

Beatrice held it open for Jasmin, and said, "Good luck, kiddo." Turning to Matthew, she said, "Good evening, Sir."

Jasmin held one edge of her dress as she ascended the stairs. Matthew stretched his hand towards her and bent his elbow to assist her up the last two steps.

"You are a vision of loveliness, Jasmin," he said while leaning over to open the lock of the passenger door.

She looked up at him and said, "Thank you," as he helped her into her seat, closed the door, and smiled and glanced back to the entrance where Beatrice still stood staring. He gave a wave with his hand, and then she waved back and finally closed the door.

When he got in, Matthew asked lightly, "Was that your 'lady in waiting'?"

Now Jasmin giggled, and said, "In a way."

Matthew started the car, drove off, and said, "You deserve attendants and 'ladies in waiting', Jasmin."

Jasmin

"Oh, I don't know about that," she said. "I would probably be bored with that. I prefer 'gentlemen in waiting'."

He laughed and remarked, "Touché."

When they arrived at the Lodge, Matthew went around the back of the car and opened the trunk to retrieve the box with the corsage. Then he opened the passenger door for Jasmin. He let her out and said, "I have something for you; I will give it to you inside."

He took the box to the cloakroom and set it on the counter. The attendant took his hat and coat and then Jasmin's jacket. Matthew opened the box and said, "Jasmin, this is a Jasmine wrist corsage made especially for you for this occasion. Let me assist you in placing it on your wrist."

Jasmin gasped, awestruck, and lifted her hand closer to her face to inhale the fragrance. "It is absolutely divine." She looked at Matthew with the most endearing expression.

He said, "Your glowing smile is worth it all."

He turned to the attendant and asked, "Would you please keep the box safe until we leave?"

"Yes, of course, sir; I'll put it right next to your hat." The young man stared in wonder at the scene while Matthew put a quick tip on his tray. "Thank you, Sir."

Matthew offered his arm to Jasmin as they rounded the corner to the dining room. Mr. James spotted them and his eyes lit up as he recognized Jasmin. "Miss Claudius, what an absolute delight it is to see you." He stretched out his hand. She shook it and then introduced Mr. James to Matthew.

Mr. James, acting as the master of ceremonies, encouraged the guests to form a line up so that when Rose and Pete entered the door, they could be greeted by everyone. Carla beamed as she showed off her corsage that Roger had bought her. Jasmin smiled approvingly, and then everyone turned their heads to the opening door to see the photographer come in backwards, camera pointed at the advancing couple.

As Rose and Pete became visible, everyone clapped and cheered for them. The couple were greeted and congratulated by each guest as they inched their way to their table. Maureen and Martin sat beside them at the head table.

Mr. James directed the Worthingtons, the Harmans, and Mrs. Tyler to their table and Matthew, Jasmin, Roger, Carla, and Jeff Kerr to the opposite table. Pete's father and Mrs. Goddard shared a table with friends of Rose and Pete.

Mr. James announced that dinner would be served, and then he poured the wine for the toast. Since there was only one waiter, the barmaid and Mrs. Tyler's chauffeur helped serve the meal of roast turkey with sage and onion stuffing and all the trimmings, so that it was done speedily.

Pete's father offered the first toast and for the next hour all the men offered up toasts. Then began the clinking of the glasses to encourage the couple to kiss. After the dessert of plum pudding and crème brûlée was served, the band began to play some favourite numbers.

The bride and bridegroom took to the floor and danced the first dance. Rose then danced with Martin. Pete danced with Maureen, followed by Pete dancing with Jasmin, and Matthew dancing with Rose. Pete said to Jasmin, "Thanks for everything; this is a great party."

Jasmin replied, "Are you glad you're tying the knot?"

"Absolutely," he answered. "You will be the first one we'll invite to our housewarming party."

Matthew asked Rose, "Who would have thought I would be dancing with a bride?"

"Have you caught her yet?" Rose asked.

Jasmin

"Pretty soon," he said.

Rose commented, "The way you are looking at Jasmin I have no doubt it will be soon."

"I'm working on it," he said.

Roger danced with Rose and Pete danced with Carla. Then Pete said he was going to sit the next one out so that Rose could dance with Jeff Kerr.

They alternated until everyone had taken a spin with either the bride or the bridegroom. Then everyone was encouraged to dance.

Matthew bowed before Jasmin, "May I have this dance, fair lady?" Jasmin rested her hand in his and rose smoothly from her chair. "You may, noble knight," she consented.

"I don't know which is more intoxicating: Jasmine or Jasmin," he whispered in her ear.

"Take your pick," she said.

"The next beat do you want to do the toe tap?" he asked.

"Go ahead; you lead," she said.

When they had finished and were about to return to their seats, the music began to play again. Matthew said, "Your dress is definitely a Rumba dress. Let's do this."

They held their position, counted quietly, and moved in unison. He led her into one variation, then another, and he whispered, "Wave step." She complied. They did the patterns they had practiced and didn't even notice that everyone was staring at them. Matthew and Jasmin finished the dance and stopped as if they were in a trance; the applause broke the spell.

Mrs. Tyler whispered to Mrs. Worthington, "I wish there was a way I could hurry up the wedding for these two."

Emma laughed and replied, "It will come soon enough."

Matthew and Jasmin had barely sat down when Roger asked Jasmin to dance with him.

Jeff Kerr said, "You beat me to it." Leaning towards Jasmin before she advanced to the floor, he asked, "Can I be next?"

"Sure," Jasmin said.

Matthew stated, "I'm sitting these ones out."

Roger said to Jasmin, "I see Matthew is sweeping you off your feet."

"Oh," Jasmin corrected, "we're just practicing what we learned at the dance studio. Would you like to join us? There is an open session for new guests. You can bring Carla; it costs nothing the first time."

"Really?" Roger asked.

"Sure," she said. "We'll talk about it before we leave."

Jeff Kerr waited for the music to start and bowed before Jasmin. "Shall we dance?"

They had danced a couple of rounds when Jeff said, "You don't happen to have a sister like you, do you? I sure would like to meet her."

Jasmin laughed as they twirled around for the last time. "Not exactly, but someone might come to mind some time."

He said, "You are exceptional and you're full of surprises. I'm a better person for having made your acquaintance. Thank you for this dance." He smiled and led her back to Matthew, Carla, and Roger. Mr. James joined them in saying goodbye to Pete's dad and Mrs. Goddard, Martin, and Maureen as they were leaving.

Jasmin said to Mr. James, "Thank you for making this evening's celebration such a success." Matthew added, "It's a fine establishment you have here."

Mr. James accepted the compliment, saying, "Thank you. I hope to see more of you in the near future."

Mr. and Mrs. Worthington had already left, giving a ride to the photographer. Mr. Harman got up to fetch his wife's coat. Mrs. Tyler

Jasmin

said to Mrs. Harman, "Would you and your husband like to come for tea tomorrow at five?" Mrs. Harman answered, "Oh thank you, that is most gracious of you,"

Mrs. Tyler's chauffeur announced that the car was out front. So she rose and walked over to Matthew and Jasmin, saying, "I've invited some people over to our house for tea tomorrow. Please bring Jasmin, Jeff, Roger, and Carla."

"Will do," Matthew nodded. He looked at Jasmin and asked, "Shall we leave then?" He gently took her arm when they reached the cloakroom and said, "Shall I take the corsage off your wrist?"

"Please do," she answered. Matthew adeptly removed it and held her hand with the flower up between their faces so that they could both take in the fragrance. He looked long into her eyes and kissed her palm. She felt a tingle all through her body and blushed; he let go and smiled.

He looked for the attendant and saw Mr. James, who offered to help. "Let me get your coats. Is this the box for the Jasmine flower?"

"Yes," Jasmin and Matthew said simultaneously.

Mr. James handed Jasmin's cape to Matthew, who placed it over her shoulders. He gave Matthew's coat to him.

Roger and Carla came around the corner for their coats. Matthew asked, "How are you getting home?"

Roger replied, "We're going to call a taxi."

"I can give you a ride," Matthew offered.

"Really?" Carla shrieked.

"Sure," he said, turning to Roger. "Are you O.K. with that?"

"Fine, thank you," Roger acknowledged.

They squeezed into the back seat, and then Matthew flipped the front seat back in place to let Jasmin inside. He put the flower inside the trunk, secured it with a strap, and then he got in the car himself. "Is everybody O.K.?" he asked.

"Yes, great," was the unanimous answer.

"Don't forget to put on your seatbelts," he admonished, looking to see if Jasmin's was also strapped in. Then he put the engine in gear and cruised at the speed limit through the city to the hotel. When they got out, Matthew said to Jasmin, "I'll be here at ten thirty in the morning to take you to church, alright?" Then turning to Roger and Carla he said, "I'll pick you up in time for tea tomorrow." Jasmin and Carla went to the staff door, while the guys watched till they were inside.

"O.K.," Matthew said to Roger, "now you can get in the front seat."

"I see you've swept Jasmin off her feet," Roger blurted out. "Just so you know, she's a special person and deserves the best. I value her friendship."

Matthew answered, "I appreciate and respect your feelings, but I can assure you I've only the best in mind for Jasmin. I have honourable intentions. Furthermore, she has given me permission to court her."

As they drove the short miles to the university campus, Matthew said, "I've been meaning to see Professor Mayberry tomorrow anyway, so why don't I pick you up afterwards from the library at around four fifteen, unless you like me to come earlier. We can have some fun on the road. I know a different route for a fast run. Maybe I'll let you take the wheel!"

"Not unless you let me teach you how to fly an airplane some other time," Roger inserted.

"Deal," Matthew said. They parted jovially. Matthew parked the car in his garage, took the box with the Jasmine flower out of the trunk, and went straight to the conservatory. He opened the case a sliver, blew air into it, and closed the case tightly as the florist had instructed him.

THE MATCHMAKER

As the girls entered the elevator, Carla said, "What a night. That was amazing. Thank you Jasmin for everything, for acquainting me with Roger, for arranging this party in that place, and now for getting me invited to tea tomorrow. I can tell Matthew's mother really likes you, and for that matter, so does Roger still, and of course there is Matthew."

Jasmin giggled, and said, "That was quite a mouthful, and thank you for doing your share to make this party complete. As far as Roger goes, I think Matthew will win him over. They could form a good friendship. That reminds me of something," she stopped as the elevator door opened. "Let's unwind in the room and I will tell you before we turn in."

In their room, Carla said, "I'm going to soak in the tub, so tell me now."

"O.K.," Jasmin said. "Do you remember Mrs. Benson who invited me to her house when I still worked at the Danish Snack Bar?"

"Vaguely," Carla admitted.

"Well, I have corresponded with her daughter, who said she might want to see me on her Christmas break. If she shows up at the Danish Snack Bar and asks for me, give her directions to come over to the Concordia Bar, O.K.? Tell her I serve lunch too."

"O.K., why?" Carla asked. "Oh, never mind; I know you have something up your sleeve."

"Thanks," Jasmin yawned. "I'm going to bed now; I have to get up early in the morning. Can you undo my zipper?"

"Alright. Goodnight, sleep tight."

On Sunday morning Jasmin took the jewelry case out of her memory box and put it in her purse. She went downstairs to wait for Matthew, who was prompt as usual. Inside the car, before he started the engine, Jasmin asked, "Matthew, would you put the bracelet on for me?"

He said, "I would be delighted." He clasped it on her wrist and stroked her fingers lightly.

As they drove, Matthew asked, "Have you rested up and recovered from the hectic day yesterday?"

Jasmin said, "Recovered, yes, from a beautiful day and evening, but not rested enough. After church I would like to take a nap until you pick me up for tea, O.K.?"

"Glad to oblige," Matthew said.

In church they sat with the Harmans again. Mr. Harman said, "The decorations are very festive."

Mrs. Harman added, "They're beautiful."

Matthew whispered, "You've done a magnificent job, Jasmin; you've created an elegant, inviting Christmas atmosphere."

The service was very uplifting and ended with a children's choir. Matthew had a vision of seeing children of his own there one day

Jasmin

- he looked at Jasmin. She looked at him with big eyes and then lowered them. Her blush was visible.

Mrs. Harman said to Matthew, "I notice you've been transporting your friends around; are you picking up Roger?"

"Actually, yes, I am," he answered.

"Mr. Harman and I would be happy to pick up Jasmin and Carla on our way into town and bring them to your place for tea," she offered.

Matthew turned to Jasmin and asked, "Will that be alright with you?"

"Oh, yes, certainly. Thank you very much, Mrs. Harman," Jasmin said.

"We'll be at the hotel at four forty-five," Mrs. Harman confirmed.

Matthew and Jasmin drove in silence for a while, and then he asked, "What are you thinking?"

"Secret," she said.

He said, "Do you want to know what I am thinking?"

"No," she answered.

"That means that we are both thinking the same thing," he laughed. "One day the secrets will be revealed," he carried on.

"I'm not nosy," she tilted her head up.

"I am," he said. "And you know what; I will know by Christmas," he stated with certainty.

"We'll see," Jasmin smiled.

They arrived at her hotel. Matthew took her to the entrance and said, "Have a good rest; I'll see you later."

Matthew went home to change and have some tea and toast, and then he set out to see Professor Mayberry. After a few pleasantries, the professor walked with him to the library and directed him to the *Law Society Gazette* so that Matthew could find a case law precedent. Matthew thanked the professor and walked with him over to the copy centre. They said goodbye and Matthew busied himself making a few copies. He looked through the glass partition just in time to see Roger entering the other department. He tried to catch his eye and when he did, he waved to him, and Roger waved back.

Matthew perused more of his reading material for some time until he heard a slight knock on the window. He looked up, and there was Roger pointing at his watch. He nodded in acknowledgement and rose to leave. When they met outside, Matthew said, "Let's take a detour home, shall we?"

"I'm game," Roger agreed.

They took a fast run up to an abandoned parking area near an old air strip. Matthew stopped and asked Roger, "Have you driven a car before?"

"No," Roger said, "but I know how to taxi an airplane before take-off and after landing."

"Well, you know the functions in principle. When are you going to get a car?" Matthew asked.

"When I graduate," Roger said.

"When is that?" Matthew enquired.

"Next spring," Roger replied.

"Come on, I'll show you, follow my movements and then I'll let you take the wheel." Matthew demonstrated how to check the mirrors and showed Roger where the reverse, neutral, and drive shifts were. Then he got out and let Roger sit in the driver's seat. Matthew talked him through the motions and Roger followed carefully. Matthew encouraged him again to go for about twenty feet and then stop. Roger did that precisely.

"Enough for today," Matthew laughed. "The ladies are waiting." They changed seats again and made it home in the nick of time before the Harmans arrived with the girls. Jeff Kerr came a few minutes later.

Jasmin

Earlier, when Jasmin had come into her room at noon, Carla had a tray with Danish pastries and tea, which she was ready to pour. "Oh, thanks," Jasmin said. "Perfect timing. I'll have some of that and I will take a nap afterwards."

"Good idea," Carla said. "I slept in, so I'm alright. I'm going to Room 608 to spend some time with the maids and catch up on their news, so you won't be disturbed. I'll be back by four."

While they were eating, Jasmin said, "You can pin your pink carnation corsage on again; it will look good on any dress. By the way, we'll be picked up by the Harmans at four forty-five."

"Great," Carla said before she left.

After her nap, Jasmin looked over her school material to refresh her memory. She checked her notes, made some additions, and put everything into a folder for the next class. She also did some typing drills to keep up her speed. Jasmin selected her outfit for the evening, feeling the thrill of anticipation for when Matthew would again pin the Jasmine corsage onto her dress. He had said yesterday that it could be converted into a regular corsage.

When Carla came back to their room the girls reminisced about the wedding and how pleasant it had been. Jasmin asked Carla, "Did Roger say anything about the possibility of going to the dance studio?"

"Now that you mention it, he started telling me about it when we were interrupted."

"We'll see if it comes up tonight. Maybe even Jeff Kerr might go. It's free the first evening for guests. After that they just pay at the door, unless they take private lessons. There are only two more sessions and then they'll close for Christmas."

"We have to go downstairs," Carla said. "Our ride will be here."

The Harmans arrived just as Jasmin and Carla reached the door, and so they went out and got into the car.

When they reached the Tyler home, Matthew came out and opened the back door for the girls to exit. Then he opened the passenger door for Mrs. Harman. Mrs. Tyler welcomed them inside the house. Matthew looked behind him and saw Jeff Kerr arrive. He waited till Jeff got out and patted him on the back.

By now everybody had made their way to their designated seats. Jasmin was seated between Matthew and Jeff Kerr, which suited her just fine. Mrs. Tyler occupied the end seat. She started the conversation by drawing each guest out with questions, so that their answers made an interesting story. As the maid brought platters of croissants, mini sandwiches, scones, and raisin bread, the cook helped serve the tea.

After they had eaten, Mrs. Tyler encouraged everyone to visit the conservatory. They all stood up and stretched their legs. Matthew asked Jasmin, "Would you like to wear the corsage on your dress tonight?"

"Sure," she replied.

Matthew turned to Emily who was about to clear the table, and he asked, "Emily, would you bring us a pair of scissors please?"

In the meantime Roger struck up a conversation with Jeff Kerr about his car. "Is it a similar model as Matthew's?"

"Mine is a Porsche, a German import," Jeff replied. "I can give you a ride in it to the dance studio."

"That's just swell," Roger said, who now followed Carla to see the Christmas cactus that Mrs. Tyler pointed to as well as the Oleander from Bermuda.

Jasmin whispered to Jeff, "You might stay for the free dance sessions too."

"O.K. it's settled then," Jeff said, as he proceeded to catch up with the tour.

Jasmin

Matthew came back with the scissors that Emily had found for him and opened the plastic flower box. He took the Jasmine out and cut the strap off. He found the pins and said, "I wouldn't like to hurt you with these; I'm going to let a lady do it." He saw that Mrs. Harman had finished the tour and beckoned her over.

"Let me do it," Mrs. Harman said, knowing exactly what it was about. She pinned the corsage securely just below the shoulder onto the left side of Jasmin's dress. Matthew looked at Jasmin and Jasmin held his eyes.

Jasmin thought, "He only has to keep looking at me like that and I'm dazzled."

Mr. Harman said, "I'm amazed how well the Amaryllis andAfrican Violets are doing."

Thank you," Matthew said. "My mother has a green thumb."

Mrs. Tyler came out of the conservatory trailed by the young people who made admiring comments. She spoke to Jasmin, "Jasmin, dear, which afternoon will you have time off for the dress fitting?"

Jasmin thought for a moment and said, "Most probably on Wednesday, yes, between two thirty and four thirty."

"Fine," Mrs. Tyler said. "I shall meet you at the Society Attire Store at that time and, before I forget, if you ever need to get in touch with us, here is our telephone number. Somebody is always in the house to answer it." She gave Jasmin a small card with her name, number, and address on it.

Carla thanked Mrs. Tyler for opening her home to them, as did Roger and Jeff Kerr. Mrs. Tyler said, "I enjoy having young people around." Mrs. Harman stood with Mrs. Tyler for a moment, as Mr. Harman brought his car to the front.

Mrs. Tyler whispered to Mrs. Harman, "I do hope something significant happens between those two." She looked over at Matthew and Jasmin. "I'm inviting her to our house over Christmas. If it is convenient for you, would you join us for Boxing Day?"

"That offer is kindly accepted. Thanks for having us; we'll be in touch," Mrs. Harman said.

As Matthew drove with Jasmin he asked, "Jasmin, I do cherish these moments alone with you. Are you comfortable in my presence?"

"Comfortable?" she asked, pondering the question for a moment, and then she nodded her head. "I can say, yes."

"I will ask you more when we get together next week after the last dance lesson. We could go to the Ceylon Tea Centre, do you like that idea?" he questioned.

"I do, actually," Jasmin replied. "I enjoy being with you. It's a long week till we get together again."

Matthew gave her a concerned look. "Jasmin, if there's anything that can't wait till we meet again, please call me at my office. Here's my office number, and you already know my home number from my mother. Please!" He gave her his business card, and suggested, "Put it safely into your purse, O.K.?"

When they stopped in front of the Worthington Mansion, Jeff, Roger, and Carla had already arrived and were waiting for them. Matthew helped Jasmin out of her seat, took her arm, and greeted Jeff with "You beat us here."

"Not by much," Jeff said. "We weren't speeding, with the lady present."

Other couples arrived and they all entered the salon. Matthew introduced his guests to Mr. Townsend. Lloyd and Verna came up and encouraged the group to sit with them in the far corner.

"For the sake of the newcomers," Mr. Townsend said, "I'll show a few basic steps, and then we will do the round so that each experienced student can dance with a novice and vice versa."

Jasmin

Since Jeff was the only one without a partner, the lady who was supposed to teach the feature dance of the evening stepped in to even out the odd number. After the intro without music and checking if everyone had done it right, Mr. Townsend started the music and called, "Change partners." After everyone had gone through a routine, he called again, "Change partners." He did that ten times until everybody was back with their own partners. For the next few dances, some couples sat it out, but Matthew and Jasmin danced the familiar routines they had learned. Lloyd took Carla, Verna took Roger, and the new teacher took Jeff around the floor.

During the break, Roger said to Matthew, "That was great; thank you for inviting me."

Jeff said the same to Jasmin, "Good idea, thanks."

After the break, the guest instructors showed them the Jive. "It's American," they said. Jasmin's ears perked up, and Matthew noticed. He thought, "Is that another hidden desire of hers? The dance, or because it is American?"

As they observed the Jive in silence, Jasmin thought, "I'm not too keen on that over the head and on the floor, it is too much gymnastics, but I do like the twists and spins. I'm sure it will make my skirt flare up sharply."

Matthew thought, "I'm not so sure about the gymnastics of it but I do like the twists and spins; I bet Jasmin's legs will look good when her skirt flares up."

The instructors finished and Mr. Townsend said, "This was an exhibition routine. We will now show you the basic principles that will look sharp." They counted the beat and showed the easy steps of how to lead the lady into the spin and catch her so she doesn't overturn. The teacher showed the men's steps; the lady showed the ladies' steps. They made everybody copy them, then dance together, and then dance with music, all the time counting the beat.

The instructress partnered with Jeff. After the groups dispersed, Jeff and Roger took Carla home first.

Jeff took Roger for the promised spin on the fast track and said, "Next time I will let you take the wheel in the daylight."

As Matthew drove away, he asked Jasmin, "Did you have fun tonight?"

"I did indeed," she responded. "Matthew," Jasmin continued.

"Yes?" He looked expectantly at her.

"What I wondered," Jasmin continued, "is what kind of dress you would like me to wear for the formal party. I mean, I know it has to be long, but what kind of fabric do you like?"

He slowed down near a quiet street, stopped, and tried to formulate the words that cruised around in his mind. "You look amazing in anything you wear, yet the feel of velvet comes to mind. Does that help you?"

"Sort of," she mused. "We also have to consider what type of dance music they play. Will it be only Waltz and Foxtrot?"

"I hope Tango," he cut in.

Jasmin said, "I doubt they will play Jive, but I am going to be prepared just in case. I am forming a picture in my mind."

"I am sure you have a vivid imagination," he said. "Whatever you come up with will be outstanding and breathtaking at the same time."

He gently stroked her cheek with the back of his hand, then he started the car again and drove her home.

Before he opened his door, she gasped, "Oh, I almost forgot, the bracelet." She took the case out of her purse, held it open, and raised her wrist slightly. Matthew took the bracelet off, slid his hand under her fingers, and smiled. "I do look forward to seeing you next Saturday afternoon, and do you need the box for the corsage?"

"Oh, yes," she answered. "I can put it into my small fridge at work."

Jasmin

"Did I show you how to blow air into it then close it tightly?" he asked again.

"Show me again," Jasmin said.

He did and then he walked her to her door, held it open, and gave the box to her. "Goodnight, sweet dreams." He gave a quick wave and smile.

Matthew was elated when he got home. "She asked for my opinion, but more than that, she asked what I like. Does that mean she is beginning to want to please me? Well, I'm not going to be presumptuous. I'll take her advice and sleep on it," he chuckled to himself.

On Monday lunchtime, Mrs. Benson and her daughter Alicia came to the Danish Snack Bar. They were about to take a seat at the food counter when Mrs. Benson asked Carla, "Is Jasmin not here anymore?"

"No," Carla said, "she is in the Concordia Bar next door. She serves lunch and hors d'oeuvres too. Would you like to see her there?"

"Yes, we would," Mrs. Benson said.

The head waiter came by, having overheard the last part. "I'll direct you," he offered. He walked ahead of the ladies and held the door for them. Then he stepped out far enough to point them to the sign next door.

Jasmin saw them enter and smiled in recognition. They came directly to her food bar. "Mrs. Benson, Alicia," Jasmin exclaimed. "What a delight to see you both."

"It's a great pleasure to see you too," both ladies said in unison. "We'll have our lunch right here." They took a seat on the comfortable bar stools, and as the barman approached, they ordered ginger beer and lime for two.

"This is an exquisite place," Alicia said. "It has a French flair. I will certainly have escargot, followed by French bread with Gruyere and chutney."

"Let me heat it up for you; it'll take four minutes." Jasmin went out the swinging door to put the serving plate of escargots inside her mini grill, turned the timer on, and came back to take Mrs. Benson's order.

"Marinated trout," was Mrs. Benson's choice.

"Tell me what's new with you, Alicia," Jasmin said, as she busied herself getting the orders ready.

"First of all, I adore your hairstyle, Jasmin," Alicia raved.

"Thank you, it's called a flip," Jasmin explained. "I have it done by a Swiss hairdresser."

"You don't say," Alicia inserted. "England is becoming more and more internationally minded. Here we are in a mainly French atmosphere, with a Danish restaurant next door, and the Ceylon Tea Centre across the road, you don't have to go anywhere. It is right here at our own doorstep."

"Not to mention Italian coffee bars," Jasmin interjected.

Mrs. Benson enquired about that particular beauty salon and when Jasmin intended to go there next. "I go to Steiner's here in the hotel, but I could take Alicia to meet you at yours," she considered.

Jasmin cautioned, "You will have to make an appointment as soon as possible to get in for Saturday morning; that's when I am going. The hairdresser's name is Kurt. Tell him Alicia is my friend. By the way, do you want highlights too? That will take longer, but they would look terrific on you." She looked at Alicia and continued, "My appointment is at eleven, so if you make Alicia's for ten, we'll both be finished together."

"Terrific," Alicia said.

"We'll do that," her mother decided.

Jasmin

"What else is happening with you lately?" Mrs. Benson asked.

"On Wednesday afternoon I'm meeting Mrs. Tyler - she's the mother of the gentleman who is courting me - at the Society Attire Store for a dress fitting for the Regency Ball on Christmas Eve. I have reduced my afternoon classes to Tuesdays and Thursdays at Worthington's Tutorial School and on Saturday afternoon I have dancing lessons at the same school. Sunday mornings I go to church," Jasmin informed them. "Alicia, would you like to meet me at the Attire Store on Wednesday, to give me an opinion on the dress I am choosing?" Jasmin asked.

"We'll both come as casual observers," Mrs. Benson suggested.

"Excellent idea," Jasmin said happily.

After lunch, Alicia said, "We'll see you on Wednesday then."

Jasmin tidied her stuff away, made sure there was enough room in her little fridge for the Jasmine corsage still in the box, and went up to her room. She decided to take a nap while she was alone. When Carla came in, Jasmin woke up and thanked her for encouraging Mrs. Benson and Alicia to come over to the Concordia Bar.

"I'm going to do some typing," Jasmin said. "Or are you going to have a nap?"

"No," Carla said, "I'm going out shopping."

Before she began her homework, Jasmin took a blank piece of paper and sketched a dress design she had in mind for the ball. She spent a good hour on typing drills, charts, and business letters, and she also completed her accounting assignment.

The next day was routine and uneventful. On Wednesday afternoon, Jasmin walked briskly over to the rental store. Mrs. Tyler was already there chatting with the clerk. "Oh, here you are, dear. Lorraine has some sample outfits selected for you."

"Thank you, Mrs. Tyler. I'll look them over first, and then try some on." One by one Jasmin held up each dress. She looked in the mirror, felt the material, and set them aside. She pulled out her design sketch and showed it to Mrs. Tyler and Lorraine. "This is what I have in mind: royal blue velvet on bodice, and satin or netting in a contrasting colour below the hips to flare outwards."

Lorraine was taken aback. "One like that just came in today; I'll bring it out in a moment."

Jasmin turned to Mrs. Tyler, who had taken a seat. "Matthew likes velvet."

Mrs. Tyler perked up and said, "Does he now?"

"Yes," Jasmin said. "Of all the dresses I wore at the dancing classes, he liked my velvet one the best. So what I'm looking for now should have velvet on the bodice and satin, silk, or nylon on the lower part to allow freedom of movement for the steps we've learned."

At that point, one could hear the doorbell ringing and the owner of the store speaking with customers. As the voices came nearer, Jasmin recognized Mrs. Benson's and then she saw her and Alicia come into the show area.

"Mrs. Tyler," Jasmin said, "may I introduce Mrs. Benson and her daughter Alicia, my friend. They have come as casual observers."

"It's a pleasure to make your acquaintance," Mrs. Tyler said.

"It's a pleasure," Mrs. Benson echoed.

"Likewise," Alicia added.

They took seats next to Mrs. Tyler, just as the manageress, Gloria, entered carrying a gown in both hands. She showed it to Jasmin.

Jasmin looked at it critically and commented, "That's just about what I am looking for."

"I will help you into it," the attendant said.

"Excuse us," Jasmin said, and went into the mirrored fitting room.

In the meantime Mrs. Benson told Mrs. Tyler how they had become acquainted with Jasmin. She explained that Alicia was now

Jasmin

home for the holidays and the girls were renewing their friendship. Mrs. Tyler, who was always open to hosting new society people, suggested that they meet at the new country club on Sunday. She explained that they shared a table with Mr. and Mrs. Worthington, and of course Matthew and Jasmin would be there also. "It's fascinating how women's emancipation has come into British society; I want to hear more," she told them. "When you call in your reservation and they are booked, tell them you know me and we will make room at our table."

A soft swoosh could be heard as Jasmin entered the semicircle. All heads turned and gazed at her, stunned. Mrs. Tyler broke the spell, and said, "Jasmin, you look like a princess."

Alicia added, "You look like a dream."

Mrs. Benson raved, "You look majestic."

Jasmin said, "The main thing is if I can spin with it." Then she made a full turn and stopped before Gloria, who had pins in her hands so that she could mark where to adjust the straps.

"This is the only necessary alteration," she said. "Now we have to decide on the accessories." She brought out a white mink stole and a white fox stole. She held these around Jasmin's shoulders and let the others, who were still speechless, admire it.

Once again, Mrs. Tyler found her words first. "The white fox is more becoming."

"I agree," Jasmin said.

Gloria also helped with the long satin gloves, zipped right up to the upper arm.

"Perfect," Mrs. Tyler declared.

"I must get back to work," Jasmin announced.

"You go ahead, dear. I'll make arrangements with Gloria and let you know when the next fitting will be."

"I'll walk you home," Alicia volunteered.

Mrs. Benson said, "I'll be at the front lobby with a taxi."

"No need to call a cab," Mrs. Tyler cut in. "I'll come around with the limousine and take you home. Just give me a minute with Gloria." She beckoned to Gloria to go with her to the office, closed the door, and whispered, "I am going to buy the entire outfit. I wouldn't want anyone else to ever wear it except Jasmin. This is made precisely for her. If she comes for the fitting and wants to pay the fee, just tell her - you'll think of something, won't you?

"I certainly will, Mrs. Tyler," Gloria assured her.

As they walked down the block, Jasmin asked, "Alicia, did you make your hair appointment yet?"

"Yes," Alicia said, "we did it before we came to your store. I'm going at ten as you suggested. Kurt said he knew you, and he will put us together when you arrive. Now that my mother and I are going to the country club for brunch, I'll be able to show off my new hairstyle."

Jasmin thought, "You will be doing more than that if I can help it." As they entered the main lobby, Mrs. Tyler's limousine was just driving up for Alicia. Jasmin waved goodbye. She took the guest elevator up to the fifth floor and walked up the last set of stairs to her room.

The rest of the week went by smoothly without incidents. Jasmin had a fleeting thought of whether Matthew would approve of the new matchmaking role she planned to play.

On Saturday morning, as Jasmin and Alicia waited for the taxi, Alicia anxiously asked, "What should I wear tomorrow?"

Jasmin advised, "High heels, pencil skirt, soft nylon or silk blouse, and suit jacket. Wear the same as you would for going to a meeting at the embassy. Your hairstyle gives your entire look that extra esprit."

"Thank you, Jasmin," Alicia said. "Wait for me at the entrance so we can walk in together in front of my mother."

Jasmin added, "Make sure the seams on your nylons are straight and have a spare one in your purse in case they get a run. Also get used to receiving admiring looks from men, and do not be flustered by it."

Mrs. Benson arrived with the taxi. "Alicia," she exclaimed, "what a transformation." She looked at her daughter with delight. "We'll take you around the corner in the taxi, Jasmin," she offered.

Jasmin thanked Mrs. Benson and advised Alicia, "One more thing: in the morning, tease the flip curls and add more of the hairspray you bought from Kurt. Don't forget to brush mascara on your eyelashes."

Jasmin was excited about seeing Matthew. Matthew had the same eager anticipation to see her. A whole week had passed without communications. He stepped out of the car, leaned against it, and waited. When he saw her through the window panes of the door, he rushed towards her. As she opened it, he took her hand and greeted her. "Good afternoon, what a lovely afternoon it is with you in it."

"Thank you," she said, "and a good afternoon to you too."

When they were settled into the car, Jasmin held the jewelry case open. "Please," she looked at him, meaning he should put on the bracelet for her.

"Glad to," he reached for it and clasped it around her wrist, held her hand for a minute, and breathed a kiss onto it.

They drove and he began, "So how was your week so far?"

Jasmin took a deep breath and said, "It was eventful to say the least. I will tell you later. How was yours?"

Matthew paid attention to the road and after a minute he said, "Extremely busy and trying, but not too busy that I couldn't think about you every free moment." He glanced at her for a second to see her reaction. She looked straight ahead. He pried, "Did you at any time manage to think about me?"

She put her nose up and conceded, "I might have on occasion."

"Might, or did?" he started again.

"Mr. Tyler, is this an interrogation?" Jasmin pretended to be appalled.

"Yes," he simply answered.

"Do I have to answer that now?" she questioned.

"Not necessarily, but sooner or later. Case adjourned, we're here." He laughed. As he assisted her out of the car, she laughed too.

In the studio Mr. Townsend encouraged them to take longer strides in the slower dances and to remember to bend their knees in the Tango because the twists were faster. He also showed them a double spin in the Jive that would look attractive and said, "Memorize the figures. If you intend to do something unusual, say it out loud to prepare the lady for the step sequence. I notice you know enough about the Rumba routine; let me see you do it once more."

When they arrived at their reserved table in the Ceylon Tea Centre, Matthew chuckled, "Did you remember any of those steps?"

Jasmin thought for a minute before she answered, and said, "Actually, I wrote them down somewhere in my notebook."

He queried, "What do you think about the whole dancing business?"

Jasmin responded, "To me it is an elegant and healthy exercise; I love it."

Matthew started again, "I do like to spend time with you in a relaxed, unhurried atmosphere and get to know you better. I enjoy learning what your likes are and what your dislikes are, or what would break your heart. I think it's really important to verbalize

Jasmin

one's feelings and to understand each other. I recall you had a sad memory as a teenager; do you want to share that with me?"

"Matthew," Jasmin began, looking seriously into his eyes, "supposing I were to do something that doesn't fit your image of me or that you would consider unusual, or let's say you heard a false report about me, would you just drop me, or would you still pursue me?"

"Jasmin, dearest," Matthew took hold of her hand, "I would pursue you even if adverse circumstances took you away from me. I would seek you out, even if you did something unspeakable or if you rejected me. That would not quench my love for you. Does that answer your question?"

She smiled and answered, "Yes it does, and to answer your earlier question, I do think about you sometimes and I extol everything you write to me in your letters. I treasure them and keep them in my locked memory box."

The waiter came with more tea, which they accepted. They ate some sandwich wedges and made small talk. Matthew mentioned that his mother had booked brunch on Sunday unbeknownst to him, and wondered how Jasmin felt about that.

He probed, "I see a gleam in your eyes. Is there something else I should know about you?"

"Yes, Matthew," she declared, "the events this week happened so fast before I consulted with you."

"Consulted with me about what? I am listening," he said.

"An idea was forming in my mind." Now she giggled, and he took that as a happy sign. He waited with baited breath. She continued, "I know you have a sense of humour. Let me start from the beginning."

He relaxed, sat back, and indicated she had his full attention. He said, "I am intrigued about what is going on in that pretty head of yours."

"At Rose's wedding, when Jeff Kerr danced with me he asked if I had a sister, because he would sure like to meet her. I took it as a fun comment. I told him, 'Not exactly, but if one comes to mind, I will let you know.' As it happens my friend Alicia, a political science student with whom I have corresponded, has come home for Christmas from Brussels. Alicia and her mother Mrs. Benson visited me at the Concordia Bar. She had first befriended me when I worked at the Danish Snack Bar. We shared all kinds of girl talk and she asked me for advice about hair styles and my activities. They ended up coming with me to the dress fitting and meeting Mrs. Tyler. Your mother took a liking to Alicia and Mrs. Benson, and she suggested that they also book at the country club for brunch. So yesterday, Alicia came with me to the beauty salon and had my Swiss Coiffeur Kurt do her hair similar to mine."

An idea dawned in Matthew's mind. "Carry on," he encouraged her, smiling. He had guessed what would come next.

"Well," Jasmin hesitated, "it occurred to me that perhaps Jeff Kerr might be at that brunch and sit at our table too."

"And you could introduce him to Alicia," Matthew completed the sentence.

"So you approve?" Jasmin asked.

"Absolutely," Matthew assured her.

"You don't think I am manipulative?" she asked, somewhat uncertain.

"Jasmin, manipulative is not in the vocabulary of my description for you. You are pure minded, tenderhearted, kind and always concerned for the welfare of others, irresistibly lovely, and above all, I am honoured you trust me with your thought process by analyzing your emotions and motivations." He added, "Leave Jeff Kerr to me; I'll see to it that he comes. Does it make you happy that your little plot is working out?"

Jasmin

Jasmin had gathered her wits together again and picked up on the jesting mood. "Does that mean you're my fellow conspirator?" She looked at him sideways.

He laughed out loud. "If we were really alone, I could hug you and lift you up in the air and kiss you and dance a jig all at the same time; you are such fun."

She moved out of her chair, raised her eyebrows in a mock frown, then smiled and said, "There is a time and place for everything."

"Indeed," he admitted.

Jasmin announced she was going to keep the bracelet on overnight, as she would wear it tomorrow. "One more thing," she remembered,

"Yes?" Matthew smiled at her expectantly.

"Matthew, would you raise the passenger seat in the Jaguar? Because I will be wearing a tight skirt and it is difficult getting in and out of the seat," she asked with the kindest voice.

"Of course, gladly," he assured her.

They walked across the road to her staff entrance. He came all the way down the steps to hold the door for her and said, "I'll be here at ten thirty sharp. Have a good evening, precious."

"Thank you, Matthew, for everything." She raised her hand in goodbye.

Matthew raced through town. Luckily the streets were deserted this time of night. He needed to get home as quickly as he could so that he could call Jeff Kerr on the telephone. Then he changed his mind and took a shortcut to Jeff's apartment. He rang the doorbell and waited. Finally the door opened. Jeff stood there, flabbergasted. "Matthew, what brings you here?" he asked.

"Let me in and I will tell you," Matthew demanded.

"Right, come in please," Jeff invited him.

Matthew began, "Whatever plans you have for tomorrow noon, drop them."

"Why?" Jeff asked.

"Do you have any plans tomorrow?" Matthew countered.

"Not yet," Jeff said.

"O.K. I'll make the plan for you. You are going to be at my table tomorrow for brunch at the country club. Do you want to drive there and meet me and Jasmin, or do you want to go with my mother? She is going too."

"Oh, no, I'll drive myself. Who else is going to be there?" Jeff now asked curiously.

"Well, there are the Worthingtons, Mrs. Benson, and Jasmin mentioned something about a sisterly friend," Matthew slowly interjected, watching Jeff closely, who in turn put on a look of contemplation.

"Jasmin's sister, eh? What time did you say?" Jeff enquired.

"Twelve fifteen," Matthew informed him. "Do you know how to get there?"

"Vaguely," Jeff answered.

"It will take you about twenty minutes from here," Matthew estimated.

"I will leave early and wait for you in the parking lot in front of the entrance," Jeff promised.

"See you there," Matthew said.

Carla was in the room when Jasmin came up. Jasmin asked what was happening with Roger. Carla said that he had to study all day Sunday but he would like to go to the open session at the dance studio in the evening. He would get a taxi to pick her up. In the meantime she was going to learn something about flight science so that she could have an intelligent conversation with him if he so desired.

Jasmin

Jasmin said she was going to turn in early. She laid out her outfit for the morning, removed her make-up, and put a silk scarf on her pillow to protect her hairstyle.

Before she drifted off to sleep, she thought, "I'm feeling secure with Matthew."

Matthew went to his library when he got home and read some of his law books. He sorted out his notes and filed them together with copies. He went to his desk and began making personal notes about Jasmin. He thought, "She's beginning to trust me."

On Sunday morning, as Jasmin came to the exit door, Matthew was already waiting. She hesitated and he came down the steps to take her arm. Jasmin discretely pulled her skirt up slightly at the side seam because it was difficult to go up the steps with high heels. As Matthew opened the car door, she graciously slid into the seat backwards and with a quick motion pulled her knees inside.

Matthew grinned, "That was an elegant maneuver."

As he got into the car, he looked over at Jasmin and greeted her with, "Seeing you brightens my day; good morning."

"A good morning to you too," Jasmin said.

When they arrived at the church, he helped Jasmin out of the car and let her go ahead a few steps while he closed the door. He looked at her silhouette sideways, and thought, "That's my lady, I am so proud of how she carries herself." He caught up with Jasmin and offered his arm to escort her into the church door.

After the service they didn't stand around to mingle, but instead left to drive to the country club. Matthew spotted Jeff's Porsche as he escorted Jasmin into the foyer where the others were making introductions. He led Jasmin to his mother and the Bensons and mumbled, "You go ahead; I'll see to Jeff." He turned back and waved to Jeff, who emerged from his car so that they could come inside together.

Jasmin headed towards Alicia and nudged her, suggesting, "Let's go to the powder room."

Alicia looked sideways at her mom and said, "Excuse us."

Jasmin instructed Alicia, "Put some more mascara on. O.K. Now, where is your lipstick?"

"I don't have one," Alicia said.

"Here, use my spare one," Jasmin showed her and dabbed it on. "Now take small steps. Walk beside me and let Matthew's mother introduce you to Jeff Kerr: he's Matthew's associate and your date! Don't faint, just accept compliments with a gracious 'thank you', like you are used to it because you look ravishing. If Jeff offers you a chair, take it. Matthew told Jeff that you're my sisterly friend; he might even think we look like sisters. If you're nervous, take a deep breath and act nonchalantly."

They walked the few steps around the corner to the foyer. As they came in sight of Mrs. Tyler, she called, "Jasmin, Alicia, our party is complete. Matthew, you haven't met Alicia; Alicia, this is my son Matthew and his friend Jeff Kerr."

Matthew bowed his head slightly, and said, "Pleasure to meet you."

Alicia nodded, "How do you do?"

Jeff bowed slightly too as she looked at him. "Pleasure to make your acquaintance, Alicia," he said.

Alicia tipped her head, saying, "How do you do?"

Matthew stepped near Jasmin as the maître d' announced, "Your table is ready."

Mrs. Tyler said to Mrs. Benson, "Shall we take our seats?"

She directed Mrs. Benson to sit between Mr. Worthington and her, and placed Matthew and Jasmin next to Jeff and Alicia. Mrs. Worthington would be seated between her husband and Matthew. Matthew held Jasmin's chair for her and Jeff held Alicia's chair for her. Mr. Worthington held his wife's chair and the head waiter held the chairs for both Mrs. Tyler and Mrs. Benson.

It was an oval table and the young couples were seated at the end. Matthew said to Alicia, "Will you resume your studies after the holidays?" He wanted to give Jeff, who was still in a daze, an opening phrase to begin a conversation with Alicia.

Jeff took the cue and asked her, "What are you studying?"

Alicia took a deep breath and replied coolly, "Political science."

"How interesting," Jeff said. "Which university do you attend?"

"Bristol University; it's the best school for this program." They chatted quite amicably some more.

Jasmin turned to Matthew and whispered, "They are off to a good start."

Matthew answered in a low voice, "You brought that about."

Jasmin saw in her peripheral vision the head waiter approach and asked Alicia, "Did you have any Mimosa when you were in Brussels?"

"Yes, I often did," Alicia confirmed.

Jasmin said, "Shall we have our gentlemen order some for us? I'm not sure if the waiter knows what it is, but Mr. Worthington surely would."

"Now, what would Mimosa be?" Matthew asked Jasmin.

"It's champagne and orange juice, a suitable drink for brunch."

Matthew looked at Mr. Worthington and said, "I'm sure you would know what Mimosa is, so you could explain it to the wine steward if he's not familiar with it."

By now the wine steward had approached the table. When he asked which beverage they would like to order, he looked at Mr. Worthington as the head of the group. Mr. Worthington turned to his wife first, then Mrs. Tyler and Mrs. Benson and asked them,

"Would you ladies venture this concoction also? And what about you, Matthew and Jeff?"

Matthew asked Jasmin, "What is the proportion?"

"Two thirds orange juice, one third champagne," she explained.

Mr. Worthington turned to the perplexed waiter and said, "Allow me to come to the bar with you and give the bartender complete instructions." In the meantime the busboy showed up with a pitcher in hand and filled the water glasses.

The hostess came to the table and asked, "Would the party now like to make their way to the buffet?"

The three senior ladies headed that way and Mr. Worthington met them halfway. Alicia and Jeff followed, and Jasmin and Matthew trailed behind the group.

Matthew whispered in Jasmin's ear, "I'm discovering a mischievous streak in you."

Jasmin countered, "Pleasantly or disturbingly?"

"Excitingly," he replied.

At the buffet, the chefs filled their plates and the guests made their way back to the table. Matthew said to Jasmin, "Let me take the plate off your hand." He set it down in front of her place next to his own, then he held her chair for her till she was seated.

Jeff Kerr followed his example and Alicia accepted the courtesy. Mr. Worthington assisted his wife with her plate and the waiter assisted Mrs. Tyler and Mrs. Benson by putting their plates onto the table. When everyone was seated, the assistant bartender brought the tray with Mimosa on it and served them all.

Mrs. Worthington, who had not said much so far, offered a toast: "To the making of happy memories."

"Happy memories," everybody echoed.

Matthew looked at Jasmin as he sipped his drink and murmured, "To adventurous new memories with you!"

Jasmin

"With you?" Jasmin quizzed.

"Indeed," he said. They put their glasses down and started to eat, looking occasionally over to Jeff and Alicia. They caught fragments of their conversation about where she was going to be assigned to next.

Mrs. Tyler said to Mrs. Benson, "It looks like our young people are getting along nicely."

"I can see that," said Mrs. Benson, still recovering from the quick turn of events of seeing her daughter with a beau at her side.

Mrs. Worthington asked the ladies what they thought of this place and the ladies gave approving comments about the food and décor. Mrs. Worthington further explained that Mr. Worthington had trained the head waiter and one of the cooks in his studio.

"Arthur, you are a genius," Mrs. Tyler proudly exclaimed.

Mr. Worthington announced that tonight was the last open session at his dance studio. Mrs. Benson listened to Mr. Worthington describe what it was all about.

Matthew asked Jasmin, "Are we still on for tonight?"

"Yes," she said, "but I shall have to go home and change out of my current outfit. What I'm wearing is only suitable for walking around art galleries or museums."

"Or walking beside me and looking great," Matthew said with a doting look on his face.

Jeff Kerr asked Alicia, "Would you be at all interested in joining my friends and me at the dance studio this evening?"

When she hesitated, he said, "Should I ask your mother?"

Mrs. Benson had overheard and looked at Mrs. Worthington, who came to her rescue by commenting, "It's a lovely activity for young people."

Jeff Kerr picked up his courage and addressed Mrs. Benson, "Would it be acceptable with you if I took Alicia to the dance studio this evening?"

Mrs. Benson answered, "If Alicia is inclined that way, by all means."

"Yes, I am," consented Alicia.

"Anyone for dessert?" shouted Mr. Worthington.

"Yes," several of them replied. The gentlemen again pulled the chairs back for the ladies.

Jasmin said to Matthew, "Please excuse Alicia and me for a couple of minutes and put something on our plates. We'll be back shortly."

She nudged Alicia and they walked confidently towards the foyer. No sooner had they entered the outer area of the ladies room then they laughed, stretched their arms towards each other, and hugged. "Jasmin," Alicia shrieked, "How did you pull off such a surprise for me? He is gorgeous. I had no idea, thank you."

"You are welcome," Jasmin giggled. "We'll talk another time about this. First things first: go home and change into a soft flowing skirt or dress with not quite so high heels. I'll do the same and we'll see you later."

"O.K., Captain," Alicia made a mock salute.

Matthew allowed a few other guests to come between him and his elder friends but stayed close to Jeff. As he leaned over to take two dessert plates he murmured to Jeff, "What's your opinion?"

"She's a knockout," Jeff raved.

Matthew raised one eyebrow and grinned. He selected a crème de menthe parfait for Jasmin and some petit fours for himself. Jeff ordered the same. The girls came back and walked to the table where the men still stood beside the chairs, waiting for them so they could eat dessert together.

Coffee was served and the party broke up.

"Shall I call for you at six thirty then?" Jeff asked Alicia. "Would you give me your address?"

"Of course," she replied.

Mrs. Tyler gave Mrs. Benson and Alicia a ride in her limousine to their house.

As Matthew, Jasmin, and Jeff made their way out the door, Matthew said to Jeff, "Remember, no wild rides on your first date."

"Ha, ha," Jeff laughed. "I'm as gentle as a dove and as tame as a lamb." Jeff turned to Jasmin and said, "Jasmin, I won't let another minute pass without saying thank you for producing such a charming 'sister' for me."

"I'm glad you approve, and you're welcome," Jasmin said.

When they were in the car, Matthew said, "I'm taking my own advice and will not drive too fast. You deserve to be pampered and the leisurely ride home should be relaxing. You have made two people happy today. Three, actually, counting Alicia's mother no doubt."

"Thank you," Jasmin said.

Matthew asked, "Did you say you like art galleries, museums, and sightseeing in general?"

"I do, sometimes," admitted Jasmin, "but I like a quiet tea for two just as much."

"I enjoy your company, whatever we do," Matthew declared. "Actually," Matthew began again, "There is an exhibition at the museum this coming weekend. I can arrange for the tickets; would you like to go there with me?"

"That would be interesting. Yes, thank you, I'd like that," Jasmin accepted.

"That would probably be our last date before the Christmas ball, other than church next Sunday," Matthew said thoughtfully.

"Everything comes to a standstill," Jasmin added. "My schooling will end too and vacation starts."

"I'm sure we will fill that time with other activities." Matthew twinkled his eyes at that comment.

"Yes," Jasmin added, "Christmas shopping and card writing."

"Are you going to write me a card?" Matthew asked her teasingly before he stopped the car. He didn't wait for an answer. At her entry door, they stood still for a moment and he said, "I'll see you later right here at six thirty, my dearest."

"See you later," she breathed.

Jasmin went upstairs to an empty room and changed into her dressing gown so as to be comfortable while resting on her bed. A couple of hours later when Carla came in, Jasmin woke up. She asked, "What did you do this afternoon?"

"Paula and I went to the cartoon cinema for a while and window shopped," Carla replied, "and soon Roger is picking me up. We are going to the coffee bar and then to the dance studio for the last time. He's going to Scotland for Christmas."

"We're heading to the dance studio as well, and Alicia and Jeff are going too," Jasmin announced. "Looks like we're going to have a mini party tonight."

"How did you get Alicia and Jeff together in only five days?" shouted Carla.

Jasmin shrugged and laughed. "Circumstances brought it about," she said.

"I bet," doubted Carla. "O.K., I need to get going, bye."

Watching Carla leave, Jasmin paused and thought about Paula. She couldn't grasp why Carla associated with her, knowing what kind of person she was. Nancy had mentioned recently at the elevator that Paula stayed out every night. When she came back to her room, she spent an inordinate amount of time seemingly mending her clothes.

Jasmin did not wish to dwell on that right now, and so she focused on her wardrobe. She chose to wear a red petticoat under her skirt, as she expected it to look sharp when it swung out doing the Jive. After getting dressed, she decided to visit her two friends on the third floor, as there was plenty of time till her date. When she entered the swinging door of the pantry, only Nellie was there.

"Jasmin," she called joyfully and hugged her. "Tell me what's going on with your beau," she eagerly exclaimed.

"Well, I'm going to the Christmas ball at the Regency Hall. My dress needs a minor alteration, and I have one more fitting. On Wednesday would you and Beatrice come with me to see my dress before it gets packed in a box?"

"Would we ever!" cried Nellie. "Beatrice and I can get the new waiter to come in an hour early to cover our absence and we'll walk with you to the store. We wouldn't miss this for the world. I'm going down with you now; I have to see your 'knight'. Let me quickly find the maid on duty to watch my post for a few minutes. How much time do we have?"

"Eight minutes," Jasmin informed her.

"Mildred, are you there?" Nellie called down the corridor, running to the maid's roomette.

"Yes," came the answer.

"Mildred, could you watch the pantry for five minutes till I'm back?" asked Nellie.

"Sure," Mildred peeked her head out from the maid cubicle. "Oh, Jasmin, long time no see, what brings you here?"

"I'll tell you later," Nellie cut in, "we've got to hurry."

"Bye," Jasmin called while rushing to get to the elevator.

They came to the staff exit and saw Matthew arriving. "That's him," Jasmin said. "Wait till he comes to our door, then hold it open." Matthew came down the steps, offered his arm to Jasmin, escorted her up the rest of the steps, and assisted her into the car. He tipped his hat to Nellie who stood staring through the open door. She blushed and smiled before going in.

THE BALL

"Another lady in waiting?" he asked, smiling.

"Yes, one of two," Jasmin affirmed. "Actually, they are escorting me on Wednesday to the rental store to supervise the last fitting of my dress."

"Will it be ready then?" Matthew enquired.

"Yes, I'm quite sure," Jasmin said.

"How are you going to transport it?" he asked again.

"I haven't thought about it really; in fact, I don't even know when to put it on and where." Jasmin sounded perplexed.

"That's easy," Matthew assured her. "You are invited to stay at our house over the holidays starting on Christmas Eve in one of our guest rooms. You will put the dress on in our home, then we'll all go together to the ball. So it makes sense that your dress should be brought to our house. My office is closed from Wednesday noon until January second. Why don't I meet you at the store and take the box to my house?"

Jasmin hesitated, "Oh, about staying at your house, I mean, I haven't thought this through yet. I've had variable emotions these last few days and I haven't considered things objectively. Matthew, can we talk about it some more in depth? I mean later, after the dance? Actually, can we leave early right after the break? At this point I need to concentrate on being friendly with friends. If it's alright with you?"

Matthew answered, "Jasmin, I'm so open and willing to listen to you." But a question formed in his mind, "You are not leaving me, are you?"

"Leaving you?" Jasmin was caught off guard. "No, I'm not leaving you." She took a deep breath, smiled, and said encouragingly, "Now let's join the others."

Matthew pondered to himself for a moment, "I don't know what I did, but whatever is bothering Jasmin, I will make it up to her!"

At the dance studio, Jeff, Alicia, Roger, and Carla had already introduced themselves to each other when Matthew and Jasmin arrived. They followed the crowd who were instructed to form two circles. Ladies were in the centre, facing the men on the outside. Mr. Townsend showed a few men's steps, the instructress demonstrated the ladies' steps, and then they danced the figure without music. The teachers encouraged the group to copy them first individually and then together, all the while counting the beats. After that round, they showed it with music, counting steps and beats, and then each couple followed their example. The teachers called, "Change partners." Each dance couple moved to the right side to face a different partner. Then they danced two rounds until the next call came, "Change partners." They continued until everyone had returned to their original partner. Mr. Townsend put on a different record and encouraged everyone to dance anything they knew already.

Jasmin

Matthew and Jasmin went through one of their familiar routines. Matthew whispered to Jasmin, "Do you enjoy dancing with me?"

"I do," she said.

He probed further, "More than with anyone else?"

"Yes," she affirmed.

The break was announced and the friends came together in one corner. Lloyd and Verna even joined the group and introduced themselves to Carla and Alicia, while Matthew took Jeff and Roger aside to fetch the beverages.

Matthew asked Roger, "Is there anything I should know when boarding an airplane?"

"If you are flying in a jet, make sure you have candies with you, because you need something to swallow to alleviate the pressure on your ears. Are you planning a trip?" Roger enquired.

"Yes, but..." Matthew put his finger on his mouth, indicating secrecy. He turned to Jeff, "Are you enjoying yourself?"

"Tremendously," raved Jeff.

"You can tell me more tomorrow at the office," Matthew said. "Jasmin and I are leaving now."

He took the soft drinks to the ladies. Then he looked at Jasmin and said quietly, "Ready to go?"

"Yes," she said to him.

"See you around," she said to the others.

In the car Jasmin started to say, "I have to fully wrap my mind around the idea of staying over at your house; I have never stayed overnight at a gentleman's apartment or house before."

They had driven only a short way before Matthew slowed down to drive into a lane that led to a park and crept to a stop. "Jasmin, dear," Matthew spoke gently, "my mother invited you to her house. There are three guest bedrooms with lockable doors. The cook and the maid live in their quarters. I live in a different wing of the house and my mother in another. She invited you over for Christmas because in our tradition the gifts are exchanged early Christmas morning and we wanted you to be there for that. The first person you see will be Emily the maid calling you down for breakfast. If you're uncomfortable with staying over, you could still come to our house. You could change from your ball gown into something suitable for travel and we could take you back to the hotel, although your curfew would be over and you would have to go into the main lobby. The next morning we would come and get you early. So think of our house like your hotel where guests live under the same roof in their own locked rooms."

Jasmin said softly, "I understand. I just had an uncomfortable flashback from last year. I wasn't aware of your Christmas tradition and I'm homesick for my mother and sisters and I haven't heard from my brother," she started to cry.

Matthew said kindly, "Come outside for a little while; it's still mild and we can take a walk together."

She came out and he put his arm around her, saying soothingly, "Jasmin, let me hug you like a father, mother, sister, brother, and friend. Go ahead and cry on my shoulder, it's alright, it's going to be alright."

She cried on his shoulders. Gradually her tears dried up and he let go of the hug. Then he cupped her face in his hands and kissed her forehead. Jasmin came back to her senses and said, "I'll have to wash my face." He pulled out his handkerchief from his lapel and gave it to her. She said, "Thank you." He could see her smile in the moonlight.

Matthew suggested, "I have an idea where we can go and talk some more. Come on, we'll go to my office; it's not far from your hotel." Jasmin nodded and got back into the car and they drove to his office building. Matthew unlocked the door, turned on the

Jasmin

lights, and led Jasmin down the hall to the ladies room. He said in passing, "Would you like to have a cup of tea?"

"Sure, thank you," she answered.

When she came out, she stood for a moment, looking up and down the hallway. "Over here," Matthew called, carrying a tea tray. He motioned with his head, "Let's go in here to this small meeting room."

"Is this where you meet prospective clients?" Jasmin asked while he poured the tea.

"Yes, most of the time," he replied. "I know you take one lump."

"Yes, thank you," she said. "How many do you take?"

"Two," he said. "I like serving you and hearing more of your dreams and aspirations. Here we can chat in leisure. You could come here during your afternoon break, now that you don't have school anymore."

"I'd like that. It doesn't always have to be a fancy establishment for a date, and here I can get to know some of your world," Jasmin concluded. She added, "I am humbled and delighted at the same time with your serving me. I like serving you too."

Matthew related his feelings for her in this way: "If I were to come to the Concordia Bar for lunch I'd be so sidetracked by your presence, I would forget my work. That wouldn't do, because I still have to earn a living so I can build that castle for you."

Jasmin giggled, "Are we back in the teasing mood?"

"Perhaps," he replied. "I see some of that gleam coming back to your face; is there another question lurking in your mind?" Matthew observed, while sipping his tea and offering her a cookie.

"Well," Jasmin exhaled, "My two 'ladies in waiting' as you call them are so interested in what's going on with me. They are taking one hour off work on Wednesday to escort me across the street to the Society Attire Store to look at my dress. When you mentioned you had time on your hands and could meet me there, I wondered if you could offer to drive them back to the hotel in your fancy car. That would be the thrill of a lifetime for them. To them you are my knight in shining armour and the stuff dreams are made of. I love those ladies as I love all the new friends I have made here. What do you think about that?"

Matthew laughed, "What do I think of giving them a ride, or the knight in shining armour part?"

Now Jasmin laughed too. "Both."

"Jasmin, dear, I like the fun loving part of you too, flattery will get you everywhere, and of course I'll give them a ride."

She said, "Now, as far as the transportation of the dress is concerned, the box will be so wide because the velvet cannot be folded, and it might not even fit into your Jaguar, so why don't you have the limousine pick it up?"

Matthew assured her, "Gladly, do you want more tea?"

"Yes, thank you," she said. "One more thing I want to talk about is a request for next Monday which is Christmas Eve. In the morning I have an appointment with my hairdresser, Kurt."

"Kurt, eh?" Matthew cut in.

"Yes," Jasmin admitted. "He's from Switzerland, he knows my hair and does it superbly, but I have to cross the road and walk one block. I can get there alright but when my hair is done, it can't be exposed to the outside air, so I'll need a ride home. If you can see it in your heart to pick me up when I'm finished and drive me home, I shall be happy."

Matthew offered, "I'll gladly take you there first and pick you up when you're finished and drive you home afterwards. What time is the appointment?"

"From eleven to twelve thirty."

"I'll be at the staff entrance by ten forty-five sharp." Matthew rose from his chair and said, "For the next three days can you manage without communications from me?"

Jasmin also stood up and replied, "I have your letters and imagine your voice often."

He assured her again, "If it is really important, please call me at this office during business hours. You can call me anytime at my house; somebody will always answer. Now, it's time to take you home," he said, while taking the tea tray and proceeding to the kitchen. She followed him, asking, "Do you have to wash the dishes too?"

Matthew was amused. "Not usually, but under these circumstances, I will."

"May I dry them?" Jasmin asked.

When they had finished the short task, he took her by the hand and said, "Let's go before the clock strikes twelve and the coach turns back into a pumpkin."

Jasmin chuckled and said, "No glass slipper though."

"But I do have one," Matthew replied.

"You do?" Jasmin asked incredulously.

"I'll show you at Christmas," Matthew said.

At the door he felt like taking her into his arms, but instead he said, "Jasmin, I think your emotions are like a fragile porcelain doll. Your heart needs to be treated with tender loving care so it doesn't break. Will you trust me?" He took both of her hands, lifted them to his lips, and kissed her fingertips - a gesture she adored. He saw her blushing.

She whispered, "Yes."

Matthew drove her the short distance to her hotel, went down the stairs to the staff door, checked if it was still open, and held it open for her. "Have a peaceful sleep, Jasmin."

"You too," she said.

Matthew rushed home and checked his calendar. "Two more busy days," he mumbled. He looked at his itinerary to see if he had time in the lunch hour to make a jaunt to the jewelry store. He went to his kitchen and scribbled a note for the cook to put a sack lunch together for him first thing in the morning.

On Monday he dealt with several cases. All were short in nature, and by noon, the judge had called for a recess. Immediately Matthew left to go to the jewelry store to see about the ring. A month earlier he had seen a solitaire diamond with sapphires. Matthew requested it be taken out of the glass case. As this was an expensive purchase, the jeweler attended to Matthew himself.

"About the size," Matthew hesitated.

The jeweler helped him out by saying, "A woman of normal weight, about 5'2" height, between the age of twenty to thirty would require approximately a size five or six ring. This ring is a size five and a half ."

"I'll take it," Matthew said.

"Very well," the jeweler said. "Should you require alteration, there's no additional charge. We are open the day after Boxing Day."

Matthew pocketed the ring box, drove back to his office, and placed the ring into his private safe. He found a bottle of ginger ale in his small fridge, took out his wrapped lunch, and ate it in the small conference room while reading the newspaper. Shortly after that he gathered the folder for the afternoon session at court and made his way out the door. On his way to the car, Jeff Kerr greeted him. "I'm going to Scotland with Alicia to see her other relatives over Christmas. Thanks for introducing us." Matthew reminded him to be back by the New Year. "Sure, second of January, nine a.m., unless you need me earlier. I am a telephone call away; the address and number is on your office desk," Jeff replied, waving goodbye.

Jasmin

Matthew returned to his own thoughts. "Tomorrow I'll have to make another important stop at the travel agent, and after that I'll devote my free time to Jasmin."

Jasmin realized she still had the bracelet on when she arrived to punch in the time clock on Monday morning. Ernest the timekeeper called, "Smiler, what do I see sparkling there?"

She admitted, "That was my birthday gift."

"Very nice," he said. "Here's a letter for you." He handed her the envelope with an airmail sticker on it. She looked and saw that it was from her brother.

At the Concordia Bar, it wasn't busy, but just as Jasmin intended to read the letter, Alicia and her mother showed up. They had a quick lunch and asked if Jasmin wanted to spend her free time this afternoon with them.

Jasmin considered their offer, but she said, "I need to go shopping uptown for a day dress for Christmas. I saw one that I liked, but at the time I didn't have any money with me, so I would like to get it this afternoon if it is still available."

"We could drive you over there and come with you," Mrs. Benson said.

"That is kind of you. I'll meet you at the staff entrance next door to the Concordia Bar. Give me ten minutes," Jasmin answered.

The women walked through the interior hotel door to the marbled-floor lobby. Mrs. Benson had the doorman hail a taxi for them and directed the cab to the staff entrance. Jasmin came out just in time and got in the taxi. She directed the driver to the store.

When they arrived, the ladies followed her inside. Jasmin went directly to the rack where she had seen the dress before, but she couldn't find it, so she asked the clerk about it, describing it in detail.

The clerk went into the back room and soon came out with a red velvet dress. She said, "It had been put aside for steaming; would you like to try it on?"

"Yes, thank you." Jasmin let the clerk take the dress into a fitting room. She saw that Alicia had also found a garment to try on.

When she came out of the fitting room to stand in front of the three way mirror, Mrs. Benson and Alicia gazed at her approvingly. "That is a perfect fit," Mrs. Benson told Jasmin, and she looked at Alicia, who nodded in agreement.

Jasmin took the dress off and said to the attendant, "I'll take it."

While Jasmin was changing into her own clothes, Mrs. Benson spoke to the clerk, "I'll pay for that dress; please gift wrap it. Would you have any gift cards available?"

"Yes," she answered, "over there." The clerk pointed to a small desk with stationery on it. Mrs. Benson chose a card, sat down, and wrote that this was a gift to Jasmin from her and Alicia.

Meanwhile, when Jasmin looked in her wallet and counted her money, she realized she didn't have enough to pay for the total amount, so she planned to pay a deposit and put it on lay-away till she was paid on Friday. With this resolve she walked over to the cashier and faced the two Benson women and the store clerk grinning from ear to ear.

She was somewhat bewildered. "What's so funny?" she asked.

The store clerk answered for the three of them: "Santa Claus is giving you an early Christmas present this year." She handed the box to Jasmin who hadn't yet made the connection.

"Read the card," Alicia said.

"For me, the dress, a gift?" Jasmin stuttered.

"Yes," Alicia said. "Our thanks to you for introducing me to Jeff. He's coming with us to Scotland to meet our relatives over Christmas."

Jasmin

"That's amazing," Jasmin said, still in wonder. "Thank you, I never expected anything for that; seeing you happy is enough for me."

"Please take it and enjoy. We'll be leaving on Wednesday."

"We'll take you back to the hotel," Mrs. Benson offered. Alicia picked up her own purchase and they all got into the waiting taxi. During the drive, Mrs. Benson and Alicia told Jasmin how they got along so well with Jeff. They had talked it over and Jeff was officially courting Alicia.

"That sure is a speedy turn of events; I'm happy for you." Jasmin thanked them again before she left.

"We'll be in touch," they called as they drove away.

In the evening, before Jasmin went to sleep she read the letter from her brother. Hans wrote that he had completed his Bible College training in Switzerland and was coming to Middleton to study at the Institute of Linguistics and would visit churches who were associated with his cause. He would need to be billeted during his one-year stay. While he was here he could do part-time jobs to finance his upkeep. He further wrote: "Jasmin, from how you describe this man in your life, he doesn't seem to be somebody I'd have to ward off. He appears to be God-fearing and respectful of you. He has his heart set on you and he will not break it. Your faithful brother, Hans."

On Tuesday, Jasmin went to work as usual. She prepared her food displays and got ready for business, and the first customer who came in was Mr. James.

"Good morning, Miss Claudius," he greeted her. "It's a delight to see you again; your smile brightens up the whole room."

"Good morning, Mr. James, how are you?" Jasmin politely enquired. "What may I serve you today?"

Mr. James ordered his drink from the bartender and then turned back to Jasmin and ordered a luncheon plate from her. He began telling her that he was looking for a security guard and had contemplated going to Mr. Worthington hoping that he would advise him.

Jasmin enquired, "What does a security guard do?"

"Basically," Mr. James informed her, "he's a person who stays in the Lodge overnight, closes up, walks around the premises, and is available for emergencies. It's only a part-time position though."

"In other words, you need a serious person, younger, but old enough to be responsible, polite, does not smoke or drink, and is trustworthy, right?"

"You took the words right out of my mouth," Mr. James answered. "Do you know a person like that?"

"As a matter of fact, I do," said Jasmin. "Would you hire someone who was trained in a Bible College in Switzerland, who is now coming to England to study linguistics, and who will go overseas as a missionary in a year? He needs a place with room and board for the time being."

"I'll take him," Mr. James exclaimed. "I am Greek Orthodox myself, but I have high regard for missionaries. I was educated in Switzerland also."

"When would you need him for?" Jasmin further enquired.

"By the first of March at the latest, preferably earlier, so I can give him a month's worth of training. I intend to take a trip in the spring to Greece and I want my place to be well looked after."

"Would January fifteenth be too soon?" Jasmin probed again.

"Not at all," Mr. James affirmed. "What is his name?"

Jasmin exhaled. "Hans Claudius, my brother," she said.

"Your brother, Miss Claudius? Of course, I'll hire him sight unseen. You just made my day!"

"Thank you," Jasmin said.

Jasmin

"I'll get in touch with you in the New Year. If not, please call me any time. Have a good day and Merry Christmas." Mr. James rose from his barstool, paid the barman, and left.

Jasmin knew she had one more errand to run in town. She went up to her room during the afternoon break and saw Carla getting ready to go outside too. "Where are you going?" she asked.

Carla said, "Downtown to buy shoes; where do you want to go?"

Jasmin answered, "I'm going across the square to the stationery store at the corner. We can walk that short way together."

"Sure," Carla said. "I also have to go to the post office for stamps; do you need any?"

"Yes, I do," said Jasmin. "Here's the money for some, thanks." She put a silk scarf over her head to cover her hair because it was misty outside. They went down the elevator together, waved to Ernest downstairs, walked across the square to the store of Jasmin's choice, and then parted.

Jasmin was welcomed by the manager who greeted her with, "Miss Claudius, we have the item you ordered. Would you like to view it before we gift wrap it?"

"Yes please," Jasmin said in anticipation. He showed her the exquisite letter opener with a mother-of-pearl handle and a fine quality desk pen with the engraved initials M.T. for a gentleman. She had the items wrapped separately and left so as to reach home before dark.

Upstairs, she let out a sigh of relief. Now she had all her Christmas shopping completed, except for writing a few more cards. She would also need to reply to her brother. She looked at the clock and saw that she still had a half hour before she had to go on duty. Jasmin finished addressing the envelopes and took the stamped ones downstairs to give to Ernest for the mail.

"Hello Smiler," he called, when she came out of the elevator.

She gave him the envelopes and asked, "Do you have a Christmas tree?"

"No," he said, "but your flowers are still fresh."

"I'll see what I can do," she said while punching in her timecard.

Jasmin did her evening chores with ease and finished up, thinking, "Tomorrow I'm going to see my beloved Matthew." She had a new excitement in her step when she hurried to punch her time card and go upstairs. She organized her schoolbooks into her drawer and finished placing stamps on the remaining envelopes. She held the one for Matthew close to her heart. She had squeezed one Jasmine petal into a fine silk appliqué. She hoped the fragrance would still be there when he received it.

Matthew had a busy morning at court. Instead of closing at noon, something unexpected came up that dragged on for another hour and a half. There was no time for lunch, so he called his secretary, Myrna, to have something brought to his office and to re-schedule the last appointment with his client. He wisely asked her to stay until he was finished and to make sure she interrupted the meeting if he wasn't done by three p.m. He added, "Have the telephone number of the Society Attire Store ready in case we have to call them."

Finally he could consult with his client who was patient enough, but took up extra time repeating himself. Sure enough, Myrna interrupted the meeting at two fifty-five, saying there was an urgent call to make. Matthew diplomatically advised his client, "We'll deal with this at the beginning of the New Year. My secretary will make the appointment for you. Merry Christmas."

He rushed to his office, took the slip of paper with the number on it, and called the store. "Hello, Gloria, Matthew Tyler here. Is Jasmin Claudius still there with her two friends?"

"Yes, they're about done. They seem to be waiting for something," she said.

"Keep them occupied for a few more minutes and tell them I'm on my way. They are waiting for me, O.K.?" Matthew hung up and said to Myrna, "I'll be back later to clear my desk." Then he rushed out the door.

Jasmin, Beatrice, and Nellie walked across the square, around the corner of a side street, and into the rental store. They were excited enough to get there as fast as they could. Lorraine showed them to the viewing room and brought out the gown. She held it up and they gasped in admiration. In the fitting room Gloria assisted Jasmin into the dress and escorted her out to turn around in front of the three way mirror.

Beatrice and Nellie almost fainted, and so they sat down in the chairs. "Jasmin," they squealed, you look like a dream, like a vision." Gloria then put the stole over Jasmin's shoulder. She pointed to the gloves, but did not let her put them on, because it would have been difficult to take them off without wrinkling them. She gently took off the stole and had Lorraine wrap it in tissue paper and place it into a large carton with the gloves. When the girls had feasted their eyes enough, Jasmin went back into the fitting room and Gloria helped her out of the dress. She still had it draped over her arm. When the telephone call came, she quickly handed it to Lorraine for wrapping.

She answered the call and came back, announcing, "Mr. Tyler will be here in a few minutes; please wait."

The girls observed how the dress was put into an even larger carton than the stole was in. Then they heard tires squealing. "That's Matthew," Jasmin stated. "Let's go." To Gloria she said, "You are aware that the boxes will be picked up, aren't you?"

"Yes, Miss Claudius, your name is on it. We'll give it to the person with a copy of this slip," she gave her the identification tag.

Matthew looked in the rearview mirror to check if his hair was straight. He put on his hat, straightened his tie, got out of his car, buttoned his coat, and entered the store. He acknowledged the attendants by saying "Good afternoon, ladies." Then he turned to Jasmin who was walking towards him and said "Jasmin." He stretched out his hand in greeting. She took it and he lifted her hand to his lips and brushed a kiss onto her fingertips. He looked deep into her eyes, and then turned to her friends. "Would you ladies like a ride home?"

They just gaped at him speechlessly.

Jasmin cut in, "Yes, they would, thank you."

"Allow me." Matthew held the door open and motioned for Jasmin to go first, then Nellie and Beatrice.

"Follow me please," he said. He opened the passenger side of the Jaguar and flipped the seat forward so that they could get in one at a time. Then he put the seat back and assisted Jasmin into it.

"How much time do you have?" he asked after he got in himself and started the car.

"Fifteen minutes," they said in unison.

"Then we'll take the avenues," he declared. He drove out of the city limits, turned onto several treed avenues, and asked, "Did you ladies have a pleasant afternoon so far?"

"Yes, thank you. We were able to view Jasmin's dress; she looks stunning in it," Beatrice said, who had finally got her tongue back.

"I shall look forward to seeing it on Christmas Eve," Matthew smiled. He took another deserted road and went a little faster, but slowed down again in time to enter their street. This time he let the ladies out on his side of the car so that Jasmin didn't have to get up.

Jasmin called, "I'll see you later."

"Bye, Jasmin," they called back. As Matthew saw them to the edge of the steps they said, "Thank you very much indeed."

Jasmin

"Don't mention it," he said, tipping his hat. He got back into the car and drove off with Jasmin.

Nellie punched Beatrice in the side with her elbow and said, "Come back to earth, we have work to do."

"How did I do?" Matthew asked with a smile.

"You are a perfect Prince Charming," Jasmin swooned. "With that charm, no wonder you win every case in court."

"Talking about court, I almost didn't make it. I'll tell you some more. We are going to my office; is that O.K. with you?"

"Yes indeed," Jasmin replied eagerly. "I also have some news."

"I have no doubt about that," Matthew laughed.

At the office, Myrna was busy filing, clearing her desk, and displaying the itinerary for the New Year. She moved from room to room, checking that everything was in order. She smiled when she saw Matthew and Jasmin come inside. Matthew said, "Thank you for holding the fort for me. Have you met Miss Claudius?"

"Yes, I have. How pleasant to see you again, Miss Claudius." She looked at Matthew and said, "I have filed your papers in your desk and your appointment calendar for the New Year is on top. I shall be leaving now." Looking at Jasmin, she said, "Merry Christmas."

"Merry Christmas," Jasmin said.

"I'll lock up," Matthew said, while ushering Jasmin into his office.

Matthew went to the kitchen and fetched a bottle of ginger ale from the fridge. Then he filled two glasses, added some ice, and brought the drinks to his office. He saw Jasmin standing there and thought, 'I wonder if her affection for me is still only a teenage crush.' Out loud he said, "Here is some refreshment after the wild ride." They both grinned.

"Take a seat," he offered, pointing to a club chair beside a round marble-top coffee table. He sat in the other chair.

Jasmin said, "You can speak first. I want to hear how your morning went."

"Harrowing," he said, and he told her what had transpired. He had almost missed meeting her at the rental store.

"I thought something like that had happened, when I heard the roar of your car and the squealing of the brakes," Jasmin laughed again. "By the way, here is the tag for the two parcels ready for pick up. Did you see how large they are?"

"I might have out of the corner of my eye, but it did not register, because when I looked at you the rest of the world melted into oblivion."

Jasmin blushed, and smiled.

"Now tell me your story," he said.

Jasmin began. "On Monday, Mrs. Benson and Alicia came for lunch and asked me how I planned to spend my afternoon break. I mentioned I was planning to go shopping for a dress I'd seen and was eager to find out if it was still available. So, they said they would love to go shopping with me. Then they picked me up in their taxi and we went there. However, I couldn't find the dress anymore and in my mind I regretted not having bought it when I had bought my black velvet one, so as an afterthought I asked the clerk about it. I described it, and she said that she had it in the back room."

Jasmin took a sip of her drink and Matthew cut in, "And she found it for you and you got it?"

"Yes, in a way," Jasmin started again. Seeing Matthew raise his eyebrows with a questioning look, she laughed. "There is that lawyer look again. After I tried it on, I gave it to the clerk to wrap it up. When I came out of the fitting room, there it was in a big gift box with a card on it, stating it was a Christmas gift from Alicia and Mrs. Benson. They insisted I take it as a token of their appreciation for introducing them to Jeff Kerr. After they took me home they said in parting that they had talked it over with Jeff and he was going to join them for Christmas in Scotland with their relatives."

"That's wonderful," Matthew exclaimed.

"You deserve a gift too, really," Jasmin said, "for bringing this about."

"You are my gift!" Matthew said endearingly. "Now tell me the other story."

"Two stories in one, really. I received a letter the same day from my brother who's studying at a Bible college in Switzerland. He's coming to England to study at the Institute for Linguistics to prepare for the mission field. He's in contact with several churches from this city and surrounding areas who are supporters of the mission. My brother wrote that he planned to finance his studies by taking a part-time job and would need billeting.

"Yesterday," Jasmin began again, "Mr. James came for lunch and started the conversation by sharing his need for a security guard and how he had planned to ask Mr. Worthington for advice, adding it was only a part-time position. Well, you can guess," she looked at Matthew and saw the gleam in his eyes.

Matthew completed the sentence, "You told him about your brother and Mr. James gave him the job."

"Exactly," she said, "Life is beautiful isn't it?"

"Life with you is beautiful, Jasmin; with never a dull moment." He rose up, took her by the hand, and spun around with her in a few dance steps.

Before he could hold on to her, she spun out of his arms and said, "I have to leave now." She looked for her coat and purse. He held up her coat and lightly kissed her on the cheek. She smiled at that.

Matthew drove her to the hotel and said, "Do you have any plans for your break time tomorrow? I can be here at two thirty and pick you up."

"Thank you, Matthew; that will be great," Jasmin said as he walked her to the door.

"See you then," he said and went straight home. He found his mother in the conservatory.

"Hello Mother," he greeted her.

Mrs. Tyler looked up from the flowerbed she was working on. "Yes, Matthew, what is it?"

"I have the tag here for Jasmin's dress. There are two big boxes - too large for my Jaguar. Would you have Charles pick them up please?"

"Yes of course," Mrs. Tyler replied. "I'll see to it that he gets them first thing in the morning." She walked to the back entrance of the house and pinned the tag onto the schedule beside the telephone.

Meanwhile, as Jasmin passed by the timekeeper's booth, Ernest called, "Smiler, what did you do for Beatrice and Nellie to put them on cloud nine?"

"Oh, that," she called back as she pressed the elevator button, "I just want to make people happy."

Later that evening when Carla and Jasmin were in their room, Carla said, "Rose wants us to come to her housewarming party on the twenty-seventh. Here's the invitation; it's inside the Christmas card. Are you seeing Matthew before your ball?"

"Yes," Jasmin said, "I'll see him tomorrow afternoon."

"Then you can give it to him, O.K.?" asked Carla

The morning session flew by in a wink, because Jasmin was filled with the joyful expectation of seeing Matthew again. He arrived at the entrance, punctual as usual. After Jasmin strapped her seatbelt on, she said, "There's a German saying: 'punctuality is the courtesy of kings'."

Matthew questioned, "Does that mean I'm always punctual, or I'm a king?" He looked at her, waiting.

Jasmin

"It could mean," Jasmin said slowly, "That your punctuality is commendable, or you are the king of my heart."

"Or maybe both?" he asked.

"Take your pick," she shrugged her shoulders.

"Where shall we go?" He changed the subject.

"I would like to shop for something small for the timekeeper, like a garland or a wreath with some mini lights to make his booth look Christmassy."

"There's a nursery with a country craft store outside of town. Would you like to try it?" he suggested.

"That's splendid, sure," Jasmin voiced her approval.

Matthew drove through pleasant treed avenues to the city limits and down several country lanes till they arrived at a quaint village. He stopped at the craft store and they went up the stone steps through the large wooden double doors. Inside everything was tastefully displayed, and perfumed candles gave out pleasant fragrances. Jasmin selected a petite wreath held by red ribbons on a stand with mini red electric candles. "This will do perfectly," she told the clerk while she paid.

"While they wrap it up, we could have tea in one of those secluded alcoves over there," Matthew pointed Jasmin in the right direction.

"I'd like that, sure," she nodded as she let Matthew lead the way.

The alcove had a window overlooking the terraced garden. Tiny lights decorated the shrubs and small spruce trees in pots along the pathways. Jasmin and Matthew sat facing each other in the high backed wing chairs with lace coverings. The waitress brought the tea tray and set it between them. After she poured, she left. Matthew lifted the tiered platter slightly to let Jasmin select a couple of treats, and then he helped himself.

"Did you get any other correspondence?" he asked.

She sighed and admitted, "Yes, from Bernhard, he's in Switzerland now, but he plans to go to America."

An arrow went straight through Matthew's heart, and he sent a silent prayer up to heaven: "Oh Lord, if you are there, make Jasmin's heart inclined towards me; you know I'm good for her and she would be good for me." Out loud he asked, "Do you want to go to America?"

Jasmin thought for a moment, sipped her tea, and answered, "I used to when I was a teenager. It was described as the land of unlimited possibilities. I had thought that maybe England would be a stepping stone for me, but now I'm not so sure."

"Jasmin," Matthew took a deep breath, took hold of her hand, and stroked it gently, "Could I be your America? The fulfillment of your dreams?"

"Possibly, but you will have to pass my brother's inspection."

Matthew looked startled, "Is he your father's emissary?"

"Something like that, but have no fear. I've already written to him about you."

"What did he say?" he asked anxiously.

She paused, and then answered, "Our conversation goes way back to a time when he described the kind of man who would be right for me. I have heeded his advice and recognized these qualities in you."

"That is a lot to absorb; thank you for trusting me," Matthew said with relief.

Jasmin said matter-of-factly, "Now I will have to go back to work, though I did enjoy talking with you, being with you, riding in the car with you, and thank you for taking me shopping too."

"That rhymes," he said.

They picked up her purchase and he put it on the back seat as he helped Jasmin into her seat.

"Tomorrow at the same time?" he asked.

Jasmin

"Certainly," she said. "I am so happy to meet with you every day now. Each time we have a new topic of conversation."

Matthew came down the steps, held open the door for her, and said, "I've got to see that timekeeper who always calls you 'Smiler'."

They came to the booth. "Ernest," Jasmin said, "this is Mr. Tyler. Matthew, meet Ernest. Here's some Christmas cheer for you; open it up," she said as she helped loosen the tissue.

When he saw the festive gift, his eyes watered. "Smiler," his mouth wavered, "you are an angel and I'll never forget you."

"I have to run," Jasmin called as she ran to the elevator.

Matthew lingered till she was out of his sight, and then he turned to Ernest with a question: "If I gave you a letter for Jasmin you would guard it with your life, wouldn't you?" Ernest nodded. Matthew said, "Give me your schedule of when you are on duty." Ernest gave it to him. Matthew tipped his hat and left with a spring in his step.

Matthew rushed home, as he knew he had two more important things to do. First, he began writing a letter to Jasmin:

Jasmin Darling,

I live and breathe your name. Time is suspended in the realm of your presence. You are the only ornament I wish to see on the Christmas tree. You are the only gift I want under the tree for me. I wait for the day and the hour when you invite me into your life completely. I anticipate meeting your family in the near future and I am honoured that you trust me with your feelings, your emotions, and your aspirations.

My affection for you runs deeply.

My devotion for you is unending.

Yours forever,

Matthew

The next day at mid-morning Matthew drove over to the complex that housed the Regency ballroom. He checked with the concierge, who recognized him, and told him he was going up to Mr. Abernathy's penthouse and would return shortly with instructions about when and where to put some flowers.

Matthew took the elevator up and opened the apartment door to see if everything was in order. He opened the drapes to a clear view of the city and positioned a floral stand in front of the window next to a Queen Anne's chair. Back downstairs he spoke to the concierge and made sure that he would be on duty Christmas Eve. He asked the concierge to place the flowers that would arrive on Monday morning on the stand in front of the window. He slipped a bill into his hand.

"Very well, Sir," the concierge said.

When Jasmin came down to the timekeeper, he had an airmail letter in his hand for her. She quickly put it into the pocket of her smock. She hoped she wouldn't be busy on this last day of work. When the bar opened for business, only a few customers trickled in and the bartender took their orders to the tables. She then went outside her swinging door and sat on the kitchen stool next to the hotplate. The letter was from her sister in Germany, stating the new address of the first floor apartment they now occupied. Her sister and her doctor husband had invited Jasmin and her potential fiancé to come and visit. They insisted Jasmin could call them anytime on the telephone. Jasmin was excited to have this news to share with Matthew. At that moment she suddenly remembered that she hadn't given Rose's card to Matthew.

Matthew decided to park his car in the usual spot near the Danish Snack Bar, but he didn't go inside. He went instead to the staff entrance and found the timekeeper. "Ernest," he said, "please give this special letter to Jasmin when she comes back in after the break this afternoon, so she can take it upstairs." Then he gave him a ten shilling bill. "Merry Christmas."

"Much obliged, Sir, Merry Christmas to you too," Ernest said. He thought to himself, "Such a generous gentleman."

Jasmin finished her chores, rushed upstairs, and put her sister's letter and Rose's card into her purse. She reached the exit door just as Matthew drove up.

Jasmin ran up the stairs and almost flew into his arms, but she caught herself, took a deep breath, and smiled. "It looks like you're glad to see me," he said.

"I am," she agreed.

"I have a suggestion," he said. "There's a Christmas concert at the high school this afternoon; would you like to attend for a little while?"

"That sounds interesting," Jasmin said with a faraway look in her eyes.

He looked at her and said, "I see the shadow over your face; is it a sad memory? Would you rather not go?"

By now they had walked across the parking lot to the auditorium.

"Oh, no, not really," she reminisced. "I was in a Christmas play once, and I played an angel. I had a live candle in my hand and when I exited the stage my hair caught on fire."

At this, Matthew impulsively put his arms around her. "Tell me what happened," he urged her on.

295

"I quickly blew out the candle and patted the flames out; it had only singed a strip of my hair, but it startled me. Eventually my hair grew back. Let's go see this," she said in a lighter mood. "Were you ever in a play?" Now she was curious.

"I was," he said.

"As what?" She smiled now.

"I played a shepherd the first time," Matthew told her.

"I can't imagine that," Jasmin laughed. "What else?"

"The other time I acted as one of the wise men," Matthew reminisced.

"I can imagine that more," Jasmin reflected.

They chose a seat in the back row, in case they had to leave early. There was still time to talk, so Jasmin said, "Oh, before I forget, this is a card from Rose. We are invited to her housewarming party." She took the card out of her purse and gave it to him.

"And this is the letter from my sister," she held up the airmail envelope.

"What does it say?" Matthew eagerly asked.

"She and her husband have invited us to visit at their new apartment anytime. Here's their telephone number and address and they speak English." Jasmin held the letter in front of him.

"Let me see that, please," Matthew said. At this moment the music began and he quickly took his pen out and copied the telephone number onto his notepad.

They enjoyed the concert and even sang along with the carols. Matthew checked his watch and whispered to Jasmin that it was time to go home. While they drove, Matthew reminded Jasmin, "Tomorrow we have a date to see the exhibition at the museum, remember?"

"What time?" Jasmin asked.

Jasmin

"Three p.m.," Matthew said. "It's about an hour long. I'll pick you up at two forty-five. I usually go to the gym on Saturday afternoons. Would you like to go there too, afterwards? They have a ladies department."

"Another time perhaps," Jasmin said. "I'm happy to go back home and read." She continued, "I might take my steno pad to practice at the Concordia Bar, if we aren't busy."

"Smart girl," Matthew said. "Say hello to Martin."

"I will, bye," she said.

After Matthew took her down the steps, he looked through the window to see if the time keeper would give the letter to her. Sure enough, he saw Ernest wave her over and hand her the envelope he recognized to be his. Then he quickly got in the car and drove off. "This will put her into a pleasant-dream world," he thought smugly.

Jasmin blushed as she took the letter from Ernest. She ran to the open elevator and got in. Upstairs she put her letter into the locked box in her closet and got ready for work.

Martin leaned over her counter. "Are you glad it's the last evening at work?" he asked.

"Yes, in a way," she said. "Matthew says hello, by the way."

"Tell him hello back. Are you seeing him again?" Martin looked like he really wanted to know.

Jasmin replied, "Yes, I'm going to the Regency Ball, and his mother invited me for Christmas."

"Good for you," Martin said. "I'm going to Rose's housewarming party, are you?"

"I expect so," she said, looking at the clock. Martin took the cue and sauntered over to the door to open it for the evening customers.

Jasmin served several hors d'oeuvres and cleared things away. A customer showed up who had been there several times before.

"Good evening Miss Claudius," he said, "I shall have the French onion soup and all the trimmings." He ordered his drink from Richie.

Jasmin tidied up below her counter and put her steno pad up at the corner, so it wouldn't get stained. The guest asked, "How is your stenography coming along?"

Jasmin said, "I have to practice to keep up with it."

He offered, "I can give you a dictation and you can take it down."

She sat on her own barstool with the pad on her lap and looked at him to signal that she was ready. He quoted the heading of a letter with name, address, and telephone number and the same of the addressee. He began with a salutation and a detailed business proposal to a potential client. He ended with "best regards" and his name and title.

Jasmin read it back to him, but he stopped her mid-sentence and added another adjective. Then he said, "Go on," until she had finished. "That is excellent," he exclaimed. "You don't suppose you could transcribe it for me, could you?"

"I could," Jasmin said, "but we're closed after tonight and won't be open until January second."

"That's perfectly alright with me. I shall be back the first week of January and will pick it up then."

"Sure," Jasmin said. She loaded all supplies onto the trolley, said goodnight, and wheeled the trolley into the kitchen.

"Finally," she said, when she got up to her room. She wanted to read Matthew's letter in private, but she knew Carla would come in at any moment. Jasmin looked to see if anyone had signed up for the common bathtub room and found a free spot. She quickly went back to her room, got into her bathrobe, fetched the letter out of her memory box, and took it with her. She decided to soak in the tub and read it there. She let the words wash over her and thought, 'He must be the right one for my future. Hans approves of him, Camilla approves of him, and I am sure Mom and Dad will too. Three more days and then I'll be with him for Christmas.'

Jasmin got out of the tub, cleaned it up for the next person, and went back to her room. She laid out her clothes for the next day, locked her letter in her treasure box, and decided to have pleasant dreams.

On Saturday at two forty-five p.m., Matthew - prompt as usual - stood at the top of the stairs when Jasmin appeared at the door. He noticed she was wearing a tight skirt and high heels, so he rushed down the few steps and offered his arm to assist her.

"You look sophisticated today with your hair up," he said admiringly.

"Thank you," she said. They walked around the various exhibits in the museum, listening to the guide and examining interesting details.

Matthew said in a low voice, "I enjoy looking at you more than all these artifacts." She looked at him sideways. "Yes," he said, "in that sharp business suit you could pose as a female executive, a financial advisor, an investment banker, or a business consultant."

Jasmin interrupted, "A real estate broker?" Matthew agreed. Jasmin commented, "You know, the virtuous woman described in Proverbs 31 is a business woman as well as an efficient manager of her household."

Matthew added, "In my opinion you could be all that as long as you're the manager of my life, Jasmin."

They looked at each other and smiled. He offered his arm and she put her hand in his bent elbow as they neared the exit.

"There's a new Italian coffee bar around the corner; would you like to go there? It's my treat," Jasmin offered.

"Your treat?" Matthew said incredulously.

"Yes," she said. When he hesitated, she repeated, "Consider it a fee for professional advice. My treat."

"Since you put it that way, I'll accept," Matthew laughed.

They walked across the parking lot around the corner to the coffee shop. Jasmin ordered cappuccino for two and the attendant promised to bring it to the booth they had selected.

Matthew started by saying, "It seems that every day we have new news for each other, and I don't know how we're going to handle it in the coming year when we're back to work. First of all, do you have my telephone numbers safely stored?"

Jasmin said, "Yes, I do."

"Now," he gently stroked her cheek with the back of his fingers, "let's hear what's on your mind."

She began, "Yesterday evening, one customer who had come in several times before asked if I had kept up with my stenography practice. On other occasions I'd practiced a few sentences he dictated to me and read them back to him for fun. I answered that I practiced when I wasn't busy. This time he asked me if he could dictate a short letter. 'O.K.' I said, and then I followed every word including names and addresses and read it back to him. Then he asked if I could transcribe the letter for him. I said I could in the New Year, and he told me that he would be back and would pick the letter up then."

Matthew interrupted, "You want to know if you did the right thing, since he asked you. And if he picks up the letter and pays you, to whom should the money go since it was done in your place of employment."

"Yes and no, because the actual typing I do in my spare time, but you are right: the dictation took place at my place of employment. In my mind it started out as practice, and when he asked it became a favour. If he offers me anything I was going to refuse or maybe let him give me something which I would put into the tip jar. You know how the tips are handled at the Concordia Bar; we're a team and we share all tips at the end of the week equally. The same as in the Danish Snack Bar."

Jasmin continued, "I don't think I want to do it again, however. A thought occurred to me of what I want to do in my future. If I don't stay in my current job, I might eventually start my own business of typing service and accounting service for people who cannot afford full time secretaries or bookkeepers. I have even thought of creating an advertising service to help small businesses off the ground."

Matthew advised her as follows: "You are handling it well by treating it as a favour and letting it be. But don't take your steno pad to work anymore, unless the hotel hires you for that extra service. In that case you would do it on their behalf and you would be paid by your employer."

"They paid me a bonus for the newspaper interview," Jasmin told him.

"I'm glad they did; you deserved that," Matthew said. "I'm proud of you. Now, how about we leave and I'll see you at ten-thirty for church tomorrow. I could take you out for brunch to the quaint teahouse; do you remember?"

"That would be lovely," Jasmin said.

They walked quietly to the car and he drove her home. Before they parted, he asked, "Did you read my letter?"

"Yes, thank you," she said. "I let each word sink into my soul, and your letter transported me into a 'dream-come-true-world'."

"That's what it is supposed to do," Matthew said as he waved goodbye.

Matthew went straight to the gym for a workout, but the whole time his mind was churning as he recalled how tense he had felt when Jasmin had talked about the frequent guest. First, Matthew had thought the guy was making advances towards her; then, when he dictated a letter Matthew had thought it was a love letter. He had held his breath because his heart had skipped a beat. He felt such relief in understanding it was just some advertising jargon. Moreover, Matthew thought, "I don't know how long I can stand seeing her in the public eye, alone and unprotected. Not that I want her hidden from the public, but I want to be beside her in the public. I'll be anxious for two more days; hopefully then there will be a decision." He went to a different set of equipment and mulled more thoughts over in his mind: "She confides in me. She values my input, yet she is ambitious. She wants to start a business, and no doubt she would be successful. Will she ever want a family of her own? Oh, Lord, could you turn her towards me?"

Silence.

He took a detour down the fast country lane and stopped to sit and think some more. "Did I promise to build a house or a castle for her? Did she say she could handle the household and a business as well? Did I promise to be the fulfillment of all her dreams, aspirations, and ambitions? Does she want to get married and live happily ever after?"

When Matthew came home he went to the library first to select a book and then to his office for nothing in particular. He turned the light on and noticed the tea tray with a letter on it. He didn't recognize the handwriting. When he turned it over, a jolt went through his body. The return address read: Jasmin Claudius.

He put the book aside and said, "I've got to sit down for this." He fiddled around with his clumsy letter opener, and finally managed to get the card out. The fragrance of the flower petal filled his nostrils. "Jasmin," he whispered, "is this from your heart, or am I just a passing fancy?"

Jasmin

On Sunday morning Jasmin practically skipped up the steps. Matthew wanted to hug her and swing her around, but as they were out in the street, he refrained from that. Instead, he held her hand and squeezed it tightly before he helped her into the car.

At the church service, they sat with the Harmans again. Matthew brushed against her hands when holding the hymn book and when she smiled, he saw that glow. His mind said, "One more day."

The pastor spoke on the book of Ruth. He related that although Ruth had lost her husband and could have disassociated herself from her mother-in-law, she chose to follow the faith path of her mother-in-law, who rewarded Ruth by introducing her to her rich cousin and advising her how to indicate to him her interest in marriage. Ruth found out where he slept and lay down at his feet. This gesture was to awaken his protective instinct and signify to him that according to law he had the right to marry her. They married and through their lineage the Messiah was born.

Matthew thought, "I vaguely remember reading about that."

On their way out, they confirmed with the Harmans the invitation for Boxing Day and wished a Merry Christmas to the pastor.

Matthew drove out into the countryside past gentle slopes amid lush fields and woods and finally glided to a stop at an empty lot overlooking a valley. He asked Jasmin to come out for a minute, as he wanted to show her something special.

She stepped out of the car and looked around. "Nice scenery," she commented.

Matthew offered his arm to Jasmin as they took a few steps to the edge of a knoll. He outlined the periphery of an invisible border for her and said, "My grandfather deeded this property to me."

Jasmin uttered jokingly, "So this is where you are going to build that castle for me?"

Matthew turned to her and said, "Yes, if that's what it takes to make you mine."

Jasmin stopped smiling and asked, "You really mean that, don't you?"

"With all my being," he assured her.

She started to go and he followed her. She said, "I am totally flabbergasted, I'm at a loss for words, you are wonderful," she caught her breath. "But I would have to have an input in the design."

"You can have all the input you want; you can even have an office built there, so you can run your business out of your own home," he insisted.

"Matthew, I have trouble wrapping my mind around all these new possibilities. I have to sleep on it."

"You have all the time in the world to become acclimatized to this idea. We have the whole of next week to talk and discuss things," he shared as he opened the car door for her.

"Well," she said again, as they drove a different route home, "You have made this an amazing day."

"It's going to be even more wonderful and amazing tomorrow," Matthew promised.

"Do you remember any of your dance steps?" Jasmin asked him.

"Yes, I do, and I'll go over them this afternoon in my mind while I think of you," he said, "as long as you follow everything I lead you into."

"Uh, oh; forewarned is forearmed. I shall have to be alert. By the way," Jasmin pondered, "Do you suppose I could give you the box with my new dress to take to your home and have Emily hang it up in the room that I am going to occupy? I don't want to squish it into my small suitcase with my other things."

"I'd be delighted to do that and more," Matthew said. "Tomorrow morning I shall be here to take you to the beauty salon at ten

Jasmin

forty-five sharp. I'll spend the hour and half in my office and come back for you at Kurt's at around twelve thirty. Then I will take you home for the afternoon and pick you up in the evening, O.K.?"

"Oh, Matthew, I feel so well taken care of by you, thank you," she gushed.

They had reached her hotel. "Do you want to get the box now? I'll wait here," he offered.

"Yes," she said, "be right back."

Jasmin rushed up the elevator (luckily it wasn't busy), grabbed the box from her room, and got down just as quickly. Then she gave it to Matthew who stood waiting at the top of the stairs. He came down the last steps and took the box, waved goodbye, and left.

Matthew arrived home at tea time, and he saw Emily come out of the kitchen on her way to call his mother. He intercepted her and said, "Emily, this is Miss Claudius's dress. Would you hang it up in her room to let the creases out? She is going to wear it on Christmas morning."

"Yes, Mr. Tyler," Emily said and took it upstairs. He made a note of which room she went in.

Jasmin decided to take a quick nap. After an hour, she studied her steno pad, typed the letter for her customer, and found an envelope. She inserted it but left it open for the gentleman to sign. Then she put it away in a folder for safekeeping. She pulled her suitcase out of the closet and selected a few outfits and nightgowns. She made up her mind not to tell Carla anything that had transpired the last few days and went downstairs for something to eat. As she stood in the sawdust-covered passageway between the hot kitchen and larder, she heard Pete calling, "Jasmin Angel, what can I get for you?"

"Hi, Pete, the usual. You know what I like. I'll be back; I need to get a few teabags and a jug of milk for the morning. Just put it into a basket tray. I'm going up to the pastry kitchen to find sweet

items." She went to the pastry kitchen where the new junior chef was working by himself.
　He asked, "Are you the one they call 'Angel'?"
　Jasmin laughed out loud. "My real name is Jasmin, what's yours?"
　"Marco," he replied.
　"Marco, are you Italian?"
　"Spanish," he said.
　"Como estas," she greeted him.
　"Bien gracias," he replied.
　"Do you have anything new baked?" she asked,
　"We've made Baklava and Danish pastries," he reported.
　"I'll take both," she said. "Nice to meet you."
　She went back to the larder, picked up her basket from Pete, wished him Merry Christmas, and told him she'd be there for Rose's housewarming party. Jasmin made tea in her room. She had the salad for supper and wrapped the Danish pastry in tinfoil so that it would stay fresh for her morning breakfast. She looked over her accounting assignments and studied the textbook for business administration, making sure to look up the word "contingency" in her dictionary. She finally went to bed, thinking of Matthew as she drifted off to sleep.
　On Monday morning she was excited about what the day would bring. She eagerly awaited Matthew. As soon as his car arrived, she was out the door. He held the car door open and she slipped inside.
　"You sure are chipper," he commented.
　"Yes, are you?" she quipped back.
　"Seeing you makes me ecstatic," he said.
　"Mr. Tyler, you are talking in superlatives," Jasmin giggled.
　"Now let's see what Kurt can do for you," Matthew grinned.
　"I'm going to have a wild style. Promise me that when you pick me up, you won't faint," Jasmin smiled broadly.

Jasmin

"The wilder, the better. Anything you offer to me, I will take." Matthew leaned over and kissed her hand when he stopped the car. He took her to the door to see her in and to get a look at Kurt.

"Pick me up right here at the desk," she whispered.

"O.K." Matthew saw Kurt walking toward him, stretching his hand out.

Matthew shook his hand and Jasmin introduced them: "Kurt, Mr. Tyler."

Matthew said, smiling, "Do an exquisite job for the lady."

"Sure will," Kurt said.

Kurt had one of his assistants wash Jasmin's hair and prepare it for curling, and then he took over. "What kind of dress are you wearing?" Jasmin described it. He gave her a pencil and paper for her to sketch the outfit, complete with gloves and stole.

"Ah, definitely up," he said, "Empire style." He used every size of curlers on her hair and special clips to make ringlets. She had to sit for thirty-five minutes under the dryer. The beautician applied foundation cream and face powder to Jasmin's face and neck and expertly applied eye shadow and mascara. Before Kurt began his creative work of art, he told her the day he would be open over the holidays and she booked her next appointment. When he had finished and showed her the back of her hair in the hand mirror, she smiled in approval. He exclaimed, "You look like Marie Antoinette."

Matthew was indeed taken aback when he entered the salon. Everybody looked at his reaction to Jasmin's appearance. He immediately took control of the situation and in theatrical style took her hand, bowed slightly, kissed the tips of her fingers, and said, "Mademoiselle enchant." The whole beauty salon applauded and cheered. Matthew put a ten shilling bill into Kurt's hand and said, "Merry Christmas." At the door, Jasmin put her silk scarf over her head for protection from the weather.

Kurt said to his staff, "If that coiffeur doesn't get her a ring, I don't know what will."

Matthew had the Jaguar parked directly across from the salon entrance so that she could slip right inside. Matthew asked, "Would you like to go for lunch? Ceylon Tea Centre is still open."

"O.K., that's unexpected, but thanks; order me something small. I'll be right back." Jasmin walked to the powder room. Matthew enjoyed looking at her slim silhouette in the soft flowing blouse, tight pencil skirt, and high heels.

When she came back, he got up from his chair and pulled her chair out so that she could be seated. She asked, "So you speak French, do you?"

"Yes," Matthew said, "enough to decipher a menu and charm a lady."

"You did that today," Jasmin smiled, while sipping her tea. "What else did you do this morning?" Jasmin asked him.

"I laid out some files to be attended to first thing in the New Year, but before that I relished in the fragrance of your endearing card," Matthew answered.

Jasmin blushed. "So you received my card?"

"Yes," he said. "I have been wondering since whether this came from your heart and soul, or am I just a passing fancy?"

Jasmin countered, "That's for me to know and for you to find out."

Matthew had an analytical look on his face and said, "I can perceive some things, but not everything. It will take me a lifetime to unravel your mystique."

She tipped her head with a flirty look that made the ringlets dangle back and forth.

Matthew grinned from ear to ear, and said, "Kurt sure knows how to create a style that makes you look irresistible."

Jasmin

"Oh, these," Jasmin fingered the ringlets, "There is an expression in German, but it would be lost in the translation."

"Enchantress!" he said.

"Matthew," Jasmin giggled, "you are poetry and I am prose."

"That's why we make a perfect match," he assured her.

"Now seriously, I have a question, Matthew," Jasmin changed the subject.

"I like the way your lips form my name," Matthew interjected.

Jasmin stated, "I agree with your comment a few days ago that it wouldn't do if you came to the Concordia Bar for lunch, because you would forget to go to work."

"And make money so I could build you that castle," Matthew completed her sentence, laughing out loud.

"Two questions I need to ask before we leave," Jasmin said softly. "One, do you place the Christmas gifts under the tree the night before? Or in the morning on Christmas Day?"

"In the evening," Matthew said. "What's the second question?"

"Would you please take my bracelet off?" Jasmin held up her wrist.

"I'd be glad to," he said. He undid it and cupped her hand in both of his, held it to his cheeks, then let go.

She placed the bracelet into its case, donned her silk scarf, and let him pull her chair out as she rose.

As they walked out, he said with a glint in his eyes, "One more thing I have discovered about us: we like to tease each other."

She shrugged her shoulders and answered, "Could be."

Jasmin kept her scarf on inside the car. Matthew reminded her that he would be back for her at six sharp as he escorted her to the staff door and left.

Jasmin put the hairspray from Kurt inside her cosmetic case. She packed the satin dance shoes and the rest of her things into the suitcase, including the evening clutch purse she had used only once when she went out with Bernhard. She reminisced for a moment about what a good friend he had been and how he had made her laugh. She hoped he would find someone nice in the future.

Jasmin puffed her pillow firmly under her neck so as not to squish the curls on the back of her head, and then she took a nap.

When she woke up and checked the time, she saw that it was five forty-five.

Carla came into the room, asking, "What time is Matthew coming?"

"At six sharp. I will be ready to go in a minute."

Carla offered to go downstairs and stand inside the door to tell him that she was on her way, and Jasmin thanked her. She put the scarf back on her hair, picked up her bags, and headed for the elevator with her suitcase and cosmetic bag.

The elevator was stuck, and fear gripped her. She ran down the stairs to the fifth floor to catch the guest elevator to the main lobby. She ran through the hallway to find that the "Staff Only" door was blocked by the catch. She frantically kicked it open with her heel, pressed through, and became disoriented as she slid into a dungeon of despair. She forced her mind to focus and finally reached the exit. She yanked open the door and noticed Carla standing beside Matthew.

She fell into an abyss of fear as her mind was clouded with a foreboding vision of the wicked stepsister tricking her prince into taking her away instead of Jasmin. Everything she had hoped and dreamed for was snatched away. She thought, "Is she stealing my boyfriend?" Jasmin yelled, "Matthew!"

At that instant he turned his head and came running down the steps. Taking her luggage, he embraced her impulsively, saying, "Jasmin, you are here!"

Jasmin

"Are you real?" she breathed.

"Yes, I am real and I am here and I won't ever let you go." He gingerly assisted her into the car.

Carla disappeared.

"Drive up ahead a bit," she requested. "I have to take a few more deep breaths so I don't cry. I don't want to think about the ordeal I just went through."

She calmed herself. He drove slowly for a few blocks and then stopped again, so they could talk.

"Jasmin," he put his hands on hers, "I must know a way to find you in an emergency. It greatly distressed me when I didn't see you at the door. I wondered how to go about finding you. Then Carla showed up and said that you would be delayed. For a moment it startled me to see her, thinking that something had happened to you. Next time, if you are not there, I will come to get you. Tell me your room number or where you might be otherwise."

Jasmin explained, "The elevator was stuck, which is unusual now with only skeleton staff. I lost several minutes, and then raced down the stairwell to the fifth floor to catch the guest elevator to the first floor. I tried to go through the blocked "Staff Only" door, finally kicked it through, and ran in my high heels that don't lend themselves for running down more stairs and a labyrinth of hallways until eventually reaching the exit. When I saw Carla standing beside you, a flashback of a betrayal seized me and I thought it was going to happen again. In fear I screamed to awaken from that nightmare, and the image disappeared when you came for me. Tell me again you are real."

Matthew held both her hands, "Jasmin, I am real, I am with you, I won't let you out of my sight, and I won't let anything come between us. This night I have a special plan for you."

"When I'm at your house, I'll draw you a map," Jasmin said. "Also, I'll tell you the staff I meet and interact with." She let out a sigh of relief and declared, "I'm ready now to go on that first official formal date with you."

"Glad to oblige at last." Matthew stroked her cheek and started to drive.

They arrived at his house to the awaiting staff and his mother. Matthew handed the suitcase to Emily, who accompanied Jasmin to her suite at the top of the stairs. Emily assisted Jasmin in fitting the new corset. Jasmin held her hand in front of her eyes and asked Emily to spray the ringlets with hairspray. Emily held the dress for Jasmin to step into, and then she fastened the hook and eye at the back and pulled the long zipper up. It took both of their efforts to slip on the long gloves and zip them also. Jasmin picked up her clutch purse and checked her compact, lipstick, tissues, and coins. Then she closed it and let Emily put the stole on her shoulders. Finally, Jasmin stepped graciously down the curved staircase. Mrs. Tyler looked, nodded her approval, and followed the chauffeur into the waiting limousine. Matthew stood at the bottom of the stairs and offered his arm. She slipped her hand onto his elbow and let him lead her to the opened limousine door. He entered at the other door and sat beside Jasmin, whispering, "You take my breath away; I am enthralled by the symmetry of your loveliness."

"Thank you," she said, "I hoped this would please you."

They stepped under the canopy into the ballroom and glanced at the welcoming smiles of the Worthingtons at their table. Matthew said, "Until dinner is served, we can mingle. Most people here are middle aged acquaintances, former clients, or former clients of my father's. There are no other guests of our age that I know with the exception of Lloyd and Verna over there. Let's walk around.

Jasmin

Don't worry, I won't let go of your hand." He offered his arm and she held on.

"I adore walking with you," she said.

"I enjoy parading you around," Matthew whispered back.

They walked around mingling until they came to Lloyd and Verna. They had been standing with them for a few minutes when Lloyd asked, "May I call on Jasmin to dance with me later?"

"One dance," Matthew said, turning to Jasmin, "O.K.?"

"O.K.," she nodded.

A few more acquaintances bowed their heads to Jasmin when Matthew introduced her, and then they took their seats at the table. The wine steward brought wine for the hors d'oeuvres as the busboy filled the water glasses. After dinner, the orchestra began to play an unfamiliar tune. Matthew leaned over to Mr. Worthington and asked, "What beat is that?"

"Quickstep," was the reply.

Matthew bowed before Jasmin, she smiled, and they took to the dance floor.

"I'll follow your lead," she said. Jasmin esteemed it thoroughly pleasurable to sway in dance with Matthew.

Matthew felt compelled to revise the timing of his proposal to Jasmin. "Are you ready for a break? Come with me; I want to show you something."

He took her by the hand to the hallway and they rode the lift up to the penthouse. He led her inside and directed her to the window overlooking the city. She looked at the dazzling view of the glistening city lights below. Inhaling the fragrance of the flowers, she asked, "What's the occasion to take me to the top of the world?"

Matthew said, "Please sit down; I want to ask you an important question." After Jasmin had taken a seat, Matthew went down on one knee and said, "Jasmin, I want to declare to you in person what

I have written in my letters. I love you with all my heart and soul, and I desire to link my life with yours. As a token of my commitment, I offer this ring to you. Can you see it in your heart to love me enough to marry me?"

He held the open box with the ring in front of her, took her hand, and slipped the ring on her finger. Jasmin gasped, "Marry you?"

He put his arm around her to lift her out of the chair. As they stood in an embrace, he held her face in both of his hands, moved close to her mouth, and said, "Say yes, Jasmin."

She whispered, "Yes, I will," before she responded to his gentle kiss.

He asked her again, "Do you love me, Jasmin?"

"Yes, I love you, Matthew." They kissed sweetly.

"Will you be the mother of my children?" He stroked her back gently, but she stiffened and pulled herself out of his embrace.

"Not now!"

He laughed. "Of course, not now; we'll have the wedding first." He pulled her back into his embrace, held her, put a soft kiss on her forehead, and said, "Don't you know we are meant for each other? You set the date for the wedding," he entreated her.

She leaned her head on his shoulder and put her arm around his neck. "Yes, I know we are meant for each other. I told my brother and he approves. My mother will be so glad and my sister made me promise to let her design my wedding dress. When it is finished, we can get married."

Matthew asked, "How long will it take?"

"I don't know; I'll have to write to her," Jasmin answered.

"So we have a deal? When your dress is ready, we'll get married." Matthew affirmed.

"Deal!" Jasmin shouted.

Jasmin

"Yes." He kissed her again. "I'm so happy we are going to get married; are you?" He twirled her around in a spin and lifted her up. "Let's go down and tell the others, O.K.?"

"O.K.," she said. "Is there a mirror here? I have to check my makeup. Oh, and the ring is too tight over the glove; can you help me undo it?"

She slipped the ring onto the little finger of the other hand to hold it, while Matthew undid the zipper of the glove. He then took the ring and placed it on her left ring finger. It fit perfectly!

He said, "The ladies room is over that way; see you in a minute."

When Jasmin came back out, Matthew was already standing at the door waiting. "Do you know what we are now? Bride and Bridegroom or fiancée and fiancé."

"Sounds fascinating," she said, holding up the ring finger to her lips. She whispered, "Fiancé."

"You'll have to keep your ring on, even at work," he admonished.

"I will for sure," Jasmin exclaimed with delight.

When they came out of the elevator downstairs, Jasmin asked, "Did you put my other glove into your pocket?"

"Yes, I did," Matthew said. "The music has started. Let's dance; it sounds like Rumba."

"It is," she confirmed.

The danced the steps and figures they remembered and lost themselves in the magic of it.

Mrs. Worthington spotted it first. She said to Mrs. Tyler, "Do you see what I see?" and pointed to the couple.

"Yes," Martha said, "they dance well together, like they belong to each other."

"More than that - look at her left hand," Emma demanded.

Mr. Worthington spotted it and cried, "The ring!"

"You mean," Martha didn't finish the sentence.

"Yes," Emma said, "an engagement ring."

"So he did it!" Mrs. Tyler rejoiced. "That boy of mine, I am proud of him; he finally caught her. Emma, we get to plan a wedding!"

"Remember," Emma said, "they have to plan a wedding."

"But I am going to have a part in it," protested Mrs. Tyler.

"Yes, Martha, you'll have the best part in it," Emma said.

Matthew and Jasmin sauntered hand in hand to the table to the three waiting pairs of smiling eyes. Matthew addressed his mother, "Mother, meet your future daughter-in-law. We are engaged."

Mrs. Tyler jumped up from her chair, "Matthew, Jasmin, I love you," she hugged both of them. "When is the wedding?"

"As soon as I have a wedding dress," Jasmin said.

Mrs. Tyler clapped her hands and suggested, "New Year's Eve".

"Not quite that fast, but close," Matthew said.

Mr. Worthington stretched out his hand to Matthew and Jasmin and offered his handshake. "Congratulations to both of you," he said.

Mrs. Worthington said the same. "Why don't we have champagne to celebrate?" she asked.

"Good idea," Mrs. Tyler clapped her hands with glee.

The music began to play and Lloyd and Verna approached the group. Lloyd asked, "Is there something I should know?" He pointed to Jasmin's bare arm and the ring on her finger.

"We are engaged," Matthew said.

"May I dance with the bride?" Lloyd asked.

"You may," Matthew nodded and said, "I'm going to sit this one out."

Mr. Worthington got up and asked Verna to dance. Lloyd led Jasmin expertly into several spins of the Jive. Matthew thought, "I know what it feels like to dance with Jasmin; now I can feast my eyes on what she looks like when she dances." Lloyd led her into a twist and double spin that resembled a pirouette and made the lower

Jasmin

part of her skirt flare to show off her knees. Matthew analyzed that and made up his mind he was going to learn that figure and would only dance it with Jasmin.

When the others came back to the table, the champagne was served and Mr. Worthington invited Lloyd and Verna to join them. They cheered and wished the engaged couple good luck. The music began again. This time it was a Tango called "La Cumparsita".

Matthew said, "That's ours." He bowed before Jasmin. "Let's count the beat," he whispered. They counted the beat and flowed with the music. He warned her before a trick step, she followed, and they had fun going through several routines before ending with a lunge.

As dessert trolleys came by each table, late night mocha was served. Jasmin took some dessert but chose ice water instead of coffee. So did Matthew. As it neared midnight they wished the Worthingtons bon voyage as they were leaving soon for their winter vacation.

Charles, Mrs. Tyler's chauffeur, showed up near the door to lead them to the limousine. While driving home, Matthew and Jasmin sat beside each other smiling and holding hands. As they entered the house, Mrs. Tyler said, "I am going to turn in, goodnight."

"Goodnight, Mother; we are going to sit in the library for a bit."

Jasmin sat on one end of the loveseat and Matthew pulled the foot stool in front of her. "You can put your feet up."

"Oh, thanks," she said. "Actually, I'd like to take my shoes right off, but..." She couldn't reach them with her hands, because of her stiff corset.

Matthew smiled and took them off for her. Then he sat down beside her and asked, "Was this evening everything you expected it to be?"

"Yes," she said dreamily. She leaned into him. "Are you real? You are not a figment of my imagination?"

"I am real and I am here with you and will entwine my life in yours. If I could help it, I wouldn't want you to go to work anymore. I don't even want other men to look at you, but I don't want you to feel trapped. I fell in love with you the day you asked me to explain the concept of 'security'. I hoped to shelter you, protect you, and express my love to you."

"I remember that," Jasmin said. "Your words mesmerized me and the sound of your voice held me spellbound. I cherish each word in your letters and I love you." Suddenly, she shrugged back from the embrace. "Oh, I forgot the gifts. They're still in my suitcase; what shall I do?"

Matthew assured her, "Tomorrow morning when Emily wakes you up, ask her to bring you a tray. You can place the gifts on it and she will take it to the Christmas tree. If you need anything, you can come to my room. I'll show you. It's the first door to the left."

Jasmin jumped up and started stomping out of the library in her stocking feet. "I'm not Ruth and I'm not going to sleep at your feet!" she told him in no uncertain terms.

Matthew caught up with her. "Jasmin, I adore your spunk." He embraced her and gave her a firm kiss. "Goodnight, precious. I'll wait until you are upstairs before turning off the lights."

She tugged the side of her skirt to give space for her feet to ascend the stairs. Then she turned abruptly and cried, "Matthew, if Emily is not here, I have nobody to help me out of my dress."

He looked stunned. "Is it difficult?"

"Yes, I can't reach the hook and eye at the back of my neck."

"I'll help you." He came with her to the top of the stairs.

"O.K.," she said, dropping the stole to the floor and turning her back to him. "You see that tiny hook? Undo it and pull the tab of the zipper a few inches. Not too much; I can do the rest."

He undid it with his slender fingers, picked up the stole, handed it to her, and opened her door.

She smiled and said, "Thank you."

He skipped down the stairs and muttered to himself, "It's going to be hilarious catching that butterfly."

In her suite, Jasmin managed to unzip the rest of the gown and slip it off. She had to struggle with the corset, but at least the hooks were in front. She slipped into the nightgown that Emily had laid out on the damask-covered comforter and wrapped a silk scarf around her hair so that the coiffeur stayed unruffled. She held her hands together, felt the ring, and visualized the memory of the sensation of Matthew's first real kiss. Jasmin wondered if this was what her mom had felt when she and her dad were engaged. She drifted off to sleep with Matthew on her mind.

Jasmin woke up at dawn, put on her robe, and took her time with makeup and such. She knew she would need help again with the new dress. While waiting, she set out her gold ballerina kidskin slippers which had been designed by her sister, complete with gold brocade bows. She looked over at the gifts for Matthew and whispered, "I hope these please you." The gift for Mrs. Tyler was a delicate perfumed stationery set, similar to the one she had sent to her own mother.

A soft knock sounded at the door. Jasmin opened it for Emily. "Good morning Miss," she said, carrying a tray. "Here's some orange juice for you."

"Thank you," Jasmin said. "Please set it down. Emily, would you help me into the dress, please?" She took a sip of the juice as Emily removed the dress from the hanger.

"It looks pretty on you for Christmas, Miss," Emily said admiringly.

"Thank you," Jasmin said, and then she pointed to the gifts. "These are to go under the tree. Mr. Tyler suggested you put them on the tray and place them there."

"Yes, Miss, I'll take the gifts downstairs and come back in five minutes to fetch you for breakfast," Emily informed her. Jasmin put on the delicate slippers and waited till Emily knocked on the door again.

"Emily," Jasmin asked her, "will you be here tonight?"

"Yes, Miss. I'm off this afternoon, but I'm coming back tonight at nine."

"Where do I call you if I need help with undoing my dress?" Jasmin asked.

"You can ring the bell right here." Emily strode into the room and showed her the pull on the wall.

"Thank you," Jasmin said.

Jasmin lifted one side of her long dress between two fingers as she descended the stairs after Emily and was led to the breakfast room. Charles stood at attention near the fireplace, and Mrs. Tyler stood behind her chair. "Good morning, Jasmin, did you sleep well?"

"Yes, quite well, thank you. Did you?"

"Very well, thank you."

At that moment Matthew burst into the room and said, "Good morning Sleeping Beauty!"

Jasmin responded with an upbeat "Good morning, Prince Charming." She smiled at him. He drew the chair back for her to sit down. Charles pulled out Mrs. Tyler's chair for her.

"Good morning, Mother; what a beautiful Christmas Day it is," Matthew said.

Jasmin

"Thank you for sending the orange juice up, Mrs. Tyler, and thank you for inviting me here. I appreciate your hospitality," Jasmin commented.

Mrs. Tyler affirmed, "You are more than welcome, dear. We love to have you with us. Now eat up and enjoy."

They had a scrumptious breakfast and made light conversation. While the servants cleared the table, Jasmin and Matthew proceeded to the drawing room. Matthew showed Jasmin to a comfortable chair and he sat down close by in another. He explained what would be happening. "Mother is going to ring the bell and the staff are going to come in and receive their presents. We will all drink sherry together, and then the staff will leave to their tasks of preparing for Christmas dinner. We will exchange our gifts after that." He patted her hand. "Are you comfortable? Will you tell me now about the layout of the hotel's staff quarters, passages, and how to locate you in an emergency? We have a half hour."

Jasmin started, "I am in room #603 on the sixth floor, which is reserved for female staff. But I have no telephone. The intercom is in the hallway near the elevator. There is a direct line to the timekeeper's booth. The housekeeper in #601 usually answers any calls. Do you know that the hotel has a house detective?"

"What's his name?" he asked.

"Slater," she answered.

"I know Detective Slater," Matthew said. "Good man, he used to be with Scotland Yard."

Jasmin continued, "There is also a doctor's office, a nurse's station, and the office on the ground floor. On the third floor is Mildred, an older maid who likes me, and in the same corridor there is the room service pantry where Nellie and Beatrice work. Sometimes I go there to say hello. Nancy, also an older maid, was the first English contact I had. We meet in passing on occasion when we book the common bath. She works on the fourth floor, she is friends with the detective, but she lives on the sixth floor as I do. Pete, you know, is in the cold kitchen. I go to the main hot kitchen to get my late lunch. I can have anything I want, from either the grill, the soup station, or the vegetable station. There is a certain alcove where I eat.

"Because of my schedule, I never have to go to the staff kitchen. The other detour I make is upstairs to the pastry kitchen during the week to gather desserts for the Concordia Bar, or to find something sweet for myself on evenings or weekends. Several corridors fan out from there to the Danish Snack Bar and the Concordia Bar and the main restaurants and lounge. You know the staff from the Danish Snack Bar and the barmen from the Concordia Bar. I believe there is a payphone at the timekeeper, but I haven't used it yet. Your endearing letters are for my eyes only; I keep them safe in my locked memory box where I honour and treasure them. I keep your bracelet in this box too. I don't even let Carla help me unclasp it, as you know by now. I always carry the key to my locked memory box with me in my purse. On Fridays I go to the office. I don't associate with any of the other maids. There's one German girl, Paula, who one year ago wanted to coerce me into something unacceptable. She is bad company, and so I haven't associated with her. Nancy once told me something suspicious about her when we met at the elevator, and I have misgivings. It disturbs me enormously that Carla chums around with her. I have tried to get Carla into a better class environment by introducing her to Roger."

Matthew took it all in and asked, "How much notice is required, if you wish to terminate your employment?"

"Two weeks," Jasmin replied, "but I can stay in England till next October. The hotel provides room and board. If I take a different job,

I'll need a place to live. Mrs. Harman has offered accommodations for me."

"Jasmin, dear." Matthew rose from his chair, took her hand, and she rose up too. He held her close. He said with all the sincerity he could muster, "I'll provide for you a place to live. I will build that house for you."

"Promise?" Jasmin asked.

"Yes," Matthew promised. "Until it's completed, will you live here with me after we're married?" After he asked this question he breathed a kiss on her mouth.

"Yes," she whispered. "I can barely imagine the delight of being with you always." At that moment the ringing of the bell interrupted them. They stood side by side, as Louise the cook, Emily the maid, Skip the errand boy, Jim the gardener, and Charles the chauffeur (who also acted as butler) came into the room.

Mrs. Tyler announced, "Now it is gift time. Please come over to the table. First, let me introduce you to Miss Claudius, who is to be married to my son Mr. Tyler in January." Each of the staff members lined up to shake their hands, knowing they would soon be serving Jasmin as a member of the family.

Jasmin sat down again as Matthew assisted his mother in handing out the gift boxes. They took seats in the chairs set out for them and started opening their gifts while Matthew poured small glasses of sherry. He gave the first one to his mother, then he served Jasmin, and finally he served each of the staff.

He didn't take anything for himself. He sat down next to Jasmin again and said, "I'm intoxicated with your presence."

She whispered, "Every day you accord a new attribute to me and I love it."

They listened to the Oh's and Ah's of the servants. "Thank you kindly, and Merry Christmas!" they said on their way out.

Jasmin had a questioning look on her face as she turned her head to Matthew.

He smiled and said, "Now it is time for our gifts."

Jasmin spotted her tray with her three boxes under the tree and asked, "May I go first?"

"Certainly," he said.

She picked up the one for Mrs. Tyler and with the sweetest smile handed it to her. Mrs. Tyler said, "Thank you, dear child." Jasmin took the two boxes in her hand for Matthew and held them while Mrs. Tyler finished unwrapping her gift. "How tasteful," she commented.

Jasmin gave the slim box to Matthew. As he opened it, she explained, "A pen to continue writing letters to me." He smiled, looked at her with gleaming eyes, and put it right into his coat pocket. Now she gave him the wider and longer packet. She paused as he undid the wrapping. "That is," she laughed, "for if and when you receive a letter from me, so you can open it properly."

He stood up, pulled her up from her chair, and kissed her on her cheek. "Do you know how long I've wanted and needed something like that? Come look at the dilapidated thing I've had to struggle with." He showed her to his office and pointed it out to her. Then he threw it away. "This exquisite letter opener is going to have a place of honour on my desk. Now come; if I have to wait any longer, I'm going to burst with excitement before I give you your gifts." He took her hands, led her to the tree, and pointed her toward the envelopes.

Mrs. Tyler said, "First mine to Jasmin." Jasmin sat down again with her gift from Mrs. Tyler. The gift box revealed a Royal Albert china figurine. Jasmin admired the delicate lady who wore a pale violet ball gown with a fan in one hand and a tiara on her head. The card read, "May this adorn the mantel of your first home."

"Thank you so much, Mrs. Tyler," Jasmin embraced her.

Jasmin

Matthew jumped up and grabbed his two envelopes for Jasmin. The first was a promise card for long distance calls to Germany. He explained, "This is to call your father and mother and sister to tell them of our engagement." Before she could catch her breath, he gave her the second envelope. "Open it and read it," he urged.

She opened the envelope and unfolded its contents. "Two airline tickets to Frankfurt?" she shouted. She jumped up and hugged him. "Oh, Matthew, the things you think about for me."

"For us," he said. "I have the telephone number here for your sister."

Matthew dialed the number for Jasmin. He held up the receiver. "Dr. Walters here," came the answer.

"Norbert? This is Jasmin from England."

"Jasmin, my little sister-in-law," he said. "Wait till I call Camilla."

After a moment of silence in the line, Jasmin heard a familiar voice. "Jasmin, is that you?"

"Yes," Jasmin tumbled over her words. "I am engaged to the man I wrote you about, Matthew Tyler. We're getting married, I need a wedding dress, and we're coming to see you!" She looked at Matthew and asked, "What day?"

He said, "On the thirtieth."

Jasmin said to Camilla, "We're coming to Frankfurt and we have to see Mom and Dad too. Matthew is going to ask Father for my hand."

Camilla cut in, "Mom and Dad are coming here for the New Year's Eve ball we are attending. You'll have to come with us and your fiancé too. You can stay with us and we will book a hotel close by for Matthew. Do you have a ball gown?"

"Yes," Jasmin said, "I have a new one. I'll bring it. All I need is a wedding dress. Does it take long to be sewn?"

Camilla replied, "I already have white satin, so I will start on it right away. It will be ready for fitting when you get here. I will purchase the trimming after Christmas and you can help me sew it on. White fox with marabou feathers for cuffs and hem, marabou feathers around the neckline, blue crystal embroidery, and you will look like a Snow Queen."

Jasmin said, "I want Mom and Dad to come here to the wedding. Matthew is going to call Dad now. You tell them to be ready to come with us."

Camilla said, "O.K. I will let you talk to Norbert, so you can give him your flight number."

Her husband came back on the line. "Jasmin, are you there? Give me the details of your arrival." Jasmin did as he requested and said, "You can speak to Matthew directly, because you speak English."

Matthew said, "Dr. Walters? Matthew Tyler here. I understand you will be picking Jasmin and me up at the airport?"

"Yes, I'll be happy to do so, Mr. Tyler. I shall meet you in the morning of the thirtieth. Have a pleasant trip."

"Thank you," Matthew said, "goodbye." They hung up.

Jasmin said, "I want my mother and father to come to the wedding."

"Yes," Matthew said. "First I will talk to your father."

Jasmin said, "They don't have a telephone. I'll have to place a person to person call to the village post office and they will locate him and bring him to the office to answer the call."

She dialed the number, gave the information to the clerk, and was told it would be about one hour. Jasmin watched as Matthew gave his gift to Mrs. Tyler, a brass planter holder for the conservatory. Mrs. Tyler gave a new desk set to Matthew for his office.

Matthew said, "I have something to do in my office. Will you excuse me for a few minutes? My mother will talk with you."

Jasmin

Mrs. Tyler said, "I want to know the details about the wedding dress in a moment. For now, why don't you go upstairs? You can powder your nose before lunch and then we can make plans."

Jasmin said, "Before I do, Mrs. Tyler, may I borrow the velvet ball gown for one more week? Matthew and I are going to the New Year's Eve ball with my parents, my sister, and my brother-in-law. I would like to wear it there."

"Of course, Jasmin dear; it is yours."

"The gown, mine?" Jasmin gasped.

"Yes, it's my gift to you," Mrs. Tyler assured her.

"That's absolutely overwhelming and unbelievable; thank you so much."

Jasmin, on her way to the stairs, turned and faced Mrs. Tyler. "Mrs. Tyler, you have raised a fine son. Matthew is so tenderhearted, sensitive, and strong of character. I promise you I will love and honour him all the days of my life."

Mrs. Tyler embraced Jasmin, patted her back, and said, "I believe you will, I believe you will."

While Mrs. Tyler and Jasmin were talking, Matthew closed the door to his office. As he fumbled for his notebook he thought, "I wonder if Jasmin is safe in the hotel with the ring on. I insisted she wear it at work, but now I am not certain. Who could be lurking in the darkness wishing her harm? Cherchez la femme."

He found a number and dialed it. "Slater here."

"Hello John, Matthew Tyler."

"How are you Matthew? Merry Christmas!"

"Merry Christmas to you. Have you made any headway with those thefts in the hotels?"

Slater took a deep breath and said, "We're narrowing it down."

Matthew probed again, "Any traces leading to the Excelsior Hotel?"

"I'm considering it," Slater admitted.

"Is there violence involved?"

"Not exactly," Slater said.

"What's not exactly, poison or chloroform?" Matthew asked. "Is there a pattern such as elevators that are stuck?"

"You got me there," Slater said. "You should be a detective, Tyler."

Matthew said, "This is serious. Are you familiar with Jasmin Claudius from the Concordia Bar?"

"Of course," Slater said, "the Angel of the staff. Everybody loves her."

"Maybe somebody loves more what she has," Matthew said. "I want her protected. We're engaged to be married in January and I want her to be safe while she still works there." He clued Slater in further. "There's one maid named Paula. She lives in the same room as your friend Nancy. This Paula has many associations with chefs from other hotels and does not come home many nights. She needs to be watched. Are you on duty on the twenty-seventh?"

"Yes, I am," Slater said.

"O.K.," Matthew said. "Jasmin is staying at my mother's house over the holidays, but on the twenty-seventh she and I are going to Rose's housewarming party. Before that she has to come into the hotel to get her passport from her room. I'll go with her. Could you please prepare the way? I know Ernest, the timekeeper. I'll be there at two p.m. Brief me, O.K.?"

"O.K.," Slater said.

Matthew came out of his office with the feeling of "mission accomplished". Out of the corner of his eye he spotted Jasmin's shoes under the footstool. He chuckled, thinking of last night. Seeing Emily returning with an empty tray from the dining room he asked,

"Emily, would you take Miss Claudius's dance shoes up to her room please?"

"Yes, right away, Sir."

She put the tray down, picked up the shoes, and went upstairs. She knocked on the door and handed the shoes to Jasmin when she opened it. "Oh, Emily, please find the tissue paper for the velvet gown. We will have to pack it into a suitcase on the twenty-ninth. Thank you. I'll come down with you now."

The telephone call came and Matthew answered, "Yes, I will accept the charges, one moment please."

He gave the receiver to Jasmin, who said, "Hello Daddy, this is Jasmin from England."

"How are you, my little Blondie," her father greeted her.

"I'm not a little girl anymore and I'm going to get married! His name is Matthew Tyler and he wants to meet you and Mommy at Camilla's house. We're coming there for the New Year's Eve party."

Father asked, "Is he a Christian?"

"Yes, Daddy," she said, "He witnessed my confirmation and goes to church with me."

"Do you love him?" Father asked again,

"Yes, I love him and he loves me. He'll tell you in person when we come."

"Can he provide for you?" her father wanted to know.

"Yes. Now I'll give him the phone and he will say hello and goodbye. You understand enough English to say that, right?"

"O.K.," was the answer.

Matthew took the phone and said, "Hello, Herr Claudius."

"How do you do?" Jasmin could hear her father's voice.

Matthew replied, "Very well, thank you. I will come to see you about your daughter Jasmin."

"Good, good," the voice said. "I'll meet you in Frankfurt. Welcome to the family. Goodbye for now." Matthew hung up and hugged Jasmin and said, "I love you, and I very much like your father."

Emily announced that dinner was served. Charles escorted Mrs. Tyler to her chair and Matthew held out Jasmin's chair for her. Mrs. Tyler asked Matthew to say grace and the servants began to fill the plates. Jasmin thought, "I love Matthew even more when he says grace."

They talked a bit about travelling plans and Jasmin mentioned the need for a bigger suitcase for the ball gown. "I could wear the stole over my suit jacket," Jasmin said. "One does not need a coat; the airports and planes are heated."

"Roger instructed me to have candies available and to chew them when the plane takes off," Matthew recalled.

"Yes," Jasmin agreed. "My sisters have flown and told me the same thing. It's because of the pressure on your ears."

"We'll have to put that on your travelling list," Mrs. Tyler noted. "What else is important for your trip?" she asked.

"Passports," Matthew said.

They decided to listen to the Queen's speech.

Jasmin remarked, "It's a wonderful tradition to hear the Queen speak." They moved to a sitting area in the drawing room and had their coffee and dessert.

"I'm anxious to hear about the dress your sister is designing for you." Mrs. Tyler looked expectantly at Jasmin.

"It will be a bell-shaped style with an oval neckline and long sleeves. The fabric is white satin. The cuffs and hem are adorned with white fox and marabou feathers. The neckline is also edged with marabou. The embroidery features tiny blue crystals which give the appearance of snow, like the Snow Queen wore. When

I was a little girl I took part in many school plays and the Snow Queen was one of them. My sister is very artistic, and she opened my mind to imagine elves, gnomes, and fairy castles. Sometimes the invisible world became as real as the visible world."

"It sounds fascinating," Mrs. Tyler exclaimed. "When will the dress be ready?"

"The dress will be ready on New Year's Eve. We'll bring it with us when we come back on the morning flight so that we can get married on New Year's Day."

Matthew jumped up from his chair, hugging Jasmin. "Are you sure?"

"Sure I'm sure, why not?" Jasmin asked.

"Yes, why not?" Mrs. Tyler echoed, clapping her hands.

Jasmin told them about her parents. "My mother and father got acquainted in the hospital. He sustained an injury in an accident with his sulky and cut his lip. As he recovered from his surgery, my mother, a volunteer nurse, attended to him. On his release, my grandmother came to pick him up in her Landau. They offered Cornelia, my mother, a ride to the place where she was staying with her relatives. My grandmother invited them all to come to my father's farm the following Sunday. On that day my father and mother strolled along the periphery of the property and ended up in the garden gazebo. Among the Wisteria and fragrant mock orange blossoms, my father proposed to my mother. Both sets of my grandparents rejoiced over their engagement and made arrangements for the wedding to be the next weekend. My maternal grandmother brought Cornelia's wedding dress from her hometown of Black Creek. As entertainment, my father rode dressage with his equestrian team to the music of the famous Radetzky March. The ceremony and elaborate reception took place in the garden and then they were whisked to the seaside resort for their honeymoon."

Mrs. Tyler exclaimed, "How romantic! Bring your parents with you from Germany; they can stay here in our house. We'll start making the wedding arrangements now. Something old, something new, something borrowed, something blue," she recited.

"Old can be my satin dance shoes, and borrowed can be the tiara my mother is bringing. All of my sisters have worn it at their weddings," Jasmin offered.

"I'll attend to the new item I have in mind, also the church, the invitations, and the reception hall," Mrs. Tyler said. "Tomorrow, when the Harmans come, we'll work on the rest of the details. The flowers and honeymoon destination are Matthew's responsibility."

Matthew firmly said, "I'll look after it, as well as the passports and marriage license."

Matthew took Jasmin to the conservatory. As he opened the French door, he said, "Jasmin, I just discovered another characteristic about you: spontaneity." They walked amid the fragrance of flowers in bloom and then took a seat on a wrought iron bench.

Jasmin replied, "It is only logical, as you asked me to live with you here after we are married. You took me from my abode and brought me under your roof."

Jasmin explained further, "In the fairytales that I played a part in, as soon as the Prince woke up Sleeping Beauty, the wedding was arranged and they got married. The Prince took Snow White's glass coffin to his castle and when she woke up, they married. Cinderella's prince, when he finally found her, took her to his castle. His mother arranged the wedding, they were married, and the wicked stepsisters were punished with blindness (in the German version). In the Princess and the Pea story, she came alone to the castle and the king's son married her after she passed the test."

Matthew laughed and commented, "I haven't heard that one before."

Jasmin said, "We can pretend we are in the Arabian Nights and I could tell you one story per night."

Matthew leaned towards her and said, "You are my story, day and night. How does the Snow Queen fit into all this? I am curious, she sounds pretty icy."

"I didn't call her Ice Queen; she is the Snow Queen. Snow is like feathers. Frau Holler makes snow by shaking out her eiderdown feather pillows, and they are soft and warm," Jasmin replied.

"I get the point," he grinned. Matthew took Jasmin by her hand and said, "We have five more days of singleness. Come on, I'll show you some brochures of honeymoon packages. Would you like to go to the Spanish island of Tenerife, or the Cote d'Azur for the honeymoon?"

Jasmin pondered for a minute and suggested, "Maybe where it is the warmest this time of the year. My sister went to Tenerife once. I leave that up to you. You are my planner, and wherever you go I am happy to be with you."

"You mean I plan things for you and you organize them for me?" he teased.

As they were rising, he tried to pull her close, but she twirled herself away from him and said, "My brother told me that until the wedding it's holding hands only."

He took her hand and kissed the inside of her palm. "What else did your brother tell you?"

Jasmin said, "You are awfully inquisitive, Mr. Tyler. My brother said that 'those who love each other, tease one another, or you can tell they are in love when they tease each other.'"

"Smart guy," Matthew chuckled.

In the evening Mrs. Tyler suggested that they watch a Christmas special on television from the London Palladium. They settled near the Christmas tree and had their late tea and cakes served while they watched the show. When it was over, Mrs. Tyler bid them goodnight and Jasmin mouthed, "Good night, Matthew."

Matthew echoed, "Good night, precious." He watched Jasmin go up the stairs before turning off the lights. Jasmin found the bell to ring for Emily to help her with her dress.

Slater got on the phone with the police force and alerted them to monitor the comings and goings of Paula. He contacted Nancy as soon as he got back to the hotel to ask if she had any success in searching through Paula's things. Then he asked Ernest to track and report Paula's exits and returns. If the elevator was stuck, Ernest was to immediately call the police.

He spent some time studying the cases of robberies in hotels over the last year to try and find a pattern in how the cat burglar might have gained entrance. This could be fire escape repairs or disruptions of elevator operations that kept timekeepers sidetracked from observing who came in with the staff. He made sure that Ernest would be on duty on the twenty-seventh and told him to allow Matthew to enter with Jasmin and take the staff elevator to go to her room and retrieve her passport.

On Boxing Day, the Harmans exuberantly congratulated Matthew and Jasmin's forthcoming marriage. They were eager to participate in the wedding plans. Mrs. Harman showed great interest in hearing about their house building intentions. She mentioned that her employer the architect was beginning to work on new housing developments. This architect designed not only houses, but also aesthetic neighbourhoods.

"Developments?" Matthew and Jasmin looked at each other, knowing they were thinking the same thing. "We'll contact them in the New Year."

Matthew guided Jasmin into his private office and said, "I'm going to show you something." He took a tiny key, opened a secret drawer, and produced a small glass box. He held it in the palm of his left hand and asked, "Do you remember when I invited you to the ball and you made up a dance card? Well, here it is." He let her read the name on the crimped slip of paper through the glass. "This would entitle me to dance only with you?"

"Yes," she whispered.

"This is my 'Cinderella's glass slipper'," Matthew said.

"And you are my prince," Jasmin replied. They held each other in an embrace for a few long moments.

"Soon our dream will come true," he assured her. He led her to the bottom of the stairs, kissed her goodnight, and watched her ascend the stairs until she entered her room.

TRAUMA

The next morning after breakfast Jasmin and Mrs. Tyler had a planning session for the wedding.

Matthew retreated to his office, as he was expecting a call from Slater. "Matthew, there are some new developments. We are on standby. I'll meet you at the staff entrance at two p.m."

After lunch, Matthew said to his mother, "Jasmin and I are going to Rose's party this evening. First we will go to Jasmin's hotel to fetch her passport. Will you be here all day?"

"Yes," she said.

As Matthew drove with Jasmin to the hotel, he said, "I'll be going up with you to your room. I have cleared it with Slater and the timekeeper. You will retrieve your passport and school papers and I will help you carry them. Trust me; I won't let you out of my sight."

Jasmin asked solemnly, "Is there something that I should be aware of?"

"Yes," he said. "Come with me and we'll see."

They entered the staff door together and said hello to the timekeeper. Slater emerged from the corner and said, "Nancy is waiting for us."

They took the elevator to the sixth floor and spotted Nancy in an alcove. She whispered, "They are in there," pointing to Jasmin's room.

"Jasmin, you go and listen to what they are saying. We can't understand it," Slater said.

Matthew held Jasmin's hand as they approached the door. Jasmin overheard Paula saying, "I've got to stash it here under Jasmin's mattress. The pawn shop is not open today and Nancy has been going through my things. We are in this together now. You've got to help me, or I'll knock you out with this."

Jasmin pulled back and whispered to Slater, "Paula has the loot and is threatening Carla. If she doesn't help her hide it under my mattress, she is going to do something to her. I'm not sure what it is, maybe a knock out drug?"

Slater told Nancy, who stood by the intercom, "Call Ernest on the intercom to get the officer up here. Then come back to help me."

Nancy came and stood beside Slater. "We're going in; you stay back," he told Matthew and Jasmin. Nancy unlocked the door with the pass key. Surprised, Paula darted for the emergency ladder out the window, but Slater speedily pulled her back into the corridor.

Nancy held Carla, who screamed, "I am innocent!"

Just before the policeman came with the handcuffs, Paula threw a vial in Jasmin's direction. Startled, Jasmin tripped and fell backwards against the wall. She hit her head and collapsed before Matthew could catch her. The vial hit the wall, broke, and then the liquid poured over Jasmin's face. Shards of glass fell on her throat and wrist and the odour evaporated into the air.

Jasmin

Slater shouted to Matthew, "Don't inhale! Take her into the room and open the window. Put a rag on her wrist to stop the bleeding and elevate her head. I'll get the doctor and nurse."

Holding his breath, Matthew carried Jasmin and put her on the first bed. He quickly wrapped his handkerchief around her wrist, opened the window, took a deep breath, and elevated her arm. He slipped a pillow under her head. He held a dry cloth against the bleeding on her neck and knelt beside her bed. He sobbed, "Oh God, don't let me lose Jasmin. She is all I have, my life, my soul."

The door opened as the doctor came in with the nurse. Matthew pointed to Jasmin's head, arm, and throat. He observed as the doctor carefully removed the cloths to reveal the gashes. "Icepack behind her head," the doctor ordered. He took a closer look and said, "The neck wound needs stitches. Nurse, please sterilize the area. Are there sutures?"

"Yes," she replied.

Matthew took over in counsel mode. He located the officer outside the door. "Did Slater give a statement yet?"

"Yes, Sir," the policeman said. "The substance has been recovered and taken to the lab."

Dr. Henley said firmly, "It smells like ether."

Matthew told the officer, "The evidence is in this room, which is still a crime scene. I want you to record what I'm taking. One, Miss Claudius's locked box. Two, her school papers. Three, her handbag. After the doctor has attended to the patient, this room must be secured until the insurance adjuster has declared the value of the stolen jewelry."

He turned to the doctor and asked, "Are there glass splinters in her skin?"

The doctor said, "Yes, and we will need a stretcher. The ambulance is on its way. The patient's wrist requires surgery."

While they waited for the stretcher, Matthew introduced himself to the police and the doctor. "I am Matthew Tyler, Miss Claudius's representative. There will be four reports to be made: one to the police, one for personal injury to Workmen's Compensation, one for the insurance, and one for the reward posted for the recovering of the jewelry." Matthew then declared, "I'll accompany her in the ambulance."

Nancy squeezed in the elevator with them and told Matthew that Paula had sewn the jewelry heist into the lining of her coat. No one had wised up to it until Jasmin had tipped him off.

When they came downstairs, Matthew told the bewildered Ernest, "I'll leave my car here until later, because I am going to the infirmary." He quickly put Jasmin's things into the trunk of the Jaguar and then entered the waiting ambulance.

The intern at the hospital attended to Jasmin immediately. The police report stated what the substance was. With this information the doctor determined which local anesthetic to apply for the surgery and which sedative to administer for the concussion. They x-rayed her arm, cleaned out the splinters, and stitched the wound. He told Matthew that it could be eight to twelve hours till Jasmin woke up.

Matthew asked, "Could she be moved and taken home? She's staying at our house over the holidays. We could take shifts in watching over her. I'll call my mother to have the bed arranged on the main level of the house."

"Yes," the doctor said. "She will have to be transported on the stretcher. The nurse will accompany her until she's settled in. If you are there when she wakes up, give her sips of water to drink. The nurse will come back again first thing in the morning."

In the ambulance Matthew watched Jasmin intensely. When they reached his home, he supervised the orderlies and nurse bringing the stretcher into the house. His mother ushered them to the sunroom, adjacent to the drawing room. The staff had prepared a large divan for her to lay on. Matthew said to his mother, "Let Emily assist the nurse with settling Jasmin in. Please keep vigil over her until I come back. I need Charles to take me to get my car. I'll attend to certain matters in my office downtown and come back shortly."

When Matthew left, Emily helped the nurse undo Jasmin's clothing while Mrs. Tyler provided a gown and robe for her to wear under the covers. The nurse checked her pulse and heartbeat and promised to return tomorrow.

Matthew called the insurance company from his downtown office, informing them that he was acting as Jasmin's attorney. He located the name of the company who handled the reward money and told them the same thing. He called Slater to firm up his testimony and Slater decisively declared that the reward should go to Jasmin. Then Matthew filled out the forms for Workmen's Compensation on Jasmin's behalf to take to the doctor to sign. He made an appointment with the police chief to clear up the situation the next day.

Finally, he called Pete and Rose to cancel their attendance to the party. Then he closed up the office and drove home. When he arrived at home, Matthew took Jasmin's belongings out of the trunk of his car and placed them into his private safe at his house.

As Matthew entered the drawing room, he saw his mother sitting in a chair beside the opened French door. She looked up from her needlework. "We can have tea in here and keep an eye on Jasmin at the same time," he suggested.

"Yes," Mrs. Tyler agreed as she rose up and put the lace aside, "you can share with me all the details."

Matthew pulled a chair close to the divan and listened to Jasmin's even breathing. She looked so pale. He touched her hand; it felt cool. He covered it with his own for a minute, then tucked it under the blanket to get warm. Emily and his mother came to shuffle the table closer, so he got up and offered to help.

"On Christmas Eve," he began when tea was served, "I waited at the appointed time at the staff entrance for Jasmin. She wasn't there, which was unusual. I looked through the window of the door and saw no one. Suddenly Carla appeared. Carla approached me and said that Jasmin would be here soon. I was bewildered about what could have happened, and intended to ask Carla to lead me to her. But then I heard Jasmin calling me. She looked frightened. Of what I didn't know, so I rushed down the steps, took her suitcase, and held her close to calm her. Then I helped her into the car. She was shaken to tears but exercised great self-control. I drove somewhere I could park safely and stopped, so we could talk. I related my distress of not knowing where to go if I ever needed to find her. She promised to tell me the layout of the hotel interior where she traversed.

"On Christmas Day, Jasmin shared with me the variety of her daily activities including with whom she interacted, where she got her supplies, when she reported for duty, what time she clocked her staff card in and out at the timekeeper, and who liked her. I have met the timekeeper who calls her Smiler. Ernest watches out for her, but he wasn't on duty that evening. All the other staff loves her dearly; she is kind and courteous to everyone and does nice things for them. They all call her Angel. When the newspaper article came out about her a few months ago, she was given a bonus check by the hotel management. Mrs. Goddard, whom you met, did that transaction.

"Jasmin was also kind to her roommate Carla. However, she was disturbed that Carla associated with Paula, one of the German maids who lived in the room with three other girls, one of whom is Nancy, a senior English maid. Nancy also liked Jasmin from the start.

Jasmin

"One year ago Paula wanted to coerce Jasmin into going out to an all-night party where an equal number of boys and girls would engage in un-ladylike activities at one of Paula's friend's apartments. Jasmin absolutely was not in favour of that and stayed home. Paula snubbed her for that.

"Shortly after that incident, Jasmin was promoted and moved to a better room that she shared with Carla. Jasmin and Carla developed a good relationship. Jasmin improved her English and as you know furthered her education. She was promoted again.

"During this past year, I became aware of thefts in several hotels in the city, but they kept it hush hush because it would be bad for business if it became public. Nothing happened at the hotel where Jasmin lived as yet. The police were baffled as to who that cat burglar might be.

"At one point Jasmin met Nancy in the corridor near the elevator, and Nancy told Jasmin that Paula stayed out many nights and came back early in the mornings. That's why Jasmin was disturbed that Carla would associate with Paula.

"In the meantime, Slater - who is a long time employee of the Excelsior and a former Scotland Yard detective - inquired of Nancy - who is also a long time employee - if she suspected anything unusual about Paula. But nothing came of it.

"On Christmas Eve, Jasmin was delayed because her elevator was stuck. Instead, she had to run down the stairs to the fifth floor to catch the guest elevator to the lobby, go through the staff's swinging doors, run down another three hallways, and finally reach the exit where she had an ominous premonition.

"In the meantime I contacted John Slater to give me an update on the hotel thefts. He told me that so far the only link he had was Nancy who had told him of Paula's nightly activities with cooks and waiters from other hotels, but not this one. I suggested that he research a pattern of stuck elevators and fire escape repairs. He called me back the next day and 'bingo'. They had narrowed it down to Paula, but had no evidence. He arranged to meet me at the timekeeper's booth with Jasmin at two p.m. so that she could get her passport. He alerted the timekeeper, had the police waiting in disguise, and came up with us to the outside of Jasmin's room. We heard an agitated conversation in German and Jasmin and I listened at the door. Jasmin understood and translated for our sake. Paula said to Carla that she had brought all the loot there and they had to hide it under Jasmin's bed. Carla protested, but Paula threatened to give her a dose of chloroform and tie her up. She threatened to use a continuous drip device that would render her incapacitated for several days. She also had a vial of ether.

At that, Detective Slater went into the room and subdued Paula. Nancy held Carla, who proclaimed her innocence. Nevertheless, before the police officer could handcuff Paula, she threw the vial of ether against the wall where Jasmin was standing. It broke and glass and liquid fell on Jasmin who tripped and hit her head against the wall and collapsed before I could catch her. I managed to get her out of that cloud and bring her into her room. I laid her on the bed, closed the door, and opened the window. I wrapped her wrist and neck to stop the bleeding. The doctor did the rest and here we are."

Mrs. Tyler said, "Should we keep her here till the wedding?"

Matthew sighed, "That thought had occurred to me more than once."

Mrs. Tyler put her hand on Matthew's hand comfortingly and said, "Everything will be fine."

"Thank you, Mother," he said and suggested, "Shall we put the couch a little closer? I will rest on it while I watch her."

"I'll get Charles and Skip," she promised.

Jasmin

While the servants rearranged the furniture, Matthew changed into leisure clothes.

He saw that a blanket had been draped over the chaise. Mrs. Tyler came back into the room and said she would turn in for the night. "However," she added, "if you need me for anything at all, please call me, O.K.?"

"O.K., goodnight, Mother," Matthew said.

Matthew knew it was important that the first face Jasmin should see was his. This would give her assurance that everything was alright. Wasn't that the first English word she asked him to translate, security? He had emphatically told her that he wanted to be her security. Her confidence lay in her conduct, her education, her skills, her relationships, her charisma, her stability, her analytical ability, her service to people, and her compassion, but her heart's security came only from someone who offered her total commitment, loyalty, and complete trustworthiness.

There must have been a betrayal once that had shook her to the core. When she had come running out of the door with her suitcase and saw him next to Carla, he could see that fear.

He examined himself. Had he answered her deepest needs when she had asked if he would continue to pursue her even if she failed in some way? Or if he had false information? Had he promised he would never leave her or forsake her?

"I did," he told himself, "and I do. I'm here for her, I will stay with her. I will shelter her. She is my life. My wealth, my health, and my love for her is unquenchable."

He sat close to her bed and looked at her sleeping face. He gently stroked her cheek with his fingertips and breathed these words: "Jasmin, which fairytale do you identify with most? Cinderella? Trust me, your wicked stepsisters have been eliminated. No one can hinder you anymore from marrying your prince."

He dimmed the lights and rested on the chaise. He slept for a few hours, and then checked her face again. There was no change.

At six, Emily took over. Matthew gave her strict instructions to call him if Jasmin even fluttered her eyelids. He said, "I'll be in my room."

Matthew laid out his plan for the day. He methodically prepared each item for the individual agencies he had to contact. He had his breakfast brought to the drawing room so he could watch Jasmin. He asked Emily to stand by until his mother joined him, and he would stay until the nurse arrived.

He looked closely at Jasmin and noticed movements under her eyelids. He moved his chair closer to the divan, leaned his head over hers, and whispered, "Jasmin, I am here." Her eyelids moved, lifted a small space, and began to flutter. Her eyes opened, seemingly not recognizing their surroundings. He placed a kiss on her lips and whispered, "Jasmin, darling."

He held her head in both of his hands so she could look into his eyes. She recognized him and smiled. She tried to pull her arm up from under the covers but it fell limply back. "Can you hear me?" he asked.

She nodded her head slowly. "You'll stay here with Mother and Emily, and then the nurse will come also. Do you understand me, darling?" She nodded again. "I am going to the office downtown and will be back by noon. You'll be alright. Here, I'll give you some water." He turned his head, motioning to Emily to pass the glass to him with the straw. Then he lifted Jasmin's head slightly so she could manage to take a sip. He gently laid her head back. She still hadn't spoken.

He heard the nurse arrive accompanied by his mother. One last time he leaned over Jasmin and said, "You're in safe hands now. I will be back for lunch, O.K.?"

"– K." She managed to get out.

His first appointment was with the police chief. When Matthew entered the building, an attendant ushered him to his office.

"Mr. Tyler," the chief extended his hand in greeting, "Chief Doyle." Matthew accepted his handshake. "Please take a seat. Quite some excitement over the holidays, wasn't it?"

"Certainly, and it isn't over yet," Matthew echoed.

"How is your client?" the chief enquired.

"Still incapacitated, but she will recover eventually," Matthew admitted cautiously.

"Here's the police report. You may peruse it, and if you have anything to add, it will be documented." Chief Doyle shifted the papers over to Matthew.

"I have my report here and it correlates with these statements." Matthew gave the document to the chief, who glanced at it and put it aside.

"Furthermore," Chief Doyle said, as he handed a document to Matthew with a bank draft, "This is the reward money. If you will sign, please."

Matthew looked calmly at the sum of one hundred thousand pounds, "Quite appropriate," he conceded.

"Also, here is the bonus reward of twenty-five thousand pounds from the hotel association for saving the reputation of the other hotels. This is for Miss Claudius, c/o Tyler and Associates."

"Acceptable," Matthew thanked him.

"Workmen's Compensation and damages are between the hotel management and Miss Claudius. Application to become a British subject will be granted without a waiting period, if she so desires," the chief continued.

"I'll take the forms, if you have them handy," Matthew said quickly.

The chief handed the forms to Matthew, pre-signed. "She will have a few days' vacation to go to the continent to visit family and be back New Year's Day," Matthew informed him. "Should it be necessary for Miss Claudius to have to sign anything else, she will be available after January second."

"The guilty party is being deported as a persona non grata to her country of origin and the other one, Carla, left on her own accord," Chief Doyle concluded.

Matthew put all the documents into his briefcase and rose from his chair, and Chief Doyle rose up as well. Matthew said, "Belated Merry Christmas and Happy New Year."

"The same to you," the Chief replied. They exchanged another handshake.

Matthew looked at his watch and saw that he still had time for the other important issue. He went straight to the front lobby of the hotel and asked to be led to the office. The Resident Manager was expecting him. While they exchanged greetings, Mrs. Goddard called the doctor on the intercom. Mr. Arlington invited Matthew to share his observations and let the doctor, who had come in, present his report. He declared Jasmin would recover, but with the wound in her wrist, she wouldn't be able to work in the food industry for a certain length of time as her contract read.

Therefore, Mr. Arlington cut in, she would be fully compensated with pay for two months and at that time she should be evaluated for chronic after-effects as a result of her injuries. Since her position included room and board, Jasmin would receive an extra allowance for accommodation outside the hotel.

Another insurance company that handled exceptional cases of trauma had offered to pay claims for damages in the amount of fifty thousand pounds.

Jasmin

Matthew perused this in detail and considered it fair. He said, "I will accept the settlement for damages now, but I will wait until after the two months' evaluation period has expired to settle with Workmen's Compensation."

He kept the doctor's report, accepted the check, signed the release, and asked for a staff person to remove Miss Claudius's belongings from her room and bring them down to him.

Mr. Arlington offered tea to be brought in for Matthew. He asked the floor manager to arrange for one of the housekeepers to have Jasmin's things packed and brought downstairs to the front lobby. Then he departed.

Mrs. Goddard set the tea tray down and poured some tea into his cup. She offered cream and sugar and helped herself as well. She asked, "How is Jasmin now?"

Matthew set his cup down and answered, "She had been given a sedative and it wore off this morning at six. The nurse gave her a pain killer when I left."

"What a brave girl," Mrs. Goddard said. "Say hello to her for me, won't you? I wish her a speedy recovery. Everyone here will miss her."

Matthew saw the porter come with Jasmin's suitcase and typewriter. "One more thing, Mrs. Goddard: Jasmin and I are going to the continent to visit with her family. We will be married after that on New Year's Day. My mother is arranging the wedding invitations. Should she direct the ones to the hotel staff c/o yourself?"

"By all means send the invitations to me at the executive office. I will be glad to forward them," Mrs. Goddard replied.

Matthew directed the porter to his car out front and had him place the typewriter and suitcase into the trunk. Then he gave the porter a good tip and drove home. As soon as he got to his house, he entered the back door, looked for Charles, and asked that Skip would empty the trunk, have the suitcase brought up to Jasmin's room, and the typewriter brought to the library. Then he made a beeline to his home office and placed the entire briefcase into his private safe.

Matthew came to the drawing room and saw Jasmin sitting in the chaise, leaning against the propped up backrest. Mrs. Tyler sat beside her in an armchair with an open wedding catalogue in her hands.

"Matthew, you're back," they said in unison.

"Hello Mother, you haven't seen me for lunch in years. Now is the perfect time; I'm starved," he replied.

Mrs. Tyler folded the magazine and laid it aside. "I will see to it," she said.

Matthew approached Jasmin and asked, "How is my patient?"

"Getting better, now that you are here," she greeted him back.

"I'm famished for your kiss," he said. Then he leaned over and gave her a long kiss.

He took a chair, sat next to her, and asked, "How did it go for you this morning?"

"The nurse changed the dressing on my arm and put a fresh invisible cover over the scar on my neck. She examined the bruise on the back of my head, and as it still hurt, she gave me a pill for pain. She and Mrs. Tyler helped me up because all my limbs were limp. They practically dragged me to the boudoir and got me dressed. I managed to drink some water, and after a while I also had coffee and toast."

"You're officially on sick leave now; you don't have to go to work there anymore," he said.

"Not at all?" she asked.

"Not at all," he reiterated, "and you get paid for it too."

"How did you manage to arrange that for me?" Jasmin sat up straight.

Jasmin

"I am your advocate, aren't I? I am your representative, I act on your behalf, and I obtained damage payment for trauma in the amount of fifty thousand pounds."

"That much?" she asked incredulously.

"There is more," he added. "The pre-set reward for the recovery of the jewelry of one hundred thousand pounds is yours, plus a combined insurance settlement from the other hotels in the amount of twenty-five thousand pounds for saving their reputation."

"That's amazing," Jasmin exhaled a deep breath. "You are a wonderful administrator, Matthew. I attended a lecture on litigation and such by Mr. Worthington, and you are a perfect example."

"Thank you," Matthew said. "I considered it wise to settle out of court, or it would have dragged on for months."

"Lunch will be served," Charles announced.

Matthew helped Jasmin out of the chaise. He put his arm around her waist and slowly escorted her over to the table and assisted her in getting seated. "Tomorrow we'll go to the bank and open an account for you," he said.

"I still haven't got a suitcase for my ball gown," Jasmin said with concern during lunch.

"We will see about that," Matthew assured her. "Good thing you wear gloves, which will cover your stitches."

"But not the ring," Jasmin said.

"We could open the seam of the one finger," Mrs. Tyler said.

"Oh, thank you, Mrs. Tyler," Jasmin said. "What an excellent idea."

After lunch, Mrs. Tyler took a note to Matthew's private office and came back to announce she was going to have her afternoon nap.

Matthew asked Jasmin to come with him to his office. "Were you glad to have me home for lunch today?" he asked her.

"Yes; because you always keep your promises," she said.

"You'll see me more often, and every Wednesday when I have my usual afternoon off, I will take you out on a luncheon date somewhere. How does that sound to you?" Matthew asked as he led her to the high backed wing chair.

Jasmin leaned against his shoulder, saying, "Wonderful; I couldn't ask for anything more."

Matthew pulled a footstool in front of her feet. "You can put your feet up, let me help you." He went to fetch Jasmin's folder and hesitated as he read his mother's note on his appointment calendar. He then brought the folder with her school papers and took the letter out. He placed a writing tablet and a pen in front of Jasmin and asked, "Do you feel well enough to write a note?"

Jasmin looked at him dreamily, "Your nearness alone gives me comfort."

Matthew was momentarily immersed in the glow of her countenance. She took the pen out of his hands and smiled.

He took a deep breath and continued, "This is what I suggest you do. Write a note to Mr. Larsen, indicating that this is the letter you drew up for him and if in the future he has need of secretarial services he could reach you at this post office box number, but leave the space open."

"I surely will do that. I know all about business mail when I worked with my sister Charmaine. She had a postal box and I used to go and get the mail for her." Jasmin leaned over her writing pad and scribbled the note.

"Tomorrow," Matthew said, as he pulled a chair beside her, "we will go to the post office and rent that postal box. That will be the number you write into the empty space. That number will also be for any future business you become involved in, as was your ambition."

Matthew began again, "Alternatively, you could just mail the letter because you promised it to him and leave no return address, because your ambitions have changed and your future plans are being a full-time married wife. I want you to have the freedom to live up to your full potential and not feel caged in."

Jasmin said very thoughtfully, "I do like the idea of the post office box. I might not necessarily want to run secretarial services or advertising services. I could run a charity organization, but not now. In any case, I don't feel caged in. Actually, I love to be totally protected and cared for by you. I don't even want to leave the house without you. You are my favourite beau. You are my permanent companion. I am just getting a glimpse of what it will be like to be here waiting for you to come home."

Matthew leaned over and said, "Your favourite beau, eh?"

Jasmin said emphatically, "You are my hero; the images in my mind are filled with only you, Matthew."

He leaned even closer before she could consent. "You deserve a kiss for that!"

After that pause, Jasmin placed the note with the letter. She asked for a larger envelope to hold all this correspondence. Then she addressed it, without closing the envelope.

"Now, my dearest, time for your nap. Would you like me to call Emily for you, or do you want to ring for her when you're upstairs?" Matthew asked.

"If you help me upstairs," Jasmin said, "I'll ring for her when I'm in my room, thank you."

After he had helped Jasmin go upstairs to her room, Matthew went back to his home office and called the bank manager to make an appointment for the next afternoon. After that he called the number on his mother's note and booked the honeymoon suite and wedding reception at the Balmoral Villa. He called the travel agency and booked the honeymoon package and airline tickets to Tenerife and asked the agency to have them ready the next day for pick up. He also ordered two return tickets from Frankfurt for Jasmin's parents.

Then he went to the back door and checked the staff schedules. His mother hadn't booked Charles, so he sought him and requested he buy a suitable travelling for Jasmin's ball gown. Then he decided to have a quick afternoon nap also.

Later that day, Jasmin felt much better. Emily had taken all the pins out of Jasmin's hair and it fell around her head in curls. Matthew waited for her in the hallway. As she come down the stairs, he feasted his eyes on her appearance. He took hold of both her hands. Though he felt the chemistry between them, he refrained from embracing her. He said tenderly, "Precious Jasmin, you have stepped into my world and you have invited me into yours." Jasmin felt the same surge of electricity come through their hands. She just let it flood through her and soaked up his words.

Matthew could see that special 'glow'. He smiled and led her to the dining room for evening supper. After supper they discussed more wedding plans. Mrs. Tyler asked if Jasmin would consider having the ceremony in her church since it was bigger than the one she had previously attended. She suggested that Jasmin's wedding dress with the long train would show up better in the larger space. Jasmin looked at Matthew, who smiled and said, "I could live with that idea."

Jasmin nodded, "Me too."

"For the reception there is an exquisite place that caters to weddings. The Balmoral Villa is somewhat larger than the Birkdale Lodge but not as large as the Regency." Mrs. Tyler recommended, looking at Matthew, who gave a quick nod.

"That sounds good," Jasmin said. "Mr. James is to be invited and the Harmans and the Worthingtons, if they are back. Also my friends from the hotel: Nellie, Beatrice, Nancy, Mildred, Rose, Pete,

Jasmin

Maureen, Martin, Mrs. Goddard, Pete's father, Alicia, Jeff, and of course the timekeeper Ernest."

Matthew told his mother that the hotel invitations were to go to Mrs. Goddard at the hotel office. Jasmin asked him if he wanted to include Slater in the list. He agreed. Mrs. Tyler eagerly offered to take on that task. "I have a hair appointment at Steiner's. I will have the bellhop take the invitations down to the office." Jasmin mentioned that Mr. Worthington's photographer student might still be available to take their wedding pictures.

HAPPY END

First thing the next morning, Jasmin instructed Emily which outfit to pack into her small suitcase. The ball gown was taken downstairs and Charles placed it expertly into the garment bag that he'd purchased. Mrs. Tyler kept the satin gloves to make the minor adjustment. Matthew called the Ceylon Tea Centre for their luncheon appointment, and then he drove Jasmin to the city via the new subdivision. He asked, "Jasmin, have you had any nightmares because of what happened?"

Jasmin replied calmly, "No, I've forgiven Carla; she was misled. I forgive Paula; she was a lost soul. You came to rescue me and that's the main thing. I love you, Matthew."

He said, "I love the way your lips form my name." He assisted Jasmin out of the Jaguar and took her right inside the beauty salon.

Kurt approached and immediately saw the ring. "Jasmin dear," he exclaimed, "is that what I think it is?" He looked at Matthew, who nodded. "Congratulations to both of you! Come look," he motioned to the other staff.

As the staff mingled around them, Matthew booked Kurt's services for the wedding morning at his house. He tipped his hat and excused himself.

"Which style shall we do today?" Kurt enquired.

"I shall need the same," Jasmin said. "Here are the pins."

"Another ball?" Kurt asked.

"Yes, I am going to Germany for two days to see my family and attend the New Year's Eve ball there," Jasmin told him.

While Kurt was attending to Jasmin, Matthew drove to the travel agency and picked up his airline tickets and the extra two tickets for Jasmin's parents. He went to his office and cleared his calendar for the next three weeks. He looked at Jeff Kerr's schedule and penciled him in to take over his January second client. He found the card with the telephone number and after a long jovial chat, invited him, Mrs. Benson, and Alicia to the wedding. Naturally, he appointed Jeff to be best man. Jeff exuberantly accepted as the Benson ladies rejoiced.

When Jasmin was comfortably situated in the car, Matthew smiled at Jasmin and said, "I booked our favourite booth for lunch at the Ceylon Tea Centre. Is that O.K. with you?"

"Very O.K. with me," she giggled.

They walked into the building arm in arm. He held the door open for her and let her step in front of him. He thought, "I sure enjoy seeing the way she walks." During their meal, Matthew asked, "Was it only last week when we decided it wouldn't do if I came to your lunch bar because I would be so mesmerized by you and forget all about my work?"

"Yes," Jasmin laughed, "and you would become a pauper because of it."

Jasmin

"I'm glad you have your sense of humour back," Matthew said. "Guess what? I took the next three weeks off. I haven't taken a vacation in seven years and this is the time to take it. We are going to Tenerife for three weeks, starting January second. Now let's go to that other appointment, shall we?"

They met the bank manager in his office. Matthew introduced Jasmin, "Mr. Rhodes, this is Miss Jasmin Claudius, my fiancée."

"Pleasure to make your acquaintance, Miss Claudius," Mr. Rhodes said, as he offered her a chair.

Matthew opened the conversation with, "Miss Claudius wishes to open an account in this bank with these checks."

The bank manager took Jasmin's information down on a form, had her sign it, and looked at the two large checks. He asked, "Do you want them deposited into a savings account?"

Matthew and Mr. Rhodes both looked at Jasmin, waiting for her answer. Jasmin said, "The larger one, yes, but for the lesser one I wish to open an investment account with growth potential over a six-month's term to be renewable at that time."

Mr. Rhodes caught his breath and replied, "Do you have stock market experience, Miss Claudius?"

"Theoretically only, Mr. Rhodes," she answered.

"We shall put this into a holding account for thirty days. At that time we will have to meet again to discuss the best options for you. Is that agreeable with you?" he asked.

"Quite," she replied.

Matthew brought out the last check and told the bank manager, "This is to go into the trust account of Tyler and Associates."

"Very well," Mr. Rhodes replied, taking the checks and giving receipts for each one. "I shall have these co-signed and bring you another copy of the deposit slips." He rose and left his office.

359

Matthew laid his hand on Jasmin's and said, "I am stunned by your keen business sense and money management capabilities. You are awesome. There isn't a day that passes without me finding something new to admire about you."

Jasmin smiled and said, "Thank you. Some of the credit goes to you, Matthew. You introduced me to the tutorial school, which brought out the best in me."

"By the way," he explained, "this trust account will stay open until the Workmen's Compensation settlement has been received. For accounting purposes it is in my name, because I am acting as your attorney."

"You should have a reward too for pulling all this together," Jasmin said.

"You are my reward, Jasmin," Matthew said tenderly.

Mr. Rhodes came back with his assistant, who handed Jasmin a bank book and a certificate for the Investment Fund. The assistant exited and Matthew rose, offering his hand to Jasmin as she also rose from her chair. Mr. Rhodes stretched out his hand towards Jasmin first, and she shook it in a business-like manner. "It has been a pleasure doing business with you. I shall look forward to seeing you in thirty days at your convenience."

Mr. Rhodes shook Matthew's hand and said, "Thank you for choosing our bank, Mr. Tyler. I expect we will see more of you in the future."

"Indeed we will," Matthew replied.

They got into the car and Jasmin was quiet. Matthew asked, "What's on your mind, Jasmin sweetheart?"

"I would have liked to go to Rose's shop and show her my ring," she sighed. "I want to brag about you. But I don't want you to disappear."

"Jasmin, darling, I am real and I am here," he said with such emotion in his voice, he almost cried. He thought, "She is probably still experiencing a flashback of trauma."

Matthew stopped his car right in front of Rose's shop window. Then they got out and walked into the store. The doorbell rang and Rose looked up from behind the counter. She flew around the corner and hugged Jasmin; Matthew stood right behind her.

Jasmin held up her ring, and Rose drew the outstretched hand closer to her eyes. "That is so beautiful. So he finally caught up with you, right? When is the wedding?"

Jasmin replied, "New Year's Day."

Rose asked, "Can I still be the bridesmaid?"

"Of course," Jasmin said. "So are Beatrice and Nellie from the third floor pantry; I promised them before. You will have to be at Matthew's house in the morning on New Year's Day to have your hair styled. My hairdresser Kurt and his crew are coming to do our coiffeurs right there."

Rose spontaneously hugged her, "Oh, Jasmin, my friend, I love you!"

"We've got to go; see you later." Jasmin turned to let Matthew open the door for her.

Matthew said, "Bye Rose."

After they had left the shop, Matthew turned to Jasmin and said, "One more thing: if you are up to it, we can go across the square to the registrar's office and sign the register of marriages."

"Sure," Jasmin consented. They drove over to the registrar's office and Matthew parked right in front of the steps to the building. He helped Jasmin up the steps and they signed the forms. Luckily Jasmin had her passport with her for I.D. Matthew showed his credentials. They were also given the form for the pastor to sign and witness on the wedding day.

"Ready to go home?" Matthew asked tenderly.

"Home, yes," Jasmin said.

Back at the Tylers' residence, Matthew put all the important papers into his safe and got organized for the trip tomorrow. Jasmin went to her room and found the suitcases already packed and her travelling clothes laid out for the trip including a packet of hard candies.

The next day, as they boarded the plane, Matthew commented to Jasmin, "We're embarking on another adventure."

"It's exciting, isn't it?" she said.

"Life with you so far has been a rollercoaster ride; I can hardly imagine what is going to be next." Matthew looked at her with a gleam in his eyes.

Jasmin cocked her head and looked at him sideways with a flirty look. "There is only one way to find out," she teased.

"You might say that," he mused.

The air hostess brought champagne and complimentary candies. This helped alleviate the fear of the unknown and they were relaxed when the preparation for take-off was announced.

As the plane took off, Matthew held Jasmin's hand and kept it there until the plane leveled out.

Matthew said, "Roger told me this was the most exhilarating moment and I tend to agree; how about you?"

"Quite so," she said.

At the duty free shop in the airport, Matthew looked around for something British to give to Jasmin's father. He asked Jasmin whether a certain gift basket with traditional English treats would be appropriate for him.

"By all means," Jasmin replied.

"How about a bottle of Scotch for your brother-in-law? I don't drink it myself, but I have it available for my clients."

Jasmin

She replied, "Since it is a special occasion, certainly. I am going to get two bottles of Chanel #5 perfume for my mother and my sister at the French counter."

They made their way to the luggage carousel and had their suitcases brought to the exit. Jasmin spotted her brother-in-law through the glass door and waved. When they came out, Norbert shouted, "Jasmin!"

He held his arms open, they embraced, and Jasmin said, "Meet Matthew. Matthew, this is Norbert."

Norbert felt an immediate affinity for Matthew and greeted him with, "It is a great pleasure to meet you."

"Likewise," Matthew said, as they shook hands.

"It will be about twenty minutes till we are home," Norbert announced. "I shall drop Jasmin off at our apartment to be with Camilla, and then I'll take you on a sightseeing tour, Matthew."

"I shall look forward to that," said Matthew.

They arrived and lugged Jasmin's luggage up one flight of stairs to the apartment. Camilla and Jasmin held each other in a long embrace while the guys deposited the suitcases elsewhere.

Then Camilla said hello to Matthew, "My new brother..." She turned to Jasmin and asked, "What is the word?"

"In-law," Jasmin completed. Camilla and Matthew exchanged a handshake, still being formal.

"I see the resemblance," Matthew said.

Camilla looked questioningly at Jasmin again. "We look alike," Jasmin told her in German.

"Ja, yes," Camilla said.

Norbert stepped in and said, "I shall take Matthew across the square to the hotel and then for a sightseeing tour. We'll bring take-out dinner later, O.K.?"

"Sounds great," Jasmin said. Looking at Matthew, she asked, "How are you so far?"

He said, "Seeing you so happy with the people whom you love and who love you makes me feel at ease. I'll see you later." He kissed her on the cheek and followed Norbert out the door.

Camilla said, "Let's have a quick coffee and then we'll get busy with the dress." They told each other about the happenings in their lives, although Jasmin left out the dilemmas of the past week.

Camilla said, "Matthew is very handsome and he has kind eyes."

Jasmin said dreamily, "He has a very kind and caring heart. He tells me every day he loves me in different ways, he likes all my ideas and helps me realize them, he always makes me feel good and smart, and when I ask for advice he leads me in the right direction. All his plans for me are beneficial and I am so happy with him."

Jasmin tried on the dress. Camilla made some adjustments and declared, "I shall do the machine stitching while you can do the hand stitching on the trimmings. You see these tiny loops? Put them on the fur and the marabou feathers. When you get home you or your maid will just have to hook them onto your dress like so." She showed Jasmin how it was done. When they had completed their tasks, Camilla folded everything into a special garment bag for transportation.

In the evening they had lively discussions and when Camilla didn't quite understand, Jasmin interpreted for her. The next day, their father and mother arrived. Norbert, as the perfect host, introduced Heinz and Cornelia to Matthew and told him that if he needed any translation he would stand by.

Matthew then addressed Heinz, "Herr Claudius, it is an honour to meet you and ask you for your daughter's hand in marriage."

Heinz asked, "Do you love Jasmin?"

"Yes," Matthew said, "I love Jasmin dearly."

Heinz whispered to Norbert, "How do you say take care of her?"

Norbert whispered back in English, "Provide."

Heinz asked, "Can you provide for her?"

"Yes," Matthew said. "She does not have to work outside of the home, and all her needs will be met."

Heinz asked Norbert again, "What were the other words he said?"

Norbert said in German, "She can stay home and have children."

At that Jasmin blushed. Matthew saw this and waited for the answer.

"Good," Heinz said. Turning to Jasmin, he asked, "Do you love him?"

"Yes, Dad, I love him," Jasmin said.

Matthew asked Heinz again, "We ask for your blessing."

Jasmin quickly said the German word to her father, "Segen."

"Yes," her father rested his hand upon her head and blessed her. Then he rested his hand upon Matthew's head and blessed him.

Matthew bowed his head and said, "Thank you."

Everybody clapped, then they all hugged each other. It was decided that Matthew would address Cornelia as "Mom Cornelia". Matthew addressed Jasmin's mother, "Mrs. Claudius, it is a delight and honour to meet the charming mother of my beautiful bride. I consider it a privilege to call you Mom Cornelia. My mother will be so pleased to meet you."

Cornelia lifted her arms and hugged him. "Welcome to the family, my new son-in-law." Over coffee and cake and much reminiscing the afternoon went by. Not much translating was necessary, as their love spoke the language of the heart. At the end of the afternoon, they prepared to go to the festivities.

Camilla helped Jasmin into her ball gown and examined it carefully. "This is good workmanship," she said.

Cornelia hugged Jasmin and said, "My littlest girl is getting married. I remember when Dad and I gave you your name, and now you are all grown up."

"Thank you for giving me my name," Jasmin said. "That's what fascinated Matthew about me. Before I forget," Jasmin gave the bottles of perfume to her mother and sister.

Matthew came over and said, "Mom Cornelia, what a rewarding experience it is to be acquainted with you. We will see more of each other in the future. May I say I'm eternally grateful to become your son-in-law; I love you and your husband."

At the ball there was lively music, dinner, and entertainment. Jasmin enjoyed a glass of wine with dinner wine along with some ice water. Then the dance floor was opened and many couples danced. Matthew and Jasmin did a few rounds on the floor, when out of the corner of her eye Jasmin saw Harry approaching, slightly inebriated.

He came up to the table and said, "Jasmin, have you come back?"

"Not exactly," she said. "Harry, meet my fiancé, Matthew Tyler."

"Oh, do I have to ask him if I can dance with you?" Harry asked.

"Yes, you do," Jasmin said.

"Will you translate for me?" he asked.

Jasmin turned to Matthew, who said, "I can guess. Go ahead, but only if you want to."

She nodded, and said to Harry, "For old time's sake." They did a Jive and laughed together. Matthew looked amused, and had no animosity in his heart toward Harry.

When it was over, Harry said, "Too bad you left; we could have made beautiful music together."

Jasmin countered, "It wouldn't have worked. I was never meant to blend in with a crowd. This dance was fun, though."

Harry returned her to her seat and bowed before Matthew. "Congratulations," he offered. They shook hands and he left.

Jasmin

Father, Mother, Camilla, and Norbert had a good time. Heinz offered to play a trumpet solo. The band let him have a trumpet and he played "Cherry Pink and Apple Blossom White" to everyone's enjoyment. Norbert asked if he could have a dance with the bride and Matthew danced with Camilla. When the music stopped, they made their way back to the table. Matthew noticed that a member of the band had come over to Jasmin and started talking with her.

Jasmin stared at Dietrich when she recognized him. "May I have this dance?" he asked her father.

Heinz said, "Only if Jasmin allows."

Jasmin didn't want to make a scene and consented. They danced to the melody of "Blue Velvet". He said, "When I saw you, I thought you had come back. I have been pining for you all these years. I concentrated on my studies to excel and finish law school one year ahead of everyone else. After I left home I asked in a roundabout way at Mannings' where you had gone, but I didn't follow through in contacting you any further. I had hoped to build an existence first and then try to find you. I supplement my income by playing in bands."

"You were always a good piano player," Jasmin said. The others had stayed seated at the table. Matthew was trying to read what was in Jasmin's mind. She had a look of resolve on her face as she made the introduction, "Dietrich, meet Matthew Tyler, my fiancé. Matthew, Dietrich is a law student."

Matthew said, "Won't you sit down?"

"Just for one moment; I have to get back to the band." Dietrich was quite conversant in English and chatted jurisprudence with Matthew. Looking at Jasmin, he told him, "I wanted to make her my princess."

Matthew answered with determination, "I'm going to treat her like a queen!"

Dietrich stood up and shook hands with Matthew. "Congratulations. What dance number shall I play for you?"

"Tango," Jasmin and Matthew said in unison.

Dietrich took the microphone and announced, "Ladies and Gentlemen, this Argentinian Tango is for this couple who is celebrating their engagement!"

All eyes were on them as Matthew bowed before Jasmin and said, "My lady." When the music began, they had the whole floor to themselves and relished in making long strides. When a difficult twist came up, Matthew whispered, "Contra check" and "lunge" at the precise moment. Her dress weaved and complemented each movement in attractive sequences. They finished with a lift to everyone's cheer.

Heinz strolled over to the microphone and announced, "My daughter is marrying an Englishman." That generated a rousing applause.

Midnight came and the New Year had begun. Following many congratulatory handshakes, they made their way home. Jasmin, her dad, and her mom stayed over at Camilla's apartment and Norbert dropped Matthew off at his hotel. Camilla helped Jasmin with the ball gown and they packed it neatly, followed by a long goodbye talk.

All four of them boarded the early flight the next morning. In their first class seats, as they were offered champagne, Jasmin declined and said, "I opt for candies this early in the morning." So did Matthew.

Jasmin smiled and said, "Thank you Matthew for making this trip possible; everything was perfect."

"Everything?" he asked. She hesitated. Matthew asked again, "Well?"

Jasmin

Jasmin laughed. "Mr. Tyler the interrogator. Yes, I have found closure. With Harry it was a fun dance, but he couldn't fathom why I did not fall for him, so I had to tell him straight, 'I am not one of a crowd.' Now I know what I instinctively knew when I broke up with him as a teenager. He talked in my presence about other girls and other things that excited him. I had expected to be his number one priority. I needed someone to be interested in me - my thinking, my feelings, and my goals - but to be compared with other girls ended the relationship. It didn't break my heart, but I didn't want to associate with a person who had no substance."

Matthew waited for more. Jasmin finally said, "When I was seventeen, I received the most endearing and adoring letter from Dietrich, almost like yours. But he didn't keep his promise. I never heard from him again. I couldn't understand why, if he cared for me that much, he hadn't continued to pursue me. My brother comforted me and said that yes, a true friend would have sought me out, but God had a better plan for me and in due time I would meet a God-fearing man who loved me, honoured me, followed through with his promise, and sealed it with marriage. You have superseded all my suitors. You are my noble hero, my dream, my reality, and you're the right man for me."

Before the plane descended, Matthew assured her, "I will always pursue you and adjoin my life with yours. I will strive to be the fulfillment of your dreams. I will never break my promise to you, nor will I ever be angry with you. You are and always will be the centre of my attention. Have I told you lately that I love you?"

Jasmin breathed, "No, but you can tell me now."

Matthew leaned over and whispered, "I love you," and he kissed her.

When they arrived at the Tylers' residence, Matthew helped Jasmin bring the garment bag with the wedding dress into the house.

Emily took it from him and Charles held the door open for the Claudius couple. Matthew saw his mother approaching and said, "Mother, let me introduce Mr. and Mrs. Claudius, Mrs. Tyler."

She greeted them with, "Call me Martha, please."

Heinz bowed his head and said, "Pleasure, Heinz."

He gestured left to give the floor to his wife, who said, "Cornelia." Martha opened her arms to Cornelia, and they hugged.

Matthew said to Jasmin, "The next time you will see me is at church." Then he left for his quarters. Charles directed Mr. Claudius to his room and arranged for the luggage to be brought to their guest suite. Mrs. Tyler and Cornelia laid out the wedding dress on the divan. Cornelia pointed out the loops for the marabou feathers to Martha.

Kurt immediately attended to Jasmin's hair. The bridesmaids, whose hair had already been styled, huddled around Mrs. Tyler and Mrs. Claudius to help put the feathers into the loops. The train was to be transported to the church separately. Cornelia took the tiara out of her cosmetic case and displayed it on a side table.

"This must be an heirloom," Martha exclaimed.

"It is," explained Cornelia. "It was from my great grandmother's French ancestors, the De Chevaliers. They were Huguenots, and the tiara is always passed down to the next bride-to-be. It stays in the family."

For the first time in his life, Matthew had become nervous. He looked in the conservatory for the bouquet, but he couldn't see it immediately. He found Charles. "Did the white roses not arrive?" he asked anxiously.

"Yes Sir, they are in the limousine. The boutonnieres for yourself and Mr. Kerr are on this shelf, because you will exit through this door. Miss Benson's corsage is with the ladies. The rings are in this box for Mr. Kerr to take."

Jasmin

"Thank you," Matthew said. "I'll be in my room. Call for me when I am to leave."

Matthew changed into the new suit that had been laid out for him and went to his private office. He looked at the portrait of his father and reflected, "You would have liked my new father and mother-in-law, and you would of course have loved Jasmin." He sat and stared out the window as he recalled scenes from his childhood and youth. "This is the day I have been waiting for," he thought.

Suddenly he heard tires squealing outside. "Jeff Kerr, no doubt," he chuckled. Charles directed Jeff to the back door and Alicia to the front entrance. Matthew made his way into the rear hallway. "Hi Jeff, how is it going?"

Jeff said, "I am here to take over for you, Matthew."

Matthew raised an eyebrow, "So you are; let's get on with it then." They turned to Charles who held the boutonniere in his hand ready to pin on Matthew's jacket first and then on Jeff's. Matthew asked again, "My father-in-law's also?"

Charles replied, "I'll do it personally." He opened the ring box with the rings he had purchased for them to show which was Matthew's and which was Jasmin's, and then he gave the box to Jeff to carry.

He instructed them, "You will drive ahead to the church and move to your designated spot inside the auditorium. I shall follow behind you with the ladies and Mr. and Mrs. Claudius in the limousine. Wait here please till I give you the cue by Skip."

Charles went to the drawing room to see that Mrs. Tyler and Mrs. Claudius were being assisted by Emily with their corsages. Alicia already had her corsage on and the bridesmaids were helping each other. He pinned the boutonniere on Mr. Claudius. Kurt placed the tiara on Jasmin's head and fastened it with pins. They were about to go into the limousine. Charles motioned for Skip to tell Mr. Kerr that it was time to leave.

The bridesmaids left with their waiting escorts. Charles escorted Mrs. Tyler to the front seat of the limousine, and Cornelia and Jasmin took the wide side. Cornelia helped her daughter to lift the train into the limousine. The seats were fitted along the windows for this occasion. Jasmin's father and mother sat on the opposite side. Alicia, holding the bouquet, slipped in behind Jasmin. Charles started to drive slowly towards the church.

The last guests were seated and music flooded into the foyer as the bridesmaids gathered around Jasmin. Cornelia attached the train to Jasmin's dress. Charles alerted Mrs. Tyler and Mrs. Claudius to enter the auditorium and they were ushered into their seats. Charles motioned for Mr. Claudius to stand beside the bride. As Alicia handed the bouquet to Jasmin she said, "These roses from Athens are Matthew's gift to you."

Jasmin closed her eyes and thought, "Oh, how I love Matthew. He goes to the ends of the earth to seek and find something that pleases me."

The photographer had his assistant stay behind to capture the image of the train. He proceeded backwards as the wedding march began to play. Alicia, Maid of Honour, took the lead followed by Rose, Beatrice, and Nellie down the aisle. A hush fell over the crowd as Jasmin appeared on the arm of her father. Matthew looked and thought, "Is this a mirage or is it real?"

With each step she took, the marabou feathers bobbed up and down in waves. Her train seemed to float as myriads of crystals sparkled in the lights. The roses in the bouquet were enhanced by tiny silver wires topped with crystals, giving the appearance of frosted snow. She held the bouquet close to her heart in her fur-cuffed hands. Jasmin's face glowed with a rosy shimmer. Matthew almost felt an urge to twirl his fingers through the ringlets of her hair, as she stood still beside him.

To the words, "Who giveth this woman away?" the answer came, "Her mother and I do." Her father released her and took his own seat.

Jasmin looked at Matthew as he spoke the words, "With this ring I thee wed, with my body I thee worship."

She repeated the words the minister had told her and ended with, "Thereto I give thee my troth."

She entered the dream world again until, "You may kiss the bride."

Amid the fragrance of roses Matthew lowered his head toward her, tilted her chin with his hand, and kissed her on the lips. The minister said, "Please follow me to sign the register." Matthew took her arm while Jasmin handed the bouquet to Alicia. Beatrice and Nellie stepped behind her, lifted the train, and carried it behind Jasmin until she sat down at the desk.

Matthew signed his name first then gave the pen to Jasmin. He pointed to the line and said, "You sign with your new name." She wrote, "Jasmin Tyler." The minister beckoned them to follow his lead and face the congregation. Matthew took Jasmin's arm and she rose from the seat as Nellie and Beatrice again carried her train until the couple stood facing the congregation.

"Ladies and Gentlemen, let me introduce to you Mr. and Mrs. Tyler." Amid a rousing applause, they stood and smiled. Jasmin kept hold of Matthew's arm as they slowly walked to the foyer. The wedding party lined up for the reception and pictures.

Heinz Claudius stood tall and erect next to his lovely wife. They received many compliments of how youthful they looked.

As many of Matthew's and his mother's acquaintances shook hands with them, Jasmin whispered, "Am I being introduced to my future society?"

Matthew whispered back, "You are my future society, Jasmin Tyler."

After the guests left for the dinner dance, Beatrice, Nellie, Rose, and Alicia continued to be awestruck by this beautiful event. They said they would treasure the memory of this forever, and hoped for pictures. Matthew said, "We'll give them to you." He stroked Jasmin's hand which was still holding his arm. He said tenderly, "We'll travel together in the limousine now, Jasmin Tyler."

Jasmin said, as they walked to the car, "I like the sound of my new name."

Matthew smiled, "You can keep it for the rest of your life."

Her train was removed by Mrs. Tyler and Jasmin wore her white fox stole to the reception hall. As they entered the hall, arm in arm, Matthew asked, "Did I ever tell you I like parading you around?"

"Once or twice," Jasmin giggled. They strolled to the head table. When Jasmin was comfortably seated, Matthew took her stole and draped it behind her chair.

Jeff Kerr took Matthew aside and suggested, "While the girls engage Jasmin in conversation, you come with me."

"I won't be long," Matthew said to Jasmin.

Jeff led Matthew through several decorative palm trees, planters, and partitions and showed him a door hidden from view. He opened it and led him through a hallway to the bridal suite. "Your change of clothes for the morning is in the closet. Charles will bring the limousine with your suitcases and tickets tomorrow and take you to the airport for your honeymoon destination." He led him back the same way and said, "As soon as you want to get away from the crowd, you and Jasmin take this exit. I will then lock it and make sure nobody follows you."

Matthew grinned, "That's my kind of guy, thanks." They walked back to the head table to find Jasmin and the girls engaged in a lively conversation. Someone rang a bell for the five-course dinner to be served.

They feasted on smoked salmon, capers, white wine, Riesling, liver pâté, canapés, French breadsticks, roast pheasant in Madeira sauce, braised celery, white asparagus, extra fine green beans, wild rice, Petit Fours, wedding cake, and crème de menthe parfait.

Many toasts were offered to the bride from her friends and Matthew's acquaintances. The bride's mother and father were toasted often. Matthew received accolades from his associates and friends of his father.

A short break was announced for the guests to mingle before the band began to play. Jasmin and the girls took this opportunity to visit the gift salon. Matthew made his way over to talk with his new "dad" Heinz and "mom" Cornelia. His mother assured him that she would spend time with them before they returned to Germany.

After everybody had come back, the master of ceremonies announced, "The first dance is for the Bride and Groom."

As the music began to play, Matthew bowed before Jasmin and said, "May I have this dance?" He offered his hand to raise her up and they floated in long strides to the foxtrot beat. The hem of Jasmin's dress flared wide in waves, making the marabou feathers vibrate in the turns. People applauded.

The bandleader now suggested that those who wanted to dance should form a circle with ladies on the inside and men on the outside. As he played the medley, he suggested that each dancer should do one turn and move to the next one till they were back to their own partners. "This way you guys will have a chance to take a spin with the bride and the ladies will have a chance to dance with the groom."

Most of the younger people joined in the activity. The bandleader, after a few bars, said, "Change your partners," until he saw Jasmin back with Matthew, and then the music stopped. Matthew walked Jasmin back to her seat and offered her champagne.

When Jeff Kerr came back to sit with them, Matthew leaned over to him and said, "The next dance is my last one. Keep your eyes on me where I am going." Jeff nodded in understanding.

The music began again and it was announced that everybody should take to the floor.

Matthew looked at Jasmin and said, "This is for us, a Rumba."

Jasmin followed Matthew to the dance floor. As they moved to the rhythm the singer sang, "Your eyes are the eyes of a woman in love and oh how they gave you away, why try to deny you're a woman in love, when I know very well what they say. No moon in the sky ever lent such a glow, some flame deep within made them shine. Your eyes are the eyes of a woman in love and may they gaze ever more into mine, crazily gaze ever more into mine."

Matthew moved smoothly towards the partitions and whispered to Jasmin, "Follow me." They slipped through the door and Jeff locked it behind them. Matthew sang along with the refrain, "No moon in the sky ever lent such a glow."

Jasmin sweetly sighed, "Only you can make me glow, Matthew!" He lifted Jasmin up and carried her over the threshold of the suite.

The next morning Matthew and Jasmin were whisked to their honeymoon destination on the island of Tenerife. They enjoyed three glorious weeks of wedded bliss. On the last day of their honeymoon Matthew and Jasmin walked along the private beach. Jasmin reflected, "Another change is coming into our lives."

Matthew asked, "Are you apprehensive?"

"No," she said. "How can I be with you in my life every which way? The first change came when I started the apprenticeship; the second, when I came to England; and the third, when I married you."

Matthew cut in laughing, "You married me or I married you?"

Jasmin

Jasmin giggled, "Matthew, are we back in the teasing mood?"

Matthew spoke softly, "Just clarifying the statement, 'When we were married.' We are one now. Did I ever tell you I love the way your lips form my name?"

"A time or two," she conceded, as they embraced and kissed.

In the evening breeze, during their meal on the terrace, Jasmin took a deep breath before formulating her sentence. "When we live in your house, there will be two Mrs. Tylers. When the staff addresses either one of us, your mother and I might both turn our heads simultaneously. Wouldn't it be easier on them if I were called Mrs. Jasmin?"

Matthew smiled. "A bit unorthodox, but if it makes you happy, sure. Your mail will be addressed to you as Mrs. Matthew Tyler though."

"Mrs. Matthew Tyler," she repeated, "I am linked with you and you with me."

"Forever in love," he affirmed.

EPILOGUE

On the first business day of the year, Mrs. Tyler called Mrs. Harman at the office asking her whom she must speak with about renovating her house. "That will be Alex Thornton," she replied. "Please stay on the line."

"Yes, Mrs. Tyler, how can be of service to you?" Mr. Thornton enquired.

"Mr. Thornton, I'm calling about the renovation of a new master suite in our house. It needs to be finished in under three weeks' time. Can you arrange it?"

"I will look into it. When can my team come to see the project? Is this afternoon too soon for you?" he asked.

"By all means, three p.m. is fine, thank you," Martha Tyler said.

"We'll be there promptly, thank you Mrs. Tyler," he said and hung up.

Martha had Charles bring the limousine to the front of the house and he took Heinz and Cornelia Claudius on a morning tour through the city. She showed them the hotel where Jasmin had been employed. They took the country road to the property where Matthew and Jasmin planned to build their house. Heinz had tears in his eyes when he viewed the rolling hills. It reminded him of his own property he had lost, but it gave him peace that his daughter would have something like it.

After they had lunch, Cornelia presented a souvenir to Martha. "This is the original Eau De Cologne perfume from us to you."

Martha gasped in delight, "Thank you, Cornelia, Heinz; this isn't yet available here in England. This is so special." At the airport she purchased an English souvenir box of Mackintosh Quality Street candies for them to take home. Martha waited until Heinz and Cornelia boarded the plane and waved till they were out of sight.

Within two and a half weeks the new flat was built for Matthew and Jasmin. After that the interior decorators completed their work. Mrs. Tyler put all her care and effort into giving it the finishing touch. The newlyweds settled happily into their new quarters. Jasmin began adjusting to her new lifestyle. As Matthew resumed going back to his office, he kept Wednesday afternoons open for their special date.

About two months later, Jasmin thought, "If this change in my body is what I think it is, I'll have to see the doctor." At the dinner table, she said nonchalantly, "I will have to get my evaluation for the Workmen's Compensation certified by a doctor."

Mrs. Tyler quickly offered, "I'll go with you."

The following evening, Jasmin instructed Emily, "When Mr. Tyler comes home, would you serve the tea in the library?"

Matthew entered his house ready to unload some files in his private office. Emily said, "Mrs. Jasmin is expecting you in the library; I shall bring in the tea tray."

Jasmin

"I will be there momentarily," he said. When he came in he greeted Jasmin, "Good evening, Jasmin darling, my one and only lady I like to unwind with." He took a seat in the other chair. "Shall I pour?"

"You pour, I'll serve sugar and cream." She smiled, and then she asked him, "How was your day?"

After he stirred his tea, he responded, "My case is successfully solved. I can leave my work behind and devote all my time to you." He took a sip from his cup and asked, "Has anything interesting transpired today for you? How did your doctor's appointment go?"

Jasmin put her cup down and said, "Very well, actually. So well, that I want to go to the Concordia Bar for lunch tomorrow."

"Do you feel comfortable enough for that?" he asked with concern.

Jasmin paused and said, "I can't think of a better place to have oysters, pickled quail eggs, and pickles."

"Interesting choice," Matthew said. "I see a gleam in your eyes. My mind is blank, tell me more."

"I'll give you a clue," Jasmin replied. "Think of the Christmas program at the Lutheran church."

"You decorated it," he said. Looking into space he pictured the scene with the children lined up in the front and how he wondered if he ever might have children of his own. Then he had looked at the blushing Jasmin. When he had questioned her later if she had been thinking the same thing, she wouldn't admit it.

Now he slowly turned his head, "You mean, you thought, you are?"

She nodded.

"Expecting," they said in unison. Matthew lifted her out of her seat, spun her around, and kissed her. "You are amazing," he breathed.

"It is amazing," she assented.

"I love you Mrs. Jasmin, mama-to-be; shall we go tell Mother?" Matthew asked.

Mrs. Tyler set her needlepoint down and looked up when Matthew and Jasmin approached.

"Mother," Matthew said, "Jasmin and I have something to tell you. We are going to have a baby."

Martha Tyler rose from her chair and exclaimed, "Jasmin, my beautiful daughter!" She hugged Jasmin first, and then Matthew. "How wonderful, when is it due?"

"October," Jasmin informed her.

"We'll have to build a nursery," Mrs. Tyler concluded.

At the Concordia Bar, Matthew and Jasmin were welcomed by Martin and Richie. "It is an honour to have you here today," Martin said. Richie bowed his head and then he directed them to the curtained alcove in the proximity of the piano.

Jasmin recognized Marco, the new food counter attendant. She waved to him and told Matthew, "That is Marco from the pastry kitchen; he is Spanish."

"We know some Spanish, don't we?" Matthew murmured.

"We sure do," Jasmin acceded.

Martin asked, "What can I bring to you today?"

Matthew faced Jasmin, "What does your crazy craving include?"

Jasmin replied, "Soda water and Angostura Bitters."

Martin nodded and said to Martin, "You heard what Jasmin wants to drink. I will have Perrier water plus half a dozen oysters, pickled quail eggs, pickles, and French sticks for Jasmin. I'll have French bread with Gruyere and mango chutney."

Jasmin watched Richie squirt drops into a balloon glass and twirl it around. She glanced over at Marco busy behind his counter. A wave of nostalgia came over her for the things she used to do.

Jasmin

Matthew perceived a nuance of change in her face and asked, "Any regrets?"

"Only happy memories," Jasmin said.

The pianist came and played melodies of "Love Letters in the Sand", "Fascination", and "Sentimental Journey". Marco brought the oysters to the table and said, "For you, Jasmin Angel."

Jasmin thanked him and said, "Marco, meet my husband Mr. Tyler."

Matthew said, "Como estas Marco?"

"Bien, gracias," was the reply.

Richie brought the Bitters frothed with soda and the other refreshments over as the place gradually got busy.

Matthew had a curious look on his face as he asked, "Jasmin, if these cravings continue, does Cook have to stock up on interesting fads such as this?"

"Even wilder," she replied. "You might have to search all over the world to find it."

Matthew laughed, "Sweetheart, I will seek and find anything for you!"

Jasmin said with a glow on her face, "I know you will!"

As Emma Worthington and Martha Tyler shared afternoon tea in the library, overlooking the conservatory. Emma mused, "Jasmin has brought so much joy into people's lives, most of all to Matthew. Do you remember the first time you met Jasmin? How did you find her?"

Martha replied with a faraway look on her face, "I had prayed many years for Matthew to find a nice young woman to marry. The answer came on a crimped piece of note paper that I didn't discard."

The name in scrolled writing was "Miss Claudius".

Jasmin is Karin Allaby's first novel. Karin draws from her experiences as assistant hotel manager, floral designer and ballroom dancing instructor. She modeled in fashion shows, piloted a one-engine aircraft and co-directed two charitable organizations. Karin lives with her husband in Ontario, Canada where she gives tours through her inspirational theme garden. She would invite reader's comments about the book on her webpage and jasminsstory.com